~DEAD GIRLS DON'T CRY~

Book One of The Dead Girl Saga

By Lorna J Welch

~Credits~

~Chief Editor~
Christopher C Gomez

~Cover Artist~
Consuelo Parra

~Model~
Maria Amanda

*~For Christopher who gave me the courage
to see this from start to finish and
always believed in me and this story, even when I did not.~*

~Chapters~

Chapter 1:   A Vampire of No Importance
Chapter 2:   An Ideal Human
Chapter 3:   Murderer
Chapter 4:   The Most Important Meal of the Day
Chapter 5:   A Day Out With Two Brothers
Chapter 6:   A Life for an Unlife
Chapter 7:   Scarlet, Day One as a Human
Chapter 8:   Jessica, Day One as a Vampire
Chapter 9:   Scarlet, Day Two as a Human
Chapter 10: Jessica, Tuesday: Day Two as a Vampire
Chapter 11: Scarlet, Wednesday: Day Three as a Human
Chapter 12: Jessica, Wednesday: Day Three as a Vampire
Chapter 13: Scarlet, Thursday: Day Four as a Human
Chapter 14: Jessica, Thursday: Day Four as a Vampire
Chapter 15: Scarlet, Friday: Day Five as a Human
Chapter 16: Jessica, Friday: Day Five as a Vampire
Chapter 17: Scarlet, Saturday: Day Six as a Human
Chapter 18: Jessica, Saturday: Day Six as a Vampire
Chapter 19: Jessica, Sunday: Day Seven as a Vampire
Chapter 20: Scarlet, Sunday: Day Seven as a Human
Chapter 21: Herb: Ghoul On the Run
Chapter 22: Jessica: Discovered
Chapter 23: Jessica: Girl On the Run
Chapter 24: Scarlet: The Makings of a Monster

~Epilogue~

Chapter 1

~A Vampire of No Importance~

"Where there is life there is hope"

I carefully outlined my lips with the new red lipstick I had bought. Liking what I saw in the mirror I attempted a smile but instantly dropped it as it revealed the tips of my fangs. I hated them, so pointy, so unnatural, so monstrous. Not how a pretty girl like me should look. It was worse when I was hungry they would tingle making them feel larger in my mouth even though they remained unchanged. At least the colour lipstick I had chosen would hide the blood. I cursed under my breath as I heard laughter echoing from downstairs. I had been hoping to slip out of the house this evening unnoticed. Grabbing my coat I cautiously descended the stairs, but before I could reach the final step I was confronted by Kristian; the youngest of my three brothers. Hanging off his arms were two girls; a redhead and a brunette; they were both dressed in black, frilly long dresses and their doting faces were embellished with layers of white powder and black eyeliner. These girls were Kristian's latest blood dolls; as with his previous dolls they were from one of the many online forums filled with humans pretending to be vampires. Blood dolls were an excellent source of sustenance, they were plentiful, willing and easily accessible, totally eliminating the need to kill. Which was a good thing, as not only did killing to feed bring unnecessary attention to our kind, but also, believe it or not, is a major taboo. The main reason kill feeds were so scorned, was MFE outbreaks - Major Frenzied Episodes. These outbreaks caused a vampire to lose his or her connection to their mortal side, instead succumbing to the demon within. Most who suffered an episode never returned to their normal state and were subsequently put down.

As I looked into the over-mascaraed eyes of these two dolls, I could not help but sense the desperation and sadness about them, it was pathetic. I noticed one had a number of scars trailing up her arms, more than likely self-inflicted as our bites rarely left scarring, the only exception being the Dark Kiss where a mortal is turned into a vampire. Blood dolls always seemed to come in two "types", there was the addicts; their arms dotted with syringe puncture wounds from years of using human drugs. The other types were pretenders, products of an unhealthy infatuation with romanticised vampire culture. The pretenders would masquerade in the human world as vampires, cutting themselves and feeding on each other in mock fashion. This was the lowest act humans' could condemn themselves to by vampire standards.

To be fed off on a regular basis, with complete disregard of the danger they put themselves into; they became merely livestock. But sadly the addiction and small hope that their vampire would sire them, meant a constant and fresh supply of willing mortals. Regardless of which path brought them here, they had merely traded one addiction for another. These two girls were no different, they probably thought my brother would turn them, I knew better.

The Red haired girl met my gaze and cooed.

"Oh Kristian, is this your little sister? She's adorable, look at that long blonde hair and button nose!"

She reached forward to pinch my cheek, instinctively I bared my fangs and hissed threateningly at her. She quickly pulled her hand away and stumbled backwards, a look of fear on her face. Kristian merely laughed.

"Careful, Mary, our little Scar bites!"

The brunette girl appeared, placed herself behind him and gave a fake nibble to his neck before softly saying. "Don't all your kind?"

Kristian smiled wickedly, tracing his hand across the back of her neck and then suddenly yanking her towards him, he opened his mouth and sank his fangs into her throat, causing her to shudder and release a moan of pleasure.

Mary, having regained her composure, pouted. "Cecile, it's my turn!" Kristian withdrew his face from Cecile's neck.

"Now, now, ladies. I have plenty of fangs to go around."

Disgusted by the display I tried to wriggle past them.

"Not so fast, little sister, where are you sneaking off to?" demanded Kristian.

I halted and turned with a scowl on my face, I hated it when he tried to act the older brother, especially when his own behaviour had resulted in him being charged with a T.R.O. - Tribune Restraint Order. The Tribune were the undead governing body that ruled our city and handing out T.R.O's to undead found guilty of violating the laws was one way they maintained control. Kristian's had been issued as a result of his association with a rogue vampire gang known as "Remnants", mostly made up of sireless vampires or, as our father called them, the 'lost youth'. It was an unfortunate by-product of immortality, especially for those without a Sire to guide them, that these individuals would group together into small informal families of their own. Being part of a vampire gang presented a distraction and a connection point for the truly lost among us. You could almost understand it from that point of view, it's not like there is a significant amount of youth clubs or outreach programs for our kind. However, the majority of the gangs were formed of fledglings, newly turned vampires, and that was something altogether different and dangerous. The rise in vampire gangs was of great concern to the Tribune; as greater uncontrolled numbers meant an increased risk of exposing us all.

There were multiple enclaves of vampire cities around the world, all of them deep underground and hidden from mortal eyes by powerful cloaking spells. The only time a human was able to see them was after they had tasted the blood of a vampire. This allowed us to build our own undead society without human interference. Trips above ground were a necessity from time to time, but hunting humans was strictly forbidden. While for the most part this arrangement worked, there was always the threat of a vengeful blood doll unveiling our existence. Should a disobedient blood doll be discovered it was the job of the Wardens, the enforcers of the Tribune, to remove all memory of the vampire realm from this mortal. However, gangs like Remnant disregarded the rules that kept us secret. They didn't harvest blood dolls, at least not long enough to bother registering them, and actively hunted the humans for sport before feeding and killing. They despised the Tribune and its rules and in recent years had become an increasingly violent threat, so much so that the Tribune decided to stamp down on the amount of time vampires could spend above ground. Wardens patrolling the human realm had been increased and a curfew introduced. All vampires and ghouls were made to wear an implant, a magic-infused accessory, which allowed them to keep track of their undead citizens above and below ground.

    I traced the raised skin on my arm where the implant lay underneath; it writhed and pulsated with magical energy. Kristian watched me, still waiting for an answer so I relented, it was easier to oblige him than try to argue.

    "If you must know I am going to Plasma," I muttered.

    Kristian raised his eyebrows in approval. "You're going to Plasma?"

"Yes, a few of the fledglings at Ghoul School invited me so I thought I would try it again," I lied.

    Plasma was the main vampire club in the Underdark. I had been once and vowed never to go back. It represented everything I despised about my kind, decadence, debauchery and depravity. They even had blood dolls suspended in cages that could be lowered by a chain and tasted for a price. But the worst part was the Rest Room at the back, reserved for VIVs only (Very Important Vampires) where retired blood dolls or humans seeking an end could go and be fed upon for the last time. I had watched them lining up for it, some old and still having not been turned, choosing a clean death instead of a dragging existence riddled with humiliation and pain. Others were part of the uninvited, humans who had sought us out in the hope for a miracle cure for their afflictions; after not finding one many chose the alternative. It is said that death by a vampire, if done correctly, can be almost pleasurable for the human, the use of enthralling one's victim helping sedate them into a dreamlike state, and as their blood is drained it feels as if they are falling into a deep, euphoric sleep. The name itself, however, had caused many a near miss for new blood dolls, who having asked to be taken to the Rest Room, were merely looking for the nearest toilet. I hoped he would not ponder my change of heart too much, his brunette blood doll, Cecile, was still bleeding and I felt my own fangs tingle at the scent. Kristian caught my eye and turned her towards me, the blood glistening as it dripped into the crevices of her collarbone.

"Have a bite, I wouldn't be a proper brother if I let you go out on an empty stomach," he grinned, exposing blood stained teeth.

"I can eat there," I said turning away from the girl's bleeding throat, she frowned looking offended at my refusal.

"Fair enough, if you can call dining on that diluted blood they sell in there a meal. Also the amount of Drakmir they charge for a shot of standard blood is getting ridiculous, it's almost the same as what they charge at Blue Bloods."

"Blue Bloods" was a vampire gentry club that our father attended, all my brothers were members except Kristian who had been banned from entering as long as his T.R.O. was in place.

"I thought you wanted me to go out more," I said.

"I do, I was merely recommending a few warm up bites to line the throat but I am in full support of you spending time with vampires that aren't brooded to you by blood."

Before I was finally free to go I had to endure another fifteen minutes of Kristian's advice on what to indulge or avoid, he was particularly fond of the cage feeding but forbade me to get involved with any of the feeding games such as gorging or guzzling which were banned from most places due to the high frequency of accidental deaths of blood dolls involved. Finally done, or bored, Kristian bade me farewell and I completed my escape. I made my way through the meandering streets of our city heading for the main hub of the Vampire Quarter. There were four main districts of our city, the Vampire Quarter, The Ghouls Quarter, The Trade Quarter and The Witches Quarter.

The integration of the witches to our city was a fairly new arrangement and was the subject of much protest from the vampires who still followed the old beliefs. Witches were the ones responsible for our existence and a great animosity had lingered between the two of our races, until the Treaty of Supernatural Unity had been created by the Tribune. However, not all of our kin felt the same way, there had always been an interest in the mystical side among the aristocratic vampire families and it was now considered fashionable to be able to dabble in the blood magic we derived from. At the centre of all four quarters was the Tribune Tower where the Tribune conducted its trials and ruling decisions for our kind. I reached Plasma and lingered outside for a moment, a large queue had already formed outside the doors and the rhythmic thud of drum and bass music sounded from within. I gave a final look until I was certain I had not been followed then headed off in the opposite direction. I made my way to the Gate, which as the name implied was the only way out of the city to the human world. I suddenly became aware of heavy, rasping breathing coming from behind me, it was keeping its distance, but definitely following. I didn't look around just in case, but instead picked up the pace. I could hear the rasping intensify, followed now by the slaps of clumsy flat feet. I chewed my lip in anticipation, considering my options, outrunning my pursuer was out of the question and would only lead to complications. So I began to slow my pace, hearing the footsteps drum closer and closer to me, I suddenly came to a full stop and swung round to face my pursuer.

"Herb! You're not coming with me!" I stated.
The gangly figure of Herb shuffled out into view.

"Ohhh, please," he rasped. "Please, Scar. I bought these new clothes especially."

He did a lopsided shuffle, that I assumed was meant to be a twirl, before facing me with a glint in his eye, he certainly looked pleased with himself. He really did look ridiculous, a pair of ill-fitting blue jeans hung off his bony legs like cooked chicken skin, the white buttoned up shirt would have been okay, if you couldn't see his exposed rib cage through it,
but the worst part was the hair. The few blonde strands he had left were combed down flat over his green tinged scalp.

"No!" I said firmly. "You stand out a mile and will scare away any potential prey."

"But my clothes are the same?" he whined.
"Yes, but that doesn't hide the fact that your flesh is hanging off and you look like that wretched thing from the Lord of the Rings."

"I do not look like Golem!" he wailed. "He has much bigger ears than me," he said feebly trying to pull down the brittle strands of hair over his large ears. Herb was my ghoul, most human girls had girlfriends, being a vampire I had to make do with ghoulfriends but what else did you expect from a member of the undead society. Ghouls were humans who failed the transition into a vampire, the demonic blood that was fed to them managed to bring them back from the dead but never succeeded into fully turning them. The result was little more than a walking corpse, their bodies varying from shrivelled husks that looked like they belonged in a museum, to the freshly dead who had skin with a greenish tinge and bloating but could pass for human, if you ignored the smell. Due to the fact that ghouls were unable to evolve fully, they have always been considered inferior and formed a dedicated servant class to tend to our menial tasks. This started off as basic slavery but over the years they had managed to establish themselves as a useful tool in vampire society, and now for all purposes ran everything for us. They have connections in every part of the city and if you wanted something rare and for a good price, then chances are a ghoul could get it for you. Their rise as cadaver entrepreneurs had gained them some respect, but there will always be those of our kind that will still treat them as a lower and weaker species. Herb had been serving me since I was first turned and had started to follow me around since I was old enough to leave the Underdark. I glared at him as he tried to plaster a bit of loose flesh back to his cheekbone. He was being very persistent tonight.

"But it will be dark in there, they might not notice," he continued to pat away at the loose bit of skin.

"True, but they will smell you a mile away. Unlike us, humans are not raised among the living dead and not accustomed to the smell of rotting flesh."

His shoulders slumped and he bowed his head in defeat before slowly trundling off.

With the worry of Herb far behind me, I joined the queue at the Gate, it was mostly undead travelling to the human realm at this time as it was past curfew, so only those on Tribune business would be allowed through now. I always got nervous no matter how many times I did this, it didn't help that the ghoul in front of me was getting a grilling from the two security guards.

"Your implant picture looks nothing like you!"

The ghoul cringed and tried to explain. "I have been under a lot of stress this week what with starting a new job so I decomposed more than usual. Once my cheekbone grows back I will look like my old self again."

The security guard took one last glance at the screen, then shook his head in irritation as he eventually let the ghoul pass.

"Damn Uncleans they look different every time you see them! I thought only Freshies were allowed to work above ground," he moaned to his colleague.

"They are but they must be getting desperate," replied his co-worker.

Both of them looked at me suspiciously as I approached the checkpoint of the Gate. Ignoring their stares I held my arm out for them to scan. The male security guard looked at the screen behind their desk, before nodding to his colleague and letting me through, I stepped through the glowing light and smiled.

Chapter 2

~An Ideal Human~

Leaving the Underdark and coming above ground was like stepping forward in time. In our cities, nothing ever changed, the same old buildings and dimly lit cobbled streets pockmarked the city. It was always night down there, the warmth and light of the sun never penetrating or reaching us. Every time I visited the human realm something was different, a full moon would have risen, stars would be out, new leaves would have grown on the trees, the place was as interchangeable as its occupants. Coming up here was confirmation that time was still moving forward, another reason I liked it so much. As I made my way through the town I passed houses with their lights on. As always I gazed in, eagerly trying to catch glimpses of the the human families sat together and settling down for the night. When I reached the centre of town it was a different story. I watched the mortals staggering from the pubs and bars, into trash-filled streets, raucous voices echoing. Most of the establishments would not be letting anyone in at this time, but there was one place that would make an allowance – Club Insomnia. The club was a rock bar filled with long-haired men and women, some with painted white faces and a general fondness for black leather garments. Blending into this crowd was perfect for a solitary hunter like myself; a young girl all on her own, lonely; it would be incredibly easy attracting the attentions of any humans trying to get lucky. As I walked past the doorman, he grabbed my wrist. Looking down at the arm restraining me I could see wire-like tendons and muscles bulging, threatening strength; one twist and I could snap the arm like a twig I thought to myself. With some difficulty, I looked up and flashed a smile.

"ID?" he asked gruffly.

Was he serious?! One of the disadvantages of being forever young, was that sometimes you got treated like it and this was just such an occasion. Luckily I was prepared and I pulled out my fake ID. I flashed him the card and he squinted at it suspiciously. After a tedious minute or so, he grunted, returned my card and released his grip before nodding abruptly for me to enter. As I made my way to the bar I spotted tonight's prey, it was a boy of about my human age, maybe a year older, he was alone and far too drunk to be on his guard, so I placed myself in his line of sight and performed my best pout. In seconds he was edging over to me.

"Hi," he slurred, the stench of alcohol was strong but not enough to mask the scent of blood running through his veins, stirring the demon in me.

It's hard to describe what it feels like when the hunger takes control. A 16th century vampire writer famously described it in his book 'Serenade', where he compared his favourite blood doll to the mythical siren. The doll's blood being as enticing as a lover's call, but with a great risk of death; albeit the blood doll's death. It is also the closest we can get to true pain, if the urge to feed is strong enough. Strange how the act of something so monstrous is the only time we feel as vulnerable as them, as if succumbing to that weakness brings us closer to being human again.

"Hi," I replied, tucking a blonde curl behind my ear, trying my best to look coy.

"Are you alone?" he asked looking hopeful.

"No," I said and he wilted as the prospects of getting lucky evaporated.

"I came with friends but haven't seen them for a while and I am beginning to worry they have left without me."

The light in his eyes came back like the flick of a switch.

"That's a shame," he said trying to hide a smile.

I nodded, adding another pout for good measure.

"I can help you look for them?" he said eagerly.

"How sweet of you," I replied fluttering my eyelashes.

I gestured towards the side exit and saw his smile widen. He dropped his arm around my shoulders and I led the way outside. It was a secluded dark alley, littered with empty bottles and cigarette stubs, the noise of the club dimly thudding in the background.

"I don't think they went down here," he said looking into the darkness doubtfully. I slid my arms around his neck.

"I think you might be right," I whispered, running my finger over his mouth.

Before he could say anything else, I planted a soft kiss on his lips and he murmured in pleasure. I traced my tongue across his lips, being careful to keep my fangs back. His hands clamped round my waist and began tracing the curve of my back, I could feel his heart rate increase as he became aroused. Trailing my kisses down his neck, I allowed myself to give in a little to the demon within, opening my mouth in anticipation of the feed. Fangs glinting in the lamplight I paused and savoured the moment. Just as the blood lust threatened to take over, his arteries appeared to me like tiny purple roads just beneath the skin. As the tips of my fangs lightly brushed his neck, he let out a slight gasp and I sensed the veins pulsating, pace matching the dull thud of his heart in excitement. Or perhaps fear. Could it be, he had sensed my true intent?

As I pressed my fangs into his neck I paused, and did something, I had never done before. I did not bite, instead I leant into him.

"Just hold me. Please?" I whispered softly.

He obediently wrapped his arms around my whole body and as I burrowed deeper, my cheek rested on his chest, rising up and down in time with his breathing. So this is what it feels like to be held I thought. For a short moment I pretended I was his and he was mine, that there was no supernatural seduction involved, he was holding me simply because he wanted to. A fleeting moment, as soon enough the boy started to stir, returning to his senses.

"Your hands are really cold," he shivered, snapping me instantly out of my fantasy.

Before he could say anything else, I lunged and gave him the only embrace I was truly capable of giving. Pulling his head to one side, my arms tightened around him, holding him in place as his body jerked to fangs piercing his neck. I sighed in satisfaction as the warm blood pumped into my mouth and over my tongue. Pulling him closer I drank deeply, each gulp siphoning a little more of his life, everything around me became a dull cacophony of sound as his blood continued to fill me up. His body started jerking more erratically, perhaps reaching close to death, so I caressed him until he relaxed, consigned to his fate in my arms, silent save for the occasional whimper. As I continued to drink, I witnessed flashes of his life, secret and private memories poured into my head. His first Christmas; a huge green tree sparkling with lights and decorations of all sorts, even tiny glass snowflakes that glistened like the real thing, large boxes of presents stacked underneath. I could feel the excitement and anticipation of the moment, and it filled me with a joy that I had never felt before. Suddenly it

blurred and the images shifted into something else; a middle-aged man with a kind smile. He was laughing and ruffling the boy's hair, it looked like they were playing some kind of game in the garden, kicking a ball around. The image changed again, sharply. This time the mood was noticeably darker. We were standing over a coffin, inside lay the same man no longer smiling, no longer alive. He was dressed in a fine black suit, a deep feeling of sadness and loss swamped me. This short moment brought waves of pain, torment and grief that I had no real understanding of, yet it pierced me to the core. I welcomed it. The memories continued to come, some happy, some sad, and I relished all of them, tiny glimmers of life in a world where I was surrounded by death. What I was experiencing was something all our kind did, when feeding off humans, by drinking their

blood the demonic powers in our own blood allowed us to recall and tap into flashes of our victims' memories, we called them 'Flickers'. Most vampires blocked them out, due to feeding from regular blood dolls, as reliving the same memories over and over became mundane and ultimately worthless, leaving just the pleasure of the feed itself. Also in recent times, most of our kind cared little for human thoughts and feelings, focusing purely on the hunt. Even the vampire gangs that hunted above ground had started skipping the slideshow and gorged straight on the fresh blood instead. But it is completely different for me, yes I still craved their blood and enjoyed the hunt, but it was my yearning for their memories that caused me to take such risks. Why? Simple really, for that fleeting moment, as I tap into that humans' blood, I am not a vampire; I am them. I am experiencing what they experienced, I am living what they lived - I feel therefore I am.

 I let out a gasp as I released him, his blood still warm on my lips as I pulled away from his neck with noticeable effort. The trick was to get only what I needed and never more, to taste but not to drain. So many vampires before me had made the mistake or choice to steal all of a human, taking not just their memories but also their life, I would not be one of them. I raised my hand to my lips and wiped away trickles of fresh blood. The boy was weak, but still breathing and very much intoxicated. He momentarily roused and looked at me groggily.

 "That was some kiss!" he blurted, swaying to keep balance. He was pale and a large red stain was pooling down his shirt, but at least he was alive.

 "That's what they all say," I replied dryly, face impassive.

 The boy let out a final giggle before slumping against the wall and sinking to the ground. The combination of alcohol and blood loss had knocked him out. With practiced efficiency, I pulled out my emergency feeding kit, selecting one of my sterilised cloths and applied pressure to the boy's neck. As I held the cloth in place I whipped out my mobile phone with my other hand, and punched in the emergency number for mortals. I answered the standard emergency questions from the operator, feigning concern and playing my part in the charade.

 "My friend has been attacked by a group of people! One of them had a knife. Please, send help!" I sniffed for effect.

The operator took down my fake details and the address of the club, then reassured me that help was on the way. Looking down once more at the unconscious boy I flicked my phone shut, before exiting the alleyway. The perfect end to the evening, I had gone out, fed and even cleaned up after myself. I pulled out my compact hand mirror from my purse and made one final check that my mouth was free from bloodstains. I should have called it a night there and then but the sounds of the club's music within called to me. It seemed that the last flickers of the boy's blood had given me sudden insight into an unfamiliar song. That was another side effect I had trained myself to tap into. Certain human emotions were so strong that it was possible for those feelings and memories to linger far beyond the time of the feed. I re-entered the club and headed straight for the dance floor, for once paying no attention to the blood pumping inside the bodies that moved next to me, I allowed myself to get lost in the song, swaying hypnotically to it. Dancing was a mortal past time that vampires no longer took part in, its purpose long lost. But tonight I danced with the same vigour and enthusiasm as the humans around me and the feeling it gave me was overwhelming. So much so that I failed to notice one of them close in behind me. His hands grabbed at my waist and he pulled my body against his, before grinding lewdly against me. This was too much, I turned and grabbed him by the throat, the music lost as anger and the sensation to feed again, rose up in retaliation to his actions. The boy's eyes widened in fear as I held him. Then the music stopped, cut short by an announcement. 'Did anyone call an ambulance? If so please make your way to the front doors to help the paramedics with their questions.'

This was my cue to leave. Releasing my grip, I dropped the boy and swiftly moved to the back door, coming out into the alleyway once again. The boy I had fed on earlier was no longer there, which made sense if the paramedics were here. He was probably receiving medical attention. With the night concluded, I decided it was time to head back, I picked up the pace but as I rounded the corner from the alley, I came face to face with an extremely drunk girl. She was pretty in a human way. Long brown hair fell below her shoulders in soft waves; her skin had a warm, golden tan and her outfit, although a tad garish for my taste, seemed stylish and expensive. She had obviously consumed far more than she was capable of, as she was leaning against a wall moaning and despite being right in front of her, she was completely oblivious to me. I could have easily fed on her without a struggle, but for some reason I was lost in the scent of her and the steady beat of her heart. I approached cautiously and raised a hand, gently sweeping her hair out the way. My hand briefly brushing against her bare neck caused her to stir.

"It's cold," she moaned, eyes flickering erratically.

"Jessica, there you are! I've been looking for you all over." A voice rang out nearby, followed by a hurried approach of footsteps. I quickly slipped back into the shadows of the alley before a girl with short red hair appeared. She was also sporting a healthy looking tan but the scent of her suggested it was not entirely natural.

"Hannah abandoned me to go make out with that guy with the tattoos, he must be at least ten years older and then you disappeared. I was left on my own like a complete idiot!" she ranted, not pausing for breath before throwing her cigarette on the floor and stamping it out with unnecessary force. The drunken girl, Jessica, seemed to rouse at her friend's shrill voice.

"There was someone else here," she slurred and as her friend frantically looked around. I retreated further into the shadows.

"There's nobody here, Jess. Come on, let's get going. I told my dad I would be home by ten and it's quarter to twelve, they are kicking everyone out soon. I told you we should have gone to Silk instead. This place is a dive."

As Jessica let herself be pulled upright and coerced towards the front of the building I could hear her faintly muttering.

"I was sure there was someone here, a blonde girl with strange eyes and cold hands."

Her friend cackled loudly.

"I think that's the shots talking. Oh look! There's Hannah, seems she's been ditched by that guy. Let's grab her and get going. Strange eyes and cold hands…whatever you're on Jess, I want some."

I know that I shouldn't have, but something about this human girl made me follow them instead of returning to the Underdark. They had obviously been drinking too much, zig-zagging their way along the pavement at a tediously slow pace. Still, I kept a reasonable distance, watching from the shadows as they laughed and talked. The one called Jessica seemed to be the centre of it all, both girls fought to gain her attention and when she spoke they hung on her every word even if they were all slurred. I felt a strange ache as I watched the unfamiliar scene unfold; I had existed over one hundred years, yet I had never had what humans refer to as friends. I had poured over my collection of mortal books describing great bonds between characters who would do anything for each other no matter how irrational and where betraying a friend was considered the greatest of crimes. I had been astounded by how much importance human authors had placed on friendship. Would Frodo have survived so long without Sam to help him through the bleakness of Middle-earth, would Count Dracula have survived instead of being killed in his coffin as he slept? If he had made a friend during his long immortal life. Anne Rice's vampire, Lestat, once said that a vampire cannot pass back to the world of human warmth with our new vampire eyes. Why is this? Is it because we are unable to seek the things that made us human to begin with? Were we not only invulnerable to pain and age but also the traits needed to build such bonds again? It seemed that reading about friendship was the closest I would ever get to it. I had tried to get a better understanding of this in the past. I had even gone so far as to join a human chat forum in Cyber Crypt; a popular ghoul café where you could get a cup of hot blood and half decent internet, by Underdark standards. Humans had used the Internet for years, but we didn't get access until much later and it was the ghouls who were the first to start using it, under the watchful eye of the Tribune of course. The idea was to use this new technology to our benefit, the use of emails proving invaluable when keeping in contact with our human representatives above ground. However, although being recognised as a useful tool, the Tribune were not ignorant of the potential risks the internet posed for our society.

This seemingly endless platform for worldwide communication would be difficult to control, therefore a number of regulations, including censorship, were immediately put in place, violators of these facing severe punishment. The first year alone, saw many of our kin being arrested for such crimes; mostly followers of Fang Fanatics, a group of vampires devoted to preserving the purity of vampirism. Their ideology based on vampires being the ultimate race, they resented the fact that humans infested the world above, while we hid underground like rats. The Internet proved to be an effective propaganda tool for inciting and organising fledglings to rise up against the mortals that kept us prisoners of the earth. The Tribune were quick to delete such websites created by the FF, lest anarchy reign supreme. I found out at first hand just how efficient the Tribune's censorship was. Most of the searches I tried regarding human lifestyle appeared to be blocked. I had already known this might be the case as they were wary of any vampire with Human Intent. But one day I managed to access a forum for humans who, curiously also seemed to be suffering from loneliness. One boy wrote how he had trouble making friends and spent his free time alone. Intrigued by his plight I sent him a message, thrilled at the prospect of a response the following day. However, the next time I visited Cyber Crypt I found the site had been blocked. I knew then my message would have been deleted and I wondered if the boy had even had a chance to read it before that happened. In that moment, as I sat in front of a computer surrounded by ghouls and vampires tapping away on their regulated sites, I became aware that not only did I have no friends but I didn't even have a voice. This was the last straw and what ultimately made me start hunting flickers. While most had been trained to ignore them, I would enhance the experience. But I was now at a point where I needed even more than that.

    As I watched Jessica pause and vomit in a bush, rather than disgust I felt a yearning. Yes, it was vulgar and unrefined but as the two other girls came to her rescue with pats on her back and pulling her hair out of the way, I wanted to be her. They continued their slow plodding pace surrounded by a cloud of nonsensical chatter, until they reached a crossroads. Stopping momentarily, Jessica's friends argued to stay with her and escort her all the way home. But she insisted she would be fine and waved them off. They parted ways, but not before giving each other one last hug. After the other two left I continued to follow Jessica, she had taken her phone out and was stumbling along chatting loudly, completely unaware of me following behind. I could take it all from her, I thought, I could drink in every memory, every experience she'd ever had, they could be mine. Although to take that much would surely kill her? But what is one life compared to the memories I could gain? After all, my life had been taken just as easily, it would make me even with the world so to speak. I played with the idea and as appealing as it was, I knew it would not be enough, the memories would be a fleeting lie. I could lose myself in them as much as I wanted but they would still be borrowed. Like a pair of ill-fitting shoes, I could force myself into them but they would never truly fit, and all that would be left would be the raw markings as a painful reminder. I had been so deep in my musings that I failed to notice Jessica had stopped. Had she sensed me? I halted in my tracks not daring to move, waiting for her to turn her head and confront me. With a hiccup, she turned suddenly and started walking up the driveway of a large double fronted house with two cars parked outside it. I lingered as she struggled to let herself in and after a few minutes of fumbling, opened the door and shut it behind her. I had missed my chance tonight, but I wasn't worried, I knew where she lived. Slowly but surely an idea was forming in my head, it was incredibly risky, and never before heard of, but still it continued to form.

Chapter 3

~*Murderer*~

When I finally got back home I found Herb waiting for me, he was impatiently hopping on the spot, clearly fretting. When he turned and saw me he lunged at me frantically.

"You were much longer than usual, Scar. Where have you been?!" he whined. I gently patted his head to calm him down before responding.

"For a walk, you know how I get after I drink, it helps ease the frenzy." It wasn't a complete lie, I did go for a walk. I just left out the part about stalking a human girl home while contemplating killing her for her memories. Herb; still distressed; started tugging at his large ears, which were twitching involuntarily.

"You don't know what it's like, Scar, I have been sooooo worried! And thinking you might lose control and actually kill someone, oh my, oh my! If your brothers find out they will finish off what's left of me." His ears started twitching so fast, I thought they were going to fall off.

"You worry too much Herb, it's not good for you, if you're not careful you'll start shedding," I told him firmly. Another common symptom of a ghoul in distress was that they would aggressively scratch their decomposed skin, causing it to shed in large dry flakes. He ignored me and carried on hysterically.

"Desmodeus even showed up and started questioning me about your whereabouts. The fact you were out after curfew is bound to make him suspicious."

That news did bother me. Out of all my brothers Desmodeus was the least likely to be fooled, he was older and more powerful for a start, he was also a member of the Tribune like Father.

"What did he say?" I asked casually.

"That he and your father are attending a meeting tonight. He insisted that you know," Herb whimpered.

"He's probably just worried I will make him look bad if I am caught breaking curfew, he knows nothing Herb, and it will stay that way as long as you stop panicking."

I glared intensely at him to emphasise the point.

"Perhaps you're right. I mean, of course you are right, Scar." He seemed to be settling down a little, his ears losing some of the earlier momentum.

"I'm always right, now go and get something for that flaking skin, if the others see you scratching like you have maggots they will know something is wrong." I waved my hand dismissively, signaling the end of the conversation.

"Okay, okay, I'll go talk to Mildred," he lamented, before shuffling off in the direction of the kitchen and Mildred.

Although technically we didn't need a kitchen, it was nice to have local stores of blood and it had been the one and only thing Mildred had insisted on having before embarking on her eternal servitude for my father. She had stated that it wouldn't feel like a proper home without a kitchen. A kitchen was the heart of the home, even if it was just for appearances sake. Father had purchased Mildred from a Ghoul Market that only sold Uncleans, these were the lowest forms of ghouls available for purchase. Freshies were readily available to members of the Tribune, from renowned traders, but father always preferred to buy Uncleans, they were cheaper for a start and because of their limited prospects had less risk of aiming above their station. In life Mildred had served as a maid for a large household from the young age of ten. She served her human family and their children faithfully until the day came in the early 1900's when hired help fell out of fashion. Unfortunately for the likes of Mildred, that meant straight to the workhouse, as no one was going to offer work to an ex head maid over fifty. It was here in the workhouse that Mildred was turned, these places making for perfect vampire feeding grounds, as most of the residents were orphans, drunks or people who generally would not be missed. Although the question of what kind of vampire would try and sire someone of Mildred's age and status remains a mystery, perhaps they were fledglings looking to experiment. Whatever the intent, they soon changed their minds and sold Mildred to the first Ghoul Market they crossed, before she had awoken. Despite her morbid transformation, Mildred had taken to ghoul life rather well. Always stating that as a human she was never much to look at, so at least by becoming a ghoul, she had an excuse. Personally, I would have minded the part about having to work as an eternal slave for a vampire but, let's face it who else was going to hire her?
Either way she seemed to thrive on her new found career.

I climbed the first flight of the stairs, still considering what Herb had said. As I walked across the hall, I passed the room of my other brood brother Dante. He was seated upright in his coffin, surrounded by tallow candles and reading his favourite magazine 'Recently Risen', despite the fact we had electricity he continued to read by candlelight. Out of all of us he was the picture of a contemporary vampire stereotype. I mean he even slept in a coffin for goodness sake! You couldn't get any more cliché than that, still I envied him. To be able to embrace his vampirism so wholly, gave him some semblance of a normal life. He glanced up and gave me a curt nod.

"Kristian said you went to Plasma?" he asked. I nodded in response and his eyes shifted back to the magazine as he spoke.

"You know, you shouldn't be lowering yourself, associating with the lower class of our kin. I could take you to Blue Bloods instead. If you spend too much time with the common vampire you will start to take on their unsavoury behaviours. Just look at what happened to Kristian, his exploits leave him housebound due to that TRO he received."

"Why don't you use the lights Herb installed to read instead of those candles?" I nodded to the spotlights on the ceiling, asking more to avoid his lecture than out of curiosity.

"They add ambiance, artificial light is so…artificial," he replied in a bored, silky voice.

"Anyway, we have to keep some traditions, if we start following every trend the humans come up with we will start thinking we are like them. There has to be certain…. boundaries."

He locked his eyes knowingly on me. The flickering glow of the candle light gave his face a look of severity unusual for him.

"I am well aware of the boundaries. I have spent my entire unlife trapped behind them," I replied, meeting his gaze steadily.

"The magical gate that separates us from the human realm is there for a reason, Scarlet. Too much time spent in their world can awaken unwanted temptations."

"Not all of us need to lock ourselves away from the world, not all of us are that weak." I retorted, before turning and walking away from him, but not before catching a flash of surprise in his eyes from my outburst. I knew my comment had been unnecessarily harsh, Dante had made one mistake in his long life as a vampire, and had already paid his dues for it, but I was feeling out of sorts. Traces of the boy's blood still flowed through me, warming me and stirring strange sensations I still did not fully understand.

After my clash with Dante, I paced the hallways of the house before returning to my own room. I turned on my CD player and laid down on my bed; the song 'Colourblind' was playing. It had been a song I had heard in the mind of a girl I had fed from a few months ago. The song wasn't related to a particular memory; they usually weren't; it was just music stored in the person's head, that had significance. The feeling I got from the song when I heard it through this girl's memories was the strangest feeling of all. It was not a happy feeling, quite the opposite in fact, but it was such a strong emotion that I had Herb hunt down the song for me. Naturally, I could have easily replicated the song myself, with instrument or voice and I was even able to appreciate the music from a technical level. But as for 'feeling' the music, it was beyond me without the girl's memory. The music they played in Plasma had no lyrics and was just a senseless repetitive beat that our kind could move systematically to without thought. I had never understood the difference until I had heard this song through that girl. Since then I would often listen to music after I had fed, still under the influence of the flickers I felt like I could sense more, and for a few hours before the effects wore off, I could understand what humans truly felt when they listened to music, and it was beautiful. I had built up a little collection of musical memories over the last month, like personal trophies, but no matter how often I listened to each one they were never the same as when I had first heard them through that person's mind.

Herb suddenly ambled in and sat himself in the corner armchair, he was liberally applying a foul smelling ointment that Mildred had concocted for him. Despite the intrusion and fetid odour I was content to lose myself in the music, even as the meaning of it began to fade away.

I closed my eyes and was all set to enjoy the final flickers from tonight's prey, when Kristian materialised. Herb yelped in surprise and nearly dropped the jar of ointment. Vampires could never bring themselves to just knock and enter, trivial things like privacy and manners were below them now. They rarely considered or cared that their presence may not be welcome. I made a point of never materialising myself; more out of the fact that it made me feel more disconnected from the world; rather than respect and manners. Despite my indifference to pain and temperature the fact that I could feel my feet planted on the ground and have contact with inanimate objects reassured me I was still here. I had already been temporarily removed from this world when my sire killed me, and when I came back I was undead. I wasn't confident that if I did decide to materialise, that I would be able to return even to that state...I could completely fade away to nothingness.

"There she is, my melancholy little sister," Kristian's voice brought me back to my, at least, half-life.

"You certainly like to live up to the self-loathing stereotype of our kin, even your music is depressing," he mocked.

I sighed and sat up glaring at him. "I am not living it up. I am trying to appreciate the calming yet confusing vocals of a human that had spent his whole life living it up. It's the closest I will ever get to the real thing."

"Human sex, drugs and rock and roll seems fun, but you know what's better?" Kristian teased.

"You not being in my room?" I muttered.

"Not even that! Oh no, my little sister! What's better is feeding off a human after they have spent an evening in decadence. We get to taste every high, every pleasure they had but mixed up with our own heightened senses. Why? because WE get to live in the now. What do Humans do? Fret and worry about the end of their short little lives, that they forget to live their lives at all."

"So that's why you are here, to enlighten me on how great being a vampire is?" I said mockingly.

"I am concerned about you. Dante said you seemed a little sensitive, even bordering on hostile?" he said with genuine sincerity.

So the self-righteous fop had decided to tell on me, I knew my comment had irritated him. I watched as Kristian slunk about my room with feline grace picking up a book on my shelf then tossing it aside with little regard.

"Worried that I will go join a vampire gang like Remnant?" I sneered.
He laughed a low rumble. "Scar, you wouldn't last five minutes in a vampire gang."

He picked up the beaded rosary on my chest of drawers examining it. Father had given us one each, after we had been turned, explaining that we were still creatures of God even if others didn't think so. Contrary to common belief we could touch religious devices without pain or discomfort.

He placed the rosary back with care, then looked at me with narrowed eyes.

"We are all concerned, Scar. You are acting even more despondent than usual. Plus you are so dead-looking lately even for our kin."

"If this is your attempt at brotherly concern, spare us both." He ignored me and instead turned his gaze on Herb who furiously started massaging ointment to the end of his shrivelled toe, pretending not to have heard anything.

"You are making sure she is feeding enough aren't you, worm bait?" Kristian stated accusingly.

I gave Herb a warning glance. He looked up guiltily but nodded an assurance to Kristian, before refocusing on his toe again. Truth be told, I didn't need to drink as many blood packs, as I was getting my fix directly from the humans above. Besides, the pre-packed stuff didn't do it for me anymore. It didn't fulfil any of my predatory instincts and it didn't give me the memories I craved. As for looking more dead I personally didn't see the difference. My skin had the same silky texture as usual, in fact the fresh blood straight from the vein had given it a more life-like glow in my opinion. It was not quite the human flush of colour but I was definitely less ashen than usual. No, I knew exactly what he was up to,
he was prying, trying to see if he could catch me out. Maybe Herb was right and Kristian was on to us.

"I'm fine," I insisted keeping my eyes on Herb who was likely to break under Kristian's interrogation if this continued.

"When are you going to realise that being a vampire is a blessing, Scarlet? You must embrace it, only then will you come to respect and enjoy its many facets."

His face took on a sinister smile and I could tell he was thinking back to his sordid evening with his blood dolls.

"The point is all this moping about doesn't change anything, you are still a vampire, Scar, and the sooner you accept that, the sooner you can start to enjoy your unlife. Do you know how many people would love to have what you have? Immortality?!

"He's right you know." I spun round. Dante materialised from the shadows.

"Throughout time, humans have surrounded themselves in myths and fairy tales of eternal youth and life. Even today they waste their lives battling the inevitability of age with these 'sciences', pills, surgery and now even freezing! However, for all the time they waste on these endeavours, they are not living longer just dying slower."

There was deathly silence for a moment while everyone took in what Dante had said, until I couldn't take it anymore.

"Will everyone stop materialising in my room?! There's a reason why I have a lock on it," I stated exasperatedly.

"Locks are for humans," said Dante dismissively. "A simple toy to give the illusion of security."

"Just like condoms," said Kristian childishly, causing Dante and I to sigh in unison, although I was quite sure I heard a muffled snigger from Herb.

"You are both wrong, being a vampire isn't the only way for a person to obtain immortality." I stated.

Dante looked intrigued while Kristian snorted.

"If you say through your kids I will remind you that having a few brats to claim your possessions after you bite the dust hardly compares to living forever."

"No. Father believes there is another way to eternal life, through the salvation of God." I said softly, knowing I was opening myself up for ridicule from the pair of them.

Both Kristian and Dante exchanged looks before Kristian snorted again. "If such a thing exists."

"Why not? After all we exist and we are meant to be creatures of myth," I said matter of factly.

It was a valid point and both of them knew it. I had never been religious like Father was, but I had to believe there was more to life than this. If a demon like the one that started all of this vampire nonsense existed, then you had to question where such a thing would have come from in the first place. After all, if there is a hell, then there had to be a heaven.

"If you and father are right, and God does exist, what makes you think any of us would be worthy of his salvation?" said Kristian a little more seriously now.

"Because we didn't choose this curse, take father for example, he was a good man before this happened, a righteous man who fought in the holy wars, surely that counts for something?" I said.

"He probably killed more humans in those wars than he has as a vampire," said Kristian dismissively.

"If you're such a non-believer then why do you wear the Rosary father gave you?" I accused.

"It's purely aesthetic, humans just love the whole repenting vampire thing," he said suddenly clasping the necklace.

Despite what Kristian was saying, I knew it was more than that. He loved to act the carefree unrepentant. But if that were truly the case, he would never have risked his life to leave Remnant.

"Perhaps joining us at the end of the month for the annual Murder Mystery weekend would do you some good?" suggested Dante in an attempt to change the subject.

"That sounds even duller than staying here," I said.

"It's really fun actually. A whole bunch usually turn up and it would give you a chance to mingle with others of our kin. I met a particularly lovely French chap last year; I am partial to an accent, as you know. His skin glowed like moonlight on the water, none of this dull ash hue that some of the younger generation are walking around with. He was the one who recommended I change my eating habits in the first place, did I tell you?"

"What Dante is trying to say," cut in Kristian. "Is, that it would do you good to mingle with some vampires your own age more often. Plasma was a good start but you should try the murder mystery weekend also. I met this ravishing young woman when I first went, back in '82, hair as black as ebony and skin like frozen silk, she really scarred me and I am not talking about the emotional kind of scars...it's a good thing we heal fast, I had nail marks on my back and even along my..."

"STOP. I get the point!" I shouted before he could finish. "Look, I will consider going." At this point, I was willing to say anything to get them out of my room.

"That's the spirit, Scar!" Kristian said enthusiastically. He looked to Herb.

"I would leave maggot face here if I were you, he'll only be a dead weight." He turned towards the door, laughing at his own joke.

Dante lingered. "I am glad you'll consider coming, I really think you'll like it. A lot of the old crowd stopped attending since they instigated the new rule; that the person murdered is not actually killed. Most of the traditional vampires thought this spoilt the fun but it's still great." With that, he began to fade before my eyes.

"DANTE, just use the door for goodness sake!" he came back into focus looking rather disgruntled.

"All right, but it's not as dramatic," he replied defeated.

With the room finally to myself; and Herb; I switched on the TV. They were showing an undead reality show, with ghouls swapping unlifes with their respective vampire masters. I was just getting into it when I could feel

Herb staring at me. I continued to ignore him staring fixedly at the screen. After a couple of minutes he finally plucked up the courage to speak.

"Scarlet..." it was barely a faint whisper.

"Don't even think about it," I said cutting him off. I knew what he was thinking.

"But Scar...they are becoming suspicious, you heard what Kristian said earlier, if he finds out he will flay what little flesh I have left." Herb's ears started to twitch a little.

"Don't be silly, if he really knew he would have killed you already." I stated matter of factly.

Herb gulped. "Oh, that makes me feel a lot better!"

"Look, I will lay low for a bit, take a week off from hunting." I hoped this would be enough to reassure Herb.

He looked at me, his yellow eyes narrowing in thought as he watched me. "You're planning something aren't you?"

"What? Don't be so paranoid, Herb. What is it with you ghouls? You're never happy unless you're accusing someone of plotting something."

He gawped indignantly. "That's not true, ghouls are known for their trusting nature."

"Right. That's why all the ghoul clans are constantly bickering. Didn't the ghoul king recently execute an entire tribe because he thought they were conspiring to overthrow him?!"

"Everyone knows that was a small misunderstanding," said Herb defensively.

"Hate to think what he would have done had it been a large one," I muttered.

"You're changing the subject, Scar, Kristian is looking for an excuse to get rid of me, what if he's already planning it?!" he continued whining.

There was a wet popping noise, as his eyeball fell out of its socket, he was clearly getting worked up again. I waited patiently as it dangled on the bloodied optic nerve while he struggled to catch the eyeball with a cupped hand. Finally catching it, he tilted his head back and squished it back into the socket.

"Look, Herb, he has no clue and even if he did he wouldn't kill you, it's all just empty threats," I said reassuringly.

"Vampires don't make empty threats," said Herb, squelching the flesh around his eye with his finger.

That was true. But I had to say something reassuring, otherwise he was going to keep freaking out until he had literally fallen to pieces.

"He knows nothing Herb. He just likes to act like he does, it's what he does to keep himself amused. For all his pro-immortality, even he gets bored at times." This last point seemed to finally reach him.

"Thanks, Scar, I feel better now," he said with a sniff. Herb was very sensitive, part of not transitioning into a fully-fledged vampire made ghouls very susceptible to emotions. I quickly looked away feeling uncomfortable, I had always been courteous to Herb and even confided in him. I had become so used to him being around, but I couldn't feel more than that familiarity; I could never care for him.

"Just try to stay calm and keep applying that ointment regularly, okay?" He nodded. "I better go, I said I would help Mildred order Dante's organic blood online, you can't get it in the Underdark, it has to be specially imported from one of those free range human farms."

I rolled my eyes. Herb didn't notice and continued.

"You know what Mildred's like, she can whip up a cure for almost any undead ailment but put her in front of a computer and she freaks out." With that, he got up, stretching with a creak as his bones cracked back into place, before shuffling out. A second later, he popped his head back through the door.

"Goodnight, Scarlet" he said smiling.

Now truly alone, I knelt on the floor and reached under the bed, pulling out a small box. Inside was my secret collection of human modifiers, different coloured wigs, contact lenses, make-up to give my unnatural cheeks that natural glow, and my retainer which I quickly popped into my mouth. It was meant to help re-contour my fangs and give them a more rounded appearance, making them less noticeable. Or so the ghoul trader at the market told me. I had been wearing them for over a year now but had not seen the slightest difference, but time was something I had in abundance so I kept wearing them. Also inside the box was a collection of human music and a small notebook, where I wrote down the latest flickers. I quickly jotted down this evening's experience with the boy, wary to note as many the details before it wore off. As I flipped through the book, I noticed it was almost filled up. I wondered how many books I would have to fill before any of it made sense to me. It seemed all too easy for my brothers, no need to research or store data. They seemed to fit into vampire society and life so easily, despite how different they were from each other. Over the ages vampire society had broken down into many subcultures to accommodate the members and quirks of our growing race. Dante was a true Historic vampire. He still dressed and acted as he did when he was turned in the 16th Century, most of the Blue Blood members were historic vampires, refusing to acknowledge any age but their own. On the opposite side of the spectrum there were the Glampires who Dante also fitted into. A fairly new vampire movement that was obsessed with the type of blood you consumed and its many benefits. Kristian on the other hand, was a Dystopian vampire. They dressed more modern in order to fit in above ground, most of the vampire gangs fitted firmly into this sub-culture.

Father and Desmodeus were part of the Conventionalists, like any strong follower of the Tribune was bound to be. Then there were other even more obscure subcultures, like the Fetish vampires who had replaced their human addictions with vampire ones, treating blood as not just a need but also a want. I supposed technically, all my brothers could fall into this category as well. Yet, with so many different subcultures, I still could never see myself fitting in. The only sub-culture I wanted to be involved in was the human one, the one that was not an option.

I returned the book to the box, attached the lid and slid it back under the bed. The TV show was still on, with the vampire talking about her week as a ghoul. From the looks of her she was a Dystopian. No surprise there, the only sub-culture vain enough to take part in such a show.

"It has made me view my own unlife differently," she stated. "I appreciate things more now than I did before, just being in someone else's shoes for a short time has helped me grow as an undead."

Ridiculous.

But despite the ridiculousness of the vampire's statement, the words she said had an effect. At the back of my mind an idea, that had started as a dream surfaced and this idea was now turning into a full-scaled plan.

Later that night I made my way down the stairs and into the kitchen. I was just pouring myself a cup of blood and heating it in the microwave when I sensed someone materialising nearby. I grabbed my hot blood and attempted to scurry out before they could fully appear, but knew I was too late when I felt a hand on my shoulder. I turned around reluctantly and met the stern gaze of my eldest brother Desmodeus. His long black hair was tied back in a ponytail and he was simply dressed in his staple black suit - he always dressed like he had come from a business meeting. I tried to picture him before he was turned, imagining warm perhaps even welcoming brown eyes as opposed to the cold calculating pale orbs they had become in undeath. It could have been my imagination, but he looked even more grave and intimidating than usual. It always felt like a test when he was around, even when he was only trying to make light conversation.

"Scarlet? I'm glad I caught you, it seems like you are always out lately." Like the others, Desmodeus still insisted on treating me like a child.

"I have been trying to get more involved with the undead scene," I said, avoiding his eyes. I never felt comfortable expressing my difficulties of acceptance in front of him, Dante and Kristian would nag me about my lack of appreciation, but Desmodeus was different. It seemed like he was always observing me, waiting as if I was a bomb about to go off. I could never admit it to Herb but I worried that if Desmodeus ever heard some of the things I had said to the others, he would have dragged me before the

Tribune on charges of Human Intent years ago. The general belief within the Tribune, was that to merely idealise humans was enough to be considered a risk, a vampire that wanted to be human would actively go out and seek ways to feel human or worse, try to find a cure for our condition. And since it was far easier to feel human again through flickers; as opposed to finding a cure; it inevitably meant, more attempts to go above ground, which meant more chances of discovery. I felt Desmodeus's eyes boring into me again as I took a sip of the hot blood. Far less enjoyable than my earlier live catch.

"The Tribune seems to be having a lot more meetings recently," I said, striking first to dictate the conversation subject.

"Yes, there has been a killing above ground, a human boy was found dead a few hours ago outside a human establishment named Insomnia. It has drawn attention in the past by vampire gangs, but never a feeding fatality."

"What?" I blurted out, nearly spilling blood down myself as my mouth missed the cup.

"Apparently an ambulance was called but he was dead before they arrived," he stated bluntly.

The news was startling. I sat down on one of the breakfast stools, the legs squeaking against the tiles as I did so.

"It's probably just another gang attack," I replied. This was no time to panic I thought, I had to make sure that this did not lead back to me.

"I don't believe so. The pattern is different, as I said previous vampire gangs have hunted this place, but never killed. If anything, they would have taken the human back to their nest to share," Desmodeus pointed out.

"The idea of a rogue vampire killing, has caused some concern for the Tribune as you can imagine. They fear this could lead to a trend if not dealt with, worse still, it would undermine the authority of the Tribune," he looked genuinely concerned as he considered this.

"I am sure the Tribune have a list of suspects already," I put forth casually.

"There have already been a few members of the FF vocalising approval of the attack, one even started a forum post about it so we will most likely start there."

I could sense Desmodeus growing more anxious as he spoke, I knew what he was considering. Every time an incident like this occurred previous law breakers had to be investigated, which included our own dear brother Dante. It had been over a century since that fatal night, and while Dante had atoned, it had not been forgotten and remained a permanent stain. While Father had still kept his position within the Tribune and even been allowed to indoctrinate Desmodeus, the events of that night had ultimately reduced Father's influence.

I decided that now would be a good time to excuse myself. I got up casually and bade Desmodeus good night before climbing the stairs. As soon as I got to my room, I closed the door and turned the TV on, furiously flicking with the remote until I came across The Daily Departed, our news channel, to my relief I had made it in time for the murder coverage. A picture of the boy I had fed on only hours before flashed up on the screen as the newsreader, a male Freshie with glasses and a literally chiseled jawline, made his report.

"The teenager was pronounced dead at the scene despite efforts made from the human medical services to revive him. No arrests have been made by the Tribune at present but, due to the nature of the injuries, they are treating it as a vampire related killing. The Tribune is urging any undead citizen with information to come forward and help them with their inquiries."

This had the potential to be problematic.

I sank into my bed and went over my predicament. There were no witnesses of me feeding on the boy, that I was sure of. I had also remembered to cast a cloaking spell, so on the off chance of anyone seeing me, they would have forgotten so immediately. I held my hands to my head as the faint traces of the boy's memories echoed through me again. A reminder of the life I had taken, his happiness and pain swirled in my mind until it shifted to his final memory, my face. I was sure I had stopped before there was any risk of it becoming fatal, I remembered him still breathing...perhaps I underestimated his strength? Surely the Tribune would see this was an accident! Stop making excuses, a small voice whispered inside my head. You are responsible for his death and you enjoyed it. You still remember his scent and the taste of his warm blood as it wet your lips. Accident, or not, you murdered him and you will do so again, it's in your nature...

Chapter 4

~*The Most Important Meal of the Day*~

 The next morning I sat in the kitchen as Herb made breakfast, he was trying to make small talk, but I was engrossed with the book I was reading. That is, until I was distracted by Dante and Kristian. They were bickering over food again, as of late Mildred rarely waited on them due to their specific needs. Dante preferred to make his own meals which comprised of a strict diet, while Kristian fed off his blood dolls or straight from a pack. I had my own dietary requirements which Herb had always tended to. Dante stood in front of the fridge scrutinising each blood pack, while Kristian rolled his eyes at the performance.

 "Come on, it's not a gourmet meal you're preparing. Just grab a packet and move along. Some of us are starving here."

 Dante ignored him and continued to sift through the packets until he found what he was looking for.

 "Finally!" gasped Kristian, as he grabbed a pack at random. He tore it open with his fangs and greedily sucked out the contents.

 Dante had just started the 'Blood Group Diet' the latest fad among the Glampires; it had been created by a vampire claiming to be a self-styled blood expert. He had even released a book about it.

 "Depending on the cultivated blood type each human would have a distinctive 'taste' and additional unique health benefits," said Dante pedantically.

 "Oh, come on! Even you can't seriously believe that nonsense," scoffed Kristian. "The whole thing is just a fad created by some vampire who found a gap in the market to exploit, despite having no proven credentials."

 Dante sniffed indignantly as he carefully measured out his chosen blood into a goblet.

 "Doctor Ervin's findings have been supernaturally proven, the amount of high sugar contained within common blood groups can, over time, affect us negatively," he said matter of factly.

 "What?! Any doctor that calls himself Ervin is bound to be a hack and anyway we're vampires. It's not like we're at risk of contracting diabetes."

I flicked my eyes between the two, wondering who would win this argument and bring the gift of silence.

 "No, but the high increase of obesity in humans can cause adverse effects on those feeding from them. Those who drink high sugar level blood put themselves at risk of reduced quality of unlife."

"Like what, fang ache?" muttered Kristian. Dante threw him a glare but continued.

"Among other things Dr Ervin's studies clearly show that vampires who are not fussy about the type of blood they consume are more likely to suffer from weight gain and frenzied episodes. I have only been on the diet for two weeks and have already noticed a difference in my energy levels. I have better digestion and more importantly I can fit back into my leather trousers, something I have not been able to do since the sixties." Dante grinned, clearly pleased with himself.

"Which is when anyone with a sense of style would be caught dead wearing them," said Kristian.

Herb let out a laugh, which turned into a gurgle as Dante glowered at him.

"The point is, the type of blood one chooses to live on could very well effect the…"

"If you dare say longevity..." interrupted Kristian.

"I was actually going to say vitality. But I wouldn't expect someone of your limited understanding of haematology to understand," he said with a condescending glare.

"I know enough to have stayed alive on common blood for the last two centuries," retorted Kristian.

Their voices faded to droning tones as I stopped paying attention, and returned to my book. It was called Perfume: The Story of a Murderer by Patrick Süskind. Set in 18th century France, the main character was a serial killer who stalked young women and collected their scents. He was obsessed with re-creating the perfect scent after having come across it in the form of a girl that had made him feel happy for the first time in his impoverished life. I wondered if I was the same, seeking out the perfect mind, convinced that one day I would experience a Flicker that would finally fulfil me enough to accept what I am.

"What in the name of all things undead is that?!" came the sound of Kristian's voice, rudely cutting into my thoughts.

He was referring to Herb, who had finished frying my breakfast. He slipped the two flat red discs onto my plate before presenting them to me with a flourish.

"My breakfast, blood pancakes," I replied as I cut a piece with my knife and fork, and nibbled it delicately.

"What is wrong with this family? Poncy blood type diets, whisked blood and syrup!" Kristian lamented.

"Actually, it's honey," I corrected him.

"We need only blood. Raw, delicious and sometimes fresh, old fashioned blood!" he paused mid-rant and picked up the wrinkled peach I had just placed on the counter from my pocket.

"What is the meaning of this?" He looked at me perplexed.

"An experiment, it's the closest I will get to the natural order of things," I replied.

"By watching a fruit grow mould? The natural order of things is that we are not natural! You cannot change that, so accept it," he said firmly and threw the peach in the bin.

Suddenly a black shadow filled the room and Desmodeus stood before us all, his expression grim.

"Eldest brother! What a pleasure it is to see you," said Kristian with an exaggerated bow.

Desmodeus sneered at him, I think he was trying to smile.

"Kristian, I am surprised and pleased to find you here, and not at one of those loathsome Blood Dens."

Kristian gave a hollow laugh.

"Just as I'm surprised you have graced us with your appearance, I hope the Tribune pay you overtime, after all you know what they say, all work and no play makes a ghoul out of you."

Desmodeus ignored Kristian and seated himself next to me as he watched Herb obediently prepare him a drink.

"Any update on that boy who was killed?" I asked trying to sound casual, I needed to know the next steps of the Tribune if I was to avoid suspicion.

"We have the Wardens patrolling above ground making their investigations. The hardest part is trying to stop the human authorities from interfering, but we have skilled enthrallers working on it," he said confidently.

"How are the old thought police? It's been a long time since I had any dealings with them," said Kristian. "In fact the last time I was in the company of Wardens, they were having a whale of a time applying red hot pokers to me in various unsavoury places."

"For good reason as I recall," said Desmodeus, swirling his blood round his glass before taking a long sip.

"I understand they have to conduct such procedures, I just wish they would keep up with the times. Pokers are so passe and have no impact on today's generation who think they have seen it all," continued Kristian. "If they really wanted to make an impact they should take something from those mortal horror films, you've got to give the humans credit, they still know their torture."

"Enough of your impudence, little brother," said Desmodeus.

"I came here to speak with Dante, you may stay if you wish but interrupt me again and I will have to indulge your idea, perhaps the flammable jelly trap? I too keep up with human cinema, in fact you would be surprised just how many torture methods I have been inspired by recently."

Kristian's eyes darkened for a moment but he kept quiet. I watched on with interest wondering why Desmodeus wanted to speak with Dante so urgently that it couldn't wait until later. Dante must have been worried because he forgot about his careful measurements and was pouring the blood bags in randomly.

"Dante, I need to ask where you were yesterday evening?" My heart would have skipped a beat if it had any beat to skip. Dante tore himself away from his special blood type breakfast to meet his older brother's gaze.

"I was in my room all evening, reading."

Desmodeus studied him for a moment before replying. "You are willing to stand by that if taken in before the Tribune?"

Dante narrowed his eyes. "Yes, what is all this about, Desmodeus?"

"A teenage boy was found dead above ground last night, bite marks on his neck. His body completely drained of blood." There was an accusatory tone to the statement.

Dante looked down at his hands. "I see."

"You understand why I had to ask?" said Desmodeus.

"Of course."

The silence in the room was deafening as the two of them stood there, then suddenly it was broken by a loud slap as Kristian swatted Herb around the back of the head.

"Will you stop that scratching, what on earth's gotten into you? Have those maggots of yours finally started eating what's left of that dried out grey sponge you call a brain?"

I jerked my head up to look at Herb and could see loose flakes of skin hanging off his cranium, where he had clearly been clawing at it with his blunt nails. He shrank away from Kristian and shot me a look. I hopped off the breakfast stool and put myself between them grabbing Herb's crusty hand and leading him away as I called behind me.

"Herb has irritable rot again, must have picked it up from one of the uncleans at the market. I'll take him to Mildred for some more ointment."

When we were a safe distance away from them I glared at him.

"Why not just blurt it out next time?" I whispered harshly.

He cringed, still rubbing the back of his head where Kristian had whacked him.

"Sorry, Scar, but I get itchy when I am nervous." I inspected the top of his head, which had broken out in a cluster of angry looking blisters and softened my tone.

"I know, this isn't your fault, it's mine but I need you to try and act normal. This whole thing will blow over in a few days," I reassured.

Herb nodded while absently picking at a particular puss filled blister. He was still fiddling with it when we found Mildred in my father's study, she was polishing a dangerous looking sword from his wall mounted collection of weapons.

"Hello, young Scarlet," she said smiling warmly and exposed a mouth full of well preserved teeth, an impressive feat considering the rest of her was heavily decomposed.

"Mildred, do you have anything stronger than that ointment you gave Herb earlier?"

She ambled over and peered closely at Herb's blistered scalp.

"Hmm not seen a case of irritable rot syndrome so bad since young Alfie, one of the blood technicians at the Blood Bank, poor thing suffers terribly from the condition. It's the job, all that interacting with humans, he looks pretty good as ghouls go but he still gets so nervous when taking samples that he sheds worse than a snake."

She appraised Herb with her mucus yellow eyes.

"I can make you up a more potent batch but it will only soothe the problem, not get rid of it. You need to deal with whatever is causing your anxiety to completely fix it."

Herb looked as though he was about to say something so I promptly thanked Mildred and started ushering him out. When we were back in my room I made sure to keep Herb occupied with menial tasks, it took his mind off the situation and meant he was too busy to vent his worries onto me. I knew once the Tribune had conducted their investigations and realised they had no leads they would close the case, all I would have to do was lie low for a week or so.

I managed to get through the rest of the day without Herb mentioning my nocturnal outings and the concerns he had about them. Mildred had stopped by with some stronger ointment and after giving Herb strict instructions on its use, she left without any further questions, much to my relief. It helped that she was already preoccupied with Kristian's blood dolls who were staying over again. Unaccustomed to servant etiquette, the pair were ransacking the kitchen. I had stayed hidden in my room precisely because of this, I was not in the habit of chatting to Kristian's blood dolls when they stayed over, I had tried conversing in the past with previous ones he had brought home and it was always the same. Most of the time they would be incoherent due to being under the influence of Kristian's blood and when you could get any sense out of them they would only talk about the dark kiss or how much they loved our blood. I wanted to learn about how to live a human life, not how to waste one. However I eventually became hungry enough to risk venturing out. All I had to do was slip past the open parlour room door and make a beeline for the kitchen.

"If you wanted to sneak past you should have materialised," came Kristian's voice.

"Get in here and be sociable for a change; you're becoming more and more like Dante each decade."

I thought about ignoring him but that usually made things worse. One time he brought his guests up to my room because I refused to come down and say hello. He was in his usual spot on the sofa watching TV with Mary and Cecile. Both girls had fresh bite marks on their necks and Kristian had cuts on his arms where he had been feeding them his own blood. The residue of the thick black liquid lingered on their smiling mouths, Kristian mistook my look of disdain for apprehension.

"It's safe to come in, the prodigal son left due to pressing Tribune matters, probably busy impaling some poor fledgling." Mary and Cecile laughed at his weak joke.

"I've never met your other brother!" said Mary indignantly like a formal introduction to Desmodeus would somehow take their relationship to the next level.

"You're not missing much, he's a bit of a stiff and I am not talking about rigor mortis." Both of the girls giggled again, more likely due to the effects of Kristian's blood, than at his bad jokes. Kristian turned his attention back to the TV.

"Aha! The Daily Departed, what new and exciting things are happening in the Underdark?" said Kristian as a female Freshie appeared on the screen. She was standing outside a shabby looking shop in the Ghoul Quarter. "That's Willy's place," he added.

"Batches of bottled blood have been withdrawn from Willy's Waterhole and the establishment closed while the Tribune conduct a full investigation after samples tested positive for containing traces of dead blood," stated the Freshie. "The discovery was made after several vampires came over with the blood sickness attributed to the intake of excess amounts of dead blood. All the reported cases had purchased their blood regularly from Willy's Waterhole, popular for having the lowest prices within the city. It is not the first time the shop has been under investigation following a recall only last year when it was discovered that a large number of his stock had been watered down with pigs' blood. Willy himself was seized and arrested this morning by Wardens at his apartment above the shop; even the High Enforcer himself was there to escort the ghoul into custody."

Footage of Desmodeus flashed up on the screen. He was frowning at the small ghoul who stood before him being held either side by wardens.

"Oh! There he is, our heroic brother saving us from the likes of Willy, I feel so safe now," Kristian stated sarcastically.

"It's no laughing matter, brother," said Dante who had, for once, used the door to enter the room. "Dead blood can be fatal to our kind!"

"Only if you drink a lot of it, not in the amounts that Willy was using," stated Kristian. "And are they surprised? The Tribune increased the cost of donated blood again so independent shops like Willy have to pay through the neck for their stock. You can't really blame the little pestilent for trying to cut costs."

"Since when did you become a ghoul rights activist?" I asked shocked at Kristian's sudden change of attitude.

"I'm not, I just think that they should be hunting down this rogue vampire that is actually killing instead of sending a team of Wardens to bring in one ghoul trying to make an unliving."

At the mention of the rogue vampire attacks, Dante faded into mist and was gone. Taking this as my queue to escape, I excused myself and made for the kitchen. Things were getting more complicated, family were involved in the investigation and also part of the investigation, on the plus side, it seemed I was a non-factor...

Chapter 5

~A Day Out with Two Brothers~

The next day Dante seemed even more interested than usual to harass me about my lack of appreciation of vampirism. I thought that secretly he just wanted to distract himself from thinking about recent events. I did feel a bit responsible for that, and it was mainly because of this that I gave in and let him take me to one of his favourite haunts in the Underdark. We were in the Vampire Quarter standing outside an ancient looking building even by Underdark standards. Two dead bay trees in large pots framed the doorway giving it an even more morbid appearance. Hung on a dusty plaque crudely nailed to the door was their price list, my eyes bulged as I took in the cost.

"45 Drakmir for one taste!" I exclaimed.

Dante looked around anxiously checking to see if anyone had heard my remark. The inner snob in him had awoken, and he smiled nervously at a passing vampire.

"Young ones, no appreciation of fine-dining you know," he uttered.

The vampire ignored him and walked straight past, heading for an all you can bite buffet across the street which was a mere 10 Drakmir.

"Explain what this place is again?" I asked, looking up at the old building with trepidation. Usually I avoided vampire-drinking holes as much as possible, they were either extremely seedy like Plasma or extremely pompous. Knowing Dante this place was probably going to be as pretentious as he was.

"This is a Blooderie, an establishment used to mix different blends of blood from donors in order to improve and sell to connoisseurs. The whole process is done by a Blood Maker, it is considered an art." Dante was in his element; having never sired anyone he had never had a protégé to inflict his teachings on.

"They collect donors from all over the world," he continued excitedly.

"Choosing only the purest and well-bred bloodlines. They hold tastings where vampires like myself can sample their stock before making a purchase, they also value our opinion as it helps them brew better beverages."

Inside, the place was almost empty. A lone vampire sitting at the bar turned in his stool to give us the once over, then nodded curtly at Dante, who nodded back and turned to me with a look of self-importance.

"They all know me here you see, I am one of the vintage crowd." A ghoul that looked even older than Mildred greeted us as we entered, bowing low. His bones creaking and cracking like dry twigs.

"Scarlet, this is Norm, the most renowned Blood Maker in our society."

He gave me what he must have hoped was a friendly smile, but the effect of the already taut skin stretching over his protruding cheekbones; one of which was partially exposed; was more ghastly than welcoming, and before I could stop him he bowed again creating further disturbing sounds from his joints.

"This is my brood sister, I am taking some time to educate her that not all vampires are depraved blood bingers."

Norm nodded sagely as he beckoned to another ghoul wearing a black waistcoat and bow tie, who scurried over to take Dante's top hat and cape.

"Very responsible of you sir, what with all the sireless fledglings running around of late. Why Oscar here is proof that it's getting worse up there." Despite the decaying traits so common to his race, it was obvious that Oscar had been a young human, younger than Herb or any other ghoul I had seen.

"Underage siring is happening more often because the fledgling vampires of today have not had the guidance the previous generation had. Oscar was only ten mortal years old when he was turned last month, no well-raised vampire would attempt the dark kiss on a human that young."

"Quite," replied Dante busily adjusting the frilled cuffs of his sleeves, not even bothering to glance at Oscar who was now performing his own little bows.

"Very quiet today, Norm," said Dante casting his eyes across the empty tables surrounding the bar as he perched himself on one of the stools, motioning for me to do the same. I joined him reluctantly, my own eyes scanning the rows of racks behind the bar holding dark bottles filled with blood, these were also labelled and priced.

"Hard times, sir, the Wardens are coming down on us ghouls. Old Gus's place was closed last week and he's got a fifty-year ban from keeping donors."

"Goodness, what for?" asked Dante leaning forward eagerly at the prospect of gossip.

Vampires rarely indulged in the affairs of others, especially ghouls, it was as if we suffered from a conversational narcissism where we would only talk about ourselves. Ghouls however were renowned for their tittle-tattle, perhaps it was due to being more human and, even though Dante would be loathed to admit it, I suspected he did not visit Norm's merely for the fine blood but also for a chance to hear about the latest scandal. If it wasn't for his perfectly preserved corpse, I would assume his sometimes human tendencies were due to some ghoulish nature. But I put it down to Dante just being Dante, I had never met another vampire quite like him and I was convinced I would have thought the same of him pre-transition. Some things do carry over in death it seems.

"For buying cheap blood from unregistered blood dolls, apparently he has been dealing with one of the vampire gangs," Norm continued.

"This is precisely why I buy organic blood, it comes with all the legal paperwork," said Dante.

"That's not all of it, he was also selling Seasons Blood!" said Norm.

Dante gasped. "I am absolutely appalled, although I cannot say that I am surprised, what with this whole ghastly affair of Willy diluting his stock with dead blood. What on earth was he thinking? I am so glad the Tribune saw fit to investigate!"

Norm nodded knowingly. "They give the rest of us a bad rep. In the case of Willy, I am not surprised, he's been in and out of the Tribune Tower since he was turned, but Gus was well respected among us ghouls, times must be bad if it's come to this."

As soon as Norm ambled off to find a suitable beverage for us and was out of earshot, I turned to Dante. "What's Seasons blood?"

Dante stared at me in disbelief. "Scarlet, you were an adult when you were turned, a young one, but still an adult, you must know about these things."

"You know very well I remember nothing of my mortal existence," I retorted.

He sighed. "Human females... in order to conceive they.... well you see every month they…"

I stopped him. "Never mind, I remember learning about that during human anatomy class, at ghoul school … that's disgusting, some vampires actually drink that?"

"Only the most vile and deranged ones, it is extremely frowned upon," replied Dante.

Just then, while I was digesting this foul information, Norm returned with two tulip shaped glasses, a large silver bowl and a silk cloth draped over his arm.

"Right, onto your first lesson, Scarlet. Now pay very close attention as I am going to share with you something that took me decades of blood tasting to perfect."

"Fine, I'm listening," I said, wondering how long this was going to take.

"The common vampire will simply quaff down blood to satisfy their hunger without taking time to appreciate the flavours contained within," said Dante, as Norm placed the silk blindfold across his eyes. Then Norm; with a flourish which would have produced envy from the very best Wine Steward; filled the glass with one of the bottles from the racks, and placed it into Dante's hand.

"There are many ways to judge on whether one is drinking good quality blood. First, is the aroma!" He held the stem of the glass below his nose and gently swished the blood around while taking a deep, appreciative sniff.

"Next is the sensation it gives you when it fills your mouth," he took a dainty sip, pursed his lips and appeared to swish it around in his mouth before spitting it out into the silver spittoon provided.

"I thought you liked it?" I asked.

"I do, however one needs to keep a clear mind when tasting. If I swallow each sample I will easily become Blood drunk."

After more swirling, sniffing and debating he finally slammed the tulip glass down.

"Dark and broody with a silky texture, it is not something I would normally go for myself but being the esteemed taster I am I cannot fault the quality of it, it is of Russian birth!"

"Your palette is unmistakable sir, would you like to view the vessel, if you are pleased with its condition I can have a bottle put aside?" Norm proffered.

Dante nodded and Norm removed the blindfold before shambling off again.

"Finally - only after you have tasted what it has to offer - do you view the vessel, far less barbaric than drinking on first sight."

Norm returned with a young girl with white blonde hair and the bluest eyes I had ever seen. She held her head high meeting my gaze with those icy irises with a look of superiority that belied her youth.

"This is Iskra, imported fresh in from Moscow, she used to be one of Dreka's girls," said Norm with pride.

Dante nodded in admiration, even I, who did not associate with the vampire aristocrats, had heard of Dreka, the Russian vampire Prince. He had gained a reputation for impaling his victims on giant pikes while feeding on them, giving him the nickname: the Sevastopol Skewer. Although the practice of such a thing had long since been prohibited it is rumoured some of the old ones still consider such displays as a dining delicacy.

"She is certainly pleasing to the eye, with a supple and firm body," Dante ran a hand along her bare arm causing the girl to shudder. "Smooth and rich in texture, although, I must admit I prefer to dine from a...different vessel."

Iskra made a noise like a huff, then muttered something in Russian; which roughly translated to calling us low class vampires; before flicking her blonde hair over her shoulder. Norm ignored her, instead smiling knowingly at Dante.

"I think I have a couple of donors in today that might suit your selective palette." He replaced the blindfold. "I have not had time to bottle this one yet, so you will sample straight from the cask so to speak, if my master would find that agreeable?"

"Live tasting is my favourite kind, Norm, you know this," said Dante clapping his hands together in anticipation.

I watched as Norm led Iskra away, who was still cursing in Russian, and returned with a male human in tow. He was younger than the woman, probably in his late teens. He was handsome but his face had a gaunt look, as if he had seen more than one of his years should have. His bloodshot eyes were wide and he was visibly shaking as the ghoul unplugged a stopper from his wrist revealing a neatly cut out hole. He tilted the boy's wrist catching the blood that flowed out into a glass before replacing the stopper. He passed it to Dante who repeated his sniff, swish and spit technique. After dabbing his mouth on a cloth Norm provided he gave his opinion.

"Fatty......, dense....., lack of preservatives within the body, excessive copper, not enough iron, and…smokey. I would hazard a guess that the mortal smokes at least thirty cigarettes a day." Dante grimaced slightly and I knew he was thinking about his blood diet. "I'm afraid this one is rather unpalatable for me."

Norm nodded and made a note in his book.

"The flaws have been noted, sir, your judgement is always received well here."

The young male looked between the blindfolded vampire and the ghoul still looking as though he would like to run away. Norm removed a large coin purse from his waistcoat then shook his head muttering.

"Wrong currency, one moment," he then pulled a leather wallet from another pocket and removed a few paper notes.

"This should be sufficient I believe?" The young male took the notes his eyes widening as he counted them, then without a backward glance darted out of the building.

"A trial sample sir, but as you yourself advised he does not meet the standards required for the blooderie stock, but one must pay them for their time," he sighed.

Dante still blindfolded, smiled and nodded knowingly. "Quite. One bad donor can spoil the whole barrel."

"I do have something else in stock that might help cleanse your palette. One moment please sir."

Norm returned with another man although this one was better dressed and noticeably older, he looked to be in his forties but still handsome. His dark hair, although flecked with grey, was full and his brown eyes were bright and warm.

He was dressed smartly in an expensive looking suit. He showed no fear or disgust as Norm led him over to us, in fact the way he held himself seemed to hint a sense of pride in his job.

"This one has more vintage to it, harvested only once since reaching full maturity." Dante took a delicate sip, and then another, all three of us waited, while he sniffed and sipped without saying a word. He was spending longer on this one, swishing it round his mouth, making his cheeks bulge excessively before finally decanting.

At last he sat back and spoke.

"Tall, dark, elegant and velvety in texture." He removed his blindfold and appraised the man.

"Beautiful inside and out I see." He turned to Norm. "Raised locally?"

"Yes, I purchased Michael from the finishing farm in the Cotts Wolds, not only do they live on an organic diet there but they are educated in feeding etiquette."

Dante tilted the glass and watched as the man's blood slid across the crystal sides. "Good clarity, a fine sample."

Michael smiled and Norm seemed pleased, his rotten face screwing up in a disturbing way as he attempted the same gesture. The next hour passed, with Dante scrutinising me as I muddled my way through several samples of Norm's finest stock, and although I could tell they were skillfully blended and better quality than the bagged stuff we had at home, I still found the whole experience rather dull. Even the live feeding seemed a little too rehearsed, the humans standing rigidly as they prepared themselves, a few had even been given vampire blood beforehand to sedate them. All seemed to be trained in withholding their memories to deter unwanted flickers filtering through, even with my skill at seeking them out, they were hazy and emotionless at best. I might as well have been feeding from a vampire. Plus having Dante sigh at me when I used the wrong vocabulary to describe the taste took away any potential enjoyment. It got a bit better when Norm brought Michael back, watching Dante's shameless and dated flirting was at least amusing. Finally, after Dante recited a particularly depressing poem he had written in his darker days we were free to leave but not before he purchased a sizeable order of what the blooderie had to offer, the majority of it being from Michael's veins. Norm bowed us out the door so vigorously he slipped a disc with an audible pop, apparently oblivious to this, he thanked us for our custom and assured us that he would send his most trusted and competent ghouls over with the delivery later that afternoon.

Just as we exited I felt my relief vanish. Outside leaning against the wall with a cocky smile, was Kristian. Laughing at my scowl he scorned.

"What!? You didn't think I was going to leave it to Dante to show you the benefits of being a vampire. One day of his unlife and you'll be practicing self-staking in no time."

Dante glowered and raised his silver-tipped cane at Kristian threateningly.

"I suppose you think your influence will be far more positive? Where will you take her first, to one of your seedy Blood Dens where they practice crimson showers? Or perhaps you intend to meet up with some of your old gang friends and get her initiated."

Kristian simply smiled. "No, I have something even more incriminating in mind. We will see you back at home, don't wait up," and with that I was pulled along by the arm like a reluctant child.

"I know you're only doing this to vex him," I said. "It worked, so you don't need to follow through with whatever it is you have planned."

He ignored me and continued to pull me through the twists and turns of the Underdark until we were in the Witches Quarter.

I raised my eyebrows. "Father wouldn't approve."

He shrugged his shoulders. "Father signed the Treaty of Supernatural Unity just like the other Tribune members." He halted outside a shop called 'Dead Canvas'.

"Here's our first stop," he said dragging me in behind him. I had read about human tattoo parlours at Ghoul School and even seen pictures and they looked far more welcoming, this place looked more like a surgery clinic, vampires laid out on gurneys while ghouls wearing medical masks and wielding large scalpels worked on them. The air was thick with molecules of acrid, sour vampire blood. I turned to Kristian waiting for an explanation as to why watching our kind being mutilated would make me appreciate my unlife more.

"I have good reason for this. As you well know but don't appreciate, our bodies although dead are surprisingly resilient. The demonic power that resides in our blood keeps us from ageing and heals wounds that would kill a mortal."

"I know all of this, what's your point?" I asked, watching as a ghoul discarded a large piece of vampire flesh into a bucket with a resounding slap. The bucket of flesh would probably be recycled for some other means, ghouls always found ways of making money out of anything, that's why we used them for all our dealings. Some say they had evolved that way, after all how else would you survive among vampires when you're so low that you're not even deemed important enough to be at the bottom of the food chain.

"My point is that as far as the less imaginative of our kind goes, this is where it ends, we are able to regenerate making us harder to kill but for those who appreciate the smaller benefits of this ability, there's a lot of fun to be had." He smiled mischievously.

"But we can't get tattoos like humans because the demon blood in us regenerates like you said, it would just heal the skin back to how it was before, the ink wouldn't even remain on us, just like we can't cut or dye our hair," I said.

One major disadvantage, in my opinion, had been our changeless appearance, staying forever young seemed great but try getting stuck with a mullet for the rest of your eternity and you would soon change your mind.

"We can now, they mix vampire blood with the ink, the same stuff the witches use for their body tattoos. It's more like a spell than a body modification. The great thing is it's only attached to the outer skin so that when they hack it off the skin grows back as naked as a baby's. They even do piercings here, best part about the witches integration if you ask me especially as I'm starting to think this is a little dated now." He stuck his throat out indicating the two puncture wounds tattooed there, part of Remnants initiation was tattooing over the dark kiss before your body became a vampire, an undead rite of passage.

"It's so important for our kind to keep up with the trends above ground, they are a great distraction and they provide a purpose, small as it may be, but the smallest of purposes is better than none. They say a vampire who cannot do this will be easily lost as the world passes them by." His face took on a serious look that I had rarely seen on him.

"That's what I worry will happen to you, little sister. Dante may dress and act like it's four hundred years ago, I mean that frilled shirt he wears…but in his own way he fully embraces what he is and if he finds comfort in clinging to a fictional icon like Dracula then so be it. You on the other hand are slowly slipping away each day, you take no pleasure in anything to do with what you are. Instead, you reach out to a past that you cannot remember and because of this you assume your human life must have been so much better." He leaned forward. "Let me tell you what I do remember of my mortal life, misery and heartache, whatever life you lived before this I can take a good guess that it wasn't as happy as you like to believe."

Our eyes stayed locked for a moment, I stared back at him waiting for more but the moment had passed and he broke eye contact to glare at a passing ghoul instead.

"Any chance of being seen today? I may be dead but I do have a life you know!" The ghoul whose gloves were covered in thick black blood quickly removed them with practiced ease and discarded them in a nearby bin before placing a fresh pair on. Why creatures that were immortally frozen in a partially rotted stasis were conscientious about hygiene was beyond me. He pointed to an unoccupied reclining chair next to another vampire who was having what looked like the remains of a name sliced off his forearm. He exchanged a smile with Kristian.

"What you in for?"

"Just getting rid of an old memento from my rebellious days," replied Kristian pulling his long hair to the side so the ghoul could begin work.

"I'm here because of a girl, a human girl," said the other vampire.

He was huge, his arm bulged and rippled as the other ghoul hacked unceremoniously into it.

"She was such a fang tease, you know the sort," he said.

Kristian nodded knowingly. "Met a few in my time, happy to flaunt their neck enough but move in for a bite and they look at you like you're a monster or something."

The large vampire continued with his story. "One minute I was her undying love the next she was chasing after my brother, damn woman couldn't decide what she wanted."

"Reminds me of my ex-girlfriend bro," piped up another voice. "She was always leading me on then shutting me out. Then whenever she got lonely she would start texting me. I was so glad when I got the dark kiss, like they say in death we are reborn. I have flown the coop of mortality and will now soar the depths of oblivion."

Kristian glanced over to the opposite chair where the vampire who had joined the conversation sat, and sighed. "Fledglings!"

"What'd you say bro?" The newcomer retorted.

"I am no "bro" of yours, of that I am certain," said Kristian.

"We are all brothers of blood once we have tasted the dark side," said the fledgling.

"Oh, shut up you imbecile!" said Kristian, the well built vampire let out a bellowing laugh and the fledgling slumped in his seat muttering.

"There's no need to be rude, bro."

I watched unimpressed as the ghoul sliced the area of Kristian's Remnant tattoo removing the layer of flesh.

"Why don't you pick a tattoo, Scar? My treat." He said earnestly.

"No thanks."

"I'm disappointed, Scar, I thought you would at least try it," said Kristian shaking his head at me.

I looked around the room at the ghouls slicing vampire flesh like meat off the bone, I felt the raised skin on my wrist, two perfect puncture wounds immortalised on my immortal skin.

"I've undergone enough body modifications, I still bear the scars from the last one."

"You always complain about not having a past, getting a tattoo can be a step into creating one, a memory etched onto your flesh, and if it's a memory you want to forget, then cut it off and replace it with a new one."

Kristian was wrong, getting rid of a scar would not change anything, I would still be the same creature, my eyes would carry the same emptiness, my teeth would stay fanged and my skin would not be catching the sun any time soon. The ghoul handed the piece of skin back to Kristian who waved it around comparing sizes with the other vampires.

"You want a piece of me?" he said throwing the limp flesh at me. I nimbly stepped to the side as it flew by and fell into the fledgling's lap.

"That was rank bro," he muttered.

"You're sick," I agreed, watching as the fledgling peeled the flap of skin off his jeans.

"What?" said Kristian feigning innocence. "It's just a memento of our day out, you're the one who gets all upset about not having anything to look back on."

"This isn't one I would choose but thanks for the offer," I said flatly.

"What are brothers for?" he said getting up from the stool and inspecting his neck in the mirror. "How long will it take for the new skin to grow back?" he asked the ghoul, who was trying to apply a gauze over the open wound.

Kristian swatted him away and he gave up. "The skin should regenerate within one to two hours, any problems just come back."

"Can I go now?" I asked, as Kristian paid the ghoul.

"If you admit that I proved my point by bringing you here." He wasn't going to let this go.

"If your point was to confirm that we can really leave no mark on this earth then yes. Even a tattoo is as insignificant as the dead skin it is inked upon, just slice it off and discard it. We are colourless; forever living in the shadows," I said darkly.

"True story bro, that is deep," said the fledgling vampire staring at me in awe.

Kristian rolled his eyes. "Don't encourage her, and no offence but a vampire that calls his undead peers "bro" would think a puddle is deep."

The fledgling frowned as he tried to interpret this and Kristian turned back to me. "Listen to yourself, Scar, you are a vampire that in death is trying to find the meaning of life, you will fail."

"Haven't you got better things to do than lecture me?"

"Not today, I purposefully made myself free so I could spend the day with you."

"A whole day out of your eternity, I am privileged," I said as we stepped out the shop back into the Witches Quarter.

Kristian didn't answer, he was staring straight ahead his eyes widened in surprise. I followed his gaze and saw a female vampire with a sharp black bob bartering with an unclean over some supernatural salve.

"Who is she?" I asked.

"Just someone that I used to know," he said and herded us in the opposite direction. Much to my surprise, he decided we should cut short our outing as he suddenly remembered he had stuff to do at home. He was unusually quiet as we walked back.

That evening I was watching films with Dante, he had decided to indulge on a vampire movie marathon. We had already watched The Lost Boys and were just finishing Bram Stoker's Dracula, when Kristian appeared. Since we had returned from the Underdark he had spent most of the evening in his room, his blood dolls had briefly visited but even they seemed to realise he wasn't in the mood for the usual blood binge and had left.

"Ah! The father of all vampire movies and clichés," he stated.

Dante didn't respond but I saw him cast a seething look at our brother, Dracula was his all time favourite vampire antagonist. Kristian, oblivious of the offence he had caused, draped himself on the other Chaise Longue, almost crushing Herb who leapt up with a raspy apology and stood there for a moment looking sheepish.

"Make yourself useful, gut rot, and get me a bloody Mary," said Kristian.

"But, sir...Mary's already left your chambers," he said apologetically.

Kristian huffed. "Be quick then and fetch me some of the pre-packed stuff and no adding any caramelised syrup rubbish like you do with Scar's."

Herb bowed meekly.

"Sometime today?!" Kristian barked, and Herb scurried off to comply.

Kristian threw an irritated glare at the ghoul's back then turned his attention to the TV. "I have to admit Gary Oldman does play a good vampire, I should turn him…"

"I think he would have appreciated that more when the film first came out," I said.

"Bram got a lot wrong though, I mean how many of our kind sleep in a coffin apart from Dante, who, let's face it, only does so because of his obsession with the cult vampire stereotype." He grinned childishly at Dante.

Dante sighed. "If you don't like the movie you can leave the room, no one is forcing you to watch it."

"I don't have to now, look the credits have come up."

I got up and put on the next film we had previously chosen.

"Aha! Interview with the Vampire, now this is a great take on our kind! Its all about Le Stat," exclaimed Kristian clapping his hands together.

"Indeed, although I do love Kirsten Dunst in this, she reminds me of a young Scarlet," said Dante.

"Don't you mean Louie?" Kristian retorted cheekily.

I stopped eating my bloodsickle long enough to respond.

"I have never once dined on rodents," I answered, quite insulted.

"No, but I did get concerned when you asked Father for a pet hamster."

"I wasn't going to eat it! I just wanted a pet," I said softly and my eyes met Dante's and he gave me a small smile.

Kristian scoffed. "You don't need a flea infested ball of fur, you have Herb and he cleans up after himself, well most of the time."

"Herb's not a pet," I said.

"Well he's as close as you'll ever get to one, although I do see your point, he doesn't exactly generate warm fuzzy feelings, and he's more crusty than fluffy with a face that even a mother wouldn't love. If you want something to play with you should take a page out of my book."

"I have no interest in obtaining a blood doll," I replied curtly.

"It would do you good, trust me," Kristian said with confidence. "If not just to give you a break from the bagged stuff."

"Dr Ervin believes that blood dolls are part of a balanced diet if accompanied by blood packs," said Dante, finally joining the conversation. "Although you must make sure the donor in question has a good blood type and is, as far as human standards go…healthy."

"See, even Dante agrees with me! It would also give you another companion to talk to other than Evil Dead over there," Kristian nodded towards Herb who was doing his best not to spill a drop of Kristian's drink as he carried it over.

Kristian took it without a thank you and turned his attention back on the film, Tom Cruise was just biting into Brad Pitt's neck.

"Makes you hungry, doesn't it," he said downing his blood and motioning Herb to get him another.

Over an hour later Kristian was still talking and I had barely been able to concentrate, despite my supernatural attention span, which was not immune to his preternatural ability to never shut up.

"Look at this poor fellow, chasing rats in the gutters. If animal blood was a suitable replacement for human blood then mortals would have carried on using it in their blood transfusions, even they realised it did more harm than good."

"If you intend on ruining this movie you should at least lecture Scarlet on the fundamental issues of her diet. I know neither of you share my interest in following Dr Ervin's balanced blood diet, but I will say that heating blood up in a microwave as Scarlet does, damages the cells and alters it," Dante stated matter of factly.

"That's it," I said, rising from the sofa.

"I may not be able to rest in peace but I would like to think I could watch a movie in one."

I traipsed upstairs to my room but once alone I found my thoughts returning to the dead boy, why couldn't I forget about it? You hear of vampires killing people from time to time, some accidental and some deliberate. They get dealt with by the Tribune and are released and reformed like Dante or, in extreme cases, executed. But you never hear about the vampires in question being sorry about it. Sure they are sorry they got caught but they don't take a moment to reflect on the effect their actions had on the human's family or the fact that they took a life, that wasn't the part that was deemed wrong. Any blood dolls that died here didn't even receive a funeral, the Tribune disposed of the body to a human rendering factory and turned it into yet more food for the undead. I decided to keep my mind occupied by rearranging my bookshelf; it lined the entire side of my bedroom wall. It was the only part of my room that gave it any personality and signified that someone lived here.

I had always enjoyed reading and collecting books had become a small obsession of mine which Dante had encouraged, being an avid reader himself. Kristian, on the other hand thought they took up too much space and caused clutter and suggested I invest in an ebook reader much to Dante's protests, he loathed them and felt that books should stay as they are, sheets of paper bound together. He believed a book that could be held, had texture and smell was far more valuable than some electronic panel that had no contact with you other than through a screen. He claimed every book he owned showed how much he had enjoyed it, by the aged spine and dog-eared pages. I felt the same as I scanned my own collection; some of these books had been with me for decades. I may not be able to change my skin, forever smooth, but these books were a testimony to my time on this earth, their wrinkled spines and yellowed pages gave me some strange comfort that time did move forward even if I didn't.

Herb appeared in the doorway and gave a polite cough; I ushered him in hastily and pushed him towards my corner chair.

"What did you find out?" I asked as soon as he had sat down.

He looked outside the open door hesitantly, I sighed and lifted my hand and the door creaked shut, with the other I pointed to my CD player and music started playing.

Herb looked impressed. "You're getting really good at channeling your blood magic."

"Never mind that," I said eager to find out his news. "They won't hear us through the music, now what did you find out?"

"Right, well they have a few suspects, one being your brother Dante, the other is some ex-FF member. The final suspect is some crazed blood doll that threatened to get revenge on 'all vampires'.

"That's good!" I said, then caught Herb's eye. "Obviously not the part about Dante, but he'll be cleared soon, they have nothing to link him to it and from the sounds of it nothing to link me either."

Herb's info was good, so I dismissed him. It seemed there was no trail to link anyone from my family to the crime. However later that evening as I lay on my bed, I still felt on edge. I knew that the Tribune were unaware of my involvement and that even though Dante was being looked at, that they would soon realise he had nothing to do with it, so why was I still obsessing over this?

Then a thought occurred to me, the last time I had seen the boy he had been alive, lethargic from blood loss but alive, maybe all I needed was closure. It was a human notion but one I was inclined to investigate.

When I got to Insomnia I kept to the shadows but I needn't have bothered, the place was deserted. There were a few fliers up on the wall showing pictures of the dead boy as well as a number for people to call if they had any information. I made my way slowly to the alleyway where I had fed on him; it was blocked off by police tape. Alongside it were flowers and small candles, left by mourners. There were a lot and I began looking at them, reading the notes that had been left. It was a strange experience trying to comprehend the meanings of these written words, the nature of my vampirism automatically slipping into its detached state of being. But underneath the emotional austerity, something moved inside me, deep within my frozen self, I felt a yearning. This dead boy, who had only spent a fraction of the time that I had on earth, had so much more to show for it. His death had left a vacuum in this world, a small one granted, but to those who wrote the cards it was significant. Who was I before this monster set up home inside me? Did I ever have friends? Would they have left flowers at my grave? I searched fruitlessly through my mind for some vague recollection of a human life before I was submerged in this eternal darkness. Nothing, the only memories I had were stolen from the living, selfishly clinging on to them as if they were the single link that keeps me connected to the life I once had. I had spent my whole unlife feeling isolated. In those darkest moments, I had even thought about ending it all but for what reason? My death would not change anything, it would be as insignificant as a teardrop falling into the ocean, in fact I was so insignificant that I was unable to create something as little as a tear, simply because, vampires cannot cry. There would be no obituary, no funeral, and no marked grave for anyone to visit. No one would care about the absence of a girl called Scarlet, a girl who had no existence be it on paper or in a photograph, I wouldn't even exist as a human memory, any real relatives I once had would be long dead. It would be as if I had never existed, and that thought scared me more than any retribution the Tribune could muster.

There was nothing here, only a reminder of just how far away I was from what I wanted. I went home, my mind resolved with what I would need to do.

Herb must have sensed something was not quite right, for as soon as I got in the house he had not left my side, perhaps he was just worried I had been out hunting again. He sat in his usual spot in the corner of my bedroom with a human beverage book propped in his lap. I decided to to keep myself busy by sorting through my wardrobe; being alive for so long meant the amount of clothes you acquired became excessive, not to mention outdated.

"Have you ever felt envious of them?" I asked Herb, out of the blue.
"Envious of who?" he asked.
"Humans."

"No," he replied without hesitation. "How about a Slushy? They seem popular above ground, freezing the blood ruins the quality, but you do seem to like the Bloodsickles."

"You mean to say that you are happier now, as a ghoul, forced to serve vampires for eternity? Herb you were once a young boy, you had friends and a family."

He looked up from the book with an odd smile. "In truth? Yes, I am."

I shook my head in disbelief; maybe years of forced servitude had institutionalised him.

"I know it may sound strange to you Scar, I was a young boy and I would have died a young boy also. I had fewer friends than I have now and that's saying something, as for family... my mother was a drunk who beat me and I never knew my father. When Master Lucard found me I was already dying and in such a bad state that I don't remember it happening."

"But you were never given a choice," I said bluntly.

"I was never given a choice for my human life either, you have to make the best with what you're given," Herb said sagely.

I picked out my blue flannel shirt and dark blue skinny jeans that I hadn't worn since the 90's.

"Oh! These are back in fashion, I'll hang onto those," I murmured, choosing to ditch my shell suit instead; a hideous shiny puffy tracksuit that Herb had got above ground, insisting they were hugely popular at the time.

"Scarlet... if you are lonely you could always choose someone," he said tentatively.

"Turn a mortal for my own pleasure? I would never create another like myself, two wrongs do not make a right!"

"Oh not the shell suit, Scar! You said you liked it!"

After letting Herb down gently, he finally accepted that not all vampires were ready for pink polyester and I was free to continue rifling through my clothes. I was just scrutinising a crushed velvet dress when a small winged creature flew out from the inside of it.

"What on earth?" I said as the creature landed on my bed shaking its fur and unfurling its leathery wings as it investigated its new landing area.

A voice called out from the hallway.

"Vlad? Vlad?! Where are you?!" I heard footsteps reaching the door of my room.

"Vlad, there you are!" cried Dante appearing in my doorway and rushing over to the dishevelled beast.

I cast Herb a disapproving look. "I can't believe you gave in."

Herb shrugged and acted nonchalant but I saw him edge nearer the bed to get a peek as Dante cradled it in his hands and made disturbing cooing noises.

"After all my warnings you went ahead and got him a pet bat? They are creatures of the wild and should not be kept as house pets, plus it's really cliché, even for Dante," I said sighing.

Dante ignored my jibe as he stared down at the bat lovingly, he stroked its small furry head as it sniffed him. Herb, however, looked sheepish as he met my gaze.

"This one was injured Scar, the ghoul at the market was going to put it down as he thought no one would buy it with a lame wing." Herb was nearly sobbing now.

I rolled my eyes, but when I looked at the creature again I noticed one of its wings hung limply at its side, no wonder it had crash-landed. I too edged closer and watched Herb and Dante both taking turns in petting and talking to the bat. Just then Kristian sauntered past my room, only to halt as he watched the scene with morbid interest.

"Dante... a bat? You really need to get out and socialise with the modern vampire community," he said flatly.

Chapter 6

~A Life for an Unlife~

It had been almost two weeks since the murder of the human boy. No leads had been found, and more importantly Dante was no longer under investigation by the Tribune. This meant once again I was able to venture into the human world. After that night at the crime scene, I had decided to move forward with my plans, the first part being to relocate the girl from that night – Jessica.

I had since been following Jessica at every opportunity and had been learning more about her, however the more learnt, the more I envied her. She had everything I wanted; friends, a normal family and a future. The turning point was when I saw her with her boyfriend. Watching the two of them together filled me with a craving comparable to extreme thirst. If I had ever experienced love as a human, I had no recollection of it, and since being turned I had given up on the idea. None of what Jessica had was for a creature like me, yet I was obsessed with her life - I wanted it! You hear all the time about humans who want to become vampires. Blood dolls being a prime example. This was popular opinion for humans, they wrote stories and made films about it. But no vampire would want to be human, most would consider it a step backwards in evolution. I wondered what Darwin would think of my plan. But then everyone knew I was different. Unlike my brothers who accepted their vampirism, I had always viewed it as an eternal death sentence. Today I felt different, today would be the start of new life filled with possibilities.

I watched as the familiar silver car pulled up outside the house and Jessica stepped out. Her long brown hair was loose and she was wearing a pair of denim shorts that showed off her shapely legs, and a pink halter-top. Her boyfriend stepped out from the driver's seat and followed her up the driveway to the house, as she stormed ahead of him. They were arguing and my keen ears soon picked up their conversation.

"You can't deny it, Jess, Phil saw you with Dean, he said the two of you were all over each other."

"And you believe his word over mine?!"

"Yes, and I believe Rob and Simon's words also, all of my friends have seen you two together, everyone knew apart from me!" He was clearly upset, his face flushed and his eyes welling with tears.

"Well, so what if I was with Dean, you're always busy spending time with your family instead of me."

"You know the situation with my family, they need me at the moment and I always invite you to come along," he was approaching her now, his arms open.

"You expect me to spend my free time at a hospital? Dean takes me shopping or the cinema and nice places to eat, while you invite me to waiting rooms for the dying."

"I can't believe how insensitive you can be Jess," he pleaded.

"Yeah, well I can't believe you expect a girl like me to wait around until you finally realise how good you have it. Do you know how many other boys I could have?" she said indignantly.

"You've been having them already by the sounds of it," he spat.

"I tried not to, I waited for you to surprise me, to be spontaneous but you haven't, you used to be so much more fun. I'm sorry about your brother, but life just doesn't stop because someone gets sick, the sooner you realise that, the better off you'll be."

With that, she turned on her heel and opened the door to her house. He followed her right up to the door, but she slammed it in his face. He stood there for a moment looking distraught before storming back to his car and driving off.

I waited a few minutes then walked up the driveway to the house. I paused for a moment, thinking about whether or not I was really going to go through with it. Casting the last of apprehensions aside, I knocked on the door. A series of high pitch barks echoed from within, it was followed by footsteps, there was no going back now. There was a crank of a handle before the door opened. And there she stood, the girl who had the power to change my unlife, change it to what it should have been. She stood staring at me in confusion, the silence was deafening even the dog which was not much bigger than Vlad had stopped barking.

"You're the strange girl that's been following me," she said at length.

She was astute, but I wasn't surprised she had noticed me. The last few visits I had become careless, following Jessica during the day when my cloaking abilities were weaker. At some points, I hadn't even bothered to channel them.

She frowned at me. "Why have you been stalking me?"

"Because I want your life," I replied simply.

She gasped, looking unnerved. I had to hurry and explain or there would be trouble.

"I'm a vampire, but I mean you no harm," I said with as kind a voice as I could muster.

She laughed nervously. "This is a joke?"

"Afraid not," I said opening my mouth and exposing my fangs, she jumped back and made to close the door on me. I placed my hand on it preventing it from closing. she struggled for a moment using all her weight to try and force the door shut, until I gave a final gentle push, forcing Jessica backwards. As I stepped through, she scrambled and backed away eyes locked on me in terror.

"You have to be invited!" she squealed.

"Only if I'm feeling polite," I replied giving up any soothing pretence now she understood what I was.

"Don't try to run, I am faster than you," I said as she looked to the open door behind me. I raised my hand and with that, all the doors in the house slammed shut one by one with loud ominous bangs.

"How did you do that?" she blurted out, curiosity overtaking her fear.

"Easily. I willed them to shut with my mind, it's a vampire thing," I said blankly.

She started to whimper in fear again and I sighed getting impatient, I was not used to human fear and the apprehension that came with it. All the people I drank from were drunk or under my thrall so they never realised what I was or what I was doing.

"Stop your sniveling. I said I wouldn't hurt you, otherwise you'd be dead by now," I barked in impatience.

She gave a final sniffle then frantically dried her eyes.

"Then why are you here?" she finally managed.

"Because you have the life that should have been mine, and because of that I have a proposition for you."

"What?" she said, her tearful expression slowly turning to one of bemusement and interest.

I walked past her and opened a door into an open-plan lounge. I paused momentarily taking in the surroundings; I was actually inside a human house, somewhere extremely taboo among our kin. There was a large fireplace with framed photographs standing on the mantelpiece, I resisted the urge to go and inspect them. I was here to make a negotiation not sight see. If I was successful I would have plenty of time to indulge my interests after.

"I suggest you sit down for this," I called behind me as I paced across a spotless white carpet and on through the kitchen-dining area. To the rear a pair of glass doors led out onto a large garden.

"Come!" I commanded as I gestured the doors open with a swish of my hand. There was a patio area with a table and chairs arranged, and to my relief, a large parasol. I took a seat, glad to be temporarily shaded from the sun's touch. I watched her as she cautiously approached, before snatching the nearest chair and scooting as far away from me as possible. I assumed she thought this a safe distance between us. She watched me with caution before a thought gave her strength to speak up.

"If you're a vampire, how come you're not bursting into flames?" she pointed at the sun above us.

I sighed at the naivety of her assumption.
"You shouldn't believe everything you read or see in the movies. We can walk around in sunlight without bursting into flames, it does, however,

cause some problems. Our eyes, perfectly adapted for night are sensitive during the day, hence the need for sunglasses."

"Anything else?" she asked as her curiosity started to kick in.

"The rays weaken us and have a strange effect on the brain, even causing seizures in the most severe of cases. And of course there's the obvious side effect of our skin blistering, but all this lessens the older a vampire becomes."

We sat in silence for a moment, while she digested the information, I could almost hear the tiny cogs of her mind ticking.

"You probably have more questions about me and my kin. Which I will be happy to answer, IF you first agree to my proposition." There was no going back now, as I considered for the last time, just exactly what I was about to do.

"What does it involve?" she asked, she appeared less afraid now, fascination had completely taken over.

"A week in your life, for a week in mine." I watched her considering it. Years of dreaming and yearning depended on her one answer.

"You want to live as me?" she finally said bemused.

"For just one week."

"Why?" she shook her head slowly, a puzzled look on her face.

"That's my business," I snapped. Why did she have to question everything?

She looked annoyed at my reluctance to confide, it didn't matter. I wasn't here for a heart to heart, mine had been still for far too long, all I needed was her consent. Her mood completely switched, as she
leant back in her chair, now relaxed and a lot more confident. She had realised that she wasn't in any present danger and, more importantly, was in a position to make demands.

"What do I get out of it?" she asked, her blue eyes narrowing and her arms folded across her chest.

I smiled at the sheer arrogance; she was actually attempting to barter with me, but I had to admire her backbone. I could pluck it out if I wanted, but I decided I would at least hear her request.

"You get to experience what no human does, you get to live a week in the life of a vampire," I stated authoritatively.

She stared back unimpressed.

"I am willing to pay you for the inconvenience," I followed up.

She held her hands out. "Do I look like I am strapped for cash?"

I had to agree, as human houses go this one looked to be expensive and lavishly adorned. I fell silent, my mind searching for something I could offer her, when she spoke softly. "How old are you....?"

"One hundred and thirty-six years old."

"You certainly look good for your age. How old were you when…?" she struggled to find the words.

"When I was turned? I do not know, I have no memories of my human life, all I know is I died in 1883 and was born again... like this." I held my hands out for effect.

"You look no older than sixteen," she said in shock.

I said nothing, still waiting on her answer; her hesitation was growing more frustrating, why couldn't she be like the others and do what I asked instantly. The thought crossed my mind, perhaps I should just go ahead and enthrall her, but I doubted as to whether I had the ability to keep her under my power for the entire week. Worse case scenario, it would wear off after the first day only for her to wake in the middle of the Underdark. No, that would be a huge liability. I had no choice, she had to do this willingly, that way we would both stand a chance of surviving it.

"And you have stayed the same ever since?" she concluded.

"Exactly the same," I replied.

"What happens after the end of the week?"

"We swap back, and I disappear from your life as if it never happened." That was it, there was nothing else to it, except for her decision.

"I'll do it," she shouted excitedly.

Despite all my eagerness to get her to say yes, I was taken aback at the suddenness and enthusiastic nature of her statement. That was the second time she caught me off guard.

"You will?" I asked, struggling to keep the shock out of my voice.

"Why not? I mean I can see it's really important to you and it sounds like it would be fun," she said jovially.

Fun? This bordered on the definition of madness! I was asking her to enter the lion's den. I had no idea if this would work and there was no guarantee that she would be coming out alive. However I wasn't about to voice these concerns; I had revealed my identity and chased her agreement; successfully; and yet I did need to warn her about some things; otherwise she wouldn't stand a chance.

"Understand, it will be dangerous, you will have to learn about my kind before hand. If they become suspicious that you are not me then it could turn nasty," I said firmly.

"I'm a fast learner," she replied with a shrug.

"You'll need to be," I responded gravely.

We sat in the garden for the next few hours while I filled her in on the minute details of my unlife as a vampire. She was very interested in how we had come about, so I told her about our history and how the witches, who practiced blood magic and demonology, summoned creatures to bind to their will. How one witch had failed to bind a creature and it had killed her and subsequently gone on a rampage killing all the humans in her village, until her sister, also a witch had managed to bind it. And finally, how afterwards, they had discovered that not all the villagers had been killed, that one had survived and it was this individual who became the first vampire.

"So how exactly did he become a vampire? Did the demon feed off him?"

"The man had fought the demon, but was mortally wounded. As the story goes, he was the lover of the witch that started the summoning ritual. When he heard the creature tearing their house apart, he tried to save her, not knowing what dark powers she had unleashed. I suppose you could say that after all that, the witch's sister felt bad for his loss. After all witches may summon demons but they are human, unlike us they still have emotions."

"So she saved him?"

"Yes, I suppose that's one way of looking at it. Using her magic, she was able to locate and trap the demon, doing what her sister could not, binding it to her will. She returned to the village and fed her sister's lover the blood of the demon, and while it saved him, it changed him forever."

"What happened afterwards? Did the witches end up controlling the first vampire?"

"No. We are not fully demonic, we are hybrids and capable of resisting witches magic."

Jessica's thirst for knowledge persisted, so I continued, telling her about the ancient feud between us and the witches and how, as we had grown in numbers spreading our pestilence like a swarm of blood thirsty locusts, we had hunted them, blaming them for our cursed existence, while they in return tried desperately to control us.

Satisfied with the history, Jessica decided to quiz me on my family.

"So you have three brothers?"

"Yes, Desmodeus, Dante and Kristian."

"I have always wanted a brother, I only have a little sister and she's a total pain in the neck." I smiled at her choice of words; hopefully for her, my brothers would not prove to be pains in the neck.

"It's Desmodeus you'll need to watch out for, he's the most observant, if you make a mistake he will pick up on it," I warned her.

"And the others?"

"Dante tends to keep to himself, preferring to stay in his room and read books. He's got the whole solitary vampire down to an art. Kristian is trouble, stay away from him and don't let his charm fool you."

"Right, okay," she said nodding; I hoped she really was taking this all in.

"What about your parents?"

"I have no Mother, my brood father is a quiet but powerful figure among our kind, he used to be a witch hunter and before that a Knight of the Crusaders, not much gets past him so you must be very careful when he is around. In fact it's probably best to avoid him altogether."

She nodded slowly and I waited to see if she had anymore questions, the human mind I realised took longer to process things than a vampire's did, I would need to show more patience if I wanted her full co-operation.

"What about weaknesses, you say you're fine with sunlight but what about crosses?"

"I don't attend church every Sunday if that's what you mean," I said flatly.

"But do they hurt you?" Her questions were becoming more specific now, which was encouraging.

"No, that's another common misconception. Vampires are not damned even though it feels like we are. Our condition is a plague but not one inflicted by God. In fact my father is an avid Christian, a custom of his former human life." I could see this concept intrigued her.

"A religious vampire? How poetic!" she said enthusiastically.

"You could say that, he views it as more of a penance."

"Do the rest of your family follow such beliefs?"

"Not at all, my brothers think Father is wasting his time, that no amount of fervently muttered words will wash away the blood of centuries of killing."

"Doesn't he kill anymore then?"

"None of us do since the changes they made to the Feeding Act in 1784. When the Tribune decided we had become a scourge to mankind and that our desire to sate our thirst would eventually lead to our own destruction." This was important, I had to ensure she paid attention to this bit.

"How did they come to that conclusion?"

"Well, if you prey on something long enough it will die out. Eliminate the source of food and you're dead, in the true sense of the word to put it simply."

As we continued our conversation, I explained to her about the basics of the Tribune and its codes of conduct, blood dolls, the curfew and the magical implants to ensure the law's enforcement. At the end we reached a moment of silence as she contemplated all of this. I waited and watched the last remains of sunlight disappearing behind the horizon.

"What about the siring you mentioned, have you ever turned a human?" Jessica suddenly said.

"No, I don't know how it's done, that knowledge is normally passed down from Sire to Fledgling."

"Didn't your father show you?" Jessica pressed.

"No, he didn't create me, he is my brood father, you would refer to it as 'adopted' I suppose."

"What about the vampire that made you?" Jessica fired back.

"I know very little of her, she didn't stick around and it's not like she left any keepsakes for me."

"You know nothing at all?" I stared down at my mutilated wrist.

"Just that she wasn't in her right mind, they found two other girls near me, both dead. Perhaps she thought I was dead too, or maybe she didn't care. Those girls could have been family to me, sisters, or just others she had taken...I will never know,' I admitted.

"So your father, isn't your father at all... he just found you and took you in?"

"Yes, but it wasn't for the reasons you assume, it wasn't love. Family is a symbol of status to a vampire, the larger the brood the more powerful the vampire leading them is as their sphere of influence is greater."

"So vampires adopt other vampires to build their own personal army?"

"Near enough."

"Does that happen often? Sires or whatever leaving the humans they have turned?"

"Sadly yes, not everyone should be given the ability to play God, the same happened to Dante and Kristian. I'm told that turning a human can be a euphoric experience for the one siring, having the power to decide whether that person lives or dies, knowing that only they can make that decision."

"So how are we going to do this?" she asked abruptly, cutting the conversation short.

I smiled and reached for my bag. From within, I withdrew a gold necklace with a red tear drop shaped stone hanging off it. Unclasping the lock, I motioned for her to lean forward, before placing it around her neck.

"Never take this off unless you no longer value your life," I warned.

"What is it?" she asked lifting the red stone in her hands to examine it.

"A magical amulet, with the power to hide the true nature of its wearer, as long as you keep it on at all times they will never have cause to believe you are not a vampire, its magic will cloud the scent of your human blood and any other attributes that distinguish you as one of the living."

"But I still look human."

"For now, but that amulet doesn't just hide your human nature. The magical stone is a Morshard, it can grant the wearer the appearance of another."

She looked back down at the amulet in awe. "Such magic exists?"

"You're sitting in your garden talking to a vampire. That alone should tell you that the world is not as simple as you once thought."

"I suppose, though while we're on the subject, what was that whole door thing you did earlier?"

"Oh, that?...just a little blood magic. The demon our kind derive from was a magical being, witches summon them to channel and use their powers. We inherited some of that power."

"What type of powers?" her eyes glinted.

"Cloaking spells to hide ourselves, the power to enthrall humans drawing them to us and making them easier to manipulate. We can also read a person's memories and; as you saw; telekinesis."

"Do all vampires have such powers?"

"Not all; fledglings are fairly limited as they are still newborn and our powers are something that develop over time. Being barely over a century myself I am regarded young for a vampire, so my own powers are weak in comparison to my brother's. Desmodeus can read human thoughts for example."

"He can read minds? Then he will surely know I am a human!" Jessica exclaimed.

I shook my head. "No, you will be fine. The amulet will not only hide your humanity, but it will protect you from vampiric abilities. The witches invented ways to protect themselves against us over the centuries of us hunting them. What you hold now is an example of just how far they have come, some might even consider what you have there – a weapon."

She smiled then looked back to the amulet, turning it so that the evening's light reflected off the smooth stone. "How did you get it?" she asked.

"I may be dead but I have connections in the right places."

"When do we start?"

"Tonight. I will return just after midnight."

"Wait, why not now?" Jessica said enthusiastically.

"The sun," I pointed to the sky. "The final part of the ritual requires me to fully tap into my Blood Magics. It must be night time when I do this to ensure it works."

And with that; before she could ask anymore questions; I stood up, announcing my intent to leave. Jessica walked with me through the house to the front door, not a word being exchanged. As I walked down the drive I called back.

"Tonight, after midnight. Don't forget."

Jessica nodded and closed the door. On my way home I felt something I had never dared to feel before. I felt...hope.

With only a few hours before the ritual, I decided to stay in. Besides by tomorrow morning I would not need to rely on the flickers of human memories, I would be busy creating my own. My bag was already packed with the essentials, I had enough blood packs to last the week. I didn't bother with clothing, as I would be wearing Jessica's clothes for the duration, if I didn't it was sure to draw suspicion. Most importantly I had managed to exchange some of my Drakmir I had put aside into human money. While I had no plans to buy anything above ground, it was better to be prepared. After packing, I spent the rest of my time sat on the sofa, a book about recent human history propped open on my lap and a bowl of blood tofu in hand. Dante was sitting on the chaise longue to my left polishing his old opera glasses, of course he never used them anymore but from time to time he liked to take them out and dust them off, admiring the polished sheen of his labours before placing them carefully back in the box. Desmodeus, was also staying in tonight, sat to my right, reading a copy of 'Mortal Coil' an undead tabloid. Kristian was upstairs with one of his blood dolls and father was at MASS; Middle Aged Spread Society - a club for vampires who originated as far back as the middle ages.

"What are you doing here Scar? Isn't tonight a Ghoul School night?" came the sound of Kristian's voice as he appeared in the doorway accompanied by his blood doll Mary.

She was sporting several fresh puncture wounds around her neck and wrists, but seemed oblivious despite blood still oozing from one. I tried not to pay attention to it, instead shoving a piece of blood tofu into my mouth. This was a dish popular among ghouls, the coagulated blood was heated up and cut into solid blocks, and yet despite its popularity, I still was not use to it. They were difficult to digest and caused a backflow of bile to rise into my throat. I sustained a gag as I answered Kristian who was frowning at my plate in disbelief.

"I thought I would study from home this evening," I said, not looking up from the section I was reading about social networking. Kristian moved his eyes from my blood tofu to the book.

"Planning on making a Twitter account are we?" he exclaimed with mock enthusiasm.

"How exciting, what would be your first tweet? 'Drank some bad blood today, not feeling too well'." He held his hand up in a fake selfie pose.

I ignored him and continued reading. Realising he wasn't getting the reaction he wanted he changed his tone.

"You don't need to read that rubbish, Scar, just talk to Mary for a few minutes and you will learn all you need to know about the 21st century."

Mary stepped forward eagerly.

"I am happy with the book thanks," I said and from the corner of my eye I noticed her droop a little at the obvious brush off.

"I'll tell you then," said Kristian completely ignoring my protest as I rolled my eyes.

"One word for young humans of the 21st century, 'entitlement'. They all believe they are entitled to something, they want money but don't want to work for it, they want relations but don't want a commitment, they want independence but are scared to be alone."

"Present company excluded," he said, turning to Mary who just giggled, probably light headed from the loss of blood because she suddenly excused herself.

"I mean it Scar. Humanity is a weakness, they are all slaves to their desires. Why are you so fascinated by them? You shouldn't be filling your head with this nonsense!" he exclaimed, suddenly snatching my book and waving it in front of my face.

"You should be studying our own histories instead."

I snatched the book back smoothing out the pages he had crumpled in his carelessness. Kristian finally gave up and addressed Dante and Desmodeus instead.

"They are holding a Speed Biting tonight, fancy coming along?"

"How improper!" remarked Dante.

"Biting one then moving straight onto the next, such methods are the poor vampire's choice for feeding, lacking the refined experience of blood tasting. You might as well just go back to street hunting," he sneered.

"What about your blood dolls?" asked Desmodeus as he turned the page of his newspaper, I glanced at the front cover for the tenth time that evening. It was a picture of the boy from Insomnia, who I now knew was called Thomas Miller. They had finally arrested a rogue vampire with alleged connections to a number of feeding fatalities in the past few months. The boy's eyes stared accusingly at me, I quickly looked away. Kristian cocked his head as if listening. Satisfied Mary was still in the bathroom upstairs and out of human earshot, he addressed Desmodeus.

"Cecile is busy with mundane human things like university exams or something equally dull and pointless and Mary…well she is starting to try and enforce even worse human aspirations onto me."

"Like what?" I asked suddenly curious, I didn't know one of his blood dolls was at a human university, maybe I should have interacted with them more, I could have learned some things.

Kristian grimaced as if he found the words hard to relate. "She wants to talk about 'Exclusive feeding'."

I returned to my book my interest completely deflated, I should have known. Kristian was wrong, the only aspirations the humans that came to the Underdark had were vampire ones.

"That's no surprise," said Dante. "I warned you that bringing them into the home would encourage such behaviour."

Kristian snorted. "Dante, you spend more time gossiping with that ghoul at your Blooderie than you do drinking there, I do not need any advice from you on these matters, thank you! I mean really, when was the last time you spent time with your own kin? I am starting to worry you are converting to Ghoulism."

"For your information, I have plans this evening with a kindred vampire."

"Well, colour me alive! With who?" asked Kristian, with a suspicious look.

"Ted," replied Dante stiffly.

"Ted?" repeated Kristian with a frown. "I've not heard you mention him before, is he a member of Blue Bloods?"

Dante appeared to take a sudden interest in the cuffs of his sleeves. "I don't believe so," he muttered.

"Then how did you meet him?" asked Kristian, now immensely curious. He glanced at me.

"Did you know anything about this, Scar?" he said accusingly.

I shrugged not even looking up. I had heard Dante mention this 'Ted' a few times but unlike Kristian, who seemed convinced that neither one of us was having as much fun as him as a vampire, I took little interest in any of my brother's social unlife.

"He's not another one of these 1990's vampires that you tend to pick up is he? I know we are limited in choices living underground and being dead, but you have to raise the bar from time to time."

"Don't be so absurd, it's not my fault, that I choose sophisticated vampires for my companions while you persist in feeding on these blood dolls that live in the city. I saw one of them gorging themselves on a hamburger the other day in our kitchen, poor Mildred was distraught. The smell was ghastly, all that animal grease and fat, it's no wonder you feel sluggish all the time if that's what your dolls feed on," Dante retorted.

"At least I feed on girls," Kristian fired back.

"How dare you! You told me you had no issues with my undead choices, and I was the same before I was turned you know this."

"No, no, no! Boy or girl is no issue to me, you know that! My point is, you don't use blood dolls at all. You constantly play it safe by ordering your free-range blood. When was the last time you indulged in some live feeding as opposed to a cask?"

"Kristian," said Desmodeus in a warning tone.

"I feed on humans at the Blooderie," said Dante defensively.

"You mean those supervised tastings! I can't imagine anything less enticing than having your blood spoon-fed to you by a rotting, creaking corpse that smells and looks as if it's just been exhumed."

"I don't have to listen to this drivel!" said Dante standing up.

It was at this point that Herb walked in.

"Dante, sir, your guest has arrived." Just behind him appeared a vampire wearing long shorts, a hoodie and wearing a baseball cap backwards. It was the same fledgling Kristian and I had met at Dead Canvas. The biggest grin I had seen, cut across Kristian's face.

"Yo, Dan! My brother from another mother, you ready to hit the UD?" Kristian struggled to contain his laughter, breaking out into fits of coughs as he introduced himself.

"Sorry, Ted is it? I am not familiar with the new vampire lingo, what's the UD?"

"Underdark, my undead friend! Our own city of lost souls," he replied enthusiastically.

"Something's definitely lost, a few million brain cells I should say," uttered Kristian under his breath.

"That's no way to greet another dark brother," said Ted, then his eyes widened as he recognised him.

"Heyyyy, you're the vamp from Dead Canvas that was getting all up in my face!" He did the same weird gestures with his hands.

"Ignore Kristian," said Dante. "He's having living troubles, you know how it is with these blood dolls."

Ted nodded sympathetically. "Ah no probs, I understand where you are coming from, my last blood doll tried to insist she was carrying my baby. So I told her, the vampire code was to feed off any children borne by the blood dolls. She soon admitted she had made it up."

"Way to dodge that bullet, because that's the main issue we have, too many illegitimate babies. You must have noticed all the blood doll mothers dragging their half vampire children around the Underdark," said Kristian sarcastically.

"Actually I've never seen any, does the Tribune keep them locked up or something?"

Kristian nodded solemnly, completely in his element now.

"That's it! They have a huge pit that they throw the children into just like the Spartans did if they sensed weakness in the child." He held his arms out for dramatic effect.

Ted nodded sagely. "It all makes sense now."

Kristian patted Ted on the shoulder. "Glad I could help, after all what are dark brothers for?"

Dante glared at Kristian, slowly shaking his head. "Come on, Ted, I had Norm set aside some fresh imports to sample."

When they were gone Desmodeus turned on Kristian. "Why can't you give it a rest once in a while?"

"Oh come on, that vampire is a stain on us all! He has been turned for over twenty years and yet he has not realised that we cannot procreate, goodness me that's the first thing I noticed, well second to my thirst for blood," Kristian said exasperatedly.

"What does that tell you?" Desmodeus said flatly.

"It tells me he probably never got any when he was human, so he doesn't notice the difference."

"No, it should tell you that Dante has taken on a vampire he can teach, a project. He needs that, in our eternal lives we all need our distractions."

"That's rich coming from you. Sorry, where were you this afternoon? Oh yes, interrogating our very same brother at that bloody Ivory Tower with your unholy officers, of born again Inquisitors." Kristian was on the attack again.

"One of those 'born agains', as you refer to them, is our father, the vampire who saved you from being incinerated if you care to remember." Desmodeus said poignantly.

Seeing no end, I slipped out of the room, glad to be getting away from the dysfunctional dead. Besides it was nearing midnight and I had somewhere to be...

The plan I concocted, was to meet Jessica at her home and escort her to a nearby hotel, which was in actual fact, one of many entry points into the Underdark. Vampire business owners had their own monopoly on profitable establishments. These could range from hospitals to massage parlours and hotels, very normal human endeavours on the front, but were in fact rich sources of potential blood dolls, human currency and of course blood itself. In total there were fifty such entry points throughout London. Hotels, however, were by far the most popular and lucrative methods for a vampire to bring potential blood dolls back; after all throughout the centuries, humans were renowned for using such places to meet and spend the night with partners of all sorts, and much like their human counterparts, a vampire would be able to book a room and bring a 'guest' up. Upon reaching the room, the vampire would conduct a basic appraisal of the human to see whether he or she would be a suitable candidate. This was often based on the satisfaction of both taste and human reaction to being fed on. The vampire would then have the option to bring them into our world, where the registration process would begin.

When I met Jessica she was wearing a leopard print mini dress that showed off her tanned legs. Upon closer inspection, she even had matching leopard print nails, bag and shoes. To my relief she had followed my instructions and was still wearing the necklace I had given her. In contrast to her garish outfit, I was wearing a black pencil skirt, a tie neck blouse complete with sunglasses. As per the plan we made our way to the
hotel, as we walked discussion inevitably broke out, leading to choices of attire.

"How cute!" said Jessica. "I love the vintage look, although I would lose the sunglasses. It's night time."

Taking note that it might look suspicious, I carefully folded my sunglasses before popping them into my bag.

"I had Herb purchase this outfit for me from Harrods in the 1950's, so vintage is the right word," I replied.

"You mean to say that I get my own personal shopper down there?!" Jessica exclaimed.

"Yes...a personal shopper," I replied vaguely, as we entered the front doors of the hotel.

As I approached the front desk. A female ghoul (who could have passed for human if it wasn't for the faint whiff of decay about her) gave me the key for the room I had Herb book earlier. As always, he had been full of questions, a hopeful look in his eye, as I spun a lie about meeting a potential blood doll I had found on 'Plenty of Flesh', a blood doll hook up agency. I could just tell him I'd changed my mind afterwards. Or at least, Jessica would have to tell him, as she would be the one going back in my place. I felt a sense of anticipation, after tonight I would not be returning to the Underdark but spending a week above ground. Our room catered perfectly for human and non-human guests. There was a bed with en-suite, TV and of course the mini-blood- bar which Jessica immediately opened and began curiously inspecting the miniature bottles of blood.

"Leave it!" I ordered hastily and slammed the door closed.
She looked shocked at my sudden outburst.

"Prices are extortionate, it charges you a few hundred Drakmir just for removing the bottle."

Jessica giggled before saying. "Hotels are all the same, no matter where you go!"

I knelt down on the floor and motioned for her to do the same, it was parquet instead of carpet and easier to clean. But Jessica was eyeing the faint red stains on the floor dubiously, looked like the ghouls in charge of housekeeping had missed a spot, if Dante were here, he would have been mortified. He was always commenting on how bad the sanitation was in the entry spots, not that he ever visited them himself.

"I am not kneeling on that floor - it's disgusting! It looks like there's someone's blood still on it and this is a very expensive outfit."

"Oh right, then it might be bad if you got your own blood on it also?" I hissed losing my patience and exposing my fangs. Jessica gasped flinging her bag to one side and kneeling into position opposite me.

"Give me your wrist," I said.

"What? Why?"

"In order for this to work I need to share your memories, I can't live as you if I haven't had a taste of your life before."

"You never said anything about having to taste me," she started to get up, but I reached across and roughly pushed her back down.

"If I had you would never have shown up," I said flatly.

"Will it hurt?" she asked, a slight tremble in her voice.

"Of course, I am biting into your flesh and drawing out blood."
She tried to get up once more, but I swatted her down again.

"It's a small price to pay for the opportunity I am giving you. I will try not to get any on your dress."

She frowned as if weighing up the options and I contemplated what I would do if she refused. I could take the blood by force but there was no guarantee the spell would work if the human was unwilling.

"Okay, fine," she said pouting. "It can't be worse than when I got my ears pierced, right?"

"Exactly!" I replied, even though I had no idea what getting your ears pierced felt like, mine were clip-ons.

She finally held her wrist out and I quickly grabbed it and bit, before she could change her mind. I felt her tense up and involuntarily try to pull her wrist away but I held on, drawing in the blood and the memories it passed onto me. Visions of her family filled my mind, I took them all in trying to learn as much as I could from the flickers. A young girl appeared but she quickly dissipated to be replaced by two middle-aged adults, her parents. Her friends came next, some I recognised from the night I had first seen her, faces of boys flashed before me, lingering on one that looked familiar, the boy I had seen her arguing with. Then came my face which was met with mixed emotions, fear, curiosity and something else that I couldn't interpret. Human emotions were still hard for me to decipher. Then the flickers started to become hazy, like something was obscuring them; for some reason I was being blocked from certain memories. I drank deeper but her resistance was strong and I knew I wouldn't be able to break through it without nearly draining her.

Reluctantly I pulled away, I felt hungrier than ever. Normally after feeding straight from a human I felt a wave of immense satisfaction, now I just felt cheated. My throat felt constricted and it took all my resolve not to grab her wrists again and empty her veins right then and there.

"That hurt so much more than getting my ears pierced!" she whined, holding her wrist and staring at the two puncture wounds.

"You're lying about something," I said flatly.

I pulled some bandages from the Hotel 'clean up' kit and proceeded to clean and dress her wrist.

"What? No I'm not!" she said, looking offended at the accusation.

She was good. If I were to take her statement for face value, I might have just believed it. However her blood did not lie, she had put up a very strong wall to keep me out, and I needed to know why.

"You are holding some of your memories back, which means there is something you don't want me to see. Now either tell me or I will have to keep drinking until you become too weak to block me."

A flash of fear crossed her face and I saw her eyes jerk towards her bag. I grabbed it before she could and emptied its contents out. It was the usual stuff I would expect someone like Jessica to carry with her, make-up, mobile phone, car keys, wallet, school books and dozens of sachets of salt.

"Salt?" I asked. "This is what you are trying to hide from me?" I accused.

"I wasn't going to hurt you, I just wanted to have some protection."

"You thought that by sprinkling cooking condiments on me I would what, melt on the spot?"

She shrugged. "I don't know, you said that none of the other stuff like garlic or crosses work so I looked it up and read that salt wards off evil."

"For the record, table salt has no effect on vampires, there are so many additives in this it's barely pure anymore."

"But salt does work? Just not this type of salt?" she asked curiously.

"I will let you off for this because you are uneducated in our ways, but do not think for a second that I am about to indulge you on my kind's weaknesses, not because I fear what harm you would cause to me, but if you are stupid enough to turn up here with table salt, then who knows what you will try to bring into my home. If Kristian even slightly suspects that you are not me and are in fact a human he will kill you on the spot, against the code or not, if he thinks you are there with the intent to harm he will end you." My eyes pierced straight into her as I said it.

"He can't, you said your father works for that vampire government thing. He would have to tell them if your brother did anything that broke their rules." She tried to argue.

"My father is loyal to the Tribune but his loyalty to his own family is absolute, it wouldn't take much convincing that your death had been necessary. An unregistered human, posing as a vampire is suspect enough, but the fact that you are carrying a magical amulet that makes you immune to our powers warrants enough of a threat to justify killing you." She looked concerned now, good I thought, I needed her to be concerned, not enough to change her mind but enough to abide by my rules.

"Okay, I'm sorry," she said, before suddenly pulling off her boots and emptying out another handful of the sachets onto the carpet.

"Is that all of it?" I asked, and she nodded sullenly.

"Good, then lets begin." I pulled a dagger out of my bag. She stared at it and edged back.

I sighed. "If I was going to kill you I wouldn't need this, I would have just drained you."

She nodded but kept her eyes on the blade. Ignoring her I drew it across my wrist then held it out, watching the black blood drip onto the floor.

"Your blood is black?" she said puzzled.

"Yes, it's demonic remember?"

"Does that hurt?"

"No, now be quiet, I need to concentrate," I snapped.

I focused using all my accumulated skills in blood magic. The blood pooled together until it was a large puddle between us. Both of our faces reflected in its black surface as we peered into it.

"Put your hand in it," I said.

"Eww no, that's nasty!" she replied petulantly.

"Do it now!" I commanded raising my voice.

Seeing no way out, she shrugged and did as she was told. I followed suit and put my own hand into the blood, it began to bubble, like tiny black skinned balloons they inflated, slowly at first and then with increasing violence, like boiling water. As the blood bubbles became more frequent and more energised, some began to pop and spit thick black globules around our hands, causing Jessica to flinch. I could sense her tensing again, instincts telling her to move away from this strange, foul looking black liquid. I grabbed her hand tighter and spoke with an even more commanding tone.

"Don't!"

"What's it doing?" she said, a hint of anxiety and excitement in her voice.

"It's working," I replied.

The blood magic hungrily poured out of the black puddle, thick gloopy tendrils lashed out and wrapped around each of our arms, like living things. The black blood crept up, climbing up us like ivy on a wall. I could hear Jessica breathing hard and a sudden squeal as the blood forced its way in, filling our mouths, eyes and nostrils. It submerged us completely until all that could be seen was shimmering black. And for that one moment, in that darkness connected by my spilt blood, we were one and the same, united in thought and consciousness as true night passed over to envelop both of us. As I began to fall into the magic induced slumber, the last thing I could hear was the muffled sounds of Jessica screaming. One smiling, the other aghast, we fell into darkness.

Had it been minutes, hours, days even? No, not days, if it had I surely would have been discovered by now, but more importantly had it worked? Eyes flickering, light filled my vision. As my eyesight gradually returned to me I noticed it was morning, there was no sign of the black ooze from last night's spell.

"Amazing..." a voice chimed in behind me. "Everything is so different."

I turned to the side and saw Jessica; or did I mean me? And the surreal nature of what had happened finally sunk in. With something resembling doubt I wondered, had I made a mistake? Still saying nothing I looked down and noticed that I had changed too, my arms were no longer the slim, alabaster white of marred perfection, but richly tanned, human. A barely restrained giggle pulled me from my thoughts as Jessica, already admiring herself in her pocket mirror, squealed in adulation.

"Your skin is so flawless!" she said, tracing her fingers across her new pale cheek down to her jaw. She opened her mouth and traced the tip of her new fangs with her tongue.

"They are so subtle, do they extend or anything?" she asked, now prodding at them with a finger.

"No," I replied, offended by the idea. "They are sharp enough, that's all that counts."

Content or unbothered by my answer Jessica shrugged and flipped the mirror closed with a loaded click.

"I just thought they might grow when you get hungry, like how boys' bits do when they get turned on."

She grinned and raised her eyebrows. The bizarre situation of seeing my face talk in such a scandalous way was mind-boggling. Seeing my face talk and act in a way so alien to my true self was like being trapped on the other side of a mirror. You could see yourself do anything and everything from within but, no matter how hard you banged on the mirror, you could not control or influence what was happening on the otherside. To see Jessica animate her face in ways I could not comprehend was fascinating, my smile, my laugh, my movements, but her feelings - the way that she was, brought me to life.

"Okay, now what?" she asked.

"Remove your clothes," I replied dryly.

Jessica looked stunned for a moment, taken off guard by the statement.

"Our bodies may have changed, but we are still wearing our former clothes. It would look incredibly suspicious if we both appeared wearing ill-fitting clothes that neither of us would normally wear, don't you think?"

Jessica breathed out and relaxed as she understood the connotation.

"Ah, I get it! I was going to say this isn't the right place to celebrate surely," she winked at me.

As we slipped out of our clothes, we both noticed the differences in our bodies.

"You're so skinny, my old clothes are like parachutes on this frame," a hint of jealousy was in her voice. Standing there completely nude and without a care in the world, she waited for me to exchange clothing.

"My wrist is no longer bleeding," she exclaimed in surprise.

"My blood from the ritual healed you, it's also how you will be able to enter the Underdark, humans need to consume vampire blood in order to get through the magical gateway that keeps our city hidden, the Morshard will play a part as well, in tricking the security guards that you have an implant."

"What's an implant?" she asked with a frown, still staring in awe at her new form.

"I told you already, the implant is what allows undead to legally travel to the human realm."

"Like a magical microchip?"

"Yes, it's the closest thing we have to an identity, or our new identity. When the guards scan it they access information about you such as who you were sired by, the date you were turned and whether you have any feeding convictions on your record; it's also used as a means to track and monitor us."

Jessica looked uncertain for a moment. "Are you sure we will be able to pull this off?"

"Yes, the magic infused in that necklace is more powerful than the scanners used," I said, with more confidence than I felt.

"Have you tested it?" she asked.

"Yes," I lied. In theory I had, the same magic used for the Morshard had been cast onto my own implant which is what had been allowing me to visit the human realm untracked for the past few months.

Jessica seemed to relax and I continued getting dressed.

"Your breasts are much larger than mine," I said flatly, struggling to remove my top.

Ignoring the comment and still naked, she grabbed her bag and skipped towards me; any sign of her concern gone.

"Remember, the dress you're wearing is the type of thing I wear on a day-to-day basis. It's part of my personality, so if you stick to this, you should blend in easily and, remember, standards must be maintained!" she cooed at me, excitement still evident in her voice. A childish smile etched on her face as she finally decided to get dressed. Feeling a little uncertain myself now; I looked down at the tight leopard skin dress that constituted 'her personality'. Looking back at her wearing my much more demure outfit I suddenly felt anxious.

"Oh, yes! There are also my school things in there, don't forget them or you will get into trouble on day one, I can't remember if I did my homework or not...Oh well, I'm sure you'll manage!" she dropped the bag at my feet with a resounding thud.

"How about me? Any advice as to how I should act more like you?" she chuckled excitedly.

"Yes. Don't be you and don't get killed," I said flatly, glaring at her. Jessica's smile quickly faded ...

Chapter 7

~Scarlet Monday~
Day One as a Human

An hour later I stood outside the building that was Jessica's place of education. According to Jessica's phone it was 8:30am, her first lesson started at 9am. I had hoped I would have had a chance to stop off at her home first, I was still uncertain that what I was wearing was appropriate attire for such a place but as I watched the other students filter through the college gates I noticed that many of them were dressed similarly. Jessica had informed me she was in her secondary education; I had read up on it and was very intrigued at the prospect of seeing what A levels were. I checked the timetable she had given me, the first lesson of the day was Drama. I managed to find my way around okay, compared to the twists and turns of the Underdark this place seemed straightforward, I only had to ask for directions once. I entered a large room with chairs laid out in a circle, no-one had taken a seat yet and instead, they stood in little clusters talking. There seemed to be no sign of an approved person to educate us so I also stood and waited. A few minutes later a boy appeared next to me, he was running his hands through his hair nervously.

"Look, Jess, I wanted to apologise about yesterday," he said, his green eyes watching me with apprehension.

I took in his face again and realised he was the boy I had seen Jessica arguing with.

"Okay," I said, still unsure as to why he was apologising, from what I had seen it had been Jessica who had slammed the door in his face.

He raised an eyebrow in disbelief.

"That's it? Normally you like to hold a grudge for at least a week?" he watched me suspiciously for a moment like I was going to take it back. When I just stood there he seemed to relax and gave a little laugh.

"Not that I am complaining, I like this new forgiving attitude you have adopted." He looked back at me and smiled, it was a nice smile full of warmth and easiness, unlike my own kin's smiles which, although mimicking humans very well, always held an air of coldness and insincerity. I had practiced and studied my own smile in the mirror before the ritual; I had mastered the gesture convincingly enough at a glance, even managing to keep my fangs hidden. However something still didn't look right, no matter how hard I tried my eyes remained cold and indifferent. I was so taken aback by this boy's genuine smile that I felt my own mouth twitching to reciprocate until I remembered that it wasn't aimed at me, it was aimed at Jessica.

"Are you okay?" he asked, concern filling his eyes; again I struggled to dismiss the nice feeling his attention gave me.

"Jess?" he said, touching my shoulder gently.

I flinched back and instinctively let out a hiss. Sam gave a sharp cry before stumbling backwards into the chairs. He regained his composure, mouth agape, not quite sure how to respond. A few of the other students looked on with the same open-mouthed expressions.

"Allergies," I stated bluntly. I raised my hand up to my mouth, feigning a sudden bout of sneezing, while inwardly berating myself. If I was going to live among the humans I must at least try to act like them, and hissing was not a part of it.

"Okay…next time warn me," Sam stammered as he bent down to pick up one of the chairs he had knocked over.

I looked around the room; most of the other students had gone back to their conversations except one. A tall boy with blonde hair and a slightly pinched face was staring at us from across the hall. Sam followed my gaze then scowled.

"I should smash his face in," he said through gritted teeth. "I don't know what you ever saw in Dean Tyler - the bloke is a complete idiot. I once saw him scratching his armpit then actually sniff it." He glanced at me.

"You and him are over now aren't you?" he tried to say it casually but I saw a slight frown crease his smooth features and I actually felt a little bad for him, looks like Jessica had this boy enthralled, if I didn't know better I would have thought she had some supernatural abilities herself.

"Yes," I said, wishing I could manage more than just single syllables.

"Jess, you're looking at me like you've just seen me for the first time or something?"

I quickly dropped my gaze.

"I'm just tired, I didn't sleep well last night," I babbled, feeling like a gormless idiot.

But he nodded. "Me too, I thought a lot about what you said and I came to realise I have been acting selfishly."

He reached for my hand then flinched away as soon as he touched me.

"Your hands are really cold."

I rolled them into my sleeves self-consciously and feebly thought of something to say, somehow explaining that I suffered from Algor mortis or death chills would not be appropriate.

"Maybe you're coming down with something?" he suggested, I decided to go along with this and nodded, trying my best to look like the doe eyed, vulnerable human who was at risk of all sorts of ailments. It must have worked because he put his arm around me and pulled me close then quite suddenly placed his lips to mine and kissed me. I had kissed boys before when hunting, but it normally followed with me feeding on them. Every instinct in me screamed to do the same now, his lips brushed against mine so softly and his hands caressed the back of my neck. As kisses go it was what I would assume was a very nice one, but all I could do was stand there with my lips partially open but unreceptive, terrified I would lose control. So I just stood there waiting for him to finish, trying not to pay attention to the blood pumping through him as his excitement levels rose. At last he pulled away from me and smiled, apparently unaware that I had been about as affectionate as a sheet of glass, perhaps Jessica wasn't a great kisser I thought.

A woman with red hair entered the room, glasses hung around her neck, a wad of papers clutched in her hand. The students, at last, began seating themselves and I followed suit taking the nearest one. Sam slid into the chair next to me. I noticed everyone had sheets of paper on their laps, I began searching in Jessica's bag but only found textbooks.

"Here you can share my script, you always forget yours," said Sam with another smile and he balanced the sheets of paper on both of our laps so we had to lean into each other to read it. It turned out Jessica's class was performing a production of 'The Elephant man'. I was not familiar with it but the red haired woman, who I later found out was Jessica's teacher Miss Fenwick, began discussing the life of John Merrick who had been the real elephant man. As I learnt more about this man a strange feeling overcame me, I had not known a human could be subject to such cruelty from his own kind purely for looking different. Vampires were not human yet we could walk among the humans unnoticed and it seemed in some cases, as long as you wore the right face, it didn't matter how monstrous you were on the inside.

At the end of the class, I was about to leave when Miss Fenwick approached me.

"All ready for Friday night?" she asked.

I stared at her blankly but she carried on talking, unaware of my confusion.

"Great! Now, Sam will be in full make-up tomorrow for the dress rehearsal, we managed to bring in a girl with actual prosthetic training who wants to take part for experience; brilliant eh? She's also agreed to help you with your wig and make–up all for the small price of taking some photos for her portfolio."

It turned out that Jessica had failed to mention she was cast as the leading lady in the play - or rather that I would be in her place. I left the classroom wondering what else Jessica had failed to inform me about. When I got outside Sam was waiting for me, he waved a plastic box in my direction.

"I bought in lunch for once, what about you?" he said.

I thought of the blood pack in my bag and shook my head. "No, I forgot."

"Not to worry, we can grab you something from Redwoods," he said, a smile on his face.

I followed him, certain that this place he spoke of did not stock food for the undead. Redwoods was not a forest like it sounded but a small cramped looking cafe where students could buy human snacks. I always loved it when human authors described the food their characters would eat. It had made me want to be human more than ever, so I could experience the same joy from food that they did. There were always so many variants that they never seemed to run out of ways to describe the feasts. There were the huge outdoor banquets deliciously described in my Brian Jacques collection with delicacies such as candied chestnuts. It was never the spells in Harry Potter that hooked me to the series, I had been created due to magic and seen its dark side. It was the feasts and shops filled with sweets that drew me in. I remember wanting to try Turkish Delight so much when I first read The Lion, the Witch and the Wardrobe that I got Herb to acquire me some and despite my lack of digestive functions, I had been determined to at least taste this human delicacy. But I was disappointed with the real thing which reminded me of the human fat Herb ate. As a vampire there was only blood, even when reading vampire books it was always the same – blood. And though some authors tried to make it sound tantalising, in the end it was just biting into someone and drinking their blood. Compared to the endless choices that humans had, my options were just plain bland.

Sam bought me a cookie along with a sandwich and a bottle of water. We found a table in the corner of the cafe and he got out his own lunch; also a sandwich; except his looked more squashed and was cut into two squares, whereas mine was cut into two triangles. Also the contents were different; mine was, according to the wrapping, chicken salad and his was filled with slices of a yellow substance, he caught me staring and nodded,

"Just cheese; I know I should be more creative but food is food."

I watched as his 'just cheese' sandwich disappeared into his mouth bite after bite until there was nothing left. He frowned after he had swallowed the last bit.

"Why aren't you eating?" I looked down at my own sandwich.

"I'm not that hungry."

"You should still eat something," he said, concern on his face.

I picked up the sandwich and bit into it. I had chewed food before, my Blood Tofu was solid in form, but once inside, my body was able to absorb it as it was still blood. This was different, I knew I would not be able to digest this and was concerned whether I would be able to hold it down and not cough it up in front of Sam. To my relief I managed to consume the sandwich and even nibble the cookie, both were foul, grainy and made my throat dry. After lunch I had dance, which took place in a white room with one side of the wall covered in tall mirrors. I was the first to arrive and took a moment to check my reflection. I had changed into Jessica's dance clothes, which were a black vest top and leggings, and tied Jessica's long brown hair into a ponytail, a style I never used as Scarlet. I watched in the mirror as the ponytail swished and flicked as I turned my head, then I saw it, a flash of blonde. I grabbed the ponytail and inspected it closer but all I could see were strands of brown, I relaxed. It had not even been one day yet and already I was acting paranoid. I was still inspecting it when the other students entered the room. I turned from the mirror and watched, motionless, as they started spontaneously jumping on the spot, some were even lying on the floor and writhing like they were in pain.

A young blonde woman entered the class; the teacher I assumed; and I watched in amazement as the students jumped and writhed with more intensity, while the teacher watched on approvingly. Was this some sort of witchcraft?

"Aren't you going to warm up?" came a voice to the right of me, I addressed the speaker and saw it was Hannah, one of Jessica's friends from that first night at Insomnia. She was sitting on the floor bent over her legs, her hands grasping at her feet. This must be some kind of human ritual before dancing I concluded, dismissing the idea of anything supernatural and mimicking the same actions.

I was copying a girl in front of me when Hannah spoke again.

"Ouch, Jess! Bending that way doesn't look normal." I glanced in the mirror and saw I had pushed too far and my leg was almost behind my head. I feigned a grimace.

"You're right, that was too far," I said moving to a more human posture. After a few more minutes of the strange movements, the teacher spoke.

"Good afternoon. We will continue practicing your dance solos, I expect to see better postures today and I hope you have selected music that suits your routine or it can be very distracting."

We were to take turns in showing our 'dance solo' in front of the class. I had never danced professionally but being a vampire, I was a quick learner and had only watched one girl perform before I had memorised the entire routine. When it came to my turn the teacher held her hand out expectantly. I stared at it bewildered, maybe I had to dance with her I thought, I placed my hand in hers and she frowned and moved her hand away.

"Your music, Jessica? You were meant to bring it in today, remember?" I shook my head. "I forgot, sorry."

She sighed. "Never mind, you can perform without it for now but you must remember it next time."

I moved to the middle of the floor and slowly skittered across the polished wooden boards on the tips of my toes, just as the other girl had. I reached up above me with my arms and performed turns, kicking my legs out at the exact same points as she had. I performed the entire dance perfectly, my supernatural limbs bending with ease and grace, my empty lungs requiring no pauses for breath. At the end I slid across the floor one leg in front, one behind and threw my arms out behind me. The teacher and students stared at me open mouthed. I smiled, they loved it, I had danced as a human and they loved me for it.

"You can wipe that smile off your face, Jessica!" snapped the teacher, which I did in my confusion.

"Would you care to explain why you have completely changed your dance and instead performed Anita's?" It was then I realised that mimicking was only going to get me so far.

At the end of the day I walked to the bus stop with Hannah. Jessica normally drove to and from college but since I could not drive she had expressly forbade me from touching her car and, instead, had written the route back to her home for me. I had intended on walking but I had never been on a bus and the whole purpose of this was to experience all aspects of human life. The most obvious difference between walking in the human world and walking in mine was the noise. As Hannah and I walked, I found it difficult to concentrate on her conversation despite, or perhaps because of, my enhanced hearing. I kept finding myself being distracted by all the other noises surrounding us, it was constant; people coughing, kids laughing, babies crying and cars beeping. The Underdark was so quiet in comparison, there are no children running about, no vehicles and certainly no coughing or other sounds caused by ailments, unless you counted the random popping of joints from ghouls. Even the tones of voices were different, we could mimic different tones to help ensnare prey, feigning concern or fondness to fool humans but I could tell the difference. However, not all human sounds appeared to be intelligible. Young girls, I noticed, were prone to random shrieks. At first I thought it was out of fear but when I saw it was followed by signs of happiness, I realised this must be a custom I wasn't aware of. The young males in contrast would resort to unresponsive grunts like some primitive form of communication. Hannah had boarded a different bus to the one I needed but she waved at me through the window from her seat and I waved back surprised by how nice such a small gesture felt. When my own bus appeared I stuck my hand out as Jessica had instructed but it drove straight past. I stared after it in confusion while a few of the humans next to me swore under their breath, one even demonstrating an impressive hand gesture. By the time the next one turned up I had been waiting half an hour, human transport, it seemed, was lacking in its efficiency, no wonder Kristian's blood dolls were always wishing they could materialise.

A lot more people had arrived at the bus stop by that point and even though I had been there first, I somehow managed to find myself at the back of the queue. When I got on I waved my ticket at the driver who watched me despondently behind a sheet of clear plastic. I waved it again at him and he nodded to a small grey machine next to him. I waited for some sort of instruction to follow but he just glared at me. A woman sighed loudly behind me, "Excuse me!" she said and leant across me swiping a square object, similar to the ticket I held, across the machine, it beeped in response and she pushed passed and found herself a seat. I tried the same and it also beeped, I looked back up at the driver.

"Well go and find a bloody seat then!" he barked, then muttering. "Bloody tourists!"

I walked up the aisle, looking for a free seat and found one halfway down. I slid across to the window side as the bus pulled away and watched with fascination as we passed the human houses. We had houses in the Underdark, but nothing like these; these had long gardens in front of them with neat little lawns and flowers. Some had cars parked in front of them like Jessica's did. Suddenly there was a sharp ring and the bus screeched to a halt. The doors opened and a little old lady got off. This happened regularly and by the time the bus reached Jessica's road I had discovered how to make the ringing noise that stopped the bus, there were small buttons on the handrails. I pressed the nearest one and the bus pulled to a stop and opened its doors, before I jumped off and watched as it drove away. Despite the obvious flaws of human public transport I felt a wave of excitement that I was now a 'commuter'.

I entered Jessica's house to the sound of barking and growling, it was apparent that her dog knew something was up. It danced around my feet agitatedly, until I hissed, causing it to immediately whimper and run off with its tail between its legs.

"Hello, dear," called a voice from somewhere in the house. "Dinner will be ready soon."

I walked into the living room and halted, the dining table was laid out. I hadn't considered that I would be made to sit down and have a family dinner. During the break in between dance class I had managed to cough up the undigested sandwich Sam had bought me and the idea of having more solids so soon afterwards was not appealing. I found Jessica's mum in the kitchen and almost gagged as the smell of what she was cooking hit me with full force.

"Your favourite tonight, lasagne," she said, looking up from the pot she was stirring and smiling at me. I forced a smile back. "Mmm... smell's lovely," I lied.

"I know, this was your grandma's recipe. Right, go wash up and get changed then it should be ready for when your father gets back from work."

I eagerly left the kitchen and went upstairs to Jessica's room. The first thing that struck me was how pink everything was, from the rose pink walls to the shocking pink bedspread. The second was how many stuffed toys she had. Jessica was seventeen years old, nearly an adult, and I had understood such things were for younger humans. I scanned the rest of the room, there were tiny ornaments on the bookshelves, some were little animals carved from crystal, others were little porcelain unicorns and fairies; I didn't understand their purpose. I sat on the bed and noticed among the animals there was also a doll. I lifted it curiously and as I did so it spoke, "I like to be held". I immediately dropped it and stamped on it. I continued to stamp on it until it stopped, when I sensed someone was watching me. I spun around and saw a small child standing in the doorway, she had short brown hair held back with a pink Alice band, her large brown eyes looked down at the doll, which still had my foot on its face. This must be Jessica's sister – Leyna, the contents of the room suddenly made more sense. I retrieved the doll from the floor and fixed its dented face. 'Here,' I said holding it out to her. She looked at it suspiciously then took it, her eyes still fixed on me. I stared back unsure of what to say, I had never met a human child; blood dolls were always adults as feeding off a child was against the Tribune's code of conduct.

"Well, I will leave you to get on with whatever it is you children do," I said, although part of me wanted to linger.

I never had a sister, or one that I could remember, living with three vampire brothers was demanding at the best of times but I imagined having a little sister would be different. I could brush her hair, read to her, teach her to draw and paint. My stomach cramped and reminded me I had not had any blood all day, the child's tiny heartbeat was loud in my ears and the scent of her blood was overpowering. I had to remove myself and get some proper food, trying to bond now would be far too risky - feeding on Jessica's family was not part of the plan. I stepped past her and entered the second room which, to my relief, looked more like the room of a teenager. The walls were a lilac colour and the bed, which had matching covers, was free of dolls or stuffed animals. The best thing about Jessica's room however, was not the absence of toys but the array of memorabilia that cluttered her shelves and walls. I explored it in awe, there were dozens of trophies, mostly for dance and gymnastics. I picked up one with a silhouette of a tiny gold ballerina poised at the top of it and wondered if I would have won anything if given the chance. There was also a large board covered in photographs, I paused in front of it. There were pictures of Jessica with her friends, pictures of her with her family and pictures of her with boys… lots of different boys. It was an entire wall of her life and I felt that same pang I had when I first watched her, out with her friends. I thought back to the stark bare walls of my own room, sure the paint was immaculate but there was no proof of existence outside of it, the room was as empty as its occupier's soul.

I moved on to inspect the walk-in wardrobe. She was obviously as fanatic about clothes as I was, except they were all a little skimpy for my taste. I picked up a lacy looking top which turned out to be a thong and quickly threw it back in the draw. I heard a low growl and turned to see Jessica's tiny dog had regained its courage and was attempting to intimidate me again. This wasn't on, I couldn't spend the whole week being chased around by the snarling fur ball. Besides being extremely irritating, having my own dog turn on me would raise questions. I knelt down to its level, it pulled its quivering lips back further showing me more of its needle like teeth, quite an impressive set for such a small creature. I focused on the depths of its large brown eyes and tapped into my demon abilities. I had never tried enthralling an animal but was relieved to find it worked, however not with the desired effect. I had intended to command the beast to leave me alone, but instead it did the opposite and was following me around like a secondary shadow.

"What?" I asked as if it were able to give me a vocal explanation of its wants.

I noticed a basket in the corner of the room, inside was a selection of toys not so different from the ones on Leyna's bed. I grabbed one, which appeared to be a pink squeaky ball, and threw it in the general direction of the dog. It stared at it blankly then looked back to me as if I was an idiot. I sat down deciding to ignore it, but I could feel the penetrating gaze still upon me. Then it reached out and placed a tiny paw on my foot. I glared down at the offensive manoeuvre but the small ball of fluff
continued to gaze at me, its round brown eyes wide and expectant.

"I give in, what do you want?!"

It ran off into the hall landing then came back and barked at me as if urging me to follow, I stood up and followed behind it as it sped down the stairs and into the kitchen where it promptly padded over to an empty pink bowl on the ground, then turned and looked up at me. It wanted me to feed it, easy enough I thought. Jessica's mother was nowhere to be seen but the cooking pots were bubbling away, the revolting smell even stronger now. I had no idea where the dog's food was kept but I noticed it was scraping its paw against a plastic bin. I opened the lid and found inside was filled with small round brown pellets that smelt even worse than the human food. There was a plastic scoop inside, I gagged as I filled the bowl, all the while it continued to observe me. I placed the bowl in front of it but it just carried on watching me with that expectant expression. Did it want me to spoon feed it as well?!

"Eat," I commanded and to my relief it began devouring the contents, I was surprised at the appetite of such a small creature. Afterwards it looked up at me and placed its paw on my foot again.

"Stop that," I said, removing my foot from under its dirty little pads.

A small whine escaped from its mouth as it pawed at me again. What else could it want?! I thought back to what I knew about the needs of the living; food, warmth.. and defecation. I grimaced as I opened the back door and watched the tiny dog sprint out and proceed to squat on the grass and deposit several steaming brown pellets which looked like a slightly wetter version of its biscuits. It then ran back into the house looking extremely pleased with itself. I swiftly closed the door on the new foul stench. I had not long returned upstairs when I heard the door go downstairs followed by a man's voice, Jessica's father, Mr Young from the sounds of it, and sure enough a few minutes later there was a knock on the door.

"Come in," I said and the door opened revealing a male human behind it, he looked to be what humans referred to as middle aged.

I had studied a book about the stages of human age from birth to death at ghoul school, curious to know all the stages I would be missing. I had learnt that I would have been an adolescent when I was turned, still considered young but changed enough by puberty physically and emotionally in preparation for the next stage of the human cycle – adulthood. Whereupon I would be expected to have obtained a job, a home of my own, a mate and then watch the stages of life proceed through my own offspring. Except I never got to that stage of the cycle, in fact it's as if I had devolved, as although I would have certainly gone through the changes needed to commence such things as a family, my condition meant I was physically incapable of bringing them to fruition, incapable of making, no leaving a mark. This man before me had clearly experienced many years of adulthood, he had followed the guidelines of conformity, he had married, had two daughters, which he would finish raising, then what I wondered? Retirement, grandparent, senility?

These stages of life were unique to humans and all were meant to play a role, but which was the most important and was it one that I was never to reach?

"How was college?" he asked.

"Informative," I replied.

He laughed but I had failed to see what was funny. "I should hope so," he said.

"How are your play rehearsals going? Your mother and I bought our tickets, we can't wait to see you in action," he smiled.

"I was about to go over a scene," I said, waving the script I had taken out of my bag before he knocked. Sam had given me his copy, advising he knew it off by heart anyway.

"Well, I am proud of your dedication darling, but dinner's ready, your mother sent me to come and get you."

I hesitated, I hadn't managed to have my blood pack. I thought of the laid out table and the family dinner conversations I could potentially miss, reminding myself this is part of why I was here, I only had one week to make the most of it. I followed him downstairs where Leyna, was already sat at the table, while Mrs Young was placing a plateful of food in front of her.

"Hi, darling," she said as I entered and took a seat. They both looked at me in confusion, I looked back wondering if I had missed some dining etiquette.

"You don't want to sit in your normal place, Jess?" asked Mrs Young, pointing to the chair next to Leyna.

"Of course, my usual seat." I moved places wondering why humans were so concerned about their seating position, at home I never thought about where I sat, even on the rare occasions where it was at the table. A chair after all, was just a chair. And yet, above ground such trappings were considered an extension of oneself.

Dinner itself was foul. Sheets of a chewy substance glued together by a sour tasting red sauce which, despite the colour, bore no resemblance to my usual diet. As if this wasn't bad enough, between the soggy sheets and sauce were lumps of a brown fatty material that looked like something that had fallen off a ghoul. The atmosphere however, made up for it. Jessica's parents conversed with me as if they had known me my whole life which, of course, they thought they had. They joked and smiled and showered me with compliments. I was, it seemed, the light of their life. I let it wash over me and knew that any disgusting food I may have to force down was a small price to pay to finally feel part of a normal family. Although I soon noticed not everyone was so chatty, Leyna was a quiet child, she picked at her food about as enthusiastically as I did. She made no attempt to join in the conversation but I put it down to not having the intellectual capacity to communicate at such a young age. After dinner, I was introduced to another human cuisine known as dessert which Mrs Young called a tart, a phrase I had always thought to be associated with promiscuous women; this was sticky and rich but nicely presented in a small triangle. At long last the food stopped coming and we retired to the lounge to settle down to watch a documentary about the planet. At eight o'clock Mrs Young took Leyna upstairs to bed; she had fallen asleep on her lap. Mr Young turned to me while they were upstairs.

"I thought you were going to practice your play before you went to bed?" he inquired.

"I'll give it a break tonight, I don't want to overdo it," I replied.

I knew, I would have all night to pour over my lines, and besides, I wasn't ready to end my family night just yet.

When Mrs Young returned she gave me a suspicious frown. "You're being very sociable this evening, normally you are glued to your phone. Are you feeling all right?" she exchanged a smile with Mr Young.

I couldn't think of a response, I had thought Jessica, after being at college all day, would want to spend time with her family, but then I thought about how unsocial I was with my supernatural surrogates, maybe Jessica, like me, didn't feel she belonged in this close knit unit, the question was why?

"Not that I am complaining," said Mrs Young, leaning across the sofa and pulling me close into a hug.

"It's nice to spend time with you, whatever the reason."

The hug was different to any kind of physical contact I had experienced, it wasn't the same feeling I had when feeding on someone and it wasn't anything like the detached hugs I received from my enthralled victims. This was real, Mrs Young was not under the influence of my charms, it brought with it a warmth and tenderness that had always been missing from my world, this was what it felt like to be loved, this was what it felt like to have a mother.

Eventually, Mrs Young became less responsive as the night grew on, her brain disengaging from the conscious world into the world of sleep where only mortals migrated to. Mr Young had already succumbed and I had been watching curiously as his breathing slowed and his head tilted forward, so his chin was touching his chest. At points his pause between breaths seemed unnaturally long and I worried that he had died, until suddenly he would make a snorting sound, briefly waking himself up before falling back to sleep again. It was a concern how fragile they were, I felt that at any moment they could be taken away from me. Much later both had dragged themselves up to bed and insisted I do the same. I locked myself in the bathroom pretending to clean my teeth but was actually regurgitating the undigested meal, the lasagne looked the same on the way out as it did on the way in, but the tart didn't look so nicely presented anymore. Afterwards I rinsed my mouth with some fang fresh that I had brought with me to remove the aftertaste and changed into Jessica's pyjamas, a vest top and a pair of shorts that seemed far too revealing, even for sleepwear. I got into Jessica's bed, pulled the lilac sheets over me and mimicked sleeping. As soon as I was certain the rest of the household was asleep I turned on the lamp and got my script out. The role I would be taking over from Jessica was Mrs Kendall, an actress that befriended the elephant man. We were to rehearse the scene where the elephant man and Mrs Kendall share their first meeting. She had heard history and out of pity paid him a visit, being told how intelligent he was beneath the physical deformities. She brings him a book of Shakespeare's works and together they read a scene from Romeo and Juliet. Overcome with emotion at seeing this charming and bright man trapped in this monstrous form she kisses him knowing that this is the best gift she can give him, as he has never known love. It didn't take me long to memorise the lines so I spent the next few hours exploring the rest of Jessica's room. I discovered more photos in her desk draw. These were of her and Sam, they were close up pictures of their faces pressed together. In some they were smiling and in others they were kissing, their eyes closed and lips touching. I put the pictures back feeling strangely empty until I remembered I had not fed yet. Grabbing my blood pack from the rations I had brought I hastily consumed it, being careful not to spill any on the carpet. I felt better immediately and decided to start on Jessica's homework. I needed to come up with a solo dance that I had not replicated from another student. I used Jessica's laptop and researched different forms of dance, watching videos I found online. My mind memorising the movements just as easily as I had the lines from the play. I even managed to find a song among Jessica's music collection that I thought would fit the performance. Suddenly I heard a muffled chiming noise, I rifled through my bag until I found Jessica's phone. I checked the number before answering and it felt strange to see my own name come up. For Jessica to be calling this early on in the switch something bad must have happened.

"What's wrong?" I asked, as I put the phone to my ear.

"Nothing, I'm just bored and I'm not allowed to tell anyone where I am, so you're the only one I could call."

"It's only been one day."

"I know, but I'm used to a very active social life, don't vampires ever go out?"

I couldn't believe my ears, I had spent over a hundred years living the life of a vampire and she was bored after less than twenty fours hours.

"There are undead clubs in the Underdark, but you won't be going to any of them," I quickly added.

She sighed down the phone in response and I knew I would have to reiterate my point, something told me Jessica was used to getting her own way. I would have to resort to scare tactics.

"Need I remind you that you are meant to be keeping a low profile? It lessens the risk that someone will see through the cloaking spell. I'm not certain how reliable that amulet is or even how long it will last for that matter."

"What do you mean you're not certain how reliable it is? I thought it was yours?"

"It was crafted for me by a witch."

"Wait a moment, are you seriously telling me this tacky accessory you have me wearing has a time limit on it? That at any moment its power could stop and every undead around me will be able to sense I'm human?!"

"I was told it would last a week, but you can't always trust witches," I said truthfully.

"Or vampires it seems," she replied. "You really didn't consider my well-being when you planned this whole thing did you?" she added sounding more annoyed than worried, which was a relief. Annoyed I could handle, hysterical would be a different matter.

"Keep a low profile and you will be fine, then you only have to worry about my family. And you can avoid them easily enough. As I told you, Dante stays in his room most of the time and Kristian is usually out or busy with his blood dolls," I reminded her.

"And your father?" she asked.

"He will most likely be working at the Tribune Tower, same as Desmodeus."

"Desmodeus.. I forgot about him."

"Stop worrying, if anyone suspected anything you'd be dead by now," I reassured.

"That's encouraging, again your casual preparation for me surviving this doesn't inspire confidence," she replied sarcastically.

What did she expect a handwritten guide on how to survive living with vampires?

"Can I trust you to try and keep it together? You're not the only one whose life is on the line," I reminded her.

"You're already dead, what's the worse they can do to you?" she argued back.

"Undead not dead, I may act like the two are one and the same but I know the difference."

"Fine. To be honest I'm starting to feel a little sleepy, I'm just relieved you have a bed."

"What did you expect? That I roost like a bat?" I hoped she would see I was being sarcastic.

"No.. but maybe a coffin?"

"Unlike my brother Dante, I do not indulge in the conventional trends of our kin."

"He has a coffin? Can I go have a look?" asked Jessica, completely ignoring my obvious disdain.

"No, you are meant to be avoiding him not inspecting the décor of his bedroom."

"Well, it has to be more interesting than yours."

"I suppose it does lack a yapping ball of fur."

"Ball of fur? Oh, you mean Princess? She's so cute, isn't she? She's a pure bred Pomeranian."

"It confuses me, I fail to see the purpose in such a creature," I said, my eyes roving to the small animal which sat on the floor with it's large eyes still fixated on me.

"Well, she's cuter than your ghoul, he creeps me out. The way he follows you around, it took me ages to get rid of him."

"Herb means well and at least he can make conversation, unlike your little sister."

She laughed.

"Leyna is strange, Mum has taken her to specialists but they all say there's nothing wrong with her, she's just very shy."

"She is somewhat of a curiosity, I wish to learn more about human children yet I find her presence unsettling, much like your dog, they both stare. Yet it's not a vacant stare; like on some of the ghouls that have brains so rotten they can't even perform menial tasks. No...this stare shows a form of intelligence that demands to be addressed, even if on the most basic of levels," I said clinically.

"Welcome to my world, you asked for it, literally," she said.

I couldn't argue that.

"Anything else interesting happen?" she said.

I thought about mentioning my meeting with Sam in drama class, but decided otherwise. It felt private and there was the possibility that she would get jealous and change her mind about the swap. I wanted my full week's worth of humanity.

"Only that it's going to be hard finding excuses not to eat your mother's cooking."

"Don't mention food to me, I had to down a cup of warm blood earlier," she lamented.

"You drank blood?!" I had to admit I was impressed she managed it.

"I didn't have a choice, your brother Kristian and that rotting heap of flesh were watching me. It would have looked suspicious if I hadn't."

I heard her gasp faintly.

"That doesn't mean I'm going to turn into a ghoul does it?"

"No, it has to be vampire blood not human, and you have to die first, it's the same process as turning a vampire except ghouls never fully turned. If a human doesn't come back to life after 24 hours after being fed our blood, chances are they are dead for real or they are coming back as a ghoul."

"So basically you're all zombies, just ghouls look more zombified because they were dead longer?"

"No! A zombie is a corpse that's raised from the dead by witchcraft, vampires are humans bitten by a demon and fed its blood," I corrected.

"But you said the first vampire was fed blood from a demon that had been summoned by a witch - sounds like you're a zombie to me," she argued.

"I am not! Zombies have no will of their own, I have free will."

"All right, no need to get your fangs in a twist, zombie or vampire makes no difference to me, I just want to get through this thing alive."

And with that, the unexpected phone call ended. After popping the phone away, I crept silently into the landing and paused at the doorway of Leyna's bedroom. She was curled up in a ball, her arms clutched around a large elephant, the rest of the soft toys had been pushed to the bottom of the bed. I guessed, like chairs, even toys had a sense of hierarchy to humans. I moved onto the next bedroom, Mrs Young was sleeping on her side, her hair splayed out on the pillow. Mr Young was lying flat on his back, snoring loudly. It was a strange sound, something I was not used to, vampires didn't sleep except when they were fledglings and even then they made no sound. They just shut off like a form of hibernation and there was no hint that they were still alive. Humans were full of life, even in their sleep, as I stood there Jessica's mother rolled over onto her other side and her husband, in an unconscious response, rolled over too. Even Princess the dog, who had settled for sleeping in the

hall, after I had managed to shoo her out, was kicking happily away in her sleep. I thought she might wake as I passed her, but she merely opened one eye briefly then closed it again before continuing her little kick routine. I went back to Jessica's room closing the door gently behind me and slipped back into bed. At home there was no difference between night and day, our city was constantly dark and in recent times, with a curfew so early that we couldn't be called creatures of the night...more like creatures of the early evening. During these periods I would read to kill time but tonight I was content to lie there and listen to the snores of my borrowed human family. It wasn't long though before the sound of snores became one less and was instead followed by a small scratching noise on the door. I threw the covers off me and got up to open the door. As I did I came face to face with Princess who was now as awake as I was. I stared down at the Pomeranian wondering what on earth she could want now, when she suddenly dashed past me and jumped onto the bed, making herself comfortable.

"Oh no you don't," I said, before picking her up and placing her back on the floor.

She promptly jumped back up again and this time I lifted her off and firmly placed her back in the hall, before shutting the door. As soon as I slid back into bed, the scratching began again. Worried it would wake the rest of the house up I jumped out of bed and threw open the door, glaring at her. She stared back up at me tongue hanging out and a stupid grin plastered on her face.

"Oh, all right!" I snapped.

She ran straight for the bed and jumped up. I got back in and rolled over, keeping my back to the bundle of fur that was attempting to nuzzle next to me and wondered why I didn't just eat the damn thing.

Chapter 8

~Jessica Monday~
Day One as a Vampire

After we had swapped bodies, and Scarlet left to start her week as me, I made my way down to the lobby. The female ghoul at the desk smiled as I approached. This one was quite 'normal' looking, the slight yellowing in her pupils barely noticeable when they met mine.

"Will you be travelling alone tonight, Miss Lucard?" She said politely.

"Yes, thank you," I said as I handed her the key back with a smile.

I instantly regretted this as a look of surprise etched the ghoul's face. I had forgotten one of the basic principles, vampires were masters and ghouls servants. To show courtesy to what was the 'underclass' would be incredibly out of place, even more so in the Underdark.

"She was an idiot!" I snapped, instantly dropping the smile.

"I would have ended up killing her," I put on a mask of authority, barely hiding my tension. What felt like minutes passed, perhaps had I gone too far?

The ghoul laughed nervously, bowing her head and lowering her eyes this time. She was scared, perfect, when you are scared you don't ask questions.

"Well I suppose you'll be wanting to return immediately then, Miss Lucard?" she held out a different key. "It's room 101 on the first floor, I hope you enjoyed your stay and find it more fulfilling next time," she said meekly, before bowing once more.

I took the key and made my way to the lift. As I waited a woman appeared next to me so suddenly I almost gasped in surprise. She had long, dark hair and pale eyes, standing next to her was a man, but he didn't look well at all, he was very pale and there appeared to be droplets of blood on his shirt collar. She caught me staring and smirked.

"Overindulged a bit. Always hard when you get a new one, you forget they are not used to it." The lift doors opened and we entered, the man staggering in behind us like an afterthought.

"You find what you were looking for?" she asked as the lift took us up, I noticed she pressed the button for the first floor.

"Not yet, but there's still time," I replied, and she laughed at this.

"There certainly is, I know I'm going to take my time with this one." The man groaned faintly. The lift doors opened and she stepped out in front of me.

"Well, back to the land of the unliving," she paused outside a door and gave a small wave before opening it with her key and stepping through, dragging the man in behind her.

I walked over and stood where she had been moments ago before peering through the doorway. But there was nothing there, except for a room similar to the one I had just been in with Scarlet. I checked the door number again.

"Room 101," I muttered, as I looked down at the key in my hand. Then had an idea, shutting the open door I placed my own key inside the lock and turned it. There was a click and creak, before the door swung open. Taking a breath, I stepped through.

I felt a tremor run all the way through me, as though my insides were being thrown into a blender. Everything went temporarily black and it was as if everything I had known had suddenly fallen down a hole. Before I could even register it, there was light again, albeit a dull light. And I was standing, but not on the carpeted floors of the hotel room, I was standing on a cobbled street. What's more, it was colder, the temperature had dropped substantially and I zipped up my jacket. I looked behind me to see if there was any remnants of the door I had passed through, but instead, there was a large wrought iron gate. On either side stood two figures, they were so still that I first thought they were statues. One was a woman and the other a man. Both were vampires judging by their old fashioned outfits and lack of colour to their skin. They fixed me with stern eyes, so I turned and started walking away, keeping my steps slow and natural even though my instincts told me to run. Suddenly one of them called out behind me.

"Wait a minute, blondie!" I froze, petrified.

Turning slowly I watched as the male vampire approached me, he was frowning suspiciously. I hadn't been here five minutes and had been discovered already, this was a disaster.

"You're not...?", he pointed a finger at me accusingly and I flinched.

"You're not...Dezzy's lil sister are ya?"

Dezzy? I had no idea what this vampire was talking about.

"It is! Hey Romy come meet Dezzy's broodling," he motioned to his colleague.

The female approached and nodded at me indifferently.

"Been out for an early morning stroll?" she asked, although I felt she was asking more out of routine, than interest.

The male vampire gave her a cynical glance.

"She's not on curfew, Rom, she's Dezzy's sister."

"So you said," she replied, her pale eyes not leaving my face.

"Besides, if anything was amiss, the gate alarm would have gone off. Plus I've seen her pass through loads of times, she's a regular commuter," Joe replied.

Romy lost interest and instead, focused on a young looking vampire who was shiftily approaching. His eyes were darting nervously from us to the gate, it was obvious he was going to try and make a break for it. His pace quickened slightly before suddenly bolting past us. As quick as he was, Romy was quicker, he never stood a chance, she grabbed him by the arm and swung him towards the floor with a bone jarring thud then pressed the sole of her boot down hard on his head, causing him to squirm underneath it.

"Got a runner here, Joe," she said flatly.

Joe, sauntered over, eyeing the fledgling with apparent amusement.

"Planning on visiting someone were ya?"

"I just wanted to see my girlfriend," he whined. "I haven't seen her since I was turned eight weeks ago!" he started whimpering even louder.

Romy and Joe exchanged a look before proclaiming at the same time.

"Fledglings!"

Romy lifted her foot off the young vampire and released his arm, before yanking him roughly to his feet.

"No passing through the Gate until you have been a vampire for over a year, got that?"

"But I can't wait that long, she will think I'm dead for certain and meet someone else," he said, dusting his clothes off.

"You're in Quarantine until you have been a vampire for over a year, too risky otherwise, you'll try and feed off the first human you come across."

The fledgling vampire made a low whining sound and Romy looked at him with contempt. "Your human is now out of bounds. Your old life is out of bounds. You're no longer part of that world. Accept it."

"But there must be a way..." the fledgling whined one final time.

Before the fledgling could say anymore, Romy struck him hard across the face leaving him blinking in shock. The slap had been so hard, that the snapping sound echoed for a few moments.

"This Gate is off limits. Pull a stunt like this again and we won't be so lenient." Her eyes narrowed as she said the last part.

Joe stepped between them.

"My colleague has forgotten how emotional the beginning can be for a newbie, soon all those old emotions will fade and it will only be their
blood that interests you. Which is why you must stay down here until you can control that part of you."

The fledgling nodded slowly, wiping his runny nose on his sleeve.

"You really think I will forget her?" he asked looking doubtfully at the older vampire. "I was going to propose this year."
Joe let out a hollow laugh.

"I forgot my wife and our four children within a week."

"How could you forget your own kids?" the fledgling asked in shock.

"It's easily done, all that conformity soon becomes alien, the need to return to it gone. Hey, it's better than killing them!" He said nonchalantly.

"What if I bring her down here instead? Like one of those blood dolls I've seen other vampires with." The fledgling inquired.

"The only way that is going to happen is if you apply through the Former Lives Association. It still has a requisite of 6 months quarantine, not to mention the additional paperwork and administration of setting up a supervised visit. Either way that is still a long time for a woman alive or otherwise, to go...unattended." Joe barely suppressed a snigger as the hope drained from the fledgling's eyes.

"But it would mean that eventually she could come and live down here with me?" asked the fledgling with determination.

"Potentially, but the success rate of pre-existing relationships are low. Our needs change but theirs don't, although we both have our own basic physiological needs such as hunger, it's their emotional needs that separate us," said Joe, in a final attempt to crush the fledgling's moral.

Romy gave Joe a long and hard stare, which indicated it was time to send the young vampire on his way, but not before handing him a leaflet from his pocket titled 'Frequently Asked Questions for Fledglings.'

"Why do you bother trying to explain it all to them, their sires don't," Romy said coldly.

"You know why, the amount of fledglings that end up being recruited to rogue vampire gangs is increasing, if we educate them earlier it may prevent this," replied Joe,

"Didn't help with your brother did it?" Romy countered harshly.
Joe made a low hissing sound.

"Nathaniel was always a rebellious git."

With the fledgling gone, they both suddenly remembered my presence and turned to look at me still standing there. Saying nothing, I quickly turned and started walking, feeling their eyes boring into my back. Around 100 metres away from the gate, I made out some bright lights and the din of people going about their business. As I got closer, I noticed a small shanty town of stalls and kiosks had been erected along the path to the Gate. I supposed it was a good idea, enterprising individuals could sell things to people queuing to leave, or catch unwary new arrivals with money making schemes. I filtered the bustling market joining the crowd's, I hoped the amulet would do its job and keep me blended in with everyone else. It was hard to keep composure as I felt at any moment, I would appear in all my human glory. Around me were ghouls; greeting and bowing before the passing undead, each wore a name badge that read 'Undead Ambassadors'. They were handing out brochures, so I took one and saw it was a guide to the city. As I opened the leaflet, I noticed there were other similarly dressed ghouls holding out various cards. One had dark red blotches on it, and scrawled in thick writing - "Would you like to try our new Unisex blood blend? 20 percent off for our International undead visitors."

I was even approached by a confident looking male ghoul, who attempted to get me to register for the City's Corpse Clubcard, '1 point for every Drakmir spent' was his catch line. I decided to move on, wary of how close these ghouls were getting and just in case they tried to sell me something else. Another kiosk I went past had a large amount of people behind the desk, it sported a sign stating - 'Change your currency here, great exchange rates available.' However, by far the largest queue was formed around a kiosk labelled 'Lost Limbs & Other Organs', there was a huge commotion going on as a female ghoul who had originally only lost an ear, attempted to claim someone else's thumb as well. I finally emerged out of the maze of markets, finding myself in a series of streets, plenty of people still wandered about, but it was less of a scrum compared to where I had just left. I flicked through the Guide I had been given, but most of it seemed to be advice on the all day friendly feeding eateries available, so instead I tried to remember the directions and advice Scarlet had given me. She had warned me there would be a lot of strange sights that my mortal eyes would never have seen, and that I should be careful to avoid staring too openly. But this was easier said than done, for a city whose occupants were legally certified dead it was bustling with life, as I found myself surrounded by the sound of coarse voiced ghoul vendors.

As I continued to find my way through the collection of narrow cobbled streets, I desperately sought out any signs or maps that might have helped. But it was the overpowering stench of rotted flesh that told me I had wandered into the Ghoul Quarter, I kept my mouth closed, and tried not to inhale too much, but even then, the smell wrapped and clung to me like a shawl. At points I honestly thought I was going to vomit, as there was no escaping it, it was as much a part of the Ghoul Quarter, as the ghouls were. I took a shallow breath, through my nose and swallowed back the bile rising up my throat. After a few minutes, I managed to get it under control and was able to focus on the nearby shops. I paused at one where several ghouls were crowded outside chatting excitedly in their dry, rasping tones; I looked at the sign over the door, which read "Flesh Fusions". Curious, I took a closer look while trying to keep my distance from the putrefied patrons, a small plaque nailed to the door read:

'We offer state of the art flesh crafting services for ghouls to help you blend in with the living. Magically fused limbs and tissue will be functional and rot resistant. All materials have been legally obtained through donors. No guarantees and no refunds applicable.'

I knew I probably shouldn't...I knew Scarlet wouldn't have wanted me to, but this was my time as much as it was hers, so without another thought I pushed open the door and walked right in.

Inside it appeared to be some sort of waiting room, a few hard wooden chairs lined the wall with ghouls sitting on them, one of them was female with no nose and one eye, she was crying hysterically as a male ghoul bent over her patting her gently on the shoulder. He looked different to the other ghouls I had seen so far, his pale face was smoother and showed no sign of rot, but it looked unusually tight. His eyes, which were both intact and a light brown colour, were a little too slanted so it gave him an overall cat-like appearance.

"I don't understand what happened to me! I suddenly woke up in some clinic surrounded by zombies!" wailed the female ghoul.

"There, there, you merely died my dear. It's not the end of the world," said the male ghoul comfortingly.

"Just look at me! I'm a..I'm a monster!" she screeched.

"A ghoul, dear. A monster is such a strong word and not politically correct," he said with a strained smile.

"I want to look like I did before," she sobbed. She scrabbled in her bag and pulled out a wallet, flipping it open, she showed a picture of herself with a man.

The male ghoul peered at it. "Hmmm yes, I can see why, you were very pretty once."

"I want to be so again, so change me back!" she demanded.

"It's not as simple as that, your skin will continue to rot as your body does what nature intended it to do...die."

She gasped and fell into silence. The male ghoul shook his head knowingly and continued.

"Do not worry, you will not, as we call it, suffer the true death, you have enough demon blood within you to sustain the unlife you were born into. It will balance out the decay process so that you remain mostly intact."

The female ghoul let what had been said, soak in, before responding.

"So you're telling me there's nothing you can do about the way I look? I was told that if I came here you might be able to fix it."

She dug into her bag again.

"I still have this if it helps? It fell off afterwards."

She held out her hand and there, in the palm of it, was the rest of her nose. The male ghoul picked it up, held it to the light and peered at it. Then with one finger tapped the end of it.

"This wasn't your original nose, was it? It has been reshaped?!" he stated knowingly.

The female ghoul narrowed the one eye she had left.

"I had a nose job a few years back if that's what you mean, what difference should that make?" she replied with obvious irritation in her voice.

"None really, I was just curious. I see myself as a contemporary plastic surgeon you see, the tragedy is that my work never gets the attention it deserves, it all being kept underground so to speak," he sighed sadly, still staring at the nose.

"Right...well can you fix me or not," she said, trying to bring the conversation back to her own dilemma.

The male ghoul turned his attention back to her as he replied.

"I can improve your appearance, make you look less like an unclean and more like a freshie but I cannot turn you back fully, not even a witch could do that."

And with that final, damning statement, the female ghoul burst into sobs again, just as another ghoul emerged from one of the operating rooms. He had bandages covering his entire face, and hands. There was a slit where his eyes were, so he could see where he was going. He noticed the pair talking, before offering a weak wave and staggering out.

"You saw Walter there, he's just had a full face fusing and reconstruction of the hands, our most asked for procedure, just check out our before and after wall and you'll be able to see the difference," he said pointing to a wall covered in photos.

The female ghoul had managed to regain her composure enough to peek a glance at the wall of photos. They showed rows of formerly decomposed faces, some had been nothing more than skeletons to start with, next to them were the pictures of after flesh fusing surgery, fully skinned and with missing body parts reconstructed. Underneath each picture was a caption advising the number and stage of surgeries it had taken to get to that point. The female ghoul stared at them then nodded decisively.

"I suppose it's better than carrying on looking like something from a horror film. How much would it cost to get to this stage?" she pointed her skeletal hand at a picture of a female ghoul who had no jawbone in the before picture, but was fully reconstructed in the after shot, and smiling, complete with shiny white teeth.

"My assistant Margery can go through the price list with you, we accept both Drakmir and pound sterling," he pointed to his assistant ghoul sitting behind a desk.

I decided that now was a good time to end my curiosity, but before I could make my exit, the male ghoul noticed me and gave a wide Cheshire cat smile.

"Would you care to make a donation, my Lady?" he asked bowing low.

"We are very short on fingers at the moment, they are always in such high demand."

He reached for my hand and started greedily inspecting it, rubbing his greasy paws over my fingers.

"Very nice, we could offer you a good price for the whole hand, and it would have grown back before you've had a chance to spend it all," he chirped enthusiastically.

"Maybe another time," I said, wrenching it out of his clammy grip. He gave me a look of disappointment but bowed again courteously.

"Suit yourself, I could give you a good offer on those eyes also, should you return," he replied, again with the creepy wide smile.

I hastily left before he could try to buy any more of Scarlet's body, alarmingly aware that whatever he would have tried to hack off would not have grown back. The body switch was just a glamour after all, behind the veil I was still human and mortal. I had barely walked a few steps when I came across another interesting looking shop called Feeding Fetish, inside was a group of humans, who I assumed were blood dolls. They were clustered round the counter where, the female clerk; who I had initially taken for being human, until I'd caught a glimpse of her murky yellow eyes; was trying to restore some semblance of order. I craned my neck trying to listen in and see what all the fuss was about, but soon got fed up as swarms of human traffic moving through the shop, got in my way. I decided to push my way through and before long, I reached the counter where several glass bottles, each filled with a red liquid stood. A sign on the counter read, *'Blood scented perfume, nothing says bite me quite like it!'* a small warning sign read, *'Not recommended for use on vampires suffering from MFE.'*.

"Crimson Cloud or Liquid Lunch?" a dark haired girl next to me said. I almost thought she was talking to me, when her petite, but curvy blonde companion replied.

"I don't know. Why are there different ones anyway? They all smell the same to me." She sniffed one of the pre-scented cards with a frown.

The dark haired girl sighed.

"I told you already, because they are different blood types. We wouldn't be able to tell but vampires can and that's what counts." She picked up the Liquid Lunch. "This is type A and that's what Tobias prefers, I am sure of it. You're an A and he always gives you more bites than me," she said bitterly.

The ghoul sales rep, sensing an impending sale edged closer to the pair, an insincere smile plastered on her blue lips. "The A type is very popular, I myself am a huge fan."

The dark haired girl turned on the ghoul.

"Who asked you? All the blood you get is probably from a bottle or a bag, no self-respecting blood doll would live feed a ghoul!" she said aggressively. It was hard to tell if the ghoul had been offended or was just in pain from holding the smile as it faltered to a grimace. I backed off and had a browse of the other wares, and found myself standing in front of a selection of glass jars filled with different coloured creams and gels.

One label read, *'Morning after balm: Relief from those lingering bites of the night before.'*, another jar read: *'Slippery skin: A numbing agent that provides easy access for your vampire'*. I felt myself begin to flush as a host of dirty thoughts flooded my mind. With a barely suppressed giggle, I fled the store before anyone could notice. It was amusing seeing all these tonics, gels and lubricants. In a way the whole feeding experience sounded like sex - intimate, naughty and messy.

With no more distractions, I remembered the directions Scarlet had given me and found the family house on Victoria Street, a road leading to the Vampire Quarter. It was a large, old fashioned Victorian style house similar to the ones I had seen around London. This was the moment of truth, the amulet had seen me through ghouls and strangers, but this would be the true test. Walking up to the door I reached for the handle and noted that the door was not locked. It seemed the undead did not worry about burglars. I stepped over the threshold into a dimly lit hallway and as I closed the door I felt the stale musky air enclose around me, a single bulb providing only a faint illumination, casting stark shadows into the corners. I half felt my way through the nearest door and found myself in a type of sitting room, that Scarlet had informed me, was the parlour room. A sofa with two chaise longues on either side, faced a marble fireplace and mounted above that, looking completely out of place, was a large flat screen TV. Heavy velvet curtains blocked the window and the room was only marginally better lit than the hallway, with a couple of lamps mounted on the wall and a few candles still flickering on the mantle place. The room had a dark overbearing feel to it but was quite stark in reality. There were no photographs on the wall or any other ornaments one might see cluttering up the shelves of an average family home. I exited and found my way to the kitchen, which, although bearing some of the typical Victorian features, had at least a few modern appliances. There was a large American style fridge, almost identical to my one at home, except this one's doors remained bare, whereas ours was covered in holiday magnets and Leyna's crayon sketches. I scanned the smooth worktops and found a large, leather bound book on the counter *'A House Ghoul's Guide to Running a Vampire Home'*. I opened it to the first chapter *'The Importance of Keeping a Blood Inventory'*. I quickly skipped this and went onto the next chapter, *'Siring and Hiring,'* - which seemed to be tips about employing other ghouls for the running of the household. I had just made it to a chapter concerning cooking human meals for blood dolls, when the candles began spluttering and the lamps dimmed. I felt a cold chill creep up my spine as the shadows began to move and shift filling the space around me. From the growing darkness a long arm seemed to stretch out, its clawed hand appearing on the opposite wall. I stared at the empty space next to me in horror as the shadowed arm formed the shape of a person, I stood petrified.

Then I saw it, a white face materialising from the gloom like some kind of phantom.

The phantom had long brown hair and eyes that were so pale they were almost white; he was dressed immaculately in a black shirt and expensive looking jeans. He was the most striking man I had ever seen but at the same time he sent a shudder of fear through me. There could be no doubt in my mind he was a vampire. Seeing crowds of them in the Underdark should have been more frightful but it wasn't, maybe because to them I was just another undead passing through the city. But this one, was up close and personal, I was on my own and I wanted nothing more than to run home but I forced myself to stand my ground. Chanting in my head, like a prayer, that as long as I was wearing the necklace Scarlet had given me, I would be fine. The vampire reached into his pocket and slowly pulled something out. It was thin and metallic, similar in shape to a needle. The amulet had failed, he was going to stab me in the neck and drink my blood!

Slowly he slid his hand into his other pocket and pulled out another smaller item, it was a clear pill, perhaps made of glass or see-through plastic. As I looked closer, I noticed a thick red liquid slowly moving within, perhaps he was going to drug me?! I finally plucked up the courage to speak.

"What are you doing?" I asked hesitantly.

He didn't look up and proceeded to pop the clear vial into the metallic tube.

"Vaping of course," he uttered nonchalantly.

"What is that?" I asked, eyeing it suspiciously, still on my guard.

"It's based on a human device, some ghoul entrepreneur thought it would be a great idea to convert them into blood vapes. It's a pure blood hit, straight to the system! Want to try?" He thrust the vape in my direction.

Relief poured through me, he wasn't onto to me. He was merely testing out a vampire cigarette!

"I think I will pass." I looked around for something else to fixate on.

"Probably for the best, I have heard these can get pretty addictive and pricey. Good business initiative, I will give them that!" he said cheerfully.

He proceeded to place the blood vape in his mouth and pressed a small button on the side. A short hiss followed as some of the liquid from the capsule decanted. A few seconds later, he exhaled, a bright crimson cloud following in its wake.

"You okay, Scar? You seem a little out of it?" he asked, as he blew another wisp of red smoke from his lips and walked over to the fridge. He opened the door and lazily grabbed for a packet of blood as if it were a carton of orange juice. His voice was smooth and velvety and I had a feeling that if I wasn't protected by the necklace it would be the kind of voice that would make you succumb to anything.

From Scarlet's description, I was sure this had to be the youngest of her older brothers – Kristian. He was still watching me as he poured the blood into a glass, I felt like I had to say something or he was going to become suspicious, necklace or not.

"Fine, just wondering where your fang fappers are?"

Lucky for me, Scarlet had filled me in on the blood dolls that her younger brother indulged in, I was hoping that by mentioning them it, I could deflect any non Scarlet behaviour.

"I gave them the night off, Mary was feeling a little light headed, I must have been too hard on her," he sniggered as he took another pull from the blood vape. "I forget how weak humans are."

His arrogance and contempt for my own race should have offended me but instead I found it fascinating; I was in awe of him.

"Where's maggot face?" he asked as he poured himself another glass of blood.

I struggled for an answer when the door opened and the ugliest creature I had ever seen entered. He moved with a slight limp giving him more of a shuffle than walk. As he drew nearer I felt the strong urge to back away, but I knew that would only give a reason for them to question my actions. He bowed his head then raised his yellow eyes to mine almost apologetically.

"Sorry it's late, Scar, I was running some errands for your father," his voice was gravelly as he spoke.

"Ugh, what is that smell? It's like rotten meat," I said, before realising it was coming from the cretin stood in front of me.

The creature seemed oblivious and instead sniffed at the cup he was holding.

"It's the same as what you always ask for?" he said nervously and held out the cup to me; I took it gingerly.

Scarlet had told me vampires could drink other liquids than blood but I was still reluctant to believe that anything this creature handed me would be safe for human consumption. I took a timid sip and almost immediately gagged, it tasted like someone had melted a handful of coins and thrown them into a cup and then added some coffee as an afterthought. It took all my strength not to spit it out in disgust. Sensing that they were both staring at me, I tilted my head back and closed my eyes which were almost watering, and took another sip. The thick liquid sloshed around my tongue and clung to my teeth, with a great effort I forced myself to swallow.

"Tasty?" the creature asked, his bloodshot eyes watching me with apprehension, searching for approval.

"I added a little caramel this time, that's what some of the humans use for their own hot drinks."

Kristian let out a low chuckle before I could respond.

"You have got to be the most bizarre of our kin, Scar! We have fresh packs of blood stocked in the fridge, yet you send your little ghoulfriend out to buy human coffee to mix the blood in with it. You can hide the fact that you are drinking blood as much as you want, but you'll never hide the fact that you are a blood drinker."

So that's what this was, coffee mixed with blood, human blood! I felt a wave of nausea as I tried to keep the foul concoction down. A dark mist suddenly filled the room and I glanced around wildly to see it was creeping in from under the crack in the door.

"Dante, why can't you materialise normally like every other vampire, why do you always have to resort to turning into mist?!" Kristian sighed.

The mist evaporated and in its place stood a tall young man with blonde wavy hair tied back with a black ribbon. He had the same white eyes and chiselled cheekbones, but his pale complexion was complimented by the dark eyeliner he appeared to be wearing under his eyes. He looked just like a vampire from a movie, even down to the dark purple velvet shirt he wore, which was slightly open at the collar exposing his pale, flawless chest. He looked at his brother with disdain as he moved to the fridge, also grabbing a blood pack from within, but instead of selecting a normal glass, he poured it into a gold chalice he had pulled out from one of the other cupboards. After, and only after, taking a delicate sip, he turned to his brother and responded.

"You may wish to dismiss the proper ways of our kin but delving into the traditional forms of blood magic is popular in the circles I associate with. Any vampire can perform a simple materialising spell but to drift into their midst as an actual element is far more eloquent," he did a weird wave with his other hand to emphasise the point.

Kristian shook his head.

"What with Scar's self-loathing and your over dramatisation it's no wonder vampires have a bad reputation."

Dante took another dainty sip, choosing to ignore his brother's comment. Kristian looked at him with a frown.

"You're not going about your usual ritual? What happened, find out that Doctor of yours is a complete phoney?"

Dante pursed his lips as if trying to summon patience.

"No, I just had a rather bad day and needed something a little bit on the stronger side." He tipped his goblet in Kristian's direction.

I had no idea what they were talking about, but I decided to linger and observe them. They seemed like two normal brothers displaying typical sibling banter; it was fascinating. I had never conceived that vampires, if they existed, would have family relationships similar to our own.

"I had an incident..." Dante started.

"I am not surprised with that idiot Ted hanging around!" Kristian chortled.

Dante took another sip, this one deeper than the first.

"No. With the Tribune. It seems they have reopened the investigation. They took me in for questioning again, they even brought in Ted."

Kristian nodded and took a long drag on his blood vape.

"Why on earth did they do that? They already cleared you from the list of suspects."

Dante sighed before continuing, clearly bothered by having to go through the details.

"There was apparently an anonymous tip, placing me at the scene of the crime."

This time it was Kristian who quietly took a sip from his cup.

"I just hope none of this gets leaked in the undead media; my reputation would be ruined!"

"Dante, your snotty acquaintances won't care if you have been accused of killing a human, they are vampires after all," Kristian said with reassurance.

Dante looked at Kristian like he was simple.

"Did you not read where the boy was found? That mortal cesspit above ground called Insomnia, why his blood could have carried any manner of filth in it, my palette will no longer be respected, they will think I drink from just any form of veins."

Kristian stared at Dante blankly for a moment.

"You have serious issues, if the only thing that concerns you about this 'new evidence', is the fact that the boy's blood was not organic enough for you."

I was getting even more lost than ever, the only thing I could understand, was 'Dante' was in trouble. Either way the conversation seemed to have lost its seriousness, so I took the opportunity to excuse myself from the kitchen. I fled upstairs to Scarlet's room, which she'd informed me was located on the third floor, after entering I closed the door, hoping to hide the exertion of climbing two sets of stairs had on me. But unfortunately, I did not even get five minutes, before a knock on the door sounded. I took a deep breath, calmed myself and cautiously opened the door. And standing right there, was the anguished face of Scarlet's ghoul – Herb. His skin actually looked like it was slipping off, barely clinging to the partially exposed bone like cooked meat. In his hands, he held the cup of coffee and blood apprehensively.

"You left this downstairs, Scar," he said with a smile.

I took the cup begrudgingly, my stomach heaving at the prospect. He was still hovering as if waiting for something.

"Yes?" I asked.

"How did the trial with the potential blood doll go?" he asked eagerly.

"I changed my mind, they weren't my type," I said abruptly, hoping he would go away.

"Oh, that's a shame, well I thought we could watch our guilty pleasure show, Morbid Makeover. They have a ghoul on tonight who's getting a new rib-cage," he attempted a hopeful smile making his already hollow cheeks almost disappear into his face, I could barely stand to look at him.

"I would like to be left alone tonight," I said as commanding as I could. He wilted on the spot.

"Oh, of course, Scar, sorry." And with that he shuffled off shutting the door behind him.

When I was sure he was gone I explored Scarlet's bedroom, which looked more like a hotel room. It was beautifully furnished, a large four poster bed dominated most of the room, which seemed like a waste of space considering she didn't sleep, but I was grateful. I had not been relishing the idea of sleeping on the floor. She had an en suite which had all the usual facilities, which surprised me, but then I remembered Scarlet telling me how vampires' homes had to accommodate for humans due to the use of blood dolls. I made full use of the added extras. I thought I felt something on my face, notable after Kristian had started blowing that blood vapour around me, and sure enough when I inspected myself in the mirror I saw tiny specks of red on my cheeks. I scrubbed and soaped my face until it felt clean again, before brushing my teeth ferociously to remove the taste of Scarlet's evening meal. Even that small sip had made me feel ill and I coughed up some bloodied mucus which, on a normal day, would have me making an urgent appointment at the doctors. Despite this, I was really hungry and I needed some normal food, but first I needed some clothes to relax in. I explored Scarlet's wardrobe, impressed with her huge collection of clothes, but to my annoyance, discovered that most consisted of evening wear. I eventually did find something that could pass as comfy clothes - a pair of black leggings and a black off the shoulder top. Scarlet it seemed, was not into experimenting with colours, the majority of her clothes were either black, grey or navy. Next I emptied the foul contents of the cup down the sink and unpacked that evening's provisions; a packet of crisps, a chocolate bar and some instant noodles. I searched the room and found, to my delight, that Scarlet had purchased the small travel kettle I'd requested. I filled it up using the tap water from the sink and plugged it in hoping, the sound of it boiling would not invite too much curiosity. From the looks of it Scarlet liked to experiment with her diet, so if anyone became suspicious I could always blame it a new diet. I rinsed the cup thoroughly and placed the noodles inside, before adding the boiled water, stirring it with the single fork I had packed. I looked for my phone while I waited for the noodles to soften, then remembered I didn't have it. I had Scarlet's which was devoid of any messages.

Noodles in hand, I stared around Scarlet's room, wondering how I was going to make the most of our life swap. Apart from giving me directions to her home and stern orders about how to act, Scarlet had not gone out of her way to concern herself about what I would do to occupy myself. I decided to call her, but as predicted, she was not enthused about my interest in fraternising with the undead. Normally I wouldn't have cared but when she let on that the amulet could stop working at any moment and reveal my human identity. I decided to listen for once, not listening to my parents could get me grounded, but disobeying Scarlet could get me killed.

Chapter 9

~Scarlet Tuesday~
Day Two as a Human

It was my second day as Jessica and I and found Mrs Young making breakfast in the kitchen. Sizzling away over a gas cooker, were two pans, the first had thick pink strands of bacon, which were reaching a crisp and light brown colour. In the other pan, were eggs, again frying, but to a rich golden yellow centre, surrounded by near perfect white.

It was almost enough to make me retch.

A sudden and enthusiastic tapping drummed at my knee, so I gathered myself and held down the nausea. I walked over to the dog food bin and dished out a couple of scoops of biscuits, before laying them down in front of Princess. That should keep her off me for a bit, I thought.

"Hungry?" asked Mrs Young.

"No thank you," I replied, eyeing the sizzling meat and sunny yokes with disdain.

She frowned.

"Are you feeling okay?"

"I'm fine, just in a hurry to get to college."

She turned the cooker off and moved the pan of frying cholesterol off the hob. Before turning to appraise me. She looked me up and down, arms held at her hips.

"I hope that you're not on some silly diet again," she said disparagingly.

"I'll grab food on the way, I just don't want to be late," I quickly replied, eager to move away.

She looked at the clock on the wall.

"You have plenty of time, you're normally still in bed and I have to drag you out to get you up."

"Well, I feel like a new person, what can I say?" I said edging away from the kitchen.

Mrs Young grinned.

"I like it, Jess, just as long as you take care of yourself, I know you're worried about this play but don't let it affect your health."

"I won't," I replied, but for a moment I didn't want to leave, despite my eagerness to experience another day at college and the smell of the fatty breakfast. It was nice having someone fuss over me.

I was used to being questioned at home but that devolved into an interrogation, whereas this felt l like someone looking over me, truly taking care of me. It was as if I too, were just as vulnerable as they were, capable of becoming stressed and ill. It was strange how such frailties could make you feel more part of the world, rather than just a bystander. I nodded awkwardly, before grabbing my things and heading out the door.

This morning's primary subject was Philosophy. I had looked over Jessica's coursebook and her last homework assignments. They were presently studying the branches of moral philosophy, which I was looking forward to. Surprisingly the undead didn't tend to contemplate life and how to live it, so I was hoping to learn a fresh perspective. Jessica's Philosophy teacher was a tall skinny man named Toby. Once we were all seated, he asked us to open our text books to the chapter, 'Good and Evil'.

"Evil is a broad term as there are different levels. Telling a white lie is often overlooked, so-much-so, it is almost common practice. Most of us have done it on occasion – 'That dress looks great on you' or...and my personal favourite 'The dog ate my homework'."

A few members of the class sniggered at the teacher's poor theatrics before he continued.

"Then, there are evil acts that are far more severe. Such as stealing, or in the worse case – murder. And of course, the punishments for these are much graver."

The face of the boy I had killed flashed in my mind's eye, I closed my eyes and forced him out. The teacher went on with his analysis.

"The earliest concepts of evil are associated with the supernatural, monsters created from fictions such as vampires and witches, creatures that defy nature and, therefore, human comprehension."

I shifted in my seat, suddenly uncomfortable, but no one seemed to notice.

"Misunderstanding of something can be dangerous in itself. Just look at the witch hysteria that went on between the 13th and 19th centuries, thousands of innocent people were tortured until they had no choice but to confess their 'guilt' to the most ridiculous accusations, for which they were then executed. And for what reason did this all stem from?"

He suddenly put the question to the class. An overweight girl with long brown hair and large brown eyes raised her hand.

"Penny?"

"Because they were different?" Penny said uncertainly.

"Go on.."

She tucked her hair behind one ear and looked down before answering.

"Well, the Salem witch trials is the one I have heard the most about, where a group of girls accused a woman of using witchcraft against them. This was woman was an outsider because she dressed and acted differently to everyone else in the village, so they killed her."

The teacher appealed to the class.

"Penny has a good point, the Salem witch trials took place after a number of girls claimed to have seizures, their accusations caused twenty people to be hanged for practising witchcraft. There has never been any evidence to prove that those accused did harm, except the word of their accusers who later apologised to the victim's families, admitting they were wrong. Were these girls evil for saying such things?"

There was a strong murmur of "Yes."

"These were times filled with religious zealotry, where death was rampant and if you did not conform your very soul was at peril. Control through fear, sounds shady in itself does it not?"

The students murmured in agreement. He continued.

"Fear is a great motivator and in order to save themselves, others were thrown on to the pyre – literally. And this is where we question evil and its motive. Are your actions evil, if you believe you are doing the work of the lord?"

I am sure those girls and the people conducting the trials thought they were doing the right thing but you can still commit a wrongdoing even when you feel you are right?"

He was staring right at me as he said this, his words cut through me forcing me to weigh up my own moral standing on feeding on that boy. It had felt right, it felt like 'my' right.

"What is good and what is evil is swayed by the people involved," What one person deems evil another person might see as good. I, personally, see no reason that true evil exists - just personal choices," said Penny.

Toby nodded in appreciation of the statement.

"Good interpretation! But let's go with the opinion that it does exist. Does an act have to cause physical pain to be deemed evil?" He looked quizzically as he once again addressed the question to the class. Penny raised her hand and I heard someone near me whisper.

"Ugh, why does she have to keep encouraging him, this lesson will go on forever."

A couple of sniggers followed, causing Toby to glance over with a frown, before nodding at Penny to answer.

"No, there are other types of pain besides physical, such as emotional. If someone says something hurtful it can hurt just as bad, if not more, than if someone hit you."

"Someone should hit her,"came the voice again and I looked over and saw a boy with blonde hair and hard blue eyes glaring at Penny. It was the boy Sam had pointed out during Drama class, Dean Tyler. He caught my gaze and smiled, I turned away surprised that I could meet a pair of eyes colder than my own.

"That is correct, Penny," said Toby oblivious to the blonde boy's comments.

"Take the recent cases of cyber bullying, with the wide access to social media you could start a post about a person tomorrow and it could reach hundreds of people within minutes. You can promote a business, product or person but can also destroy a person with the same tool. You can write awful things about a person and watch as their reputation lies in ruins, have you physically harmed them? No, but is the aftermath any less painful? There are many stories out there where young people have committed suicide because of things people have said about them online, and I'm not talking about a simple thumbs down or a few thoughtless comments. This is online harassment, where the victim cannot escape the bully. It continues after school, whenever their computer or phone is on, and the bully is empowered because they believe they cannot be held accountable from behind a computer."

Another voice from nowhere shot out.

"Stupid trolls. Think they are internet tough guys!" the voice came from a dark haired boy at the back of the class.

"Yes, thank you Chris for that analogy." said Toby.

"Bloody keyboard warriors," the dark haired boy muttered, as the class giggled.

During lunch I was looking for a place to sit outside, when I spotted Penny. She was sitting alone on a bench, I approached and sat down next to her and smiled, she looked back at me bemused.

"We're in the same class," I pointed out.

"I know," she said still looking bewildered. She had a thick book opened up on her lap, I read the cover, it was Vanity Fair.

"Good choice!" I said. "Thackeray's best work."

"You read?" Penny said, shocked.

"Of course," I said blankly.

"I just didn't think it would be top on your list of interests," she muttered carefully.

"It's one of my main interests," I said. Then I remembered I was meant to be Jessica, and even from the brief moments I had spent with her before the swap, I knew the concept of Jessica reading for fun, was an unbelievable one.

"I'm trying to improve my vocabulary, that's what reading does right?" I asked attempting to look doubtful.

Penny half frowned and smiled at the same time.

"It's one of the many benefits, yes."

That seemed to do it. I was going to have to try and cover my tracks a bit better and act the part of Jessica, if I was going to fit in. I stayed seated and made what I believed to be known as 'small talk' with Penny, until it was time for my next class. Just as I was saying goodbye I saw Jessica's friends Hannah and Nikki, both of them were staring at me strangely.

"What were you talking to her for?" Nikki hissed when I reached them.

I looked back at Penny who had returned to reading her book. "Why not?" I asked.

"Because she's annoying."

"What did she do?" I asked curiously.

Nikki stuttered, failing to find an obvious reason.

"She...she's just annoying!"

"She smells," said Hannah flatly. "I had to sit next to her in my further maths class and she smells of B.O. plus she lies all the time."

"You do further maths?" was all I could say.

"She lied about having a boyfriend. She said she was seeing this boy called Harry but he completely denied it," Hannah said vehemently.

"Humans lie about many things," I said with a shrug.

"Earlier you said Hannah didn't look fat in those jeans, which is not true. The cut of them clearly emphasises the largeness of her thighs and posterior, so that was a lie also," I stated matter of factly.

Hannah glared at Nikki.

"I knew it!!" she raged.

Nikki just gave me a look, "What's gotten into you today? All I was saying was that Penny is annoying. You always call her a nerd anyway."

I stopped myself from asking what a nerd was. I was doing it again, but it was hard to understand such irrational hatred for another person. Ghouls were treated as inferiors because they were physically weaker than us, Penny didn't seem to suffer any obvious impediments, in fact, after talking to these two, she seemed intellectually superior; it seemed that there were subcultures among humans also, only less defined.

My last class of the day was Drama and when I entered the room, everyone was rushing around with their scripts, going over their lines for the Dress rehearsal; many were already in costume. I didn't really know where I was meant to go, so I took a seat and began looking over my own script, even though I had already memorised it.

"Ready, Jess?" I looked up to see Miss Fenwick, her red hair tied back today and her glasses perched on top of her head.

I nodded and she smiled.

"Katie is just finishing the last touches of Sam's make up, then she will come and do yours, okay? In the meantime your costume is hanging up on the rails over there waiting for you to try on."

I followed the direction she had pointed to, and made my way over. Looking through the collection of outfits, I found a dress with a label on it reading 'Jessica: Mrs Kendall'. I grabbed it and popped to the girls toilets to get changed. When I came back a girl with brown hair styled into a messy bun was standing waiting for me, she had a big black bag in her arms.

"Hi, I'm Katie the make-up artist." She motioned for me to sit down. "That dress looks great on you, it'll look even better once we style your hair," she ran her hands through my hair.

"Good thing I brought a lot of pins, you have a lot of hair," she said laughing.

I remained silent, unsure of the etiquette for such a situation.

"I just did Sam's make-up, he seems nice, very nervous though."

I just nodded and she laughed again, "Sounds like you are also."

She carried on talking, while I continued giving the bare minimal responses back. But the whole time I was taking it all in, it fascinated me how all humans had different skills and different plans for themselves in life. She told me how she had just finished studying make-up at college and how she wanted to make a career out of it, but that it was hard due to the competitive nature of the industry. She was happy to be helping us out because the photos from the play would help her with her portfolio. She asked me if I wanted to be an actress for just theatre, or if I would also want to go into TV or films. I struggled with these questions, not only was I not Jessica but being a vampire I had never considered the options humans had at picking a career. Katie kept using words like "passion" and "living her dream", and despite watching her now, working free for an unglamorous college play, it was possible to get caught up in her vision. I started to picture a map in my head with all these winding roads and signs, some might be a dead end but then others would open up to new roads. I felt a sudden injustice surge through me, why couldn't I have those choices too, for vampires it was either work for the Tribune or run a business. But you never actually got to run it, you just invested money then sat back as the ghouls did the work. You would never get any satisfaction from it - not in the real sense. How much could you get back from a ghoul sending you a monthly report of figures? Vampires didn't care about money the same way humans did, it wasn't as if we went on shopping trips. What wasn't spent on blood just got invested back into the businesses, run by other people, it was as if we lacked the imagination to spend it. Katie had lots of imagination, she had lots of hopes and dreams too. She had been dating the same boy for the last five years, she was slightly older than Jessica being twenty-one, they both lived with their parents but were saving up to get their own place; they would get a dog as they both loved dogs but their parents would not let them have one. They would get married, nothing big - just close family and friends, have two children, one boy and one girl, she even had their names picked out. It was all there before her like some unpublished book and here I was without even a manuscript.

That evening at dinner with Jessica's parents, I was still contemplating the human wheel of life. There was so much to consider and balance that it fascinated me, there were family relationships, friendships, studies, work life, financial matters, leisure time, health and, if you were lucky, romance. I pictured my own wheel motionless for all these years and struggled to think of at least one category that I had fulfilled. I supposed I had health, I had even surpassed it, but for some reason that left me with all the other parts of life empty.

"What on earth are you doing, Leyna?" came Mrs Young's voice and I looked up from my plate of fish, potato and tiny green balls that I had discovered were called peas.

"I am seeing if a baby appears," replied Leyna, who was poking at her belly with one hand while the other balanced a forkful of peas. "Martha's mum is having a baby."

"That's wonderful news!" exclaimed Mrs Young, then quietly added to her husband. "They've been trying for another for ages and were considering getting 'help'."

While I pondered what this 'help' might be, Leyna continued to prod her stomach with her finger, this time spilling the forkful of peas onto the carpet.

"That's enough, eat your food like a good girl."

"But Martha said it happened because her father pressed her mother's belly button."

"That's ridiculous!" I replied, shocked at how uneducated this human child was of her own species.

"Human females become pregnant from sexual intercourse with the male species," I explained.

"A fetus is then formed in the woman and after a period of nine months, is ejected from the vagina," I finished with a smile glad to be of some help in this child's learning.

"Jessica! That's enough!" snapped Mr Young, while Mrs Young held her hands over Leyna's ears.

I stared at them confused, did they want their child to believe such nonsensical stories?

"But the naval is merely a scar left from the umbilical cord when it is cut off, it has nothing to do with procreation, although it has become fashionable to show it off by exposing the midriff, as a way to entice the human male species which could then lead to sexual intercourse..." I continued.

"Jess you may leave the table," snapped Mr Young.

"This is not appropriate dinner conversation!" he added, taking a sip of his glass of wine, while exchanging a look with his wife who was tending to Leyna like she was injured.

I left the table and returned to Jessica's room mystified, humans were far more sensitive than I had previously perceived. I would have to be more cautious in what I conversed in from now on. Later that night, Mrs Young came upstairs to see me, she poked her head around the door.

"Am I allowed to enter? I come bearing cake as a goodwill gesture." she said warmly.

I was sitting on the bed with Princess, I think we had been playing but I was unsure, she had dropped a piece of rope in my lap with a ball on the end of it. When I picked it up she tried to take it back so I dropped it and let her have it. But this only caused the creature to bring it back to me and again drop it in my lap. This time I held onto it, when she tried to grab it and after a minute of trying to tug it out of my grasp she collapsed on the bed her tongue lolling out the side of her mouth. It seemed like a frustrating game for her, but a minute later she repeated the whole thing again, so she must have gotten some enjoyment from it. Dogs, it seemed, were easier to please than humans who would yell at you one minute then bring you cake the next. Mrs Young came and sat on the bed next to me, handing me the cake.

"Sorry, Jess, I know you were probably just trying to help even if it did come across as being sarcastic," she winked at me knowingly, but as usual I felt I was missing something.

"I think your father and I are just a little stressed at the moment. Your aunt phoned earlier wanting to know why we have arranged for the Funeral reception to be at the Petersham Hotel when she could get us discounted rates at your uncle's restaurant - never mind the fact that your Gran despised that place. She even had food poisoning when we last went there."

She sighed and rubbed her temples with her fingers.

"Funerals are hard enough without other family members fighting over them," she leant across and stroked Princess who had finally lost interest in the rope game and was now sniffing in the direction of the cake which lay out of reach in my hands.

"You did say that your teachers' were fine for you to have Thursday off for Compassionate leave?"

I nodded but inside I was perplexed, why hadn't Jessica mentioned that her Grandmother had died and that I would be going to the funeral in her place? Had she got the dates mixed up and not realised? Maybe I should call her to remind her? But then I might have to end the switch earlier than planned.

I felt a hand rub my shoulder gently. "I know it's sad darling but she's in a better place now, watching over us."

With that, Mrs Young gave me a final smile, got up and made to leave the room. Once she had left, I peered upwards suddenly paranoid
'she's in a better place now, watching over us'. I shook my head, I was being silly, everyone knows ghosts had better things to do than that. I stared down at the cake instead, then to Princess who had both brown eyes

glued to the plate. I laid it down in front of her and said 'okay'. She eagerly lapped it up. On the plus side, it seemed as if I had found a solution for the human food I was being plied with.

Chapter 10

~Jessica Tuesday~
Day Two as a Vampire

After my first day in Scarlet's underground world, I was starting to realise that living as a vampire was not as glamorous as I had imagined. For a start, drinking blood was just as disgusting as it sounded and having a zombie-type creature bring it to you made the whole ordeal even worse.

Scarlet's ghoul, Herb, was a vile creature, his skin, which was tinged green, was mottled with veins and had an oily sheen to it which smelt like rotten fish. On occasion layers of skin would slip away revealing the pink tissue underneath. To my greater disgust he also has outbreaks of what he referred to as 'death blisters', which the abominable creature persisted in fiddling with, until they burst, giving off an even worse smell than what he already emitted. As planned, I had managed to stay awake the previous night by consuming large quantities of black coffee, but today I could feel the after effects. My eyes were itchy from tiredness and my concentration was scatty at best. I would have to get some sleep tonight, but the thought of Kristian materialising into Scarlet's bedroom and finding me sleeping was enough to put me off. I should have gone over this more with Scarlet, how did she expect me to last a week without sleep? I was convinced she didn't care either way, she was so obsessed with trying to have her turn at being human that my part of the bargain wasn't a factor. I got dressed finding a pair black jeans and a short-sleeved top, which I dressed up with some nice boots and a poncho, this should have been enough to keep me stylish, but more importantly warm. I checked my face in the mirror, slightly envious of Scarlet's perfect complexion. She didn't need any make-up at all, I fluffed up my hair watching how the silky blonde strands fell back into place, it didn't even seem to get greasy, upkeep for vampires was really a no brainer.

When I got downstairs I found Dante in the kitchen, if I didn't think it was possible I would have sworn he was hungover. He sat at the table staring vacantly into the bottom of his chalice, still wearing the same clothes from the night before. The table was covered with empty sachets of blood packs. Spread out on the counter in front of him was a magazine, it had a picture of a vampire but his face was marred with scars. The caption read:

'Vampire finally tells all about the night his Sire purposefully mutilated him before performing the dark kiss, leaving him to face immortality with the monstrous scars.'

When he finally noticed my presence, he looked up but seemed to have trouble focusing, before meekly looking down at the blood packs strewn across the table.

"Sorry, Scarlet, I believe I may have finished off the last packs. Mildred has just popped out to get some to tide us over until the weekly order comes in."

I felt a wave of relief. No blood packs meant I had an excuse to skip the compulsory blood breakfast. Suddenly a high-pitched scream came from the living room, Dante and I exchanged glances before both dashing towards the sound. A feeding fatality in the house was not what I needed right now, anything that encouraged Scarlet's family to be investigated while I was here, would not be good. But no, what I saw was much worse, two girls sat on the sofa giggling hysterically. From the fresh bite marks on both, and the way they were both squealing excitedly, I was certain that they must be Kristian's blood dolls. The red haired one which, from Scarlet's description I knew to be Mary, had a black cardboard box in the shape of a coffin opened up on her lap, within and buried under layers of red tissue paper, were small packaged items. The lid of the box which had been cast aside, had a large logo of a pair of red lips, with vampire fangs on it.

"It's my monthly Coffin Crate!" Mary gushed.

I rolled my eyes and sat down, watching in disgust as she went through all the contents and chatted excitedly like a child.

"They had sold out when I tried to order mine," said the other one enviously.

This one had long brown hair and looked a little younger than Mary. Scarlet had told me that her name was Cecile, both came across as complete idiots, maybe being a blood doll destroyed brain cells.

"Awwww look!! More rejuvenation balm, just as I was running out. Let's see what else they have sent me, ohhh a blood barrel! and a pair of fang earrings!" purred Mary.

Dante, who seemed a little more sober now, inspected the items curiously. I could tell he wanted one for himself but didn't want to admit it. Out of nowhere, Kristian laughed at all three of them before popping a blood vape into his mouth.

"You have to hand it to these ghouls, they really know how to market the undead scene for humans. They charge thirty Drakmir for each subscription and most of the stuff is harvested for free. Those fangs were probably extracted for a price at Flesh Fusions and the blood, collected from Dead Canvas for their tattoo removals."

The girls didn't seem to acknowledge Kristian's comments, Dante on the other hand, remained intrigued.

"You can see the appeal though," remarked Dante as he pulled out the blood barrel. It had the label *'Vintage Vamp'* written on it.

"This has even been approved by Dr Ervin, I had heard he was doing a line of products aimed at blood dolls," he said, gently swishing the small bottle in front of his eyes.

Kristian snatched it from him and opened it taking a deep sniff.

"I'm not sure I approve of you drinking some other vampire's blood," he sneered.

Mary smiled triumphantly. "Jealous are we?"

Kristian laughed. it sounded cold and I saw her face fall.

"My dear, you could feed off all the undead in the city for all I care as long as it's all pure blood." He glanced at Herb who had silently sneaked in to get a peek at all the commotion.

"If Dr Ervin produced it then it's bound to have come from the very best of our kind," said Dante coming to the product's defence.

They started talking about vampire bloodlines and I got bored. While the four of them were engrossed in conversation, I grabbed the free book that had come with it. It was titled, *'Buried but not Beaten'*, a autobiography about a ghoul who had started off with bleak after-death beginnings. According to the blurb, he had suffered decades of supernatural stigma due to being not just a ghoul, but an unclean with no above ground work prospects. But by using his previous life experience in HR, he set up his own chain of ghoul recruitment agencies and now ran a number of ghoul fund schemes to help fellow ghouls set up small businesses. A caption at the bottom of the cover read, *"As inspirational as 'From Rotten to Riches' and as funny as 'Death is Uncertain but Taxes still are: How to become a supernatural success'."* Finding the concept boring I disregarded it and instead picked up a magazine that had also come with the Coffin Crate loot.

"Oh, is that the latest edition of Recently Risen!" Mary snatched it from my hands in her excitement.

I didn't especially want to read it, I doubted it would shed any light on what really interested me, but I hadn't liked the way she snatched it, what would a vampire reaction be I wondered. I looked up to Kristian but he did not seem to think Mary had done anything out of turn as he had wandered off upstairs, probably bored of her antics. Scarlet had mentioned that whenever he grew tired of his blood dolls he just left the room without explanation and that sometimes he would even leave the house. Despite this, both girls, would wait for him until their tiny brains had established he wasn't coming back anytime. Dante had also vanished, probably to see if he could order the next month's crate before that too sold out.

Mary and Cecile sat flicking through the magazine together, the other items forgotten. I reached across and grabbed the rejuvenation balm and slipped it into my pocket before leaving the room. As I made for the doorway, I passed Herb his eyes looking at me questioningly, the vile creature must have seen me swipe the balm. I hesitated for a moment, but then brushed the thought off, so what if he did? He wasn't about to tell on me, he was a ghoul after all and more importantly, he was 'my' ghoul for the week. I didn't have to explain myself to him. But as I climbed the stairs to Scarlet's bedroom I couldn't help but feel a sense of unease, had I just blown my cover for the sake of a mere trinket? If the little wretch suspected something then it would take more than a little rejuvenation balm to save me.

Later I was inspecting myself in Scarlet's bathroom mirror. I had carefully applied the rejuvenation balm and was amazed at the instant effect it had. If this stuff was released above ground, it would sell for a fortune, maybe I could bring a load back with me and start my own enterprise I considered. I checked my phone, it was still early but I was feeling tired. I looked at the bed longingly but knew it would be foolish to try and sleep now. Both Kristian and Dante were in the house and the foul creature Herb had been lurking outside my room for most of the morning, most likely worried about my theft from earlier. I needed to get out of the house, a walk would wake me up and I would get to explore exactly what this city had to offer. I decided to tell Herb that I was going to Ghoul School; Scarlet had filled me in about her little undead college so I knew this would attract less attention. But minutes after leaving the house and walking the cobbled streets I was completely lost, panic started to settle in, would I have to ask someone where I was? What if they spotted I was human. Then to my relief, I heard the husky voices of two male ghouls passing by.

"I wish I had selected Ghoulology instead of Corpse Care, it covers more. I've been studying it over twenty years and I still don't know how to fuse a fingernail back on!" The first ghoul said.

"Doesn't Corpse Care focus more on the appearance of the skin though?" his friend replied.

"Yeah, I can now transmute skin from green to a pallid yellow," ghoul one exclaimed proudly.

"Wow, that's amazing!" wheezed his friend in excitement.

"Oh, and I finally worked out how to remove cornea clouding and reduce death bloating," said the first.

"Always a useful skill," said the other, nodding sagely.

Excellent luck I thought to myself, it didn't take a genius to work out that both were students from the Ghoul school. So I decided to follow them, putting up with their weird conversation. And to my joy, I was not disappointed, as we eventually arrived at the Ghoul Quarter, complete with its thick unmistakable fog of stench. It was a lot more crowded and squalid looking than I remembered, perhaps this was business hours. The stench was far worse again probably due to the larger number of ghouls in the area, but despite this I was ready. I controlled my breathing, making sure I didn't take huge lung fulls of the air and managed to block out the feelings of nausea that overtook me the night before. Short shallow breaths, through the nostrils, were the key. I followed the two ghouls through the busy streets, to the front of a large grey building. It was a ruddy looking building, that stood five or so floors. At the very top, perched stone gargoyles that looked like they were taking refuge from the stench fog. At the front, above the main entrance, it had a sign outside that ominously read in thick gothic lettering.

'DEATH CAN WAIT, EDUCATION CANNOT'.

The two ghouls I had followed, hopped up the stairs to the front entrance and aimed for a fast moving revolving door, that seemed to be sucking people in, while at the same time spitting them out. I gave myself a few minutes and composed myself, before ascending the stairs and quickly scooting through the revolving doors. Inside, ghouls were moving around, heading to class most likely, chattering away in raspy and high pitched voices. Just in front of me, a female ghoul sat behind a reception desk. She looked up as I approached, part of her windpipe was exposed and her collarbone was protruding through the skin.
"If you're here for the embalming class, it just finished," she croaked.
"What's the next class?" I asked firmly.
"Blood magics with Mistress Varias, would you like me to sign you up?" she asked.
"Yes. When does it start?"
"In the next fifteen minutes, it's in room 12 down the hall to the right, if you prefer you can wait inside the classroom as it's currently not in use." The ghoul said, before bowing her head respectfully.
I signed up, remembering to give Scarlet's full name and she found my details on an ancient looking computer. There was a fee of two hundred Drakmir which would be charged to Scarlet's account. I got a little worried at the cost, not knowing what the value of currency was here, but it soon passed. After all she had offered to pay me initially for the swap, so I considered this small fee as a down payment. With the admin out of the way, I took to the corridors to find room 12. Once inside I took a seat at the back. There was no one else around so flicked through the prospectus the ghoul receptionist had provided me.

Ghoulology: This course shows the learner how to manipulate blood magics to fuse skin and bone. Known as the ancient art of flesh crafting and bone blending. Many ghouls who have completed this have gone onto work at Flesh Fusions, the ghoul surgery which has won the Corpse Cosmetic award for fifty years running.

Corpse Care: The subtle art of adding life into dead flesh, changing skin and eye tones to give a more lifelike appearance. Undead undergraduates will also learn how to treat common ghoul ailments such as Cadaver callouses, death blisters, grave wax, Irritable rot syndrome and maggot infestations.

The door creaked and I glanced up to see another student entering the room. To my surprise, I recognised her, it was the same ghoul I had seen in Flesh Fusions. She was still missing an eye but her nose had been reattached. She noticed me staring and gave a nervous smile, the skin at the corners of her mouth splitting. I had to bite back my revulsion, before instinctively smiling back. I suddenly remembered, this was not correct etiquette, but before I could correct myself, the ghoul got up and approached, encouraged she took the seat next me.

"I'm Grace," she said, holding out a hand which was missing three fingers, I glared at them in horror.

She followed my gaze then dropped the hand.

"Sorry I am still new to all this, I keep forgetting I'm not the same. I'm having my phalanges reconstruction tomorrow, so that is something I suppose. She sighed huskily, it sounded like a wasp was trapped in her throat.

"Even my voice is rotten," she said on the verge of tears.

"But you're immortal," I said pointedly, not wanting to have a crying ghoul on my hands.

She sniffed and shrugged.

"I guess, but what kind of life can I have looking like this?"

"They gave you a new nose and you have only been a ghoul for a day," I reasoned back.

She nodded a little too vigorously causing her skull to rattle.

"I am happy with it, I just hope they are able to do my eye soon but they advised that due to high demand donations for eyes are hard to come by."

She squinted at me.

"How did you know about my nose?"

I had stuck my foot in it, then I remembered what the male ghoul has said to me.

"I was at Flesh Fusions also and saw you, I was considering making a donation."

Grace suddenly looked hopeful.

"Your eyes are paler than I would like but they can fix that," she said excitedly.

"Oh, I decided not to go through with it," I stuttered hastily, as she greedily reached a decaying hand towards my eye.

"That's a shame," she said, before continuing.

"The ghoul surgeon suggested I place an advert in the local paper, partially decomposed ghoul seeks single eye..." she laughed bitterly.

"Before yesterday all I wanted was my boyfriend Clive to finally propose to me, we had been dating for years with no sign of him popping the question. That's how I got in this state in the first place, we had an argument about it and I stormed out to a bar in the city. I sat there and had a couple of glasses of wine, hoping he would get worried and come looking for me but he didn't." She shook her head in disbelief.

It seemed Grace, was intent to tell to me her whole unlife story...

"He knew what I was like. Before, if I walked out he would chase after me. But now, he has stopped. Probably assumed I would come back once I had calmed down."

She laughed bitterly.

"Well, I won't this time, that's one bit of satisfaction I get, he will be stewing up there while I am rotting down here."

"You were saying something about that is how you got into this state?" I pressed.

She frowned, then nodded in recollection.

"Oh right, yes. Well I probably had a bit more than two glasses, more like a bottle, I got talking to some young man, he was handsome and he was paying me attention, I would never normally consider cheating on Clive but I was angry with him, feeling like I was wasting my life so I indulged a little, lapped up the compliments and smiles like a neglected dog. I had forgotten how nice it was to be told I was beautiful, I knew I was of course, but Clive rarely said it anymore."

"So this young man, he was the one who did this to you?" I asked leading her back onto topic.

"Yes, he invited me back to his place and then the next thing I remember is waking up in some clinic surrounded by ghouls and vampires. He left me there, couldn't finish me off. He was supernaturally impotent as they call it and because of it I will never get married now." She started to wail annoyingly.

"So you don't remember anything about how he turned you?" I asked struggling to keep the irritation out of my voice.

She shook her head slowly. "No, like I said I was quite drunk."

Grace spiraled back to talking about her ruined looks and how her transformation had been literally a life changing event. She had been informed that she could seek compensation. If a vampire turned a human, who was under the influence of drink or drugs, vulnerable or did not express their permission to the act, then the fledgling ghoul or vampire in question had legal precedence to seek compensation. The reasons being pain and suffering endured as a result of this traumatic event. According to Grace there were many ghouls that specialised in undead law, who were willing to take on such cases for a percentage of the compensation awarded. Unfortunately for Grace her sire was unknown and without his details, she would not be able to claim. But this didn't stop her trying to pursue the claim through the FPB - The Fledgling Protection Bureau, a non-profit organisation devoted to innocent victims of vampire attacks. They would look to pay her out for a 'bite and run' claim. It would mean a smaller payout but something was better than nothing as Grace put it, especially for all the upcoming flesh crafting and bone blending surgeries she was planning.

Grace's incessant conversation, had caught me off guard and I failed to notice the class had begun to fill up. There were a number of ghouls and vampires in attendance, all sitting separate from one another. Grace and myself were the only two sitting next to each other, which resulted in us attracting curious stares. I wondered why Grace had dared to approach me with such confidence in the first place. Then I remembered, she had only been a ghoul for 24 hours and was clueless to her new position in undead culture. I was sure that this additional fact would be another harsh blow along with the loss of her looks and her boyfriend. I put her out of my mind as Mistress Varias the room. She had long white hair tied in a plait and was wearing a long purple dress, an array of different necklaces dangled from her neck and her fingers were covered in huge chunky rings. The oddest thing about her appearance though were the strange spiraling tattoos that covered her neck and face, each one alive, shifting across her flesh in a writhing mass of black ink. Once at her desk, her eyes scanned the class, before pausing on me. I felt my heart beat faster, did she know? The ghoul secretary had said the teacher was a witch, perhaps she could see through the amulet's spell. Then it hit me, how could I fool a witch when the amulet meant to protect me was crafted by one? But before I could fret anymore, Mistress Varias took her eyes off me and instead addressed the class as normal.

"For centuries witches like me have used demons to help us with our magic. Demonic blood is a key ingredient for the most powerful spells, we never cared about the repercussions."

Her gaze fell on Grace who, despite her recent cosmetic procedures, was still the worst looking ghoul in the room.

"Vampires are infamous in the world above, ask any human what a vampire is and they will tell you what they have been brought up to believe. But their stories are full of misconceptions."

She emptied a bag of items onto the table and picked one of them up, holding it out to the class.

"The Crucifix, associated as a common weakness for vampires but it is in fact complete fabrication."

She placed the cross back onto the table and picked up a hand mirror.

"Reflections, a vampire has no reflection, again another untruth."

A male ghoul raised his hand and Mistress Varias nodded at him to speak.

"What about sunlight and blood, those are true," the ghoul said nasally.

"A vampire's weakness to sunlight has been greatly exaggerated. The human film industry always depicts vampires as bursting into flames instantly, or turning into dust as soon as a few rays of sunlight hit them. That is simply not the case. Yes, it burns and in cases of long exposure it can cause death in a fledgling, but even that would take hours. Older vampires condition themselves to the point of immunity and ghouls are far more resilient even when first turned."

She grabbed another item from the table, a dagger and without hesitation drew it across her hand. The red liquid flowed freely down her arm and she held it over a small bowl. I watched the undead students around me sit up straighter in their seats, Grace made a sudden involuntary snarling noise, before quickly covering her mouth in shock.

"I cannot argue that blood is most certainly a weakness, for both vampires and ghouls, but with proper training, this can be managed."

Mistress Varias grabbed a linen bandage and wrapped it round her hand, then holding her hands over the bowl began chanting. The words were strange, like she was speaking in tongues and as she did, the tattoos covering her began to move more aggressively, coiling round her throat like a mass of black snakes. A dark shadow started to fill the room, just like it had when Kristian materialised, but this form was far larger. As it came into focus I saw it was not a vampire but something far more monstrous standing in front of us. It was massive, almost reaching the ceiling of the classroom, it had grey, leathery skin and bat like ears. Coarse black fur stood out in patches over its muscular back. A pair of huge wings unfurled as the creatures black beady eyes took in the students. Its slit like nostrils immediately picked up the scent of the blood and it sniffed greedily at the bowl. Mistress Varias held the bowl away, until the creature looked at her and tilted its head as if waiting for instructions.

"This is a Strigoi. A breed of demon," Mistress Varias declared.

I looked around the room and saw the ghouls looking warily at it, even some of the vampires seemed intimidated.

"The vampire species is descended from such a demon. Hard to believe by looking at it, but just as humans share a common ancestry with apes, you all originated from something very similar to this creature," she continued.

The demon in question growled, its hackles rising as if trying to assert dominance over its smaller undead descendants.

"Humans inherited opposable thumbs, you got fangs and immortality," Mistress Varias informed.

I mused this over, somehow it didn't seem a fair comparison. Mistress Varias, walked next to the Strigoi, before lecturing us again.

"These are not the only evolutionary traits you have inherited. Demons are magical by origin the blood that runs through the veins of such creatures, is like ambrosia to a witch. And fit is or this reason witches take such risks to summon, control and harness demonic power."

I sat up straighter as she said this, curiosity taking over.

"Vampires, being half demon, carry the same blood, it is because of this that you don't grow old or suffer from the normal ailments that plague mankind. And as you are all well aware, there are additional perks such as materialising at will and the ability to control flickers. Vampires who work above ground use cloaking spells to travel unseen, and enthrallment to escape stickier situations.

Mistress Varias, paused to let the information sink in, all the while, the Strigoi stood there, breathing heavily.

"Such magic is just the beginning, and as you delve deeper into the art of blood magic you will unravel even greater spells: Shape-shifting, telekinesis and even telepathy. A vampire or ghoul skilled with these abilities will find themselves easily employed by the Tribune. Wardens have to be adept in advanced blood magic, you are not going to capture a rogue vampire by merely materialising and enthralling them to come quietly. Besides vampires are immune to such basic mind sway tricks. Telekinesis, however, can be very effective but takes considerable time and skill to master such an advanced technique."

Mistress varias turned to the demon who was still standing to attention.

"Gron is an adolescent demon so his powers are not what they should be, but I will demonstrate a few basic spells."

We watched on as Mistress Varias used the Strigoi to levitate objects on the table. She then used it to cast demonic possession on a fledgling Vampire, compelling the fledgling to attack a terrified ghoul in the next aisle. While amusing for the rest of the class, the side effect corrupted the mind of the unfortunate fledgling, leaving the wretched creature curled up in a whimpering ball. These lessons seemed harsh, but none of the students seemed to mind potentially being broken for the purpose of education. Mistress Varias went on to explain how ghouls were harder to possess or dominate due to having closer connections with their human side. A fact that seemed to cause some resentment among the vampire students, who I assumed found it difficult to accept that their lesser undead colleagues could be better than them at anything other than servant work. I wanted to ask Mistress Varias how she managed to control and summon Gron but thought better of it, I still wasn't sure if she had seen through the spell, but if she had, I wondered, why she had let me sit in on the class. Instead I concluded that while it was okay for the course to cover the teachings of blood magic, it was not okay to include the summoning or controlling of demonic pets. Perhaps the Tribune were worried about masses of demons being used as dangerous weapons.

At the end of Mistress Varias's class, Grace turned to me while the rest filed out.

"That was exciting wasn't it? Do you fancy a bite, we could go to that Mixology blood bar in the Trade Quarter, it seems more upbeat than the others in the Ghoul Quarter and the Vampire Quarter won't let ghouls in unless they are staff or have an authorised vampire escort," she rolled her single eye.

"How do you know all this already?" I asked impressed.

"Last night I went on what undead refer to as a blood binge and visited all the drinking holes. I got refused from every single one in the Vampire Quarter, but while I was having a few shots of Bloodclot in this dingy bar in the Ghoul Quarter, I overheard a few others talking about this Mixology bar that served both ghouls and vampires - it's really controversial apparently. Anyway I went and stayed for most of the night, the ghoul blood-tender is actually quite cute, apparently he was only dead for two days, his skin's a little waxy but he looks fresh enough, so do you want to come along?" She looked enthusiastically at me.

Catching Mistress Varias in the corner of my eye packing up her things, I shook my head and made an excuse about having previous arrangements. She looked a little crestfallen but to my relief shambled off without another word. As I watched Grace exit the classroom, I turned to face Mistress Varias, who continued packing away her things, ignoring me. I took a few steps forward, when Gron snarled in warning, Mistress Varias silenced him with a word, before turning to me with a smile.

"Scarlet, I was surprised to see you in my class today, Flickers aside you have always shown little interest in the demonic powers of your condition."

"I have been thinking a lot about my origins lately," I replied. That sounded like something Scarlet would say, after all she was obsessed with her origins - just not the demonic ones.

The witch met my gaze, her eyes narrowing.

"You are not Scarlet," she said frankly.

I knew it, from the moment she had entered the room, she knew I was an imposter. This woman could summon demons, possess and mind control the undead. It had been foolish to hope she would not see through the amulets glamour spell.

With a sigh, I responded.

"No, I'm not," I confirmed, sounding braver than I felt.

Her eyes fell on the necklace around my throat.

"That's a Morshard. Where is Scarlet? Human," she said, emphasising on the 'human'.

"Yes, it is and yes I am. Look...I need your help," I replied trying to sound empowered.

Mistress Varias narrowed her eyes again.

"What makes you think I would help you?" she huffed in amusement.

This was going to be risky, but I had to do it. I had been suspicious when Mistress Varias had first shown up. The fact she recognised Scarlet's Morshard gave me further evidence in what I was about to say to her, but there was still no guarantee that she would agree.

"Because I know you are the one that gave this to her. You probably even taught her the spell. If you hand me in, or I get caught, you go down also, you can pretty much ensure your name, will be the second I mention to the Tribune. And after all, aiding human intent is a very serious offence," I bluffed.

The witch smirked.

"You're a shrewd one. But I guess you would have to be, to agree to being here in the first place. Tell me child, what is it you want?

"I need something that keeps me awake, I cannot live among vampires if I have to resort to human needs. Eating I can manage but falling asleep is too risky."

Mistress Varias nodded.

"I have a draught that will suffice. But it will cost you," She said abruptly.

I reached for Scarlet's purse and begun fumbling some coins into my hand, but she stopped me.

"No, not that kind of cost, I need blood." She said in an unsettling tone.

I sighed, of course it wasn't going to be that simple.

"Surely you can purchase that anywhere around here," I tried to reason.

"They overcharge me because I'm a witch," she could not hide the resentment in her voice.

I thrust out my arm in her direction.

"Take it then!"

With a grin on her face, Mistress Varias pulled a small jar from her bag and removed the lid, inside were several green worms with tentacles, ending in suckers.

"Ugh, what are those?!" I recoiled in disgust.

"Demon worms, they store blood, so I can use them for spells at a later date. What did you expect? I can't exactly bite you, I'm a witch remember," she said with a shrug.

Before I could muster an argument, she grabbed my arm and placed the jar upside down on it. The worms latched on and she proceeded to lift the jar, letting the little worms do their work. They fed feverishly, until their slimy green skin turned to bright red and their bodies bloated into fat blobs, filled with my blood.

"How did you learn all of this?" I asked as Mistress Varias started prying off the blood filled worms.

"Blood magic has been practiced among witch families for centuries, no one knows for certain how it came about, but some believe our ancestors themselves derived from demons, how else would we have learnt such power?"

The last of the worms had been removed and traces of blood begun to stream from the bite wounds. I noticed Gron fixating on it.

"Are they all like....?" I said, still keeping my gaze on Gron.

Mistress Varias handed me a cloth.

"Here press that to the wounds, they will continue to bleed for a while, the worms saliva stops your blood from clotting. No, there are other types but Strigoi are the closest relatives of the vampires and ghouls, these are what my ancestors used in their summoning spells as they are the most powerful, but there are lesser demons like imps and, of course, worms."

I stared at her neck and face, while absorbing the information.

"Are the tattoos part of the ritual?" I said trying to put two and two together.

Mistress Varias smiled.

"You are a curious one, aren't you? But to answer the question, no. The summoning can be performed without the markings. These are Inkspells, they anchor us to the mortal plain, this stops demons from being able to drag us to their domain, during the binding process. It also has the added bonus of dampening locating spells." She raised her eyebrows as she said this.

"Locating spells? Like tracking someone?"

"Yes, vampires were not always so accommodating to us. It wasn't long ago when they would hunt us, posing as human inquisitors. The more shrewd of us were able to keep hidden by using inkspells." Anger flashed in her eyes as she recalled this.

Mistress Varias finished packing the rest of her tools away and started walking towards the door, Gron gave one last disgruntled look at my arm, before turning around and following instep behind her.

"What about my draught?" I called after her, just before she could exit.

She paused and turned to face me.

"Come by my shop this evening and I will have it ready, it's called 'Toil and Trouble'. In the Witches Quarter naturally." She flashed me a wink and left.

With no other plans till this evening, I decided to sign up for another class. I was also starting to feel the effects of no sleep, which made the idea of heading back to Scarlet's home even less appealing. Flicking through the prospectus, I discovered the next available class was *'Burial and Business'*, aimed at would be ghoul entrepreneurs'. When I got to the class, I saw some fledgling vampires also in attendance, I guessed that while not as low down as ghouls, these individuals didn't have sires or brood families and were having to 'make a go at it' themselves. The class was dull, it was run by a weasel faced ghoul who I would not have given the time of day to when he was alive let alone now he was dead.

"Success in death is even harder than success in life," he squeaked. "Sure there's less competition but there are also fewer customers."

The next two hours he rambled on about the fundamentals of Resurrection Tax and how to avoid it, the state of the undead economy and Necro Network; a supernatural site for professional ghouls and vampires looking to connect regarding business opportunities. By the time the class ended I was more in need of that potion than ever, it had taken every ounce of will I had, not to fall asleep in my seat. When I finally got outside I checked Scarlet's phone, it was still too early, but I decided to make my way to the Witches Quarter as I was unsure how long it would take me to find it. Half-an-hour and a few wrong turns later, I managed to find it by following the increasingly cryptic and vague signs. I noticed that the Witches Quarter was far less crowded than the other parts of the city, and was shocked when the distinct smell of coffee and human cooking filled the air. I went pass what appeared to be a witches coffee shop, called "True Brew". The smell of tea and cakes made my stomach grumble and I realised I had not eaten anything since the noodles last night. I looked around warily before stepping in and I was surprised to see it was quite cosy inside. There were comfy looking armchairs, a cheery log fire hearth and even live music, or unlife to be more specific. The musician was a female vampire who sat on a stool while strumming a guitar and singing a song, which sounded vaguely familiar, but with key words changed.

"I bit a Ghoul and I liked it! I hope my Sire don't mind it" rang out.

I stepped up to the counter, where a young girl courteously greeted me, her face was covered in the strange inkspells Mistress Varias had told me about.

"Can I have a cursed cookie and a glass of mystic milk?" I asked, reading from the menu.

The girl stared at me blankly as if I was speaking a foreign language.

"I am sorry, but our foods are for human consumption only. May I offer you something from our selection of Artisan brewed blood?"

Of course. I was Scarlet the vampire, a creature not expected to be buying baked treats. I had forgotten in my tiredness how unusual my request had been. There was no way I could buy food here, let alone eat it in public. I had to think of something to cover my tracks, as well as my hunger pains.

"It's for my blood doll," I lied. "I'll take a cup of that blood for me."

This seemed to make perfect sense to the witch serving girl, who gathered my order without another question. Cookie, Milk and Blood in hand I went to find a corner seat, at the back of the cafe. Hidden from view, I gulped the milk and bit into the cookie enthusiastically, while the vampire singer performed *'Like a Fledgling - bit for the very first time'*. By the end of her set, I had finished my cookie and a new performer had set up on stage. It was a ghoul comedian who decided to start the set by saying how he felt so disconnected from the world, before proceeding to pull his arm off, it was going to be a long wait I thought to myself.

By the time the ghoul finished it was, fortunately, time to go meet Mistress Varias at 'Toil and Trouble. Unsurprisingly and true to the name, it turned out to be a potion shop. Inside there were rows of glass bottles lining the shelves and boxes filled with strange coloured powders or lumps of metal. On tables were stacks of purchasable books next to bubbling beakers filled with glowing liquid, in the middle was a selection of price tagged cauldrons. All the different ingredients in the shop let off a strong smell, that reminded me of my old Chemistry class. At the very back of the shop, sat Gron. He was sitting in a large iron cage and chewing on what looked like a foot. Having noticed me enter the shop, he let off a deep growl. Mistress Varias was behind the counter, serving a female ghoul so I decided to browse while I waited. Most of the shops wares were home-brewed remedies for ghoul afflictions such as skin rot and death blisters; however there were some vampire draughts such as Flicker Blockers and Blood Suppressants, both were potion based. I suddenly heard the door close, as the ghoul exited the shop. Mistress Varias has escorted her to the door and once certain no one was else was coming toward the store, she locked the door and flipped the sign to closed. Walking past me towards the back, she called out.

"I have the draught ready."

I made to follow, but as I passed Gron's cage he tried snapping through the bars, the witch turned and uttered some harsh sounding words I couldn't understand, which settled him. He let off a small disgruntled huff, before returning to chewing the foot. I followed her down a narrow staircase and into, what appeared to be a living area. A small fire burned low and a cauldron bubbled over it, emitting a rank smell. She motioned for me to take a seat in an armchair by the fire, I sat down, while she approached the cauldron and ladled some of the contents into a glass bottle.

"Here," she said handing the bottle to me. I peered at the dark green liquid doubtfully.

"This will stop me needing sleep?" I asked sceptically.

She nodded before going through the instructions.

"Two spoonfuls tonight should do it, when you feel the effects wearing off just take another two."

"Any side effects?" I asked cautiously.

"When you return to your human life and stop using it, you will suffer from some temporary fatigue but a week of normal sleeping will remove any lingering effects," she confirmed.

"Thanks," I said, slipping it into my pocket.

"That, I believe, concludes our business; unless there is anything else you wish to blackmail me for?" she smirked.

I gazed around the small room curiously.

"Is this where you live?"

"Yes, it suits me fine," but I could detect the defensive tone in her voice.

"It just seems odd that a woman of such power would have such a humble abode."

She narrowed her eyes at me, clearly offended.

"Did Scarlet not tell you anything of her world?"

I could sense the mood changing, and the last thing I wanted was to anger Mistress Varias, but I was curious, so I continued.

"She told me that witches summoned the demons that created the first vampire. And as a result the vampires hunted your kind for vengeance, but that it's over now and you're all friends," I blurted.

She scoffed.

"Friends is a strong word, they tolerate our presence as it benefits them. We help keep their city hidden and in return we can trade among them." Her voice was thick with resentment.

"Why would you live among them then?" I pushed.

"The same could be asked of you," she said with a wry smile.

"I like trying new things," I replied matching her smile.

"I see. Well for us the reason is simple, vampire blood is a potent ingredient in many of our spells, almost invaluable in fact, and worth sacrificing any desire for more spacious living quarters, if that's what you were wondering."

"I suppose there's a price to everything," I looked down at my arm which was still tender.

"Be careful of that," she said. "If anyone spots you bleeding human blood it will become clear you're not a vampire. Use some of this, it's a rejuvenation balm, ghouls and blood dolls use it to heal wounds and rejuvenate areas of decomposition." She handed me the small tin of balm.

I decided not to tell her I had stolen some earlier that day, the more supplies the better I thought. So I took the tin and began rubbing a small amount of the balm onto the wounds. I felt a tingling sensation and watched in fascination as they slowly grew smaller, before vanishing from my arm completely. Nodding in gratitude, I decided now was the time to leave, Mistress Varias said nothing as she saw me out the shop.

When I got back to Scarlet's I found Kristian and his blood dolls watching TV, the smell of vampire and human blood was heavy in the air. Cecile was inspecting herself in a hand mirror.

"Your blood is better than botox, look how smooth my skin is now," she gushed.

It was true, her skin did look better than usual and I wondered how long the effect lasted for. With that in mind, it was easy to see why drinking vampire blood became such an addiction. After all, who could possibly resist getting high and staying forever young in the process? It was the next best thing to being a vampire. Mary however was sitting away from them, reading a book titled *'To be Sired or not to be Sired: The vein hope of a blood doll.'*

"How was school?" Kristain suddenly said.

He had noticed I was there without glancing from the cooking program. A female ghoul was chopping up a block of fat, she was clearly a freshie as her pale skin was almost as flawless as a vampire's. She had thick dark hair which seemed full of life, but it was her eyes which gave her away they were a murky shade of green.

"I love the way the fat squelches under my knife," she was saying to the camera.

"For a lesser undead this Gourmet Ghoulia is rather entertaining," said Kristian, still not looking away from the screen. "I'm not a ghoul and yet I want a bite of that fat for some reason."

Gourmet Ghoulia was now moving onto the next stage. "Now, firmly roll out the spleen, I always soak this in full fat blood of course."

"It was good," I replied in answer to his original question. "The teacher summoned a Strigoi."

"See, much more interesting than reading a book about Instagram," Kristian said triumphantly.

"I agree," I said. "In fact it has got me thinking about the siring process." He turned abruptly and gave me a sharp look. Mary and Cecile also looked up, their faces full of hopeful intrigue.

"Siring is overrated," he said bluntly and slowly. Before turning back to the TV, both Mary and Cecile's faces fell in disappointment.

"I used to think that," I continued. "But I am starting to see the benefits of it."

"Siring without the Tribune's permission is illegal, Scarlet. You know this. If you want to go through all that paperwork that's your choice, but a fledgling is for eternity not just a few months," Kristian warned.

I decided to say no more, it seemed, that if I wanted to learn about siring, I was going to have to ask someone other than Kristian.

__Chapter 11__

~Scarlet Wednesday~
Day Three as a Human

Wednesday morning I came down to the kitchen to greet Mrs Young, much like the other days, but something was playing on my mind. I was musing over how fast the time was going, I was already at day three and yet it seemed that there was still so much to experience. Earlier I had received a text from Sam saying how well I had performed in the dress rehearsal yesterday, he stated how he thought I looked 'strangely sexy in a Victorian dress' but was quick to assure me, that this was not a fetish he was suddenly getting into. I found him quite witty for one so young and surprisingly well read, even though his main passion was music. Last night I had discovered some old compilations he had made for Jessica, and having nothing else to do during the night hours, I listened to them using Jessica's headphones. I felt a strange bitterness over the fact, that in my long life no one had ever dedicated a single song to me, let alone a compilation of them. He had included one of his own songs on there that I found I didn't dislike. In fact if I had been more capable of emotion I was certain I would have found it quite beautiful, this frustrated me even further. I wanted to truly feel that song, more than any other song.

"You're awfully pale, darling, are you sure you're feeling well enough to go in today?" asked Mrs Young, as I took my place at the table.

She laid out a plate of fruit for me, along with a croissant, being curious to try french pastry I bit into it. But immediately wished I hadn't.

"Have you got a temperature?" She came over and pressed the back of her hand to my forehead and immediately flinched. "You're like ice!"

This wasn't good, if Mrs Young thought I looked pale then maybe the spell was wearing off.

"I'm feeling normal," I replied as I slid away from her.

Ditching the croissant and grabbing my bag, I made for the door. I needed to get going before she started asking more questions. She was still shouting concerns after me as I dashed out the house and headed to the bus stop.

The first class was Drama, during which I spent most of my time helping Sam with his lines. Despite stating that he had learnt them all, he continued forgetting them during rehearsal. Playing the lead role he had a lot more than me to remember, so I tried not to judge him for how bad his memory was compared to mine, his brain was only human after all. Miss Fenwick, who had been rushing around even more than usual, suddenly paused as she passed us and looked at me properly for the first time since I had arrived.

"You look different, Jessica, are you feeling okay?" I could see panic starting to fill her at the thought of her starlet being ill so close to opening night.

"I'm fine," I said reassuringly.

"Are you sure you don't want me to fetch the nurse? You look awfully pale, dear."

"I'm okay, really. I've just been using less make-up."

She frowned unconvinced, but finally gave a nod.

"Alright then, but if you start feeling queasy go straight to the nurse's office."

That was the third human to have commented on my health, Sam had also asked if I was feeling okay, something was wrong. I excused myself to the bathroom, but this seemed to cause even more concern. When I arrived at the toilets, I was relieved to see that the face greeting me in the mirror, was still Jessica's. But as I looked closer, I noticed it had lost the healthy glow, the once golden skin was nearly chalk white. The amulet's power must have started fading, I needed to get to the bottom of this and find a solution – fast.

After Drama I rushed out of class without waiting for Sam, in case any of my other vampire traits started resurfacing. I went behind the corner of the building and flipped out my hand mirror. To my relief it was only my undead skin that had reverted, so the glamour was seemingly intact and I was confident in proceeding with the rest of the day. I decided to see if Penny was in her usual spot for lunch.

Same as yesterday, she was reading and as I approached, she looked genuinely shocked. Despite this, she didn't tell me to go away, so I sat down next to her. I didn't notice any unusual smell about her, which confused me as I was no longer sure what Hannah had meant the day before. Being a vampire my sense of smell was far superior, so with that in mind, I established if Hannah had been wrong in that sense, then she must also be wrong about Penny being a liar. So far I had found Jessica's friends unremarkable, their conversations were less stimulating than I had hoped; Hannah had phoned me last night to update me on her latest love interest – Rob. I had, at first, been delighted at the opportunity to hear the concept of love at first hand, but Hannah's version differed to the romantic accounts of Jane Austen that I had been basing my expectations on all these years. From what I could construe, Hannah thought Rob was still in love with his ex-girlfriend. She then constructed a number of mundane reasons to build up her case regarding this; a text message on his phone, a message on a social media site, an instant message, an email, a voice mail, a video call, a missed call. I got so confused with all the different forms of communication between him and his ex that I failed to keep up with the content of these messages. Hannah went to great lengths in reading me each one and urged me to read in between the lines of a 'Smiley Face', and a 'Like', and then a 'Smiley Winking Face', which only added to my confusion. It got so bad, that Hannah accused me of not listening to her and opted to call Nikki instead.

I enjoyed my lunchtime spent with Penny. I found her company relatively peaceful. She didn't question why I wasn't eating and she didn't confuse me with the significance of certain emojis. Instead we discussed the homework and I found her views relevant, she had been bullied a lot which is why she was so interested in Psychology, her other main subject along with Philosophy, as Penny explained more of the course to me, I felt myself wishing Jessica had chosen that instead of Dance. It turned out that Penny wanted to become a Counsellor to help people that suffered with mental health issues. She explained how her own mother had become obese as a direct result from her depression, which had affected Penny's childhood and was still having a massive impact on her life. Her mother had become so large that she was no longer mobile and needed Penny to look after her, it had got to a point where Penny would worry about her mother, every time she left the house. Only last month she had returned from college to find her mother had fallen over and not had been able to get back up without help. This was another side of humanity that I had not experienced, I was well aware humans were fragile and prone to ailments of all kinds, but I had never considered the effect it could have on the offspring, and that the two roles of parent/child could become reversed. So engaging was the conversation, that I failed to notice the lunch break had ended and our next lesson was due – Philosophy. I decided that I would sit next to Penny, which I noticed, drew a few shocked glances and hushed whispers from the rest of class. For once, even Dean kept quiet when Penny participated in discussions. It seemed, my simple changing of seats had once again had major implications.

At the end of the day, Sam caught up with me at the bus stop. He seemed breathless like he had been running.

"Didn't you get my text?" he asked.

I fished inside Jessica's bag for her phone and saw there were lots of unread messages flashing up. I had heard it go off earlier and had even been told off in class for not having it on silent, but I had forgotten to check the messages afterwards. I wasn't used to receiving calls or texts, not having any friends myself. The only texts I got were from Herb and that was only in regards to meals he was getting me, or if I needed anything from the ghoul market.

As I looked through the phone, I saw there were two messages from Sam: one was asking if I wanted to meet him for lunch, obviously too late now. The other was asking if I wanted to come over to his house after college.

I glanced back up from the phone.

"So?" he said, smiling.

"Yes," I said flatly, but a million thoughts sped through my mind.

Going to Sam's house was something that Jessica might not be happy about, considering it was 'her' boyfriend. I weighed up the options, they had been fighting recently, maybe she was planning on breaking up with him. From what I gathered, she had been spending time with Dean, maybe he was her new boyfriend, which meant Sam was nothing to her. I battled with it in my head; Jessica had given me permission to swap lives with her, so even if she did have any lingering feelings for Sam it didn't make a difference to the conditions of our agreement. I was entitled to experience her life for the entire week and that meant spending time with her family, friends and yes, even her boyfriend.

"Well we don't need to get the bus then," he said when I still hadn't moved to follow him. "I have my car."

I nodded and he grabbed my hand in his, this time he did not mention how cold mine was, but he did shove them both in his pocket as we walked along as if to warm them up. When we got to his car, he gave me my hand back and got his keys out. I stood by, waiting for instructions, but instead he came round and opened the door for me, motioning for me to get inside. From the outside, Sam's house was similar to Jessica's, but within it was very different. There was a lot more ornamentation, in the lounge there were shelves upon shelves, displaying decorative plates. Sam followed my gaze.

"Her collection is getting bigger, isn't it? I keep saying she's going to need another room just for them," he chuckled.

"What's the purpose, do you eat off of all of them?" I asked doubtfully.

Sam laughed. "No, Jess, she just likes collecting them."

There were pictures on the wall of Sam and another boy who looked slightly older. There were also lots of books, mainly on self-help and homeopathy. I followed Sam into the kitchen, where his mother was stirring the contents of a large pot over the hob, I stayed back a little, avoiding most of the cooking smell. Sam's mother I discovered was Filipino and very pretty, she had black hair that was cut into a stylish bob and was smaller than Jessica, so when she came to welcome me I had to bend slightly as she pulled me into a hug, kissing me on both cheeks.

"Hello, darling!" she said, before holding me at arm's length. She paused and seemed to appraise me in a scrutinising fashion, before turning to Sam.

"She looks different, is she ill?"

"I'm fine." I piped up even though she had not addressed me specifically, I felt the need to speak up for myself and mentally made a note to visit the bathroom and apply more make-up.

Sam leant in towards the cooking pot and sniffed appreciatively, "Mmmm Sinigang, dinner I assume?"

Sam's mum smiled faintly. "I haven't cooked it in a while so thought it would be a nice change."

"Yeah, we haven't had Sinigang since Ben was with us," said Sam.

Her smile faded and her voice had an edge to it when she spoke. "He's still with us, Sam."

Sam's face fell, "I know, I just meant since before the accident."

Sam's mum had stopped listening and was turning the heat down on the hob, before muttering to herself. "Right, I will let that simmer."

"We'll go watch TV then?" Sam asked.

She nodded. "Yes, I'll call you when it's ready."

We sat on the sofa while Sam flicked through the channels. He asked me what I wanted to watch but I had no preference, so he selected a film. It was about a group of people that had super powers who were trying to save the world from an evil force, but I was unable to concentrate fully on the plot, as about a quarter of the way through, Sam had slipped his arm around my shoulder and gently pulled me towards him, so that my head was resting against his chest. The sound of his heart beating steadily reverberated through me, reminding me he was a living breathing thing, I could feel my hunger rising, so tried harder to concentrate on the film. If I did that, I hoped it would be enough to stop me wanting to feed on him. I had not managed to have my blood rations at lunch as I had sat with Penny and while we were progressing in our familiarity I didn't think we were quite there yet for me to openly use a blood pack in front of her. I instinctively began turning my head towards his neck, my mouth opening slowly, fangs tingling at the scent of warm blood... his throat was inches away.

"You're not watching this are you?" he asked.

"What? Of course I am," I said defensively, paranoid in case I had released an unbidden hiss or growl.

"I'm not either," he said and turned towards me. "I keep thinking about how much I want to kiss you."

He searched my eyes for permission, I sat there muted by his desire. I had enthralled boys to want me but it was never real, the glazed look in their eyes and lack of emotion in their voice made them puppets. This is not real either I told myself, you are still using magic, he thinks you are Jessica, if he knew what you were, he would hate you, he would run from you. I knew it was true but I couldn't stop myself, I was overcome with something stronger than blood lust, I pressed my lips against his, kissing him the way my mortal self would have, no blood, no pain, just the warmth of his mouth on mine. If my own lips were cold he didn't show it, he moved his hand to my face holding it as he kissed me deeper. My own hand moved to his neck stroking the back of it. This is it, I thought, this is why I risked so much.

I had never felt this alive, this is what being human was about, connecting with someone, not killing them.

"Ouch!" I pulled away immediately and Sam was touching his lips where a small droplet of blood had formed. I had bitten him accidentally, I was mortified. He saw my face and smiled. "I guess we both are a little eager."

"Sorry," I smiled weakly.

"It's okay, you might need to kiss it better though," he grinned as he leaned in for more.

"Actually, can I use the bathroom?" I gently pushed him back.

"Of course, you know the way," he replied.

"Thanks," I said before grabbing my bag and slipping past him. I dashed up the stairs, hoping that it was up there.

I found it on the first floor and quickly closed the door behind me. I opened my mouth and saw Jessica's normally blunt teeth had turned into a set of fangs. I sat down on the edge of the bath and tried to calm myself, it's because I'm hungry, I reassured myself. Grabbing my bag I pulled out a blood pack and emptied the contents down my throat in one go. I decided to wait a few minutes to let the effects kick in and was rewarded when I started to feel better again. I stood up and checked myself over for splashes of blood. With relief, I discovered that my fangs had retracted and were back to normal. I was still pale so I decided to add some blusher. Finally I checked my hair for blonde strands and my eyes. A little paleness I could explain, my eyes changing colour would have been a little harder.

When I finally came back down, dinner was ready and Sam's father was home from work, so we ate together. I sipped the Sinigang making sure to make complimentary noises; it was a soup dish with meat and vegetables floating around in it. If I had not met Sam's mother I would never have guessed Sam was half Filipino, his father was English and Caucasian. Sam's mother still carried a slight accent and would often break into her native tongue – Tagalog, especially when she was cursing. I liked her, she was different to Jessica's mum, more forthright. Decoding all the hidden meanings of human conversation had been the hardest part of the swap so far, so the relative bluntness was a welcome change. After dinner, which I had managed to finish; it helped that it was mostly liquid; we went upstairs to Sam's room, it was the same size as Jessica's but again very different. The walls were a simple white and his bed had navy covers on it. A guitar lay propped against the wall and there was a desk with a computer on it. There was a single picture of him and Jessica in a frame on the desk, which I quickly turned away from, I didn't need another reminder that I was usurping. Sam put some music on and sat down on the bed, patting the spot next to him. I sat down warily, I didn't want another embarrassing situation so I was going to have to control myself. He reached a hand and stroked my hair from my face.

"You sure you're okay? you seem quieter than normal."

I turned to meet his gaze, feeling surprisingly uncomfortable about lying to him.

"Sorry, I'm not feeling myself at the moment, but I will be soon, I promise." I contemplated the irony of my response.

It wasn't a complete lie, soon I would be back underground where I belonged and Jessica would be back in my place, I wondered if she and Sam would stay together. I felt a small tightness in my chest, my body must have been trying to reject the Sinigang.

"I'm glad you agreed to come over, I know things haven't been great between us lately, but I still care about you," he said softly.

"I can see that," I said, and meant it. It was obvious Sam still had feelings for Jessica.

"I know you've said before you don't want to, but I have to go and see Ben in a bit and it would mean a lot if you came along; I'll understand if you decide not to though."

I wasn't sure who Ben was, but if it meant a lot to Sam, I should go I thought. After all I was supposed to be fulfilling Jessica's role as a girlfriend, it seemed the least I could do. So I agreed. Just after a knock sounded on his door and his mother popped her head around it.

"Sam? Sorry to interrupt but we're leaving now," she said.

"Right, erm is it okay if Jess comes with us?" he turned to me. "Are you sure you still want to come? because if not I understand."

I nodded and his mother looked at me as if she was also uncertain that I should go.

"Of course, I'm just surprised as she never showed any interest in the last month that Ben has been at the hospital," she said without restraint.

"Mum!" said Sam, giving her a hard look.

"Well, it's true. We'll be waiting in the car," she snapped, before disappearing downstairs.

"Ignore her, she's just stressed out about this whole thing, we all are," he said apologetically.

Before we left the house, I managed to gauge between Sam and his parents, that Ben was his older brother who had been in a motorbike accident. This had caused traumatic head injuries and left him in a coma, Sam's father was a doctor himself but he was a cardiologist and didn't specialise in coma patients. I sensed this caused some frustration and I imagined being trained to save people's lives but unable to save your own child must have felt awful. At the hospital we washed our hands in steriliser and walked through the corridors in silence, our shoes squeaking on the floor all the way until we arrived at the correct Ward. When we entered the room, someone was there already; a nurse. She smiled and greeted Sam's family as if she knew them, I supposed that if they have been visiting Ben at the hospital for a month, you would get to know the staff. She excused herself and Sam's mum moved towards the bed where the boy I had seen in the photo lay, except in those photos he was awake and laughing. She brushed his hair back.

"He needs a haircut," she murmured.

Sam's father joined her by the bed, staring down with a grim face. There was silence except for the steady beep of the machine.

"I'm going to speak with Dr Philips," he said.

"I'll come with you," Sam's mother replied with a nod.

They left leaving Sam and I alone with Ben, my eyes roved to the tubes and the beeping machine. Sam noticed me staring.

"Feeding tubes," he explained. "The machine helps him breathe."

I nodded, not knowing how to respond. I still found it fascinating how humans had created these methods of sustaining life. Sam leaned in close to his brother's ear and spoke softly.

"Ben, it's Sam, can you hear me? You've got a visitor today, it's Jess, you remember her don't you? Open your eyes and look at her, open your eyes, Ben."

Ben didn't open his eyes, he didn't even twitch, he just lay there, his chest steadily rising and falling in time with the machine.

"Playing hard to get." He laughed before gently patting Ben's shoulder. Just then Sam's parents returned.

"What did Dr Philips say?" he asked them.

Sam's mum was holding a tissue and wiping her eyes, she had been crying. His father wasn't crying but he looked like he had aged ten years. They both glanced at me then back at Sam.

"Jess, will you keep Ben company, while we go grab some tea?" he said.

I nodded but I was not certain what good keeping a comatose person company would do, it's not like he could hear me. After they left the room I stared at my surroundings not sure what else to do, taking in the white crisp bed sheets and the matching white washed walls. I browsed the gifts that had been left by visitors and well-wishers cards, flowers, even a few balloons, some of which were starting to shrivel. My gaze slid back to Ben, it felt odd watching over this human that I had never met, he looked like he was sleeping. I suddenly had a thought, what if he wakes up now, while I was the only one here. I subconsciously edged closer to the door, I could hear the sound of Sam and his parents talking in low whispers from down the hall.

"The doctors say any future recovery is slim, the damage he has suffered to the brain is substantial, even if he did wake up he would be in a minimal conscious state." It was Sam's father talking.

"What does that mean?" asked Sam.

"That he will not fully recover, he may open his eyes and even seem to acknowledge us but he would not be truly aware of who we are." Sam's father said clinically.

"But he might do, they don't know for certain that he won't," Sam responded, still hopeful.

"Sam, the prognosis is not good," his father said bluntly.

"I know but you hear about cases where the person wakes up and, at first they need to go to rehab and learn to walk again and sometimes they even need to learn how to speak again, but with the support of their family they get through it. Couldn't we be that kind of family?"

"In almost all cases like Ben's the patients are unable to communicate properly, they even seem to be incapable of experiencing pain or suffering, you're blinded by your own emotions, Sam. We have to face facts that he may not wake up and if he does, he may not be Ben at all."

"That's your professional opinion but this is not just some other patient this is your son! - my brother!" Sam responded heatedly.

"Charles, we should just bring him home! He would feel more comfortable there," sobbed Sam's mum.

"We both work full time, Maria. Who would take care of him? He can't even breathe on his own! He would need feeding, washing, full time care," he responded wearily.

"Dad! What else would we do? Surely, you're not suggesting switching off the life support?" Sam said raising his voice.

"No, of course not, I'm sorry… this is hard on us all." His voice cracked and I moved away from the door back to the bedside of Ben.

I could still hear them but at least it felt as if I was trying to give them privacy. I didn't know much about human illnesses, but I had attended a class on 'Death and Serious Injuries in Mortals' and it had briefly covered comas. I had interpreted it as being similar to the transition stage from human to vampire, which puts you in a sort of stasis, except instead of it being between life and death it was between death and undeath. "Minimal conscious," that sounded worse than being a ghoul. I looked down at Ben's still face, he looked different to Sam, his hair was a lot darker, more like his mother's and his skin was slightly more tanned, his eyes were closed so I couldn't tell what colour they were.

In the car, on the way back I thought about what Sam's father had said about most coma patients like Ben that recovered being "Unable to communicate, seem to be incapable of experiencing pain or suffering." I could not help but wonder, is that what I live in, a 'minimal conscious state'. If I was tied to these machines and examined would they think it better to pull the plug on me?

Later that evening Sam dropped me back at Jessica's house and after exchanging farewells, I settled in the kitchen. Once there I couldn't stop thinking about Sam's brother lying motionless in that hospital bed. How his family watched over him and held onto the hope that he would one day wake up. Had my own human family clung to such hopes? Had they looked for me? Sent out whispered prayers for my return? For the first time I hoped they hadn't, I hoped they had carried on with the rest of their lives, seeing how Ben's condition affected Sam and his family I would not have wished that on anyone, especially those I once loved. When I got back to Jessica's, her mother was still worried about my pallid appearance, and seemed to think that my visit to Sam's brother had not been a good idea.

"It's a shock to see someone in that state, I don't know why he dragged you along, it's all very morbid." Mrs Young started as I hung my coat up.

"If it were me I'd want to be switched off, what quality of life will the boy have even if he awakes? Sam's father should know better being a Doctor himself." Jessica's father was even less sympathetic.

After their opening statements, I was in no mood to chat, so I excused myself to regurgitate the undigested sinigang, unsure as to whether it was my allergy to human food, or the lack of empathy Jessica's parents showed that caused it. Regardless, the sounds of me retching caused great concern to Mrs Young, who even banged on the bathroom door asking if I was okay. After reassuring her it was just the food disagreeing with me, and that I was neither suffering from some stomach illness or an eating disorder, I escaped to Jessica's room and changed into a pair of her pyjamas, before acting out the motions of a human going to sleep. Once the rest of the house was sound asleep I switched on the lamp and decided to flick through one of Jessica's beauty magazines as Princess nuzzled against me. Talk about emaciated! Some of these models were skinnier than me and I lived on a liquid diet, I paused at a picture of a model sporting a natural sun kissed tan just like the one Jessica had, the caption at the bottom read *'Spray tan for that healthy glow that makes your skin look alive and fresh! Open late every day!'*. There was a phone number at the bottom asking to contact the shop for more details. It was late, but within the opening times listed, so I grabbed Jessica's cell phone and dialled the number; after a few rings a young woman answered.

"Hello, Top Tanning, Tina speaking," she said brightly.

"Hello, I would erm.. like my skin to look like the girl on your advert," I answered, unsure.

"Erm..okay sure, when would you like to make an appointment for?" Tina continued.

"Tomorrow evening," I replied.

"We have a free appointment tomorrow evening at seven."

"That's fine," I replied. Jessica's grandmother's funeral would be finished by then, I thought to myself.

"What's your name?" Tina asked.

"Scar...Jessica, it's Jessica Young." I corrected myself.

"Okay, Jessica, I'll pencil you in. Have you been to a tanning salon before?" Tina inquired.

"No," I said flatly.

"Okay, that's not a problem just remember to exfoliate before you come and make sure your skin is free from any products and wear something loose fitting," Tina said in routine fashion.

"Right. Thanks," I said.

That wasn't too bad I thought as I hung up. By this time tomorrow I was going to experience my first spray tan and if it went well, it was something I could do on a regular basis. This could be the key to sorting out the issues of paleness I had experienced today, I would finally look just like the rest of them. I smiled to myself as I took one last look at the picture of the girl in the magazine before closing it.

Chapter 12

~Jessica Wednesday~
Day Three as a Vampire

The draught Mistress Varias had made worked perfectly. I was still wide awake by the time Wednesday morning came. I spent it lingering in the kitchen with Mary and Cecile, hoping I would get a chance to bring up the siring process without Kristian interfering like before. He was currently out, part of his Tribune Restraint Order involved him visiting his assigned Watcher once a month. The process consisted of a ghoul monitoring and essentially tick boxing Kristian's routines. However, my hopes of gaining any insight from the blood dolls were dashed, as not only had Dante materialised but both were suffering from the 'Gluttons', an overwhelming urge to eat large quantities of food, an apparent side effect of binging on vampire blood.

"I'm starving, why is there never anything to eat around here?" complained Mary as she peered into one of the cupboards despairingly.

Dante looked at her like she was simple, she noticed and merely rolled her eyes.

"I know vampires don't eat human food but I thought Kristian would have at least gotten the house ghoul to buy some, we practically live here!" she said exasperated.

"You are mistaking my brother for someone who cares for human needs," Dante retorted.

Mary ignored him and, instead, grabbed a tin from the cupboard.

"What's this? Looks like some sort of casserole?" she said swishing the tin about.

"That's ghoul food, if you want human food, Mildred will happily oblige, she doesn't get to cook much for obvious reasons," Dante said.

"Oh yeah, ghouls don't drink human blood like vamps do they?" said Mary scanning the label on the tin.

"They do, it's just the lingering human in them still craves solids," he replied.

"What does human derivatives mean?" asked Mary, squinting at the list of ingredients on the tin's label.

"It's the undead food industry's way of advising that inside that tin are all the parts of a human that would not be considered edible," said Dante.

"Edible human parts?" said Mary and I could see why blood dolls irritated Scarlet so much; these people spent so much time around vampires and ghouls on a daily basis, feeding on each others blood yet still knew nothing about them.

"Come, dear, you didn't think the animated corpses walking among us live on a diet of fresh fruit and veg did you? Just look at him!" said Dante, pointing at Herb. "As I mentioned, they need solids not just blood, and solids would constitute as human remains."

"That's disgusting," she said placing the tin firmly back on the shelf.

"Indeed but necessary, prime cuts such as lean muscle are hard to come across. What that cheap substitute contains are the leftovers after everything else has been stripped away, such as the stomach, brains and intestines," Dante continued, ignorant of Mary's growing discomfort.

"Okay, now I'm hungry," said Herb shuffling over to the cupboard and claiming the tin. Mary watched in disdain as he ripped it open with his bony fingers and began eating the mashed pulp straight from it.

"At least use cutlery!" said Dante disparagingly.

The smell combined with watching Scarlet's zombie BFF shoving remains of jellied brains into his mouth was too much for me to handle. I held my hand over my mouth and willed myself not to be sick, Dante noticed.

"What on earth's the matter Scarlet?"

"Nothing," I replied hastily, but he continued to stare suspiciously until Mildred appeared and enthusiastically set about trying to create a human meal. Both blood dolls squealed with delight and even Dante and Herb seemed intrigued by the idea. An hour later though, the premature thanks seemed to have died in their throats as they watched Mildred stir her famous 'Ghoul Gruel' which she had modified for human consumption. Her change to the recipe didn't make the grey slop look or smell any more appetising. Despite this, both girls must have been hungry, because they ate it. Mildred, mistaking their grimaces as they spooned it into their mouths for appreciation, eagerly dished them up seconds. Herb thinking I must be hungry also, handed me a glass of blood with a sprinkling of cinnamon on it, causing me to form my own grimace. I excused myself and dashed upstairs to throw it down the sink. By the time I came back down, Mary and Cecile had migrated to the living room. Their hunger sated they were now napping fitfully, having claimed a chaise longue each. A pile of magazines lay nearby on the floor, I grabbed one called 'Gossip Ghoul' and opening the first page began to read.

"After much speculation the reality vampire star Eva Vonkarstein, famed for her risqué selfies with blood dolls on Nibbler, has admitted to getting fang fillers. Eva shot to fame through her vampire vlog 'How to Look Good Undead' but what every undead really seems to be interested in is the size of her fangs which have grown visibly over the years. A number of photos have been posted by rival vampires showing Eva with a much more modest set of fangs."

I flicked the magazine shut with disgust, and picked up a copy of Recently Risen instead which had done a spread on blood dolls. This was more like it I thought as I flipped to the article, there was bound to be something about siring in here, so I started reading eagerly.

A blood doll is a life not just for feasting on: Choosing a blood doll can be the simplest of acts or it can be a very long process depending on the standards of the vampire. Those who enjoy brief encounters visit the Blood Dens where the Mademoiselles in charge will ensure a sated visit and the efficient staff quickly clean up any mess.

Others, who want one for an extended period, will take their time in searching out one with just the right qualities. There are many ghoul-run blood dolls agencies for this, such as Plenty of Flesh, Mort-Match and Bloody Good Times. Obviously any human who has a tendency to be squeamish will not do.

Manners and Meals: Increasing Abuse of Blood Dolls
Some blood dolls are easily misled vulnerable to members of our kind who wish to dominate and control them. A mortal who is quick to learn will not fall prey to this easily as they would soon realise that we need their blood more than they need us. However, inexperienced blood dolls will suffer regular abuse from vampires who think they can get away with it. The Tribune are looking at ways to stop this - the mandatory procedure of registering blood dolls is part of this. This ensures that if something untoward happens, the Wardens are able to track the vampire down. There are also outreach programmes in place where blood dolls who feel they are being abused can seek advice.

Many of our kind view blood dolls as prostitutes for the undead and publicly verbally abuse them.
Clementine Cooper, a blood doll for the last ten years, speaks out against this behaviour.

"We are not blood whores or fang fappers or any of the other things they call us. We are more like you than you think, we are lost souls in need of companionship, it's not just about being fed on, it's about finding a connection."

Clementine has released a book about her experiences called 'Vampire Addict: Passion with a Parasite.'

Are you guilty? Recognising whether you are guilty of this type of abuse is the first step a vampire needs to take.

Do you constantly make condescending comments about the shortness of your blood dolls' lives, talking about their certain death to cause them distress?
Do you stop feeding when they give the safe word or do you carry on regardless of their pain?
Ghouls are not blameless, often seeing blood dolls as targets for easy business sales, flogging samples of blood, pretending it will give them immortality if they drink it.

What a load of rubbish, I thought as I discarded the magazine with a frustrated sigh. This was useless, it seemed that vampires were willing to publish any old drivel except something relevant, like how you became one. The magazines had given me an idea though, I would have to investigate these Blood Dens, anywhere that had a multitude of vampires desperately seeking blood, was bound to be a good idea. So with that in mind, I went back upstairs and looked for the city guide I was given when I first arrived, lucky for me there was a section on Blood Dens.

According to the guide there were a few in the Vampire quarter, but most of the Blood Dens were in what would pass as an undead slum, which lay between the Trade Quarter and The Ghoul Quarter. I hoped there would be less chance of someone recognising Scarlet there. I kept my eyes open looking for hidden signs or shady individuals, but to my surprise, they were not the inconspicuous buildings I would have imagined. Flashing neon lights declared services on offer such as live feeding shows, one place had window displays of humans performing self-mutilation then wiping their blood on the glass to attract customers. One human behind a window was even erotically washing herself under a shower of blood.

All of these places were in direct competition with each other and so put on the most lively advertising possible to sell their wares and trade. I headed towards one called the 'Quick bite', two vampires were just leaving as I approached the door, one had a backwards cap on, a long thick gold chain around his neck and jeans so big they looked like they were falling down. The other was wearing a hat that was so loose it looked like a floppy sock, a checked shirt and a pair of jogging bottoms that were tucked into his trainers.

"Fancy another?" said the one with the backwards cap on. "We could try Dolls House in the vamp quarter, it's more pricey but they do a lot more blood play in there, think of it as starter before you get to the main course," he nudged his companion enthusiastically.

"I'd better not, two humans a night is my limit, otherwise I start trying to sire them." The other slurred back.

They staggered past, but as I did, I caught the eye of one of them.

"Hey! It's Scarlet isn't it?"

I eyed him warily and he removed his cap.

"It's Ted, I know your brother Dante," he said while making gestures with his hands.

"Oh right, of course," I replied stiffly.

He looked back at the Blood Den, then to me, his face breaking with realisation.

"I didn't know you visited the dens?" Ted said.

"Yes, although I would rather you kept this from Dante, I don't think he would approve," I warned him.

"Yeah, Dante's so fussy about where his blood comes from, don't worry, Scar, your secret is safe with me," Ted replied, nodding knowingly.

I watched them walk off before finally entering 'Quick bite'. I had seen documentaries about human brothels so I had a certain expectation of what a vampire's version would be like, but I was still shocked by what I saw. It looked more like a scene from a horror film, the room was dark and grimy. A male ghoul with a handlebar moustache and greasy slicked back hair greeted me with a smile, exposing yellow teeth and rotten gums.

"Whatcha looking for?" he rasped.

I scanned the room, there appeared to be no separate rooms, just beds with dirty looking curtains pulled closed; through each one I could see shadows of figures embracing each other, and from each one the sound of grunts and gasps could be heard. I watched the shadow of a particularly large figure clinging to a smaller figure, a guttural roar emitted from behind the curtain and a high pitched scream followed in its wake. The ghoul followed my gaze,

"There's an hour wait for a bed, what meat you after?" He asked.

I hesitated, I hadn't been planning on actually booking a session with a blood doll, I was no real vampire after all. What I wanted was one of the vampire patrons.

"We have Weeping Willow in tonight, she's one of our best bleeders to date," said the ghoul, wiggling his eyebrows and grinning suggestively. This already creepy little scroat became even creepier as his entire face sagged during the attempt to hold a smile. The ghoul procurer interpreted my repulsion for a 'no' and instead handed me a brochure.

"These are the other humans we have on offer, for one hundred Drakmir you get an hour's feeding time, we ask that you don't feed the dolls your own blood as we need them to stay sober to work," he said with a low bow.

I took the brochure and sat down next to the other waiting vampires, flipping through it.

"What you going for?" asked a male vampire.

I flipped through the pages of humans, next to a photo of them was a small caption listing the services they provided.

"I'm still debating, how about you?" I asked eager to keep the conversation going.

"I picked a deep throat service, I haven't had any throat for ages. My ex-blood doll kept saying she understood my condition and would support me, but every time I tried to go for the throat she said I was moving too fast and that she "needed more time," the male vampire said woefully.

"Yeah, most humans don't like neck biting because of the whole power thing, wrist biting is just as dangerous though," chipped in a female vampire with the red mohawk.

"It was mainly the mess that put her off, it's a lot bloodier, plus the horror stories of feeding fatalities that spread around this city don't help, she kept saying a blood doll has the right to choose," the male continued.

"You should've just lubed her up with your vamp blood, she would soon have come round," said the female vampire.

"I told her straight, I'm a jugular vamp and if she didn't let me feed from there, I would feed on it from someone else. I mean you don't read about Dracula taking it slow, no, he goes right for the throat."

"Did it work?" I asked.

"No, she's now sharing blood with some New Age vamp who apparently is a lot more patient and gentle than me."

"Damn!" said the female vampire shaking her head.

"Worst part is she let him feed off her jugular, I saw them at 'Plasma' last Friday. When I asked her, she gave me some crap about how he explained the fact that the blood in arteries along the neck are richer in nutrients, and that is the true reason vampires feel the urge to drink there."

"That's smart, you gotta give the vamp credit for that line," the female vampire countered.

"She said once she realised it wasn't just a power trip, she was fine about it and if I had bothered to explain it to her she would have happily let me feed there."

"Could have been worse, I once fed from a girl who wouldn't even let me drink from the wrist, I had to settle for biting her inner elbow, you know the part where human doctors draw blood from. She was never really interested in being fed on anyways, she was just in it for the potential of being sired."

"You can always tell when you get one of them, withholding blood unless you give them a set date when you will turn them," the female vampire said, nodding in understanding.

"So glad they brought in the 'One Sired Policy', now I just quote that. Anyway she ended up getting what she wanted though, she found one of those illegal siring pits," the female vampire concluded.

My ears perked up, this was intriguing and just what I was looking for.

"Siring pits?" I interjected.

"Yeah, the Wardens closed most of them down but they started another in the basement of Willy's house," the male explained.

"That's risky," said the female vampire. "Isn't he currently on trial with the Tribune for selling dead blood?"

"Yeah, but he's desperate, the amount of legal fees he's having to pay have almost bankrupt him."

They started discussing the state of the undead legal system but I was no longer listening, I was heading straight for the door.

"Where ya going?" yelled the ghoul procurer but I was already outside, spurred on by new hope.

Becoming a vampire legally was such a long-winded process that I could see why human blood dolls would opt for something as medieval sounding as a Siring Pit. Luckily for me, I had educated myself a bit on the laws down here. After I had taken the draught from Mistress Varias, I needed something to help pass the time and had gone for a wander within the house. I had found one of Scarlet's father's books about Vampire Law in his study, and read all about the SRA (Sire Regulation Authority), every siring had to be authorised by them otherwise it was viewed as illegal. They would do all sorts of background checks such as checking if the human is certified as a blood doll and also if they had any criminal convictions, the SRA believed that if a mortal cannot abide by human laws then they will not abide by undead ones.

I only had to ask one ghoul for directions to Willy's, it was a dingy looking building with no doorbell. I tried the door, but it was locked, it seemed ghouls actually locked their doors unlike vampires, so I started banging on the door instead. It opened a little and a ghoul, wearing a purple velvet jacket, orange satin shirt and a large pair of gold aviator sunglasses, stared back at me, to top it all off he was sporting a lopsided 70's perm. He squinted at me suspiciously.

"Yes?"

"I heard you are siring vampires?" I declared.

He jerked his head left and right.

"Keep it down will you!" he hissed. Then he looked at me properly.

"I know you, you're one of Desmodeus's brood, got his family watching me now has he, well I ain't telling you nothing!" he said, slamming the door in my face.

Slightly shocked, I gave myself a minute and knocked again, but this time I got no answer. Getting sired in a city filled with vampires was surprisingly hard it seemed but it was almost impossible trying to do it in the guise of Scarlet, who was not only already a vampire but also related to the members of the institution that enforced the laws restricting it. The disguise was now necessary and a hindrance.

When I got back to Scarlet's home, the rest of the family were in the living room. Kristian was back from his TRO meeting and in a foul mood. Apparently his Ghoul Watcher wanted him to help out with a program they were trialling through the undead clinic 'Coffin Crisis'. It would involve weekly visits to the clinic, to talk to fledglings about how he managed to successfully leave one of the most notorious vampire gangs.

"This is a new form of torture, it's not as obvious as being chained up and stabbed with hot pokers but it is torture none the less," he seethed.

"I think it's sweet they want you to help the newbies," cooed Mary.

"I think it says a lot about today's vampires, the new generation of undead have it a lot harder than we did," said Dante, looking up from a book he had propped open on his lap.

"What makes you come to that conclusion?" Kristian challenged.

"In this book I am reading, Dr Ervin mentions how much more of a struggle immortality is to vampires sired within the last century," Dante proclaimed.

Kristian rolled his eyes.

"I'll probably regret asking this, but let's hear it then, I want to know how this quack justifies such a statement."

Dante turned to the page he had open and began reading aloud.

"Young vampires have it harder than their ancestors due to having higher expectations at living a normal life. With the rise of vampire fiction, they feel that humans will be accepting if they discovered our existence. They have become resentful to the ancient codes and rules that forbid any human and vampire integration above ground. This pent up frustration and anxiety from wanting to be accepted can lead to EDS (Early Decomposing Syndrome)."

Dante stopped reading to glare at Kristian who had burst out laughing.

"Vampires suffering from anxiety? Does this tripe constitute as writing nowadays?" Kristian exclaimed.

"You are ignorant to the issues among the newly bitten, I have learnt a lot from Ted, being younger than myself he has helped me see things differently," Dante responded.

"Our father's generation had to live through vampire hysteria, they were hunted by zealous demon slayers throughout their fledgling years. Do you recall father telling us his own wife's grave was dug up, a stake driven through her lifeless body and then set on fire? Yet Fledglings of today are upset because they can't create a social media account or stream a youtube channel, excuse my lack of empathy," Kristian argued back.

After more bickering about modern day vampires, Kristian eventually got bored and turned the TV on to watch an undead Game show called NewlyDead, where the contenders had to guess who the fledgling was when they were alive. As I stood there, watching the undead equivalent of junk TV, I realised with panic, just how much time I was wasting. I was going to have to throw all caution to the wind if I wanted to get turned before Sunday.

Chapter 13

~Scarlet Thursday~
Day Four as a Human

*"The busy world is hushed,
the fever of life is over
and our work is done"*

The next morning I made sure to check myself in the mirror, I was still pale but my eyes remained the same bright blue, more importantly, my fangs hadn't returned since last night's kiss with Sam. Perhaps it was just a minor glitch in the spell and out of all the vampire traits that could come back, paleness was not the worst of them. But if all went well tonight, a solution for that was already arranged. Just in case, I decided to ring Jessica.

"What's wrong?" she croaked groggily.

She didn't sound as if anything bad had happened just annoyed at having been woken up.

"Do you still look like me?" I asked, trying to keep my voice casual.

"What? Of course I do, is why you woke me up at 6am? Are you drinking enough blood or have you just gone senile in your old age?"

"Just check for me, go to the mirror and make sure nothing has changed," I told her.

"Ugh!" she huffed and I could hear her down the phone, throwing the duvet off in irritation and stomping across the room to my mirror.

"Yes, I still look like I'm anaemic and need to gain at least a stone…why?"

"Just checking that the spell is still working," I replied.

"It's working, calm down, it should be me that's paranoid, at least you can do that vanishing thing if you get found out."

"I don't partake in materialising," I responded, rather more defensively than I'd intended.

"Well, you can run fast then. Anyway was that all you rang for because I would like to get some sleep while I can, today is the first time I don't have your ghouls hovering over me and I need to catch up on some serious z's, being a vampire is tiring." A small yawn followed her statement.

"Where are they?"

"I gave Mildred a long list of chores to do downstairs and sent that cretin Herb on a shopping trip, so no need to worry, okay bye!" She rushed her words, trying to end the conversation.

"Wait!" I snapped.

"What now?" she huffed.

I gave a brief pause, conflicted by what I could stand to lose, before I forced myself to continue.

"Your Grandmother's funeral is today," I declared.

"Oh yeah," she laughed. "I completely forgot about that."

"Well, don't you want to attend?" I said, more than a little confused.

"Why would I? She's dead - it's not like she will notice I'm not there, besides you're there in my place so no one will ever know," she said nonchalantly.

When she put it like that it made sense, but even with my lack of emotion it seemed a little odd, but I was starting to learn how complex human relationships could be, and how strangely fickle they were in some ways. Just looking at her relationship with Sam for instance, one moment they are an item the next she is chasing someone else. I put it down to options and having too many of them; why would a person want to settle when there were so many other opportunities out there, especially when humans had so little time on earth? Even as I contemplated this I couldn't help but think of my previous evening with Sam...maybe some opportunities were better spent than others though.

We arrived at the funeral home a little after ten in the morning. The service would begin at eleven in the morning at the local church, before moving onto the reception. I calculated, that it would finish at six giving me enough time to get home, get changed and make my appointment at the beauty salon. The funeral home itself was about as well lit as the Underdark, I guessed viewing the deceased required little light and as I stood in the corner of the room feeling awkward I watched the people in attendance; everyone was speaking in hushed tones and looking sombre. Even Leyna, who was too young to fully understand the concept of what was going on, merely sat quietly on her father's lap, her small fingers clutched around his tie and her eyes fixed on the coffin in the centre of the room. The humans took turns to walk up to the coffin and pay their respects; they would stand there for a few moments, utter something, then move on, it seemed quite orderly.

I remembered reading about the natural state of death in ghoul school and how, when an animal loses its offspring, it will often carry it around with them for a while afterwards or linger near it. When it came to my turn, I followed everyone else and walked slowly and deliberately towards the coffin, bowing my head, I stared at the body and was filled with curious thoughts. I had seen photos of what Jessica's grandmother had looked like before in her photo albums, her short hair styled in tight curls of a pale blonde, large glasses and a warm smile that seemed to be permanently on her face, except for now. Now, lying here in her wooden confines, mouth pulled tight in the rictus of death, eyes sealed shut in eternal sleep. Her hair was uncurled, slicked back in limp strands that looked more green in the dim light than blonde. I reached out a hand and touched her cheek, it felt clammy and clay-like. I half expected her to move, the dead skin stretching itself into a smile like I had seen so many times among my own kin, the creaking of joints as stiffened limbs reanimated themselves. But this was not a vampire's death, this was real death, the type I would have suffered had I not been turned. She looked so fragile that I thought my touch would leave a mark, but the skin had taken on a rigid quality.

I sensed the hand before I felt it on my shoulder yet still I flinched, human touch was something I was struggling to get used to. My own kin didn't tend to touch each other, the only thing close to intimacy we had was when we were feeding.

"Everything okay Jess?" a deep voice asked.

I turned to look at Mr Young, his grey eyes were brimming with tears.

"Yes," I mumbled as he squeezed my shoulder.

"People are waiting to say their goodbyes." I looked behind him and saw the queue of people all dressed in black wearing solemn expressions.

I moved aside so those waiting could look upon the body, I listened to them paying their last respects and noted that some spoke as if they were paying a normal visit. "See you again someday," they whispered, others like Mr Young openly wept, their shoulders shaking silently as their grief took over.

Once everyone had paid their respects, she was carried down the hall and delicately placed into the back of a black car. We drove to the service with the coffin in the back of the vehicle, the scent of flowers and death as heavy as the silence. We pulled up at a church and I entered it with trepidation. I was old enough to know such places did not hurt my kind but it still didn't feel right being there. As we walked down the aisle and filed into one of the benches, I looked up at the effigy of Christ, hanging from the cross. His eyes seemed to move and fixate on me, the shepherd spotting the wolf among his flock. I quickly looked down at the programme I had been handed, *"In memory of Joan"*. I flipped through the few pages, hymns, a poem, then some more hymns. I frowned, thinking back at what Mrs Young had said about her mother not being religious, it certainly seemed like a religious funeral to me. I suppose some humans had to keep up certain appearances even after they had left the world.

I managed to sing the hymns out of time despite following the programme and copying everyone else, singing like a human was difficult, despite the fact that, unlike ghouls, vampires had pleasant voices. This was because of the amount of emotional content carried in it, a vampire could sing a song beautifully but it would not sound as beautiful as the way a human singer could sing it, we have the talent but not the tenderness. Even harder than singing, were the prayers. It didn't feel right for me, a creature part demon, to be uttering words deemed holy. I knew my father prayed regularly but he had once been a religious man, he had carried that belief on through death. I had no recollection of such devotion and it seemed unnatural for me to start now. But I read them anyway, after all, the point of this experiment was for me to experience all aspects of being human and blind faith was a part of that. After the prayers, Jessica's father took to the altar, his hands were visibly shaking as he read from a card. I felt uncomfortable watching him so I let my gaze sweep across the other guests. It was a mistake. They were all weeping silently into their hankies, some held hands in support. If I had felt uncomfortable before, I felt more so now. I was like a visitor from another world staring at an alien race where I had no understanding of their customs or emotions. I shifted my gaze again, this time choosing to focus on the coffin; it was made from mahogany. Dante's was not dissimilar except his had silver handles and this had brass. The flowers on top were white lilies and covered almost the whole lid. I carried on with this train of thought throughout the rest of the service; it seemed to help.

Afterwards, we were driven to the reception in the same black cars, to a posh looking hotel. As I followed the mass of mourners I wondered how long these things went on for, my natural instinct was to prey on the weak and the lamenting mortals were like ripe fruit for the picking. I reached inside my bag and felt better when my hands touched the plastic case of one of my blood packs. As soon as we were inside I excused myself to the toilets, managing to slip away before Mrs Young could offer to come with me; that was another strange thing I was noticing about mortals. They did absolutely everything together even defecate. As I entered the ladies I was about to dash into an unattended cubicle when a high-pitched screech stopped me in my tracks. I turned my head to see a large middle-aged woman applying bright pink lipstick to herself in the mirror, her eyes fixed on my reflection.

"Jessica, is that you!" She turned and gave me a huge smile. I noticed some of the lipstick had gotten onto her teeth.

As soon as I nodded with acknowledgment, she engulfed me in a tight embrace, despite her heavy fog of perfume I could feel myself attuning to her pulsating blood. I bit my tongue to distract myself until she released me and stood back, her eyes tracing my face.

"You've grown so much since I last saw you! You were always pretty of course but now... well, you're the picture of your mother when she was the same age," she said.

"Thanks," I replied, unsure of what else to say.

She looked down and then squealed again, taking me completely by surprise.

"This must be little Leyna. Oh, what a precious thing you are!" She cooed.

I scowled, Leyna must have followed me in here. The woman squeaked again as Leyna too was made to suffer the ritual crushing embrace. I took my chance and dashed into the cubicle, closing the door and locking it behind me. To my horror the woman continued to talk to me through the door.

"So sad about your grandmother, although she did live a long and happy life." she said.

I ripped off the cap of the blood bag and sucked hard on the nozzle with practiced ease.

"Did your mother mention anything about the house in France?" she asked.

"No," I said, the sound coming out as more of a gurgle than a word through the mouthful of blood.

"No? Oh well, of course she wouldn't, much too early to be discussing such things I suppose," she murmured. "Although," the woman prattled on, "It is such a lovely property, with such a pleasant location it would be a shame if your mother did not inquire, I could even come and help her modern up the place if she liked. I've always wanted to go back there for another visit, I could even bring my daughter Molly and her boyfriend," she went on.

I finished the last of the pack and let out a relieved groan as my hunger diminished.

"Are you alright, Jessica? You've been in there for awhile? Is it that time of the month? If so I have some pads on me, I know you youngsters prefer the tampons but I just can't get used to them myself."

"Er... yes that's it," I called back, hastily wiping the blood from my lips.

"Here, I'll pass you some under the door," she replied.

I stared down as a small purple packet appeared; I opened it up and found a wad of white spongy towels. I inspected one, curiously unfolding the small white wings, then shoved it in my bag.

When I opened the door the woman placed a hand on me.

"All better now?" she cooed.

I nodded and went to wash my hands, scrubbing the red stains from my fingers. My throat still felt like it had a lump in it but the dryness had gone and I had stopped shaking. As we went back out and joined Jessica's parents in the lobby I discovered the woman was an Aunt of Jessica's.

It intrigued me how large human families could be, grandmothers and grandfathers, aunts and uncles, cousins, nephews and nieces, and then relations created by affinity. I had learnt in my human studies how important families were for the socialisation, as this was how humans learnt how to behave.

A train of waiters and waitresses had started to move around the room holding out trays of miniature food. I felt a wave of nausea as one waved rows of small squares topped with something pink and slimy under my nose. I shook my head firmly and he moved onto the next person. I spent the next few hours doing this as more trays were brought out. Throughout the whole event, people kept coming over to take Mrs Young's hand in theirs and give condolences. Some even took my hand, flinching at its chilling touch. I forced what I thought to be a smile of thanks, but it only seemed to encourage further words of pity. After the humans had their fill of rich food and alcohol, more speeches were made in honour of the departed. As I listened, instead of feeling closer to them as anticipated I felt detached and undeserving, I had no right to be here. I didn't know this person they all spoke of so fondly as they reminisced. I was surrounded by people but felt more alone than ever. I thought about all the blood dolls living among vampires in the Underdark, how they all knew this would happen to them one day, that it was the natural order. But it wasn't, they knew there was an alternative. It made me finally understand why they gave themselves to us like they did, maybe the fear of death was worse than any pain or humiliation we could inflict. I watched them all, now knowing their curse. They were doomed to die and knew it, they went through life facing that fear. I had always taken my immortality for granted, even hated it because it was linked to my condition, the reason I needed blood - my eternity's price. Everyday humans faced the struggle of keeping their frail bodies going, vulnerable to diseases, freak accidents, homicide or in some tragic cases suicide. If they were lucky enough to escape these threats they would eventually fall to old age, where they would slowly deteriorate until their body could no longer keep up. I felt very foolish, my whole time as a vampire I had been wishing for a mortal life, I had grown tired of immortality. Yet after seeing all of this I feared the idea of death more than ever.

When we finally got home at six, I had almost forgotten my appointment at the tanning salon until I checked my phone and saw a reminder text. Jessica's parents didn't seem happy that I was going out straight after the funeral but they were both too tired to argue and so let me go. For a moment I contemplated staying with them instead, but then I caught a glimpse of my pale face in the hallway mirror and darted out the door.

I entered the tanning salon a few minutes before seven. I had taken the advice of the girl on the phone and chosen to wear a pair of Jessica's grey sweatpants, a loose black t-shirt and some flip flops. Underneath I wore her black bikini, as they had recommended a swimsuit. A woman in a white smock stood behind the desk, she had a very orange face and when she smiled her teeth were so white it was almost blinding.

"I have an appointment for seven," I said.

She scanned the book in front of her with a long pink nail.

"Jessica Young?"

I nodded as I took in the surroundings, apart from some shelves lined with tanning products it was quite bare, the white washed walls and polished wooden floor gave it a clinical feel. There were some seats and a table stacked with glossy magazines, all showing models on the cover with perfect looking tans. I felt a shiver of excitement run through me.

"Are you over eighteen?" she asked frowning at me.

I was probably older than this building.

"Yes, I just don't look it," I said.

"Appreciate it while it lasts," she said blinding me with that smile again.

She looked at me closely taking in my translucent skin.

"Do you have any pre-existing medical condition that we should know about?"

"Yes, I am a creature of the night!" I said.

She looked at me and then laughed.

"Very good, well we'll soon get some colour into those cheeks and you won't have to worry about those type of jokes," she replied, with a wink.

"I think for your skin type we should start you off at a 3 minute session, next time we could increase it, I just don't want to risk you burning."

The idea that I could obtain a tan in 3 minutes was baffling, what human invention could hold such power?

"The beds are through here," she said with a smile and wandered off into a room.

When I entered the room, I gripped my towel tightly with both hands. The bed looked like a large coffin filled with tubes of light, I froze as an angry hiss escaped from my throat, causing the receptionist to step back in fear. Another lady quickly entered the room.

"What's going on?" she said her eyes roving between the receptionist and me.

"I'm not sure, she just froze on the spot when we came in here?" The receptionist said.

"Maybe she's having some sort of panic attack?" The newcomer replied.

The receptionist stood directly in front of me, her large orange face blocking my view of the vampire torture device.

"What's the problem my love?" she said brightly, while casting anxious glances at the other clients watching on curiously.

I pointed wordlessly at the machine with a quivering hand.

"I was meant to be sprayed," I managed.

"Sorry it must have been a mistake, we had down a pre-sunbed booking beforehand but we'll just go ahead with the spray," the receptionist reassured me.

She motioned for the newcomer to move me away from the machine and into another room where the spray booths were. I got unchanged and was then led to one of the tent-like booths. Jessica's bathing suit was smaller than the underwear I normally wore, so I was feeling suitably exposed, but the lady remained impassive to my near naked state.

"Now step into the sticky feet," she instructed.

"What?" I asked in confusion as she pointed to a pair of black foot-shaped pieces of foam on the floor.

"They protect you from getting the tan on the soles of your feet," she explained.

I stepped onto the sticky feet and into the tent where the lady proceeded to hose me down with brown liquid, occasionally calling out instructions such as 'Close your mouth' or 'lift up your arm'. Next I was blasted by another hose, but this time it just shot air at me. Finally I was told that I could get dressed. I admired myself in the mirror, I was a few shades darker than Jessica's normal colour, but I didn't look pale anymore. I smiled, happy with the outcome, after paying and reassuring the manager I was no longer traumatised, I left.

It was late when I got back to Jessica's. For a vampire who had lived over a century it had felt like a very long day, the longest of my long life. I also felt very empty so I drank another blood pack as soon as I got back. Jessica's parents were in the lounge watching TV, Leyna was in bed and I was thankfully alone in Jessica's room. I could have gone downstairs and watched TV but it still felt like I was intruding on their mourning. I suddenly had the urge to talk to Sam, but had no idea why. It wasn't like I had spent a lot of time with him but when I had, I had found his presence comforting. I scanned the photographs on Jessica's walls, searching for one of him without her. It was petty but I wanted to appreciate him without having Jessica smile back, reminding me of what I already knew, that 'he' just like her 'life' was only on loan. Then I had a thought and grabbed her phone from inside my bag. I flicked through the hundreds of selfies and finally came across a single photograph of him. His green eyes were squinting at the camera, it was a sunny day and his hair was shorter. I think I preferred it now. I thought of the way he ran his hands through it when he was nervous. I sat back on the bed, fully absorbed in his image and finally realised why I felt so empty.

Chapter 14
~Jessica Thursday~
Day Four as a Vampire

I couldn't believe it was Thursday already! And I was still no closer to becoming a vampire. It didn't look like my progress was going to improve much today either as Desmodeus had materialised in the early hours of last night, with news that there had been an outbreak of FF rioters in the Ghoul Quarter. He had returned with his father to the Tribune Tower very early this morning, to assist with the patrols. It must have occurred a few hours after I had left the Blood Dens. The Wardens were on patrol now, so my hopes of finding a siring pit were growing increasingly unlikely. With the Tribunes eyes and ears sniffing around and FF members stirring trouble, ghouls like Willy were going to be even more suspicious of anyone inquiring about such things. The sound of Scarlet's phone ringing startled me, I quickly answered it, trying to keep my voice as low as possible. It was Scarlet of course, no one else knew I was here, she wanted to know if the spell was still working. For someone who had been on this earth for such a long time, she could be extremely dense. If the spell had worn off I would hardly be answering my phone. From what I had learnt so far about the way their society worked, I would have been hauled up in some cell of the Tribunes being interrogated by now. I had read a lot about the Tribune over the last few days, especially their methods of punishment. Which ranged from being buried alive to 'The Walk of a Thousand Bites', where the accused vampire was marched through the four quarters of the city surrounded by crowds of bloodthirsty undead, who would throw themselves upon them and take turns in biting them. Not too different to how crowds of humans would throw rotten vegetables at a criminal in the stocks, but with teeth...lots of teeth. This form of punishment seemed common. True Death, as they referred to it, was less so, probably due to the effort it took. I read about one case where a vampire lost control in one of the Blood Dens, afterwards he was forced to drink the blood of the twelve blood dolls he had killed during the rampage. Dead blood it seemed was the vampires equivalent of food poisoning, it made them very sick and could incapacitate them for a short while. The most interesting fact, was that if drank in large quantities, it would even kill them. Scarlet's sudden panic did have me slightly concerned though, so I humoured her by checking myself in the mirror. The smooth pale face that stared back was enough to reassure me. I decided to pretend to Scarlet that I still needed sleep, I didn't want to mention my dealings with Mistress Varias, or anything that might arouse suspicions. I had little time left and the last thing I needed was her returning early because she was worried about me being found out. Herb was still out shopping for me and Mildred was repairing a load of Scarlet's clothes that I had purposefully damaged.

With my ghoul shadows dispensed with, I made my way to the living room to determine what the rest of Scarlet's family were up to.

Kristian was there with both blood dolls as per normal, all they ever seemed to do was lie there feeding off of each other, it almost made me see why Scarlet thought being a vampire was dull if this was what she had to learn from. Cecile was lying on her back in the middle of the floor staring up at the chandelier and muttering about how pretty the crystals were. Mary, who was a slightly more lucid, was cross-legged on one of the chaise longue's reading a human fashion magazine. She had gone back to her own place last night, wherever that was, to get fresh clothes, after hinting loudly how nice it would be to have a place to store her things here. Subtlety didn't work on vampires, Kristian bluntly retorted back that he did not want human clutter littering his immaculate bedroom. Kristian himself was leaning over Mary as she read, feeding from her neck, and kept stopping in between mouthfuls of blood to comment on the articles.

"Ten ways to make your boyfriend want you more," he read aloud.

"Less is more, by not telling him about your day at work or the latest gossip from your girl pals, you will make him even more interested in you, a mysterious girl is far more alluring." He laughed.

"Is this what human males crave? A woman who keeps secrets just to appear interesting, what utter idiocy!" he proclaimed.

Mary pouted.

"Don't you ever wonder what Cecile and I are up to when we're not here with you?" she pined.

I couldn't give a fiddle what you girls do above ground," Kristian replied.

"What if something happened to us, like we died, you would notice if we didn't return wouldn't you?" Mary continued.

"Yes, and I would miss your veins. But don't see that as an excuse for me to turn you, before you start harping on about that," he said coldly.

Mary sighed and snapped the magazine shut, Kristian, ignorant to her frustration, wiped the blood from his mouth and, grabbing the magazine for himself and began flicking through the pages.

"The current generation of vampires complain about being undead, but do you think humans are happy with their appearance? Just look at what their perception of beauty is." He held up a perfume advertisement with a human female model on it, she was pouting at the camera with a faraway, look in her eyes.

"A photoshopped stick insect with a mouth like a duck. They've taken out all the life from this woman, no sign of a vein anywhere, it barely makes me peckish."

The door bell sounded and both Mary and Cecile jumped up, looking at each other excitedly. Kristian raised an eyebrow unimpressed.

"Let me guess you've ordered another one of those crates?"

In waddled Mildred carrying a box and before she could speak it was torn from her arms and ripped open as both blood dolls snatched at tiny plastic figurines, they started squealing over them.

"You've got to be kidding me, they've now made dolls for blood dolls..." Kristian laughed at the irony.

"Not just any doll," said Mary defensively. "These are Dead Dolls, a new range from the ghoul brand 'Mortal' who make lots of collectables for blood dolls."

"It's to resemble our idea of what beauty is," explained Cecile, pointing out the tiny fangs that had been painted on the doll's face along with the pale eyes and vampiric skin tones.

"You can even buy ones with their own blood dolls," she added.

"So it's a blood doll, with a doll, who has a blood doll?" said Kristian in disbelief.

Ignoring what Kristian had said, Mary followed up.

"But the best thing is that you can get them customised to look like your vampire, as well as get the blood doll to look like you, so they can be together for all eternity!" she cooed, as she hugged the doll.

Kristian laughed cruelly.

"Well, that's the closest you're going to get to it." Then he stopped and glared at them both, as a thought occurred to him.

"If either of you dare get one of me, I will kill you both. Vampire laws aside," he said with a scowl.

Dante wafted into the room forming fully by the box, his face full of curiosity.

"Oh no, not you as well!" said Kristian pulling out a blood vap and shoving it between his lips.

"I just wanted to see what all the commotion was about, it was disturbing my reading;" said Dante.

Both blood dolls jumped up, eagerly showing him their dead dolls.

Mildred shook her head.

"Back when I was among the living, young ladies filled their time with going to dances or having afternoon tea. Not playing with children's toys," she tutted.

"You have to admire the details they've gone into," said Dante, examining a miniature-sized blood pack.

There was another knock on the door, Mildred went to answer it and returned some moments later, she was even less amused than before. It turned out not to be another delivery for Mary and Cecile, but an undead reporter from the Daily Departed looking for Dante. He was searching for a story on Dante's previous brush with the law, it seemed being taken in by the Tribune this week, had made him popular with the undead media. Despite their positions of power, neither Scarlet's father nor Desmodeus had been able to stop the story being leaked to the public.

"I sent him away, but that will be the first of many now that your past has become public knowledge," said Mildred before returning to finish her chores.

Dante put his face into his hands.

"I cannot abide this. Soon every vampire will think I have been trawling above ground feeding off any intoxicated mortal; no one will trust my tasting skills ever again!" He lamented.

Luckily for Dante, he would not have to focus on the press for much longer, as the next knock at the door turned out to be a pleasant surprise. It was Michael from the Blooderie, a high-class blood doll. It seemed that the two had formed an attachment to each other. Michael entered the parlour room and took his place by Dante's side, while Kristian turned up the TV as footage of Dante's face flashed up on screen.

"Why are all the news channels still covering you as being a suspect? You were already cleared!" demanded Kristian. "What about other news, I haven't heard anything about the raid on the Ghoul Quarter last night. It seems they are using our brother's scandal as a smokescreen to distract the undead community about the real issues."

"A human still died," said Mary, taking me by surprise that she knew what was going on, let alone had an opinion on it.

"Humans die every day, and my brother had nothing to do with this boy's murder. It was probably some sireless fledgling. They should be focusing on trying to prevent such occurrences instead of using Dante as a scapegoat. They have nothing to tie him to this boy's death, it looks as if someone is trying to discredit our family," Kristian said irately.

There was another knock at the door.

"Who in blazes is that now?!" yelled Kristian.

Mildred went to open the door, but shuffled back in shortly, looking at the floor.

"Sirs..." She sniffed.

Following just behind her were two large vampires, dressed in black suits with long dark cloaks. They looked at the family members with scrutinising eyes and after a long minute, one of them finally spoke.

"Dante Lucard!"

Dante and Kristian turned and looked at each other.

"Enforcers...What are you doing here, do you know who's home this is?!" said Kristian aggressively.

"Dante Lucard, new evidence has arisen, implicating you in the murder of a human boy. Under the authority of the Tribune, I place you under arrest for suspicion of a Feeding Fatality!" the Enforcer shouted back.

Barging past Mildred, the two Enforcers moved forward and took Dante by the arms, escorting him out of the living room. Kristian and the blood dolls jumped up in protest and followed straight after, Mildred lagging at the rear. There was raised, but muffled voices, before a slam of the heavy front door.

Well...that was unexpected, I thought to myself. Just when I thought time wasn't on my side, it suddenly was. With the entire household now out, I grinned and said out aloud.

"Whatever, shall I do now..."

The after effect of last nights FF raid was evident even on the streets of the Vampire Quarter. Already the ghoul shops had started investing in better security, as I strolled through I noticed the Blooderie had installed new heavy iron bars across its front windows and door. The atmosphere was different too, vampires in support of the FF were lingering on the streets in groups casting harsh eyes and jeering at passing ghouls. But it was when I reached the Ghoul Quarter that the aftermath was most obvious.

"Having lower supernatural status we get little or no help from the undead authorities," moaned one ghoul to his friend as he swept up broken glass from the front of his shop.

As I reached the Ghoul School I found it too had been a target of the FF riot, the tall windows smashed in and the plaque torn from the wall and smashed into pieces. As I was still taking in the carnage, the double doors, which surprisingly had remained intact, burst open as undead students milled out down the stone steps. Among them was Grace.

"Hi Scarlet," she rasped. "All lessons have been cancelled until further notice due to last night's events. A group of FF managed to break in and set fire to the classrooms; it's frightening isn't it? I thought this type of thing only happened above ground but obviously not," she said, a slight frown on her face.

"What sparked it all?" I asked. "There's been no coverage on the news at all."

"Word among the ghouls is that it broke out in the Mixology bar I was telling you about. A ghoul was accused of feeding on a vampire's blood doll, so the vampire and a few others dragged the ghoul outside and set fire to him. A few ghouls tried to intervene and call a Warden but then the FF showed up and, taking advantage of the chaos, began ransacking all the ghoul shops. When the Wardens did finally show up they arrested the ghouls that tried to help but didn't make any attempt to arrest the vampires responsible for the ghoul who had been burnt to death. The FF soon cleared off once the Wardens arrived so they got off scot-free also," she explained. Grace continued to comment on the unfair treatment ghouls received while I pondered what to do about this news. With the school closed Varias would be at her shop, she had said previously that she did not want me coming to the store to discuss anything regarding the life swap but if she was not at the school it left me little choice.

Grace invited me to join her for a drink, not wanting to be on her own in the aftermath of the riot, but I made my excuses and headed for 'Toil and Trouble' in the Witches Quarter instead. When I got there the door was open, but the witch was nowhere in sight and even more odd was that Gron's cage was empty. I considered leaving, but stopped and listened as I heard something. There was the faint sounds of chanting coming from the quarters below so I made my way to the staircase and quietly crept downstairs, the sounds of chanting getting louder. Everything I had seen about witches from films, books and the internet flashed in my head. I expected the worse, were they summoning a demon or perhaps sacrificing some poor innocent? Maybe this was a trap, maybe Varias was planning to sacrifice me?!

None of it could have prepared me for the scene that met my eyes. Sitting on the floor in a circle were four witches, the fire in the hearth gave them an eerie glow, each had their own ink spells which slithered about in the firelight. One witch had her arm raised and was waving something, while yelling some word. As I crept closer still I started to make out their clothing...they were wearing... onesies! More than a little confused I approached the group and noticed on the floor in front of them lay a board, at first I thought perhaps it was a Ouija board. But no, the board they had in front of them was a Scrabble board. Scattered around the board were empty bottles and what looked like a bowl of crisps along with a purple dubious looking dip. I noticed Varias on the other players, a tiny white kitten, that I had never seen before, curled up on her lap, fast asleep.

"For the last time Sebastian, 'AFC' is not a word!" protested a witch with large black rimmed glasses and red hair held scrappily into a floppy bun.

"Show's what you know, Fiona. It's text speak in the witching community for 'Away From Cauldron'," Sebastian said.

"That's such rubbish and you know it, and for the love of Baphomet will you stop chanting, Audrey!" retorted Fiona.

The witch Audrey who had been sitting cross-legged chanting with her eyes closed opened them and glared back resolutely.

"I am merely invoking the blessing of the Fates, there was nothing stated against it in the rules."

"Can't we ever just play a normal game?" moaned Fiona.

"Witches, we have company," said Varias, suddenly fixing me with a glare.

They all stopped talking and looked up at me with intrigue, Varias rose and motioned for the others to do so.

"I think our game has ended for tonight, I will see you all again next Thursday. Remember it's your turn to bring the dip next time, Sebastian," she said pointedly.

The other three witches gathered up their belongings and filed up the stairs, still arguing about the game they had just left. Varias and I were finally alone.

"Scrabble?" was all I that could manage after a minute.

She shrugged.

"There's not a lot of social events for witches down here, once a week, one of us will host a gaming night, we also play Ludo and Monopoly," she said matter of factly.

"How exciting! And here I was expecting to find a coven summoning demons," I said condescendingly.

Varias frowned.

"Never mind what I choose to get up to during my free time, why are you here? If it's to purchase something from my shop let's go upstairs and I will assist you but if it is for any other reason I'm afraid I cannot help."

"I'm running out of time, I only have three days here after today and I know you can help me get what I want," I stated.

"You want me to help you turn into a vampire? Do you know what could happen to me if I got caught aiding a human in receiving the dark kiss? My licence to trade as a witch among the undead would be taken away from me for a start! Then serving a long sentence locked away in the Tribune Tower, which I am told, makes the Tower of London look like a five-star hotel," Varias said darkly.

"It can't compare to the punishment you will receive if the Tribune find out you gave Scarlet a Morshard necklace to perform a glamour so she could live with my family, while I was forced to stay here in her place," I replied in a warning tone.

"Forced? You willingly agreed to come here, my dear. I am a witch living alongside the unliving, I may play board games but I could also make you disappear without a trace. Gron could slice through your bones like they were butter." The kitten meowed in agreement, I looked at it again more closely and noticed it had red slits for pupils.

Varias laughed.

"Yes, that's right, it's Gron. I don't just do glamour spells for vampires, this is his friendlier form that I use for trips above ground and on the odd occasion I entertain here. He can come across intimidating even to other witches," she smirked.

The kitten version of Gron sidled up and pressed himself against Varias's legs as if he knew she was talking about him. I saw, dangling from his collar, a small red stone identical to the one in the necklace that Scarlet had given me.

"He's wearing a Morshard?" I asked, but deep down knew the answer.

Varias picked him up and stroked him.

"Yes, as you are well aware they are the key ingredient for glamour spells as well as possessing other powers. On that note I would like to remind you that your necklace only protects you against vampire blood magic not witches' magic, which I can assure you, is far more potent. So I don't think it wise to threaten me, especially since I am the only person who can help you," Varias said with a smile.

I opened my mouth to argue but then thought better of it and said quietly.

"I thought you said you wouldn't help."

She motioned for me to wait and went upstairs, I heard her locking the shop door, when she returned she had two glass vials and a syringe in her hand.

"Take these, they won't turn you. But they will aid you."

I stared at the vials curiously as she handed them to me, one was filled with a white crystallized substance and the other a dark red liquid.

"I will tell you what to do but as before there is a price," Varias continued.

I rolled up my sleeves to offer my blood again, but Varias stopped me,

"No, not now, I will let you know when I need it," she said calmly.

And with that, I listened and made my second pact with the witch, hoping that this would ensure me a place on the siring waiting list.

Chapter 15

~Scarlet Friday~
Day Five as a Human

Tis true my form is something odd. But blaming me is blaming God
Could I create myself anew, I would not fail in pleasing you.
John Merrick

College passed by in a blur, I managed to perform Jessica's solo in dance class, I didn't get the best marks, in fact to my surprise I scored the lowest, but at least it was my own creation. I hadn't borrowed it from anyone else and Mrs Darcy, the Dance teacher had said that it was seamless in its presentation but needed more emotion. I took that on board as constructive criticism. Drama class, however, was a much more frantic affair. It was the final rehearsal before tonight's opening performance, Ms Fenwick rushed about, making sure stage positions were correct and cues on time. I however was calm, I knew my lines, I knew my spots, I just hoped that somewhere I could find the emotion needed to make my character believable. In a mere few hours, I would be up there, revealed to crowds of humans.

The play, was like nothing I had ever experienced, I could finally see why Dante loved the theatre so much. The rehearsals had been a pain but the actual performance was worth it and the audience clapping thunderously as we all stood in line and bowed was exhilarating. Throughout the duration I had experienced something I had never thought possible, I was no longer Scarlet, the girl who died so long ago, I wasn't even Jessica, the girl whose life I had stepped into. I was a character telling a story to the audience. I was acting, playing someone else, but for the first time I felt as if I was exposing myself, showing some real part of me that had never been shown before. I even found myself surprisingly moved when at the end Sam recited a diary excerpt from Treves, the actual doctor who took in the real John Merrick, regarding the poor man's death.

"He often said to me that he wished he could lie down to sleep 'like other people'. I think on this last night he must, with some determination, have made the experiment. The pillow was soft, and the head, when placed on it, must have fallen backwards and caused a dislocation of the neck. Thus it came about that his death was due to the desire that had dominated his life - to be 'like other people."

The last sentence rang in my mind in with the applause.

After the play Jessica's parents wanted us to go out to celebrate and even invited Sam's parents who politely refused as they were going to visit Ben instead. It worked out for the best though because Leyna started fussing as she had caught a head cold, so they decided to go straight home and put her to bed. I lingered and said that the student cast were going out for drinks, but really I wanted to spend time with Sam. I found him backstage with Katie who was removing the prosthetic pieces from his face; it reminded me of Herb when he exfoliated. With his make-up removed, we finally got outside and Sam went to help Katie load her make-up kit into her car. I stood there waiting when I felt a hand on my back, I flinched and spun round to find it was the blonde boy, Dean, from Jessica's Philosophy class, he was holding a bunch of flowers. He handed them to me with a smile so predatory that he could have been mistaken for a vampire.

"You were magnificent tonight, Jess," he said, then casting a glance over to Sam who had joined us as Katie drove off.

"Shame the same can't be said for others," he added in a voice so full of scorn it made Kristian's jibes sound respectful.

"A group of us are going to 'The Crow' for a few drinks with the rest of the cast if you fancy ditching the Elephant man," he followed up.

"No," I said, hoping he would leave without an argument.

But he laughed bitterly at my response.

"What has happened to you, Jessica? You've spent the whole week acting like a different person. You don't bother with your friends anymore, Hannah said she can't have a proper conversation with you, while Nikki says you snub them to sit with that loser Penny."

He leaned close and spoke in my ear.

"That's not all that's changed, you used to have a better taste in men. Have you forgotten me so easily, or do you just need a little reminder?" He wrapped his hands around my waist, but was suddenly pulled off me.

"Get off of her!" growled Sam, a look in his eyes of pure hatred.

"I was merely commenting to Jess on your poor performance, you're vegetable brother would have injected more life into it," Dean sneered.

You didn't need to be a vampire to know what was coming next. I could have prevented it easily but instead, I watched as Sam's fist hit the side of Dean's head, knocking him to the ground. He stood over him breathing hard, both fists clenched. Dean crawled backwards on the ground looking with a mixture of fear and outrage. He touched his head which was bleeding.

"You're out of your mind!" he spat. "I could do you for assault!"

Something within me knew I had to pull Sam away, but with Dean bleeding I was finding it hard to concentrate. Dean was now looking at both of us wide-eyed.

"Jess, you can't seriously want to be with this psycho over me!" he pleaded.

My throat tightened and my fangs tingled under their glamour, but I found Sam's hand and grasped it. When our hands met I felt the primal urge to feed slip away and as I turned to Sam I noticed that his rage had also faded, he looked at me his eyes large and fearful.

I threw the flowers on the ground and turned to leave, Dean shouted abuse at us, as we walked, Sam didn't seem to hear as he led me to his car parked nearby. It must have turned colder because his breath, which was coming out fast, became clouds on the air, proof of the life within him. My own remained stagnant and absent of occurrence and I stared at it wistfully, as we walked in silence. Until quite suddenly he stopped and turned to me with a determined look in his green eyes.

"If you wish you can join the others tonight, I won't be welcome now but you can go and have fun," he said in earnest.

"I would rather stay with you," I said without hesitation.

He smiled, and reaching out, stroked my cheek before frowning, "You're still cold, let's get you in the warm."

We drove straight to Sam's house and he cooked Pizza for us; it was just as bad as the other human dishes I had been forced to consume during my time as Jessica, but I did find myself making more of an effort to enjoy it. Ultimately it was futile, my demonic body could no more tolerate the food Sam created as I could appreciate the songs he wrote. I sat in the company of this human male whose gifts were wasted on me, yet I still continued to pursue this fruitless quest. After food we talked, or more accurately I listened, as Sam talked. I found I had little to confide, not being Jessica, but I was fascinated by learning about Sam, so I found it easy to contend myself with hearing about him. He apologised for losing his temper at Dean, although I had thought the reaction more than justified. The boy had not only been having relations with Jessica, who at the time was still with Sam, but had also insulted Sam's brother who was seriously injured. Even I could see the callousness of that. He explained that he just snapped, he was worried about Ben the doctors had spoken with his parents the night before and said they wanted to take him off life support.

"They said we should start looking at end of life care and consider their organ procurement policy." He sat back on the sofa and shook his head. "I was with Ben last night and I was playing his favourite song on my guitar and he opened his eyes and looked at me, when I told the doctor that he said it was an automatic response," Sam said, eyes welling with tears.

"My brother looked at me, actually at me, not an automatic response. He recognised the song.... and all they care about is taking his organs," he continued exasperated.

I was well aware of the need for organ donors, it was one of the highest commodities among the undead, so I could only imagine how valuable it must be for the humans who needed them to stay alive.

A body with failing life versus a life with a failing body.

I could see why doctors would make such suggestions. But seeing how much Sam believed his brother still had a chance made me wonder, if I were in the same position, would I be so logical. I was still struggling with the ethics of it all when his parents returned, they greeted me and asked if we had eaten already, before giving an update on Ben. It was all very positive, too positive compared to Sam's account. One risk of Ben's coma was that he is more susceptible to infections and respiratory problems. When Ben had first fallen into coma, these things had been a major issue, however it had since improved. In fact the doctors had advised that this very night his lungs had shown no signs of congestion. I wondered if the conversation would have been so optimistic if I had not been there. Sam's father seemed tired and said goodnight, but Maria made herself a tea before going to the computer in the living room. After a few moments, she called me over to show me Ben's social media page, which consisted of lots of photos of him along with comments from well-wishers, she talked for a while, reminiscing on Ben growing up, it was a verbal catalogue of his existence.

Afterwards, Sam gave me a lift home, when we got to Jessica's front door we stopped and looked at each other. I knew from human films that this was a common spot where the boy would kiss the girl, so I stood ready and waiting, but instead, he frowned at me searching my face as if confused.

"What?" I asked after a suitable amount of time had passed, without so much as a peck on the cheek.

"I don't know, you just seem so different," he said with a smile but still a slight frown.

I stiffened, I had become too relaxed. I had been acting on my own needs and not thinking how Jessica would act, first Nikki and Hannah, then Dean tonight. And now Sam could see I wasn't the same person.

"I like it," he said softly and stroked my hair from my face.

"Coming to the hospital to see Ben, helping me learn my lines in the play, coming over tonight and listening to me moan about my problems when you could have gone out with your friends. I appreciate it, I'm just not used to it," he said smiling.

I didn't know what to say, it surprised me that such simple gestures seemed out of character for someone who he was supposed to be in a relationship with. Jessica didn't seem to be performing any of the needs expected, physical or emotional, it baffled me as to why she even dated Sam.

But before I could think anymore on it, he suddenly fulfilled my needs. That kiss I had been waiting for, he took my face in his hands and pressed his lips against mine. This time I tried really hard, I kissed back, unlike our first kiss in drama where I had been like a statue. But I also tried to be gentle and kept my demonic desires in check. He ran his hands gently through my hair and I reciprocated, running my hand up the back of his neck until they were in his hair holding the back of his head. I was completely caught up in him, I wanted him like I had never wanted anything in my life – but not in that way, not in the way I was used to. This ran deeper than any need for blood, into the hidden human within me, long dead urges rose up unbidden. I released a sound involuntarily but it was a moan, not a hiss, growl or snarl, it was the most human sound I had ever made. Sam was moaning too and it was also unlike anything I was used to hearing because it was unaccompanied by pain, just pure pleasure. I felt his hand move from my hair and on my chest, running over my breast or Jessica's breast, I didn't care anymore, I just wanted him to continue touching me. I grabbed his other hand and placed it there also and he willingly obliged. I moved my own hands to his belt and began undoing it, like I had seen in the human films, but then he pulled his mouth away from mine,

"Jess, not here - not like this, we're on your doorstep," he said quietly.

"So?" I murmured as I found his lips again and continued pulling at his belt.

He moved his hands away from my chest and gently placed them on my shoulders to restrain my advances.

"Because your dad could find us here any moment and I really don't want to be in that situation. Look I want you so much, but we have to be sensible, I don't even have protection on me."

"Protection? I'm not going to hurt you," I laughed. "Unless you want me to." And I spun him and pinned him against the wall kissing him again. I didn't care if Jessica's parents or the whole street saw us, I wanted to feel him against me, I had been waiting for this for so many years. This was the connection I needed and now I had it, I didn't want to stop.

"Jess, you don't know how much I hate saying this but we have to stop..." Sam said.

"No!" it had come out as a growl, it seemed it wasn't just the human in me that wanted this but the demon had also decided it didn't want it to stop.

I tore his belt loose and threw it on the ground, before tearing at his jeans.

"Come on, Jess!" Sam said, more serious now. Before trying to remove my hands. But I was stronger, much stronger and in the process my hand which was now inside his jeans, slipped and I heard him gasp as one of my nails scraped against his lower abdomen. My nails had turned to their glass like claws again, but I hadn't noticed, I was too fixated with Sam.

"Jess, you've made me bleed..." Sam said, a little shocked

"Enough talking!" I snarled, slamming him again against the wall, but this time so hard it winded him. Then I saw his face under the porch light, his eyes searching mine again but this time in fear.

"Your face...," he said.

I let go of him and reached for my mouth before quickly covering it. My fangs were out and Sam had seen them. And if my fangs were out, then the rest of me must be.

"I don't feel well," I blurted out, before turning my back on him. I fumbled through Jessica's bag, desperately searching for the door key.

"What just happened?" asked Sam.

"Nothing. I feel unwell. Must be the stress of tonight's performance, good night!" I stammered, as I finally found my key.

I scrambled in and locked the door behind me, without a backwards glance at Sam. Once upstairs I checked myself in the bathroom mirror and saw to my horror, that not only had my fangs returned, but my eyes were milky white and my skin had paled to match them. I moved to Jessica's room and grabbed my supplies from under the bed, before draining two packs of blood. I sat there for awhile, trying not to think of anything. When I had finally calmed down I went back to the bathroom and checked myself again. The glamour was working as intended, I must have just become overly excited. It didn't make any sense for me to become so out of control like that, I was acting like a fledgling and it hadn't even been over blood, it was over sex. A human need that didn't hold any purpose or attraction for my kind. I had never craved such a base form of human intimacy before, a hug yes, a need to be embraced, even a kiss. But the full messy process of human intercourse, never. Yet I could feel the way my body tingled when Sam had laid his hands on it. But now I had a bigger issue, Sam had seen what I really was. Maybe he would shrug it off, a trick of the light, the effects of all that caffeine earlier, bad pizza, a bad dream? But as I sat and waited the night out, I couldn't shake the feeling that I had broken yet another undead law.

Chapter 16

~Jessica Friday~
Day Five as a Vampire

There was a solemn mood in the house, I had overheard Kristian talking to Mary and Cecile in the living room. Herb and Mildred were in attendance also, so were fully appraised of the situation. Within hours of Dante being taken away, the Tribune had ruled that he was the number one suspect and was to be put to trial immediately. Kristian supposed that political enemies of House Lucard had bribed or influenced the Tribune into pushing for an immediate trial. With Scarlet's father out of the city and Desmodeus distracted with the FF riots, it would have been impossible for either of them to return in time and intercede on Dante's behalf. Dante had been made the scapegoat and the Tribune was intent to throw the full weight of the law at him.

I found it amazing that such a thing could happen so quickly, but I supposed when you dealt with impossibly old and powerful creatures, who didn't sleep, things would naturally move faster. With the household appraised of the situation, we each made preparations. I knew there was no way of avoiding this one, not turning up to court would have sent clear messages to the rest of the family that something wasn't right. I had intended on using the vials today, but sadly due to this inconvenient court case it would have to wait.

We met Desmodeus at Tribune Tower, he had been the one to insist all family members attend. It was a show of broodling support and familial strength. The Tribune Tower was the equivalent of the local Civic Centre in the human world, except a lot bigger and the fact that it was also the place where interrogation and torture occurred. Its tall foreboding structure seemed more like a statement of power than an architectural signature. It had twelve levels in total, in addition to the Chamber of Decree; which was the courtroom; and the lower level dungeons. The rest of the tower housed Divisions specialising in overseeing different departments of the Tribune. These consisted of the FSA (Feeding Standards Authority) where Desmodeus worked, they were responsible for regulating feeding issues, such as the quality of blood on the market and whether it was legally obtained. Then there was HR (Human Resources) who oversaw the treatment of the Underdark's human citizens, ensuring blood dolls were registered and regulating the health and well being of blood dolls and witches residing in the city. The Division which sounded the most interesting was the one Scarlet's father worked for, The SSA (Supernatural Sorcery Authority) which oversaw magical practices such as maintaining the supernatural security spells which included the cloaking spells over the Underdark, the magic gateways which provided access to and from the city and the tracking of its citizens by magical implants. They also regulated the witches by making sure they and their summoned demons were registered legally.

A female ghoul was sitting at a large reception desk as we entered through the revolving doors. She nodded in greeting to Desmodeus and passed us a book to sign in. As we took turns to sign a male vampire in a pinstriped suit approached the desk.

"Jenny, cancel my 10 o' clock and send a cleaner to level four, I just had to fire three employees for gross misconduct and there's ash everywhere." he said.

After Jenny the ghoul made arrangements to sweep up the three vampires, she advised us that the hearing would be held on level nine. I eyed the marble stairwell with trepidation until I saw with relief Desmodeus marching over to a set of lifts. As we got out at level nine a large vampire, wearing black robes with a hood obscuring his face, approached and shook hands with Desmodeus.

"Good morning, Desmodeus. How's the dead blood case going?" he asked in a deep voice.

"Good morning Gideon. Slowly, the accused ghoul Willy claims to have been tricked into buying the botched blood," Desmodeus replied.

"A ghoul like Willy tricked into buying something he didn't want? He just needs someone to help loosen his tongue, let me know if you need my assistance," Gideon said eagerly.

"You have my gratitude Gideon." He pointed to the large sledgehammer the vampire was carrying. "A new form of punishment?"

Gideon gave a dry chuckle.

"Yes, you know how I love to embellish. I call this the Hammer Horror experience, makes them go weak at the knees every time."

Desmodeus turned to us once Gideon had disappeared into the lift.

"Gideon is our Head Executioner, he is known as Gideon the Destroyer in smaller circles," Desmodeus said with pride.

"Nice work colleagues you have, I always wondered why you never invited them over," muttered Kristian.

Desmodeus led us to the waiting cells next to the courtroom. This was where Dante was being held. There were a number of cases scheduled before Dante's, so Desmodeus decided it was prudent to prepare Dante for his hearing one final time. We all filed into the cell, where Dante already sat at a table. Desmodeus took the spare seat while we took to the side benches. Desmodeus opened up his briefcase on his lap and sifted through some documents.

"Lets see who's up first, ah! Winifred the Wicked vs Liam Hickey; a witch on trial for Possession. The ghoul claims he was forced to act on behalf of Winifred for several months, illegally importing vampire blood above ground to her coven before he was able to break free of the binding spell cast on him."

"I thought ghouls were immune to witch binding spells," I asked.

"Most are, but fledgling ghouls are more vulnerable, but it is still very rare. Although don't think that hasn't stopped some ghouls from trying to claim differently, the first thing that Willy said when we arrested him was that he was forced into it by a witch." He shook his head in disbelief, before turning to the next page.

"Igor the Impudent vs the Sire Regulation Authority. Aha! Yes, I remember an email about this one! A vampire who faces sterilisation by having his fangs removed. He is responsible for the siring of over forty ghouls in the last year, all authorised by the SRA but the fact they all failed to fully transition has raised concerns. Currently, the number of ghouls being created is a lot higher to that of vampires. It is quite a controversial case, if the Tribune decide that Igor is a valid candidate for sterilisation it will be carried out even against his will. It's all part of the new legislation for reducing the growth of the ghoul population," Desmodeus informed.

"Hmmm forced sterilisation, now where have I heard of that being done before? Oh yes, didn't some German politician invent that and it led to...what was it again? Oh wait, World War two!" Kristian responded baitingly.

"Human history is irrelevant," said Desmodeus. "This is about our world and how we protect it. Undead population control is essential for keeping our existence a secret. Just because we have the ability to create more like us does not mean we should. It's not like we're in danger of dying out. If everyone just adhered to Sire Planning the Tribune wouldn't have to resort to such methods."

"Oh, so it's really an undead alternative to birth control, except it's more rebirth control, and here I thought it was a way of weeding out the weak, controlling the blood pool to what you deem to be fit, similar to what the FF advocate."

Desmodeus sighed. "Really, Kristian, I thought your anarchist days were behind you, stop trying to be a white knight about everything."

Just then Desmodeus's phone rang, after answering it, he handed it over to Dante.

"It's at the Tribune Tower," Dante paused, there was a garbling sound from the phone.

"The tall tower in the centre of the city," Dante paused again, to more garbling.

"Level Nine...." Dante said wearily, before hanging up the phone, he looked concerned.

"Was that your lawyer?" asked Desmodeus.

"Yes, he... er...had a little trouble finding the place," Dante replied, sounding disconcerted.

"He had trouble finding the Tribune Tower? How can you miss an eyesore like this?!" said Kristian, before narrowing his eyes in suspicion. "You never mentioned how you found your lawyer?"

Dante suddenly became very interested in the frills of his cuffed sleeves and started tugging at them, before answering quietly. "He was recommended to me by Ted."

Even Desmodeus looked shocked by this news. "Dante, you told me you found him through an acquaintance at Blue Bloods?"

"Ted has been to Blue Bloods as my guest," muttered Dante now looking deeply distressed.

"You let that feeble minded fledgling talk you into using his lawyer? Dante, socialising with the fool is one thing, taking legal advice is another entirely! Probably the difference between proving your innocence and being chargrilled on a wooden stake!" yelled Kristian.

Dante didn't respond but it was clear he was growing more concerned as the minutes passed. Eventually, almost half-an-hour later, a ghoul with a briefcase, a bright pink tie and polyester suit entered the cell. What made him look especially bizarre though was the Barristers wig he was wearing, which was far too large and kept sliding off his head.

Dante rose from his seat and stared at him in disbelief. "You're my defence lawyer?"

The ghoul blew his nose on a handkerchief, examining the contents carefully before replying. "Yes, Mikey ...I don't have a surname yet but I've applied for one," he offered the hand still holding the used hanky then thought better and lowered it.

"But..but...there must be some mistake, you're a ghoul," spluttered Dante.

"The first ghoul qualified in Undead Law, I have all the required documents if you wish to see them," said Mikey with an obvious sense of pride.

"I would like to see them immediately!" demanded Dante.

Mikey opened his briefcase on the table and pulled out a soggy looking certificate. "Oops, left my Stomach and Kidney pie on top of it, some of the digestive juice may have stained it, I wrapped it up in greaseproof paper but you know what it's like."

Dante looked at him, clearly insulted that anyone could suggest he would know what it would be like to have anything to do with a Stomach and Kidney pie.

"Well...Mikey, it looks like you're qualified for the job," said Desmodeus peering at the certificate.

Dante made a faint moaning noise, before passing the certificate back to Mikey, he sat back down, staring blankly at the wall, with a look of defeat. Kristian's phone suddenly rang, it was Mary.

"I told both of you I would be at court today, can't you do without for one day? I don't care if you have a migraine, take some paracetamol like any normal human, my blood is not an open all hours pharmacy!" He hung up in outrage.

Mikey pulled out a small card from his top pocket.

"I also represent ill-treated blood dolls," he said, handing it to Kristian with a grin, which turned into a wince as the former grabbed him by the throat.

"Listen you swindling, smarmy git! If my brother gets found guilty for this I will show you the real meaning of ill-treatment, now get preparing, we're due in court any moment."

With introductions out of the way, Mikey and Dante went through their defence strategy, Desmodeus occasionally interjecting to add points while Kristian continued to glare at Mikey menacingly. I sat quietly, debating when I would be able to sneak off.

An hour later an Enforcer entered the cell, informing us that it was our time. Dante and Mikey entered the chambers courtside, while we exited and went through the main doors to the stalls. We took the seats at the front of the gallery, just behind Dante.

Mikey, Dante and the prosecution were seated at their tables on the other side of the bar. The jury was present and seated, with just the judge to enter and begin proceedings. A few moments passed before a voice bellowed, 'ALL RISE!'.

We did as commanded before an ominous figure in black entered the courtroom, his long, flowing cloak draped behind him, making him look like a floating apparition. The cloak was hooded and loosely draped over his head. He walked with heavy, deliberate footsteps, each pound of a boot ringing out like a metallic cacophony as the loose buckles rattled in time with his steps. When he reached his bench, the judge finally turned to look at the assembled court, I held back a gasp, he had no face. The judge wore what seemed to be a brightly polished gold mask, devoid of any features. The only noticeable thing were two thin slits where his eyes should have been, which emitted an eerie red light. The dress, movements and actions, all gave the
impression of malign power. After what seemed like an age, the judge finally and slowly sat down, the creaking of leather ripping through the silent auditorium as it adjusted to his form. With the judge finally seated, the courtroom followed in suit in total silence, before a final voice echoed;

"Court is now in session."

The judge addressed the room in a cold voice that resonated through the Chamber.

"Mr Dante Horatio Caspian Elliot Lucard, you are here today, because you stand accused of a Feeding Fatality of the first degree. You failed to take adequate precautions thus resulting in the loss of life of the said human, Thomas Miller. This crime was committed above ground at a human hotspot, risking the exposure of our kind, as well as costing the Tribune a huge amount in undead funds to cover up. A number of human authorities who witnessed the bite wounds had to be enthralled and an increased number of Wardens put on patrol, in the belief that this may not have remained an isolated incident."

"Oh, because that's what really matters, how much Drakmir the Tribune had to pay out," muttered Kristian.

The Prosecution opened with their first witness. Their lead was a tall, modern looking male vampire, who was well groomed and had a chin-strap goatee, he wore an expensive looking dark navy suit, a total contrast to Mikey. It was more than possible that he had been a lawyer before he was turned.

"I would like to call my first witness to the stand, a Mr Todd Wake."

"That's Vincent Lapelle," murmured Kristian before looking at Desmodeus in shock. Desmodeus returned the glance, also worried. Lapelle was known as one of the best and most aggressive lawyers in the city, winning large payouts for his clients, along with the most severe punishments for his opponents.

A young male human sauntered in, he was covered in bite marks and had dark shadows under his eyes which darted nervously around the room.

"Who's this blood junkie?" said Kristian quietly.

"Quiet!" Desmodeus warned him.

"Mr Wake is a regular donor for the Blooderie in the Vampire Quarter and has had many dealings with the accused," said Lapelle.

"How dare you! I tasted him once and sent him away, just look at his veins sticking out like ropes under that sallow skin," said Dante rising from his seat in outrage.

"The accused will take his seat and refrain from speaking in the Chamber until his turn in the witness box," said the judge.

"Mr Wake, how do you know the accused?" asked Lapelle.

Mr Wake hesitated then at a nod from the prosecutor started to speak.

"He comes in the Blooderie, he fed off me there."

"Was it just the one occasion?" Lapelle continued.

"No, he took me back to his place after and continued to feed, even though I said I did not want to." Todd sniffed for effect.

"You're suggesting that Mr Lucard forcibly fed off you?" Lapelle confirmed, before turning to the jury.

"Yes, he used that mind trick."

"Oh? So in fact you're saying Mr Lucard ENTHRALLED you so that he could feed off you without your protest is that correct?" Lapelle said before turning to the jury and raising his eyebrows, clearly trying to evoke a response from the crowd.

It worked, as a gasp followed by a low mutter echoed around the courtroom.

"What preposterous lies!" bellowed Dante.

"Mr Lucard, you shall not be warned again," said the judge.

"Did Mr Lucard pay you for your time?" asked Lapelle.

"Yes, he gave me fifty Drakmir to keep me quiet, he said he already had a previous history and didn't want to get into any more trouble," Todd confirmed.

"If you had not been under the influence of the enthralling charm would you have considered sharing blood with the accused?" Lapelle was leading to a conclusion.

"No, he made me feel degraded, he did not disguise the fact that he wanted to, in his words, 'Mutilate me'. He was very rough and did not care that he was hurting me, in fact he seemed to take more pleasure in this." Todd was on the edge of sobbing.

"It must have been so traumatic for you, you have my sympathies. Thank you Mr Wake, no more questions." He finalised. It was a strong opener, the witness had been very well rehearsed, right down to the timed sobs, Lapelle also had a strong sense of charisma, that had the jury and crowd hanging off every word.

It was now the defence's turn to lead with questions, so Mikey approached the witness box, his wig lopsided.

"Mr Wake, it states on your feeding forms that you were only employed at the Blooderie for one day before your services were no longer needed, do you know why you were unsuccessful as a donor there?" Mikey began.

Mr Wake shrugged. "It's a snobby place, they were prejudiced against me."

"Or perhaps it was because your blood did not meet the standards required?" Mikey went back to the table and opened his briefcase, he removed and held out a piece of paper for everyone to see.

"Norm - the Blooderie's proprietor - keeps records of all his donors, this is a document stating that your blood contained too much cholesterol and that there were traces of supernatural drugs in your system such as blockers to suppress flickers and lucidity, a pain suppressant commonly used by humans that work in the Blood Dens as the feeding is a lot more - 'unsupervised' shall we say?"

"So what? There's nothing illegal about taking those, they sell them in all the shops around here," Todd retaliated.

"You are quite right about that, quite right," Mikey nodded his head, the wig jiggling.

"The defence will get to the point," said the judge.

"The point, Your Honour, is that Norm prefers his blood dolls to be clean of supernatural stimulants and suppressors, and this is one of the reasons Mr Wake was let go, another is because his blood was noted to be unpalatable to one of Norm's biggest customers, Mr Lucard." He held the document up.

"It's all noted here, Mr Lucard did not like your blood, he has a reputation of being a fussy feeder and this document proves you're not a human he would consider fit for consumption. Therefore it would make no sense for Mr Lucard to have invited Mr Wake back to feed upon if he had already rejected him as a donor."

Mikey turned to the judge. "No more questions, Your Honour."

Mr Wake was led off, before another witness was called to the stand. This time it was a ghoul, a very ancient looking one.

Lapelle approached the box. "State your name and occupation to the Chamber."

"The name's Norm, sir, I am the proprietor of the Blooderie in the Vampire Quarter."

"And for how long have you owned the establishment?" Lapelle quizzed.

"For the last eighty-two years, sir," Norm replied.

"What were you doing before that?" Lapelle quick fired.

"I worked as an apprentice in the Blood Vessel."

"Ah yes, which was closed down in 1935 for blood doll trafficking?" Lapelle asked.

"Well, yes, but I was cleared of all charges," said Norm defensively.

"So I see. Your co-worker was not though, a ghoul by the name of Gus, who recently received a fifty-year ban from selling donors after being found guilty of buying blood from the rogue vampire gangs above ground," said the Lapelle confidently.

"Yes that's true..but I would never.." Norm didn't get a chance to finish.

"Gus was also found to be selling Seasons blood," oozed Lapelle with a tone of utter revulsion.

Tuts of disapproval and disgust filled the courtroom.

"This is the ghoul who taught you the art of blood blending, a ghoul who uses cheap and illegal resources, it makes me wonder what else he taught you," said Lapelle mockingly.

"Sirs, I would never...my humans come with all the correct paperwork..they are raised locally on free range farms," Norm stuttered.

"So you say, but paperwork is easy to forge is it not?" said Lapelle.

"Objection!" shouted Mikey. "Mr Norm's previous working relationships are irrelevant to this trial, the questions asked are an attempt to discredit the witness."

"Objection sustained," said the Judge.

Lapelle smiled disarmingly. "No more questions, Your Honour."

After Norm's grilling, a tall man with dark hair was called up, from his beige complexion and brown eyes I could see he was human. His name was Michael and he had a determined look on his face.

"Please explain to the jury how you know the accused," Lapelle began.

"I am a donor at the Blooderie and Dante... I mean Mr Lucard is one of our regulars," replied Michael.

"Has Mr Lucard fed from you before?" Lapelle quizzed.

"Yes, many times," Michael confirmed.

"How would you describe his nature? Has he ever shown signs of feeding aggression?" Lapelle fished.

"No, Mr Lucard has always been courteous and respectful, he is a gentleman," Michael said.

"A gentleman you say, a term rarely used for a vampire." Lapelle baited.

"But appropriate, I feel safe when I am with him," Michael flushed and I saw a flicker of a smile on Dante's face for the first time that morning. Michael handled the rest of the prosecutor's interrogation well, remaining composed and diligent. It was starting to look good for Dante, most of the attempted character assassination had been deflected, that is, until the last witness was called. At first I thought it was another ghoul, as the man's face was so misshapen, but then I realised it was not decomposition that distorted his features but severe scarring. He was, in actual fact, a vampire, his pale eyes gleaming out from the marred flesh.

"Please state your name to the court," said Lapelle.

"Dalmar Montague," he replied.

"You were once the blood doll of the accused, is that correct?"

"That is correct," as he replied Dalmar cast his eyes to where Dante was seated, his face, heavily disfigured as it was, could not hide the look of hatred that crossed it.

"Mr Lucard is the one responsible for turning you into a vampire, is this correct?" Lapelle stated.

"Yes, he...did this to me!" Montague said harshly, pointing at Dante.

"By 'this' you are also referring to the severe level of scarring?" said Lapelle, regaining control of the questioning.

"He mutilated me, he tore chunks out of my face, when I awoke I was covered in blood and looked like this. He took my life and gave me this hell in its place, I have tried to kill myself numerous times but each time I survive and wake again to this horror," Montague said lamenting.

"No more questions, Your Honour," said Lapelle.

Mikey stood and slowly approached the stand, Montague stared at him like he was something unpleasant he'd discovered on the sole of his shoe.
"Your relationship with Mr Lucard was reported to have been tempestuous - even hedonistic," Mikey began.
"Objection, the defence is making assumptions based on hearsay," interjected Lapelle.
The judge's blank face rotated and in its place was a sad face, much like the tragedy mask from the human theatre.
"Objection sustained, stick to the facts, Mr Mikey," stated the judge.
"My apologies, Your Honour," said Mikey with a quick bow before continuing.
"Mr Montague, is it true that along with vampire blood you used other stimulants during your human days?" Mikey pried.
"I'm certain I do not know what you are referring to," replied Mr Montague coldly.
"Oh, well according to our records, in your previous life, you were an excessive user of illicit human drugs. Having been arrested by human authorities for possession, distribution and use. Do you confirm or deny these facts?" Mikey said casually.
"Objection! In accordance with section twelve of the First Lives law, the witness's pre-death history is merely for ancestral records and cannot be used in Undead Law. Human law is for humans, Undead law is for vampires and ghouls. As it is written, it is obeyed," interjected Lapelle again.
"Even I knew that..what is this ghoul doing? Dante should have hired a proper lawyer instead of listening to that fool of a fledgling," whispered Kristian loud enough to cause Desmodeus to glare at him for the second time that afternoon.

The judge's face switched again this time to a smiling mask, "Objection sustained, Prosecution is quite correct. The jury is to disregard the defence's last statement. Please continue, Mr Mikey but within the realms of Undead law."
"My client was not himself that fateful night, Your Honour. The victim, Mr Montague, had been drinking heavily and when Mr Lucard showed up to escort him home, Mr Montague had insisted he enter his home – a direct formal invitation."
Mikey paused for effect to punctuate the non-forced entry.
"With regards to 'history' then perhaps we should look at my client's history. We must note, that my client and Mr Montague had a long term relationship, one which was registered with Human Resources and spanned decades, involving many nights spent together. In all of these prior

instances, my client had always controlled his urges. So the question is, what changed that night?!" Mikey raised his voice, attracting the Jury's attention.

"Objection, the defence is leading the witness!" Lapelle declared.

The judge's face changed back to sad. "Objection sustained, Mr Mikey, please refrain from ambitious storytelling."

Obviously flustered, Mikey paused before asking the next question.

"The facts are this, for a sustained time frame, my client has never suffered a feeding frenzy. I postulate that in order for my client's character to so dramatically change after hundreds of years without incident, something else must have happened. Do all present agree with this? Vampires are creatures of habit, one does not change habit for the sake of it, it is simply out of character, as out of character as it is for my client to be an aggressive feeder."

Mikey edged back towards his desk and picked up a set of papers, before returning to the witness box.

"Mr Montague, in your human days did you ever take additional substances during your revelries in the Underdark?" Mikey asked.

Mr Montague glanced over to Lapelle who rose to object. "Objection your Honour, Mr Mikey is repeating the same line of questioning which has already been overruled."

The judge stared at Mikey, eyes blazing brighter in furious red anger.

"This is a complete shambles," said Kristian not bothering to lower his voice. This time Desmodeus didn't correct him but stared incredulously at the defence lawyer, Dante was holding his head in both hands, while Mr Montague smiled cockily.

But Mikey seemed unphased. "The prosecution is correct in stating that the First Lives law protects the privacy of your previous life, Mr Montague... but only above ground, in the human world. The moment you set foot in the Underdark, you were subject to quarantine and border control, after all the state has a responsibility to monitor and prevent any potential human based epidemics. This means any records are conducted by citizens of Undead law and kept on file here; for legal access. In other words your movements, criminal activity and, most importantly, health records made within the Underdark are not protected under the statute of the First Lives Law."

Mikey raised his right arm in the air, drawing focus to the papers in his hand.

"So, Mr Montague, I ask again. Were there, or were there not, human stimulants in your blood while you were present in the Underdark?" Mikey said authoritatively.

Mr Montague's smile vanished and Dante looked up, a glimmer of hope on his face.

"May I remind you, Mr Montague, that you are under undead oath..." said Mikey.

Mr Montague looked nervously around the courtroom before turning to see the judge's face switch back to a smile.

"Well, I may have brought some additional narcotics with me when I visited, it was all the rage above ground especially among the thespians...I thought it would take the edge off, it was only some opium, I hardly see how this is relev..." Montague was cut off.

"So you admit to having foreign substances in your blood?" demanded Mikey, drowning out the witness's attempts to pander to the jury.

Kristian was breaking out into fits of laughter now, Desmodeus even dared to smile, which was hideous.

"Objection! The defence is badgering the witness and trying to use human history to further his case," Lapelle pleaded.

The judge's smile remained fixed. "Overruled."

So Mikey continued.

"By your his admission, the witness is stating he had foreign objects within his bloodstream. I have here in my hands a scientifically proven document. In here it states the relationship of drugged blood and its effect on vampires, it is unofficially known as 'spiking'."

Mikey approached the bench and handed a copy to the judge.

"The combination of forbidden drugs and high passions caused Mr Lucard to lose his normal restraint finding a new euphoria as the opium-laden blood of Mr Montague coursed through his veins and warmed his dead heart. Caught in the moment of intense excess, he lost control. Only afterwards did he see the extent of the horrific injuries he had unconsciously afflicted to Mr Montague. It is a fact, my client suffered an episode of feeding frenzy. We do not dispute this, however what we dispute is the nature of its occurrence. My client was illegally coerced by the use of spiked blood and did not willingly commit so heinous an act as knowingly force feeding." Mikey approached the jury, right hand raised as he emphasised each point.

"My client narrowly escaped execution, he paid out a large sum in compensation for Mr Montague who accepted it at the time, he also offered to donate any flesh needed for future flesh crafting but Mr Montague refused all such offers. Would an unrepentant force feeder do such a thing?!"

The jury was fixated by Mikey's passionate performance, for a single moment, this mere ghoul was a true vampiric lawyer. However, his conclusion was to be the most thundering.

"I postulate that despite being illegally drugged by Mr Montague, despite offering compensation to the witness and, most importantly, the fact that Mr Montague ultimately got what he desired – which was to be turned. And finally the fact that my client had been acquitted from this case centuries ago, leads me to believe someone is attempting to paint my client as a monster. The question is who and for what purpose?" Mikey turned to address the court, his eyes accusing.

There was a gasp around the courtroom, Mikey's outburst was taking centre stage.

"I believe that the case of Thomas Miller and Mr Montague are not directly linked and, in fact, we will sue Mr Montague for perjury in regard to this new admission of blood spiking that was previously withheld from the initial investigation," Mikey thundered.

The court burst into uproar, the noise so deafening that it drowned out Lapelle's attempts to object. There was a loud series of bangs and the court quickly settled down again. The judge was standing, gavel in hand, glowing red hot as if his anger at the chaos had become physically manifested. He looked down at the witness, Mikey and finally the rest of court. Slowly but surely his face shifted to a smile.

"The evidence of Mr Montague is invalid. Blood coercion by a human, whether past history or not, is a most heinous crime. To take away the control from our undead, is to invite chaos. The most dangerous and savage of chaos. As a result I will not allow Mr Montague's statement to affect this case, additionally, I am demanding the arrest and interrogation of this witness for further 'questioning' concerning blood spiking." The Judge proclaimed.

There was a gasp around the court as the judge continued.

"In light of today's events, court is adjourned for 24 hours, both parties will present new data concerning the case at hand."

Two Wardens appeared at the witness stand and grabbed Mr Montague, a look of fear etched on his face. Lapelle had lost his temper and swatted at his notes in disgust. Mikey walked back to his desk and addressed Dante.

"That's the key element of this case removed, I think you will find," said Mikey with a gummy toothed smile stretched across his face.

"I am grateful, but did you have to get Mr Montague into so much trouble? I do feel a little a responsible for his condition," said Dante, slightly despondent.

"Nonsense! He deliberately spiked you all those years ago, it was a violation of trust. The worse thing a blood doll can do is intentionally contaminate their blood. He knows you had no involvement in that human boy's death, he wanted a chance to punish you and by making you relive that night was a perfect way to do it, plus the added bonus of incriminating you for a feeding fatality would have ensured you didn't escape execution this time," Mikey said firmly.

"I am just glad today is over," Dante sighed.

"Clearing you of the boy's murder should be straight forward now, they have no evidence to link you to the boy's death. And it turns out that the true victim is you," Mikey assured.

"Well, thank you for your work today, I believe I misjudged you, you are more than competent," Dante responded.

"Just doing my job, but believe me this case promises to bring big things, a counter-suing on the cards and a possible defamation charge, the undead media have been writing some nasty things about you, there's big Drakmir in slander and libel. We look to make a large settlement out of this before it's over," his yellow eyes glinted at the prospect.

He may have been a good lawyer but he was, after all, still a ghoul at heart, and Scarlet had told me how obsessed with making money they were. I turned to watch the rest of the court leaving, the judge, the bailiffs and the Wardens, the jury. As the attending crowd started to leave, I spotted someone at the back of the room making a quick exit, it was Mistress Varias and the look on her face, as she stormed out, was murderous.

Chapter 17

~Scarlet Saturday~
Day Six as a Human

I stared at Jessica's phone as it rang for the third time that morning, Sam's name flashed up on the screen. My hand hovered over it, torn between wanting to hear his voice and fearing the questions it would have for me. As before my fear won and I let the phone ring out, a minute later the phone vibrated as a text came through.

"Jess, we need to talk, I'm not sure what happened last night but I have all sorts of crazy things running through my head right now," it said.

My hope that Sam would have put my vampire lapse down to a trick of the light or hallucination, were vanquished ever since he started ringing. I had until tomorrow before Jessica and I would swap back to our own lives, I could avoid Sam until then. A pang of regret rose within my chest, I had not planned for it to end like this, I had wanted to spend my last days with Sam. Finally, I had felt what it was like to have someone. I had always believed that love was something that could be controlled; a form of science made up of a chemical process which resulted in a physiological need. I had witnessed proof that it could be controlled, a manipulation of the mind through the blood magics I had learnt, enthralling humans to succumb to me, to bend to my will, to devote themselves until I had taken what I needed. But I knew this was not true love, it was magic, but I had thought the process of human love to be somewhat similar. What then could explain what I was feeling now? I was undead, surely immune to such things. Love, from what I could make of it, was a form of sickness, it made humans irrational, depressed and provoked jealous rages giving way to acts of madness. Had what happened last night been just that? Was I suffering some form of mental illness brought on from my time as a human? It would explain why I had practically assaulted Sam.

Jessica's phone rang again and I was about to switch it off but stopped when I saw a different name flash across the screen, it was Nikki, I answered it hesitantly. I had not spoken to her since the beginning of the life swap.

"Hi Jess, what are you up to?" she asked.

"Nothing much," I said truthfully, I had no plans for the day now, other than avoiding Sam.

"Well Dean invited us to a house party tonight, he asked if you would want to come, as Hannah and I are both going."

A house party, I had learnt about them during human studies. They were popular among teenagers and usually involved loud music, alcohol and other recreational drugs. I had not taken a liking to this Dean character that Jessica had obviously been involved with, but I was interested in going to a human house party. There was never anything similar among my own kin, the idea of a group of vampires gathered together at one vampires house, feeding together and sharing blood drunk tales was bizarre, we were not social predators after all, with the exception of the gangs above ground who found safety in numbers. Vampire residents of any major undead city had no reason to form such bonds, blood was readily available if you had the Drakmir and most did.

"Whose party is it?" I asked.

"Some boy from Dean's Creative Media class, bit of a weirdo, really quiet but his parents have gone on holiday so he has a free house," said Nikki enthusiastically.

"Sure why not," I said.

The party was at seven but we would be arriving at nine as, according to Nikki, parties didn't start until two hours after they started which confused me. It was near Jessica's house so both Nikki and Hannah would knock for me and we would walk there. When I got off the phone I searched Jessica's wardrobe for something suitable to wear, I found a nice white bodycon dress that showed off my spray tan with a pair of nude heels. With my outfit sorted I was left with nothing to do but clock watch, it was strange, I wasn't used to having to keep tabs on the time. Everything in the Underdark was open 24/7 so you never had to worry about catching the shop before it closed. There were no set routines, even Desmodeus, who was the only one of my vampire siblings currently in work, was able to do what hours he wanted and seemed to materialise in and out of the office whenever he pleased, I supposed it wasn't as if they had to worry about him not being able to do overtime or the prospect of retirement, his contract was as literal to permanent as you could get. It amazed me how humans discovered so many ways to fill their short time on this earth. Along with obtaining their life cycle goals such as education, a career, a home and family, they then carried on searching for other ways to complete themselves. Mrs Young loved to cook, not just because food was a necessity but because she enjoyed creating food. That made me think about why Mildred got so excited at the prospect of making food for Kristian's blood dolls. Mrs Young had books upon books about cooking and watched shows about it. This morning she was baking a cake for Leyna, who as it happened was turning seven today. This was another surprise Jessica hadn't prepared me for. I was intrigued about experiencing a child's birthday party, as I had no recollection of such a
thing myself. I was astonished Jessica hadn't mention the fact she would be missing her sister's birthday.

"Now crack six eggs and beat them," said Mrs Young. She had asked me to help her make the cake, but so far I was proving more of a hindrance than a help.

"Eggs," I repeated, I knew what eggs were, and I had seen humans crack them open on the cooking channels that Mrs Young watched, it seemed easy enough.

I stared down at the smooth oval object and tapped it on the side of the glass bowl; it exploded covering me with translucent gloop.

"What on earth are you doing, Jessica? They're eggs, not walnuts!" she said in shock.

"Sorry," I replied wiping off most of the goo with a cloth she handed to me, I selected another and this time was careful to only tap it gently. My efforts were rewarded by a cracking sound and, under Mrs Young's watchful eye, I carefully pulled it into two halves and emptied the contents into the bowl.

"You've added half the shell to the mixture, you'll have to fish it out," she said with a sigh.

I picked out the tiny pieces of shell and for once appreciated how much easier it was to just open a packet of blood and drink it, even hunting seemed less effort. Following her instructions I proceeded to mix the eggs with milk and sugar until she passed me yet another bowl filled with something called flour.

"Sift this into the mixture while I finish melting the chocolate in the pan." she said.

"Sift?" I asked.

"I don't know what's wrong with you today, I have shown you how to bake a hundred times before."

She sighed. "I'll do it, you stir this." She passed me the chocolate covered spoon and I timidly began stirring the melting chocolate.

I fruitlessly smeared the thick dark liquid around the bowl when I sensed Leyna enter the room, she never announced her presence, she would just appear; it was quite disturbing. I turned and attempted to smile at her but she looked straight past me to her mother who tutted.

"Still in pyjamas, I thought your father was going to help you get ready..." she muttered more to herself. "Jess, can you take your sister upstairs and help her into her birthday dress, it's hanging on the wardrobe door." She took the bowl off me and eyed the lumpy mess disparagingly.

"I'll manage without you, don't worry."

I took Leyna upstairs as asked. The dress was light pink with layers of lace ruffles and tiny rosebuds sewn onto it. Leyna didn't speak a word as I struggled to get her out of her pyjamas. It was strange thinking I had once been a child myself. I folded up her tiny clothes marvelling at the human growth process, when I spotted a long scar running down her chest to her stomach. I was no stranger to scars, every undead had one from their transition but this scar was different and seeing it on a child made it look so much more vicious. I wondered how such a thing had come about. Leyna saw me looking at the scar and immediately covered her arms over it. Surprised at her self-awareness I looked away and grabbed the dress before hurriedly pulling it over her small frame. After a brief struggle, I finally managed to get her arms through it.

"There," I said attempting an encouraging smile.

"Don't you look beautiful," and without thinking it through I moved towards her and wrapped my arms around her tiny frame.

I wasn't sure what I had expected to happen but it was somehow an anti-climax, she just stood there frozen. When had I become better at showing emotion than an actual human? I released her and stepped back but was not even rewarded with a smile, maybe Leyna was in agreement with Jessica's friends and sensed something about me that made her wary. As if confirming my suspicions she ran past me and downstairs, confused I followed and found her sitting on the floor in the living room in front of the TV. Deciding to give up on sibling bonding I returned to the Kitchen. Mrs Young had put the cake in the oven and was now washing up. I picked up the bowl with its smoothly mixed chocolate and started to whisk it.

"Mum?" I asked hesitantly.

"Yes, dear?" she said frowning as I accidentally let some chocolate dribble onto the kitchen counter.

"Well... I just wanted to check... you see while I was helping Leyna get into her dress I noticed something."

"Hmm?" she said as she scrubbed harder at the cooking pot she was rinsing.

"Did you know she has a scar across her stomach?" I blurted out.

She stopped and looked at me, her face had paled and her mouth was pressed together in a thin line.

"Is that a joke?" she demanded.

"What? No of course not..I just.." I tried to find words to respond.

"I thought we had put this all behind us, Jessica!" she left the washing up and started banging pots and pans around. I stood there holding the chocolate covered whisk unsure of what to say, then the jingle of Jessica's phone sounded.

I put the whisk back in the bowl, Mrs Young carried out her unexplained outburst on the kitchen utensils so, with a final glance at her back, I left the room to take the call. It was Penny, she wanted to know what time I wanted to meet. In the anticipation of going to a House party, I had forgotten that I had invited Penny over this evening.

"I'm sorry, I'm going to a party tonight now," I said.

"Oh, that's okay. I understand," she said.

Then I had an idea.

"You can come with me."

She paused before asking. "Are you sure?"

"Yes, of course. Why wouldn't I be?"

"Well, your friends probably won't want me to come."

I considered this before answering. "They don't know you, they just need to talk to you like I have." It made sense, all of Nikki's and Hannah's judgments had been based on hearsay, or because Jessica didn't like Penny. Now if they saw Jessica inviting her to a party they would have no reason but to accept her.

When I returned to the kitchen Mrs Young was still banging pots about so I went outside into the garden where Mr Young was overseeing the outside entertainment. As I walked out the patio doors I felt the morning air on my face and closed my eyes a moment, appreciating being outside, I took Jessica's slipper boots off and stepped onto the neat lawn feeling the grass beneath my toes. I could feel the morning sunlight dappling on my face, it didn't hurt, I had conditioned myself enough during my vampire life to sustain its touch for a reasonable amount of time. I opened my eyes and admired the clouds against the blue sky, it really was beautiful, better than any paintings I had poured over as a fledgling.

I hadn't realised how nice it was just being out in the open and surrounded by nature. My senses were uplifted by an abundance of new sensations, Mrs Young was an avid gardener and had created a wondrous outside space for the family. I had not fully appreciated it when I came here on that first visit, I had been so preoccupied with convincing Jessica to agree to the life swap. But now I could see the beauty of it, I had seen real magic, even the very blood in my veins had magical properties, but this simple garden was more magical to me than any of that. I took in the unfamiliar scents and was suddenly hit by a powerful feeling of nostalgia, I had smelt flowers like this before. I opened my eyes in astonishment and scanned the coloured petals peeking from the assorted pots, I had to find the origin. I had never remembered anything from my past before, yet this sudden smell had brought back a feeling of such familiarity that it had to be a memory. I tried to latch onto it but it was fading, and as I dashed among the flower pots trying to find the suspect it had gone, it was an awful feeling like losing part of you.

"Having a go at the treasure hunt?"

I turned to Mrs Young who was pointing at a wrapped little box poking out of the soil in one of the flower pots I was standing over.

"You have to leave some for the kids, Jess," he said with a smile.

I smiled back and surveyed the garden, my vampire eyes spotting the hidden gifts straight away now I was concentrating. There was one protruding from the bird house, one in the watering can and dozens in the flower pots. Gazing around the large garden I felt my frustration melt away, maybe I had imagined it, I had spent so long trying to force memories it made sense that I would start forging them one day. False

memories aside, I was enjoying Jessica's garden. I could hear birds in the trees and the wind rustling the leaves, I thought about the lack of nature in the Underdark, how long had it been for some of those undead since
they had felt a breeze on their face? Walked on grass? Seen the sky on a summer's day? There were some undead that had not ventured above ground since they were turned and it was worse since the curfew and implants were enforced. An immortal world left in the dark, forgotten and buried, such simple sights becoming mere myth.

"What do you think?" asked Mr Young as I took in the new feature of the garden - a large inflatable castle.

"It's big," I replied, unsure of what else to say. It was a strange sight to me, castles were meant to be impenetrable fortresses not brightly coloured structures that bounced but Jessica's parents seemed to think Leyna and her friends would love it.

Soon enough they all arrived and I was no longer alone in the garden, I was surrounded by hordes of screaming children, I stood paralysed as they ran circles around me. I was surprised by the amount of energy they had, Jessica's parents were right, they loved the Castle, jumping up and down repeatedly until they got dizzy then rolling off only to return a moment later and do it all over again. Along with the inflatable castle, they had arranged for a lady to come and paint faces, another curiosity to me. It seemed very tribal at first when I heard them discussing it, I had pictured dozens of children wearing war paint, hoisting spears and chasing a large pig. Instead, a rather normal looking lady arrived with a stack of tiny paints and brushes. The children were made to line up to receive painted creations of their choice, girls opting for brightly coloured strokes that spiralled off into wings as if an oversized glittery butterfly had landed on their faces, the boys chose tigers or pirates and charged around the garden growling or yelling "Arrggh!"

Mr Young laughed as he saw me watching with interest.

"You fancy having your face painted? I won't tell your friends, but your mum might sneak a picture of you if you do."

I glanced at Mrs Young who was refilling a bowl with some sort of children's snack that was so full of colours it looked more like the face paint than food. She didn't seem to be thinking about taking pictures, in fact she seemed distracted. Ever since I asked her about Leyna's scar she had become very quiet and barely said more than two words to me. Leyna was also acting strange, being the first child of my acquaintance I hadn't noticed it much before, but seeing the other children today, there was a clear difference. The other children laughed, yelled, cried and generally ran around ignoring the adults. But Leyna remained quiet as usual and stood firmly by her mother's side, refusing to mingle with the other children. I thought about Penny and how she chose not to spend time with humans her age. Perhaps this was something that afflicted some humans like ghoulism did in the undead. But then I remembered I had seen Penny watch Jessica's friends with that same wistful expression I once had, how she had let me sit with her and gradually opened up to me. It was my feeling that Penny had always wanted friends, just like me, but she had never been given the opportunity.

    I saw a number of children approach Leyna during the party trying to get her to play but she turned away and buried her face in her mother's skirt. What would make a human refuse friendship? She was alive and capable of human emotions, so why was she paving her own social isolation? Jessica's parents seemed unconcerned, her mother made no attempt to encourage her to play with the other children and her father was busy conversing with the other adults who had been invited. I recognised a few of them from Jessica's grandmother's funeral, they had tried to talk to me but I must have been doing something wrong, because after a short while each found an excuse to edge away from me. I complied with what I perceived to be appropriate behaviour for chatting with adults, I maintained good eye contact, I nodded to acknowledge I was listening and even attempted laughter when they made a joke, but it was my strong opinions on current affairs that seemed to discourage them. I picked subjects that I thought would pose an interest such as human politics, economics, religion and how changes in climate would eventually cause the mass extinction of the human race. It seemed as if popular belief was, that teenagers like Jessica should not have an interest in such topics, as most seemed shocked at my involvement in such discussions. The fact that I eagerly tackled the harsh facts of each one did not go down well, in fact some guests even seemed offended by it. For the second time this week I had come to the realisation of why conversation was called an art. It seemed my social skills at this party were about as good as Leyna's.

I progressed better with Jessica's own age group, I found adults and children a lot harder to talk to than teenagers, maybe because they were also conflicted with the world. Children seemed oblivious to it, more interested in the toy their friend stole off them or the piece of cake in their hand. Adults, having a developed frontal lobe, seemed more rational. They accepted things the way they were. Children questioned, adults accepted and teenagers argued it. They had asked the questions, been given the answers but were not ready to accept them and that is how I felt and probably the reason why I was a vampire gate crashing a seven-year-old's birthday party.

    Much later the guests had gone home and I was dressed and waiting for Nikki and Hannah. While I waited I checked for any more texts from Sam but he seemed to have given up. Although this was for the best I couldn't help checking the phone every now and then. It felt strange walking along with Nikki and Hannah just as I had seen Jessica do. Even stranger, was the fact that now I was doing it myself, it didn't seem to be half as fun as I thought it would be. Nikki had bought a bottle of wine along which we drank on the way, swigging it from the bottle. I had tasted alcohol before but it was normally clouded by the taste of human blood, the pure undiluted version was something else entirely. It was my understanding that, as demons, blood was our drug but human drugs could still affect us. But it seemed that it took a lot to do so and perhaps required the conjunction of live feeding, as the wine seemed to have no affect on me other than leave a bad after taste. The change in Nikki and Hannah was obvious though, both became a lot louder, cackling loudly on the bus and swearing profusely. A lot of the other human commuters were glancing over at us and I was almost relieved when we got off and arrived at our destination.

There was already a large number of people there, the front door was wide open as groups of teenagers clustered outside smoking. Inside there were even more people, some were draped on the sofas while others were in the kitchen, which was where Nikki and Hannah immediately headed. The boy's parents were nowhere to be seen except in the photographs on the walls, apparently they were in Spain for a week. Dean was there and he hugged them both. He saw me and paused then, seeing Sam wasn't with me, smiled.

"Come to your senses at last, Jess," he turned to the others. "The fridge is empty but there are some beers on the side there, Joe just went out to get more."

As Nikki and Hannah eagerly helped themselves to bottles of beer I took in the rest of the scene. A group of people sat round a large table, shot glasses lined up. Dean caught me staring.

"After something a bit stronger than beer I see," he said laughing and leant in close to me, the only thing stronger I craved was not contained in tiny shot glasses but pulsating through every human in the house. I moved away from his neck which was precariously close and he looked annoyed.

"Maybe I was wrong? It seems like you'd still prefer to be in someone else's company." When I didn't answer he snorted. "I don't have time for your mind games, Jess, I'm not as well trained as Sam!" He pushed past me and stormed into the living room.

Hannah raised her eyebrows and Nikki frowned at me. "I don't get you, Jess, you've been sneaking around with Dean for months and now you're suddenly not interested. You haven't really gone back on Sam have you?"

"Sam is fit though," purred Hannah in between sips of beer, her cheeks were flushed and her pupils dilated. "If you don't want him I'll happily step in," she giggled and dribbled beer down her chin.

I didn't fancy having a debate with them over Jessica's taste in men, I had absolutely no interest in Dean. But Sam... well Sam was off limits, my demonic outburst had ruined any chance of that happening. Nikki and Hannah thankfully moved onto another conversation, and I was free to people watch in peace. It surprised me how much underage drinking was going on here and we had only just arrived, but some of the humans had clearly already had a lot to drink. They also stood around in little clusters, not yet drunk enough to integrate properly.

After an hour of watching people drink, I noticed they had finally built up enough confidence to dance and a bunch of them were jumping around in the centre of the living room, a few ornaments had already been broken in the process but the resident (Dean's friend) didn't seem bothered. He was sitting in the corner with his mouth locked to Hannah's, who had somehow cornered him after finishing her beer and been kissing him ever since. Nikki had managed to get hold of a bottle of Vodka and was pouring it out for us as she pointed at them in disgust.

"Why does Hannah always have to go pull the weirdest bloke in the room, I know it's his party but it doesn't mean she has lock lips with him all night."

I took an experimental sip of the vodka, it wasn't as bad as the wine but it was still rancid. It was a good thing I had a pack of blood before coming out as the alcohol and close proximity of humans was making me hungry again, not wanting to take the risk I slipped upstairs in search of a bathroom. I found one but the door was locked, I waited and after ten minutes knocked on the door. The sound of a small groan greeted me and someone telling me to "Fuck off!" assured me it was going to be engaged for a while so I resigned myself to going without.

When I reached the bottom of the stairs I felt an arm grab me, I looked up and saw a panic-stricken Penny.

"I've been outside for half an hour, I tried calling you but you didn't pick up," she said.

I had forgotten I had put Jessica's phone on silent in case Sam tried calling.

"Why didn't you come in and try to find me?" I asked, slightly confused.

"I didn't want to come in by myself, I don't know anyone else here," Penny said uncomfortably.

"Well lets go change that, I will introduce you properly to the others," I said reassuringly.

This didn't seem to reassure her and as I beckoned her to follow me into the living room she clutched my hand tightly. When we entered, Nikki who was still drinking the Vodka, glared at Penny then back to me. "What's she doing here?"

"I invited her," I responded.

"Why? No one likes her, tell her to fuck off!"

I couldn't understand why Nikki was being so hostile, I had never seen

Penny do anything to deserve such treatment.

"Why don't you try and get to know her before you insist that you don't like her?"

Nikki stared at me for a moment looking confused but then she smiled. "Oh okay, that makes sense now, we should get to know Penny better."

I smiled pleased with myself, I had spent so long feeling alone and apart from the world, if I could help someone avoid that then doing this swap would have been worth the risks involved. I was starting to learn that maybe the human way of life was not so perfect after all, I had always thought being human would make everything better, and a lot of things were better. The connections they built with each other were as real and heartfelt as I had always believed. But there was also a lot of pain and sadness, maybe that was the price you paid for the good parts.

Nikki invited Penny to sit down next to her and began making conversation, Penny looking frightened, barely responding, but then after a while she seemed to relax and even began enjoying herself. Satisfied I excused myself, I was still feeling the urge to feed, the alcohol wasn't getting me drunk but it was playing havoc with my appetite. This time the bathroom was free, but it was a mess, I glanced at the state of the toilet glad I no longer had that specific human need.

When I emerged Dean was waiting outside the door, I made to move past him but he grabbed me and pushed me against the wall and started kissing my neck.

"Dean, stop!" I said but he kept on going, is this what I had been like with Sam? I pushed him away and his face twisted with anger.

"I already told you, Jess, your games don't work on me. If I want something I take it."

He made a grab for me again but I was quicker and I caught him by the throat, my hand gently squeezing it, feeling the arteries throbbing underneath. His eyes bulged slightly and he wheezed as I applied more pressure.

"Jess!.." He pleaded.

I let go and he gasped and choked. "Next time you try and take me, I won't be so forgiving." I left him there slumped against the wall, still gasping for air.

What had Dean been planning? Would he have really taken Jessica by force? I tried not to think about it. When I returned to the living room Penny and Nikki were no longer there, I looked to where Hannah had been but she was missing also. Dean's friend, who she had been kissing, was still there. He was fairly incoherent but I managed to decipher that Hannah had gone outside with Nikki and another girl. I felt an overwhelming sense of pride, I had used the influence Jessica had over her friends for good, by showing my acceptance of Penny I had caused Nikki and Hannah to accept her. But as I walked outside and away from the loud music I immediately sensed something was wrong. At the bottom of the garden a large group of guests had gathered, they appeared to be watching something, some had phones out and were filming. My ears picked out the sound of someone crying, I walked over and the familiar smell of blood met me as I pushed my way through the crowd. There in the centre was Penny, curled up on the ground crying and moaning as both Nikki and Hannah viciously beat her. For a moment I could do nothing but stare in shock, Hannah was pummeling Penny with blows to the head using her fists, while Nikki stamped hard on her ribs, the group watching were laughing and cheering. Both girls suddenly saw me and laughed.

"Good idea, Jess, luring her here so we could do this," said Nikki wiping some of the blood that was on her hands onto her top.

"I didn't bring her here for this!" I exclaimed, still in shock, the blood was distracting me, I couldn't think straight, this was not what was supposed to be happening, it didn't make any sense.

Penny was trying to crawl away but Nikki grabbed her and dragged her back through the muddy grass as Hannah aimed a kick to her face, Penny was crying louder now, high pitched raking sobs, it seemed to snap me into action. I bent down and tried to help Penny get to her feet, her face was a mess, blood was covering it and her eyes were almost swollen shut.

Nikki and Hannah seemed confused asking why I was spoiling the fun, I ignored them and carried Penny through the crowd. I kept walking hoping they would let us go as they continued to shout after us, I didn't know what I was going to do otherwise. I could feel the disgust rising in me, if they tried to stop me I might have to use force against them and right now I didn't know if I could restrain myself. What they had done to Penny was horrific but I knew I was capable of worse. Luckily, they didn't follow, perhaps they still respected or feared Jessica enough to comply or perhaps they just preferred opponents that wouldn't fight back, either way I was glad for it. When we were a good distance from the house I gently sat Penny down against a wall and inspected the damage done, she had a broken rib and cuts and bruises to the face. She was still crying.

"I'm sorry," I said, meaning it, then I bit into my wrist and made her drink from me.

"It will heal you," I said coaxing her as she tried to resist, she opened her swollen eyelids and looked at me and then nodded, somehow she still trusted me. I let her drink, just enough to heal her, then I sat down next to her and waited. It took over an hour before her wounds had fully mended.

"Does it feel better now?" I asked, the skin looked better, the dried blood still covering it but the bruises had gone and her face was no longer swollen.

She touched her face, her eyes incredulous as they looked at me. "I feel fine now, but that's impossible.. I just got kicked in the face and stamped on."

I closed my eyes, I could enthrall her but my powers were not strong enough to remove her memory like the Wardens could do.

"My blood fixed you. Look, I am a vampire but don't worry, you won't turn into one, but you might feel strange for the next 24 hours, like you've had a lot of caffeine."

She laughed light headedly then stopped. "I do feel strange..but in a good way, like I could do anything." She stood up and wobbled a bit. I steadied her. "But you're still human so you need to go home and rest, I'll walk you back," I ordered.

We walked together and I told her everything, I didn't care that I was breaking even more rules, what I had seen tonight had shaken me and I needed to talk to someone about it. Penny believed everything I told her, the good thing about vampire blood is, it makes you see things how they really are, just as it removes the glamour cloaking our world and allows mortals who have drunk it to enter, it made Penny see my true form. She had a lot of questions as to be expected.

"I knew it was odd that Jessica would suddenly start being nice to me," she said. "So what made you choose her?" she asked, she sounded almost jealous as if in her opinion Jessica had been undeserving.

I explained how I had crossed paths with Jessica and wanted her life. She nodded knowingly. "I can see why. She is popular, pretty, well off... if I could pick a life I probably would have done the same. I suppose she has a nice family as well? I have never met them, but I bet her mother is really pretty like her." Penny said almost in admiration.

"Yes, she is," I said factually.

"It makes you wonder why she does it," she said.

"Does what?" I pried.

"Hurt people. If she was happy, there wouldn't be a need for that."

"It was her friends that attacked you not her, she's not here." I pointed out.

"True, but they did it because they thought it was what she wanted, they thought you'd bought me tonight for that very reason," Penny replied.

I remembered what Nikki had said about me luring Penny there, is this what the real Jessica did for fun? When we got to Penny's house she invited me in but I politely refused.

"You can call me you know, after all this, if you want a friend. I know what it's like to be lonely, I won't tell anyone what you are."

I thanked her and felt hopeful despite the way the evening had turned out, it would be nice if I could see Penny again, as myself. On the way back I tried to make sense of what had happened tonight. I thought it would have involved spending time with friends, something I had not experienced. But the brutal acts I had seen were far from what I had in mind, I had never seen anything like it. Gang violence happened among the undead, when you have been around for hundreds of years grudges and for hundreds of years, grudges and blood feuds are bound to mount up.

But there were rules and a code of honour, this was nothing like that, this was harming an individual for the sake of it, almost like out of childish curiosity. What I had witnessed tonight had been unprovoked and the execution in which it had been carried out, had been one of sadistic pleasure.

"Did you have a good time?" asked Mrs Young as I got back, she was in her dressing gown and I could hear sounds of the TV from the living room, mingled with Jessica's father's snores.

"Yeah, great!" I replied as I rushed past her.

When I got upstairs I scrubbed the blood off my hands, watching the water run red over them until it was clear again, as if trying to cleanse the memory of what I had seen tonight. I stared at my reflection, I was still Jessica, but for the first time I didn't feel relieved, I wasn't sure if I liked being Jessica anymore. When I had washed up and changed I shut myself in Jessica's room and reached under the bed with shaking hands and unzipped the cooler bag, ripping open one of the blood packs with my teeth I drained the contents in one go. My throat still burned for more so I guzzled down another and sat back waiting for the hunger to pass. Jessica's mobile was flashing with new text messages, I opened it up, it was a video message showing them kicking Penny on the ground. A written message from Nikki followed.

"Will upload this tonight along with last weeks clip," I deleted both messages with disgust.

Yet you wanted to be one of them I thought, you risked everything to be here and live in their world. I curled up on the large bed feeling more conflicted than ever, Princess jumped up and nestled against me, I reached down and stroked her soft fur finding comfort in the small act. I stayed like that for a long time, while my mind kept going back over the night's events. Then I remembered what the text had said and realised with alarm they had done this before, this was probably something Jessica took part in regularly.

Chapter 18

~Jessica Saturday~
Day Six as a Vampire

I was in Scarlet's room sat at the dresser, in front of me, lay the glass vials Varias had given me. As I casually spun one of them in circles, I stared at myself in the mirror thinking through my plan again. I was still irritated that I had lost a whole day watching Dante's trial yesterday, so I was determined to take action. I pretty much had the house to myself, while the ghouls still pottered about, Desmodeus, Kristian and their father were at Tribune Tower, the Jury had come to a swift decision concerning Dante's case. While they were out, I planned to go into the city. I wanted to make sure I was as well informed as possible about being turned, my main concern was exactly what was I going to become? The idea of spending my immortality like Grace was not appealing, I needed to find out why some humans did not fully transcend and if there was anything I could do to prevent that. Mistress Varias had not informed me either, but I was sure she would know, maybe she had some potion that would help. I heard slow footsteps in the hall and froze, grabbing the vial in my hand. Keeping wary, the last thing I wanted was Herb lurking outside, hoping to tag along. There was a knock at the door, before it creaked open, I gripped the vial tighter. It was only Mildred, she paused just in the doorway, carrying a large basket filled with clothes with surprising ease considering her bony frame.

"Any laundry my sweet?" she croaked eyeing the bedroom with a slight frown.

It was a bit of a mess, but in all honesty I had little care for Scarlet's collection of boring old books and had left most of them scattered on the carpet, while I had been doing my research. The bed was unmade and a pile of dirty clothes lay next to it, which I had piled up during my stay here. I got up and gathered a bundle, before adding them to Mildred's basket. She gave a curt bow, before leaving, mumbling to herself how *this would keep her busy for a while.*

I went back to the dresser and checked myself in the mirror, the glamour was still working. Instinctively I grabbed for the Morshard. In all my days here, I hadn't really considered what would happen if the spell on the Morshard broke, would it just be the glamour that stopped? Or would the stone itself lose all its power, leaving me vulnerable once more. As I was coming down the stairs I paused on the landing, next to Dante's room. There was a strange noise coming from within. Curiosity got the better of me and cautiously I entered and looked over to where a bat sat, squeaking in its cage, it sounded like a baby crying. I walked over and peered through the bars, it was chewing on a moth and looked up at me with large brown eyes, before uttering a squeak in greeting or fear, I couldn't tell which. This must be Vlad, I thought. Scarlet had mentioned that Dante had a pet but this had been the first time I had actually seen him. I opened the cage door and slipped my hand inside, gently picking him up. I cradled him in my arms as I sat down on the bed, he struggled feebly, but I held him tight, after a while he relaxed and nuzzled his furry head against my hand. I peeled open one of his wings and traced a finger along his wingtips marvelling at how delicate the membrane was.

There was a sudden high pitch squeal, followed by short huffs of pain as I bent Vlad's wing back sharply, breaking the bone. He struggled desperately and as I watched him writhe in pain, I felt my frustrations of the week melt away, listening to his pathetic cries of pain and suffering, I smiled in satisfaction as I held the power of life and death over something again. This whole swap had been out of my control from the start and I had thought it would be easy. But I had underestimated the bureaucracy of existing among these creatures of the living dead. Laws, legislation's, policing just like it was above ground. Rules had never bothered me before, I had always given the impression I was following them, but I never saw the benefit of complying with them. Any consequences from breaking them were a mere irritation nothing to be feared, but down here, in Scarlet's world, I felt stifled...I despised it.

"What in the name of all things undead was that noise?" I turned to see Mildred in the doorway.
"It's Dante's Bat, I only wanted to hold him and he began screaming," I lied with practice ease.
The old ghoul came closer and gently picked up the distressed creature.
"Looks like his wing is broken, he will need some nursing. Poor little beast has been through the wars alright, got two damaged wings now," Mildred said, stroking Vlad's head.
"Oh dear, the poor thing," I said, not meaning a word of it.
I left the creature with her and headed to the Witches Quarter, desperate to further my plan. But when I got there Varias's shop was closed, I called the number she had given me and it rang out, I tried it again, but the same result. I glanced around, I would just have to find answers somewhere else I decided. I made my way to the busier streets of the quarter, bypassing stalls and open markets.
"How about a nice hearty breakfast to start the day," rasped a ghoul vendor as I passed by. He held out the bloodied organ to me. "Freshly donated a few hours ago."

I ignored him and searched for a bookshop, if anything would have details on what I wanted, a book shop would I thought logically. But to my disappointment the ones I discovered only sold vampire literature similar to Dante's diet collection, or the rubbish the blood dolls read. In one shop, there was even a huge display of Dante's idol Dr Ervin's latest book 'Blood for the body conscious'. As I stood there looking at it, I hoped deep inside that the Tribune found him guilty of that boy murder, and tortured him.

The concept cheered me up and I continued on and discovered another series of shops on the border of the Vampire and Witch Quarter that looked promising. One had an aged and faded sign that read 'Vampiric lore and ancient artefacts'. This was more like it, surely there had to be something in here about how it all began. I felt a rush of excitement but was wary to suppress it, I didn't want to draw any unwanted attention. I pushed open the door and at the sound of the bell, a tall sinewy vampire appeared from behind a stack of books at the back of the shop.

"May I help you?" He asked, managing to be both courteous and sinister at the same time. I cleared my throat before responding.

"I'm just looking," I said, while scanning the shop's wares. I paused to pick up an elaborate looking ring which resembled a sharpened thimble rather than a piece of jewellery. With impossible speed the vampire shop owner was next to me prising the object from my hand.

"Looking does not involve touching merchandise that has been around since before you were sired," he said haughtily.

"Sorry," I said, suddenly very aware of his cold grasp on my wrist. He nodded slowly then slithered his hand off me, subconsciously I looked down at my hand half expecting to see a glistening trail where he had touched it. There was nothing there of course but I quickly wiped it against my jumper anyway.

"I am looking for a book," I said trying my best to sound assertive.
His face remained unimpressed.

"As you can see I have plenty of books" he waved a hand dismissively at the dusty stacks.

"This is one about siring," I said.
His sharp eyes narrowed and I knew I had said the wrong word.

"The ritual of siring is not something one writes about. It is a sacred ceremony passed down from sire to brood, if any old fledgling knew how to do it we would soon be overrun. If your own sire did not think you worthy enough to share the secret of the Dark Kiss, why on earth would I?" He seemed to loom over me as he said this, so I backed off and left the shop. Clearly, I would not be getting any assistance here. Frustrated and more than slightly creeped out, I decided to end my search for the day. With time running out and still plenty to take care of before tomorrow, I decided perhaps I should just leave it all to chance, a flip of the coin, vampire or ghoul.

Later that evening, I was sat in the parlour room with Mary, Cecile and Kristian, who had returned early from court. Both blood dolls had just awoken from a nap. Their sleeping habits were all over the place, I guessed that having a relationship with a creature that didn't sleep would do that. And from what I had seen throughout the week, Kristian would keep them awake for nights on end, only allowing them rest when he had used their bodies up or the blood dolls had succumbed to exhaustion.

The candles flickered and for a moment, the room grew darker. For the first time since my stay here I didn't startle, I was getting so used to the way vampires would just randomly appear out of thin air. Although when I saw that three shadows filled the empty space between the TV and the sofa, I instantly became alert. The first to appear was Dante, who seemed to be in the best mood I had seen him in since I arrived, a superior smile on his lips as he greeted us. Next Desmodeus materialised into view, his face as stoic as ever, finally an older looking vampire materialised after them. Like

Desmodeus he had long, dark hair, but it was flecked with grey. His pale skin bore the signs of mortal ageing, suddenly stopped in its tracks, a few crows feet and subtle lines around the mouth, but smooth cheeks and full lips. At first, I was confused then it dawned on me this must be Scarlet's father. He made my own father look ancient in comparison. Kristian eyed them cautiously.

"The full clan is here, that must mean only one thing...."

"I have been cleared of all charges!" Dante said, before anyone else could.

"As I said you would, those prissy fools had no evidence to link you to that boy's murder, turns out that ghoul knows a thing or two about undead law after all," Kristian said triumphantly.

"Yes indeed, I said all along I was right to take him on, never doubted him for a second," gloated Dante.

Rather than correct him, Kristian merely smiled.

"In light of this unsurprising, but still good news I demand we go out and celebrate, I believe a night at Plasma should suffice?" Kristian suddenly said, arms wide open.

"Oh yes let's!" squealed Mary.

"Yeah we haven't been out in ages!" joined in Cecile

"I'd rather not, I was more inclined to a quiet evening at the Blooderie." Winced Dante, expecting to be chided by his brother.

"Oh come on, you have gone there almost everyday of your undead life. Try something different for once, you could even bring that blood doll you like, what's his name again?" Kristian said winking.

"Michael, and I do not like him. His blood just happens to suit my dietary needs," Dante said unconvincingly.

"Fine, just invite him and lets go!" Kristian said impatiently.

"Michael did say he had the night off tonight," admitted Dante hesitantly. "But I don't think Plasma is his scene, he's far too sophisticated for such things."

"Rubbish, he'll love it, it screams Anne Rice, any true vampire fan will love Plasma. It's like a fantasy come alive for them, all that attention they get from the vampire patrons," Kristian continued to sell the idea.

"Oh alright!" said Dante relenting.

Scarlet's father and Desmodeus having witnessed the exchange, looked at each other and shrugged, before excusing themselves from the night's revelry. With the 'drama' over, it was time for both of them to return to their work commitments. Kristian rolled his eyes but didn't seem surprised. He then turned his gaze on Herb who had just entered the room with a silver tray and glasses of blood for the new arrivals. Herb suddenly wilted.

"Well? How about you worm-bait, are you coming?" he asked. Herb nearly dropped the entire tray as Kristian's offer sunk in. Herb overcame his shock and nodded eagerly, I felt my own anticipation wavering, so hastily spoke up.

"Herb can't come out tonight," I said, Herb's face fell, while Kristian frowned.

"Why not, surely you can give him the night off for once, how urgent can the mundane tasks you get him doing be?" Kristian pried.

"I have an assignment due in and I need Herb to visit the ghoul library and get some books for me," I said flatly.

"Surely he can do that after?" Kristian argued, while Herb shot me pleading glances.

"I would prefer him to do it sooner, rather than later, in case someone else takes those books out," I said firmly. Kristian shrugged, while Herb dropped his head in disappointment.

"Alright, the rest of you get a move on and get ready, we get a free blood clot if we get there in time for Haemo-hour," Kristian motioned.

Dante insisted on Michael coming to the house first, he was worried that if Michael arrived at Plasma alone he might get poached by other vampires. This gave Mary and Cecile ample time to get changed. I also went to freshen up, I was starting to feel the effects of lack of sleep, so I used the opportunity to pop upstairs and take a dose of the draught Varias made me. I decided to change from Scarlet's jeans and top I was wearing, exchanging it for a long black dress with the back cut out. I found some red lipstick I liked among her collection of human cosmetics and pinned her long hair into a sophisticated updo. It was true Scarlet could not cut or dye her hair it but she could at least style it differently from time to time. As I came down the stairs, in my new attire, there was a gasp.

"Oh Scar you look divine!" It was Dante, Michael was standing by his side.

"Yes you look very Queen of the damned, can we go now? I thought humans took ages getting ready but Mary and Cecile were down long before you," Kristian huffed, the comment annoyed me far more than it should have.

Mary and Cecile were not so formally dressed, both were wearing matching T-Shirts that said *'Dogs never bite me, just vampires.'*

When we got to Plasma there was already a queue outside, Dante immediately began ranting about how he would never have to queue at Norms, but then the Doorman who I recognised as the Gate Warden 'Joe' waved us over.

"Kristian! I haven't seen your fangs around here for ages!" Joe shouted out.

Kristian gave a smile in thanks, before nodding to Mary and Cecile, who were tilting their necks flirtatiously.

"I prefer to eat in lately," Kristian said, winking. Joe gave a slow nod before winking back. He then set his pale eyes over the rest of our group.

"Whole brood out tonight?"

"Almost. Father and Desmodeus wouldn't be seen dead here, literally," Kristian mocked.

As Joe and Kristian briefly chatted about the 'good old days', I learnt that Kristian used to work at Plasma as a doorman, which explained why Joe let us jump the queue. Mary and Cecile made the most of it, by throwing superior looks at the other blood dolls still waiting in line. Inside, the club was huge. It had high ceilings with cages suspended by chains, tables and chairs, a dance floor and a bar. Loud electronic music thumped throughout the club, but I noticed it was only the blood dolls dancing. There were also feeding booths, which were balcony rooms, with heavy velvet curtains pulled across for privacy. Human blood dolls walked around with trays of bloodletting tools to accommodate vampires who practiced the art of feeding foreplay, or so I overheard Dante explaining to Michael, a hopeful hint in his voice.

We found a table in the corner and sat down just as a large male vampire was escorting a fledgling out the doors. The fledgling protested loudly as he was dragged away.

"Get off me! I could kill all of you!" Another burly vampire came to assist and shook his head at his colleague knowingly.

"Immortal complex. Happens every time, they get all carried away with their new found supernatural powers. They get so blood drunk, they end up thinking they can take on the world." The fledgling continued his threats to no avail, before being thrown head first out the doors,

"One thing I miss about working here, throwing all the stupid fledglings out on their ass," Kristian laughed.

On our table was a menu with what was on offer, along with a note advising that all staff were qualified first aiders. Shortly a male ghoul came over to the table holding a pile of papers which he handed to each of us.

"Listen to this!" demanded Kristian as he read the document aloud.

"I hereby agree to take full responsibility for any blood dolls I have brought along with me and acknowledge that any action leading to their deaths is not through any negligence of the establishment Plasma." Kristian shook the papers with disdain, before dropping them on the table.

"It's enough to make your fangs go soft, having to sign a waiver as soon as you get here, they never used to do this!" Kristian continued.

"They had to introduce it due to the rising amount of lawsuits going on at the moment," explained the ghoul.

"Last month, a blood doll tried to sue us for feeding negligence, when her fledgling vampire failed to feed her enough of his own blood to heal her and caused permanent scarring to her neck area. We've also got an ongoing lawsuit from a blood doll that used to work in one of the cages for us, apparently for mistreatment and being treated like an animal." The ghoul went on.

After we had all signed; but not before Dante commented on how he never had to sign a waiver at Norms; Kristian went to get us drinks. I tried to talk to Michael hoping to get him comfortable enough to talk about the blood doll relationship. Being an educated man, I thought, that he had to be more in the know than Mary and Cecile, who were both idiots as far as I was concerned. but Dante was so possessive of him, it was impossible to have a proper conversation. Kristian returned and placed a tray laden with shot glasses on the table.

"Two for the price of one Blood Clot! Get these down your throats, I even got some vamp blood for the humans under our care." He handed Mary, Cecile and Michael small glasses filled with black liquid. Dante snatched it off Michael and sniffed it suspiciously before handing it to Mary who happily downed it.

"Michael is on a strict diet, only my own blood will suffice," Dante responded and with that, he drew the sharp blade tip of his ring across his arm and filled the glass with his own blood. I appraised my own drink, as Kristian raised his in a toast meeting my eyes.

"To our brother Dante and his questionable choice in lawyers!" he chortled.

He tilted back his shot of blood and downed it, nodding at me to follow suit, I swallowed my own back, hiding my disgust as the thick liquid slid down my throat, it was hard not to gag. Just then, a large group of blood dolls entered, all laughing and clearly already intoxicated. A young woman with long blonde hair seemed to be at the centre of them all, she was wearing a black t-shirt with pink writing on it that said 'Vampire to be' the rest of them held balloons with 'Keep calm, he's turning her'.

"Oh goody, it looks like a Sire party!" said Kristian with relish.

"Ugh I thought they stopped doing those decades ago, how uncouth," said Dante.

"I think they're great, celebrating your last night as a human before you get turned. Not a lot of us got that chance," said Kristian, as he eyed the girls approvingly.

"I find groups of sire party's to be a lot easier to feed on, they are all so caught up in the whole spirit of it that they are that much more willing to take a chance on an unknown vampire," he said with a smirk.

Mary glared at one of the girls who was wearing only a pair of hot pants and a boob tube. She turned and waved her wrist provocatively at Kristian, who needed no second invitation, and was immediately by her side taking full advantage of the exposed flesh.

"He always does this," moaned Cecile.

"I know, he calls it playing the feeding field," said Mary glumly. "You would think the two of us would be enough to keep him satisfied."

Michael watched Kristian taking his turn feeding on each girl in the Sire party and turned to Dante almost apprehensively.

"If you wish to join your brother, I am happy to wait here for you."

Dante eyed the girls disdainfully.

"That will not be necessary, I have no idea what those girls have been living on. As I stated before Michael, I am very selective about what I put my teeth into." Dante said, giving him a meaningful smile.

Michael blushed and then gasped, as Dante grabbed him close and sunk his fangs into his neck. With Dante and Michael feeding on each other and Kristian feeding on everyone else, Mary and Cecile decided to keep themselves busy, by taking selfies and uploading them onto the blood doll social media site 'bitebook'. I decided now while everyone was suitably distracted, would be a good time for me to find the opportunity I had been waiting for. To my relief, not many vampires had brought blood dolls with them and those that weren't sampling the hired humans, were being served at the bar. I positioned myself between a couple of male vampires, one of them turned and smiled at me.

"Oh hey Scar, it's Ted, Dante's friend? I bumped into you the other night outside the Blood Dens?"

"Oh of course," I said quickly, checking none of the Lucards were listening but they were still engaged in their own feeding activities. "How are things?" I asked Ted, only half interested.

"Great, being one of the chosen ones has really turned my life around you know, except for the part about being dead. But I'm not really dead I'm like that dude from the Highlander movies."

He then started quoting something about being 'the only one'. I had no idea what he was talking about so I just nodded.

"I always felt like I had a link to vampires, even that vampire puppet that taught me how to count," Ted went on.

When I failed to think of an appropriate response other than 'Uh huh' he changed the subject.

"I hear Dante's been cleared of all charges?"

"Yes, that's why we're here tonight," I replied.

"Dante's here?" he laughed. "That must have taken some persuading! Between you and me I didn't really like that posh ghoul bar he kept taking me to."

This could turn to my advantage I suddenly thought, here I was looking for a vampire that either didn't know or didn't care for the law, and Ted seemed to be a perfect candidate. He was the epitome of a human turned during the height of the vampire phenomenon, sireless since his transition and preyed upon by vampires like Dante, who didn't educate them with anything worthwhile, but their own beliefs of what a vampire should be. So far that had only included a snotty blood type diet and bad poetry.

"Scarlet!" my thoughts were interrupted by a hoarse voice and I turned to see Grace waving at me.

"What are you doing here? I thought you said they don't let ghouls in without an escort?"

"They don't but I work here now. Before I died I was a Marketing Director for a big company with an impressive wage, but since I became a ghoul my credentials above ground mean nothing, I am having to work my way up again," Grace informed.

"So you're starting out as a barmaid?" I asked.

"Yes, it's strange, I never considered such a job but I am finding it quite refreshing. My manager is quite cute too, he has no skin on the right side of his face but other than that he barely looks dead." She pulled out her pocket mirror that she seemed to carry with her everywhere.

"Wish the same could be said for me, I had a formaldehyde facial today, for that recently deceased look but I am not sure if it worked, what do you think?" she asked.

"It really makes a difference," I lied.

"Do you really think so?" she gushed.

"Absolutely," I pandered and she smiled happily, she really was a fool, I wondered with amusement how a creature so ugly could believe anything nice said to them. Maybe it was because they desperately wanted it to be true.

"I have just finished my shift actually, so will join you. I am only allowed to stay for one though, then I will be told to leave as per the contract I signed, ghoul staff are only allowed to stay on the premises for thirty minutes before or after their shift," Grace recited, as she rolled her one good eye.

Ted gave Grace a forced smile then excused himself as she sat on a bar stool next to us, she stared at his back sadly.

"Sorry for making your friend leave, not many vampires will be seen socialising with my kind, you're the exception it seems," Grace said apologetically.

I tried not to show my anger. It was only half an hour I thought. I could always find Ted after Grace left, but I couldn't help but feel resentful at her interruption.

"I joined that undead clinic today. Coffin Crisis and it really helped! I saw this ghoul there who believes our condition is all in the mind, basically if I believe I'm beautiful I regenerate faster, it links in with the idea that negative thinking causes adverse effects even through death, that's why I didn't fully complete the transition into a vampire, I brought along too much human negativity," she babbled on.

I was only half listening to her, when I felt a sudden wave of nausea, I looked wildly around me, sudden panic rising. I could not allow myself to be sick here, in front of all these vampires. Nothing said human more than puking in a vampire club. Telling Grace I'd be right back, I dashed off until I found a sign saying Restrooms. I burst through the door only to be met with a room full of what looked to be very ill or old looking humans forming an orderly queue. At the front of the queue were three vampires sat in throne like chairs, as each human approached they bowed before them.

"Scarlet, what are you doing?" came Grace's voice behind me.

"I was looking for the toilets," I said, my eyes fixed on an old man bowed before a female vampire, he seemed to be praying, then he kissed her hand and gazed into her pale eyes as she spoke soft words to him, he smiled and seemed completely at peace before suddenly, the vampire struck like a snake. It was quick, not like any of the feeding I had witnessed during my visit so far. The man let out a long sigh, his eyes rolled to the back of his head and closed, as his lips parted into a small smile before slumping forward. The vampire withdrew, delicately dabbed her mouth and clicked her fingers. A couple of ghouls ran forward and took the man's limp body away. This was, it seemed the undead version of assisted suicide for mortals, I was fascinated and wanted to watch more but the feeling of sickness urged me to leave. Turning I scanned the walls of the club searching for a sign.

"Toilets are this way," said Grace leading me down a staircase nearby. It was filled with blood dolls, mostly standing in groups chatting, while they did their make-up in the mirrors, some were taking selfies.

"Check out the bite this vamp just gave me, he had the biggest fangs I have ever seen, this is going straight on bitebook," one of them tittered.

I passed them and dived into one of the cubicles, before throwing up the blood I had downed earlier. I leant against the closed door for a moment trying to regain my composure. My head was spinning, this wasn't just the effect of the blood I had drunk, something was wrong. I got Scarlet's phone out and called the number I had for Mistress Varias's shop.

"What was in that draught you gave me?" I demanded, as soon as she answered.

"Hello Scarlet, or should I say Jessica," she replied calmly, ignoring the question.

"Enough with the pleasantries, what was in it?" I asked again.

"A few herbs, a bit of demon blood, nothing that could cause you harm."

"I don't feel right!"

"Have you considered, that it might not be the draught causing that? I'm not the only one to have given you something magical."

I looked down at the amulet Scarlet had given me.

"You think it's the Morshard?!" I exclaimed.

"It could be, when the glamour starts to wear off it can cause nausea in humans. It's to do with the shift of magical energies. How do you look?"

I came out of the cubicle, ignoring Grace who was still hovering outside and checked myself in one of the mirrors.

My eyes were no longer white, but blue and my face was flushed and very much alive. The rest of me was still Scarlet, but I didn't know how long that was going to last for.

"You have to help me, I am turning back," I pleaded down the phone.

"I cannot help you now, the Wardens are patrolling and if they see you and become suspicious, they will follow you here. Which means the amulet will be linked to me. I cannot allow that," Varias said softly, but firmly.

"But I can't go back out there looking like this!" I tried to reason.

"I'm sorry but you're on your own now," Varias replied coldly and with that, she hung up.

"Stupid Bitch," I muttered as I put the phone away, trying to think what I would do. But now I had another problem, in the mirror staring wide mouthed at my reflection was Grace.

"What just happened?" she croaked.

"Look I can explain..." I began.

"You're human? All this time I've been opening up my heart to you and you've been a human!"

"It's a spell, a vampire talked me into it," I said quickly. "I had no choice."

"You got a spell to pretend to be a vampire? Is this some kind of sick joke? My skin is falling off. Every day another piece of me starts to rot and I don't know what will fall off next and you're alive and well and probably laughing at me." Grace said, realisation dawning.

"Look just keep your voice down and I will explain," I pleaded.

"Don't bother, you have issues from the sounds of it and my Guru ghoul advised I stay away from those who harness unproductive energy, you're stopping me from healing," Grace said indignantly.

"Guru ghoul? Grace, thinking positive thoughts will not make you look any better!"

"What would you know about it!" Grace retaliated.

"I told you to keep your voice down!" I said, trying to regain control of the situation.

The blood dolls were looking at us now, but to my relief, they seemed more interested in finishing their make-up and their cravings for vamp blood. They left casually, leaving the two of us alone.

"Who were you talking to on the phone? Was that your vampire? How did they make you look like them?" Her eyes fell on the amulet.

"It's that necklace, isn't it? I thought it looked a bit tacky, but I just thought you had bad taste. But this is what's making you look different isn't it!" Grace reached out to grab it but I moved backwards quickly, despite the nausea.

"Give it to me! I need it more than you, you're already human, you can go back to your life and then I can be this vampire and look pretty again," Grace screeched.

She made another grab for it but I swatted her arms away, frustrated she gave a guttural hiss and lunged at me, her hands; which now had all fingers; gripped me with surprising strength. I fell back hitting my head on the hard tiled floor, pain flooded my vision momentarily adding more confusion to the nausea, and her hands clutched the necklace ripping it from me. She stood up triumphantly, staring at it longingly.

"If this can change you, it might be able to change me."

She tied it around her neck and then turned to the mirror, waiting, I sat up and touched the back of my head wincing as I felt blood.

"Grace, I need that necklace. It doesn't just change what I look like, it protects me also."

She had stopped listening though and was peering intently in the mirror, waiting, but her face remained the same. She rounded on me viciously.

"Why isn't it working?"

"Because it's a spell, it only works on me and the vampire that cast it," I tried explaining.

"You're lying! You just don't want me to look like I did before...you're jealous that's what it is!" Grace screeched again, before punching the mirror, shards of glass falling into sink along with thick droplets of her brown blood.

This was getting ridiculous, Grace was clearly falling apart mentally as well as physically. I needed to get the Morshard back and find Ted before he left. I stood up ignoring the wave of dizziness. The feeling of nausea had lessened, but now I was concerned my fall had given me a concussion, but I would have to worry about that later.

"I'm sorry Grace," I said.

"No you're not!" she spat.

"I am. You see, a creature as hideous as you should not be allowed to live, you were a mistake," I uttered with contempt, her face contorted with rage but was replaced with confusion as she looked down at the syringe suddenly buried in her chest. She pulled it out and stared at it, then back at me bewildered.

"Dead blood," I said simply.

"Injected directly into the heart, not enough to kill a vampire but enough to stop the body from rejuvenating itself. However..it's fatal for a ghoul, as that's the only thing that keeps your kind alive, without it, your body will now decompose fully like it was supposed to," I said, eyes locked.

"What?!" she gasped.

"See, I did a lot of reading up and it seems, euthanasia for ghouls is a recent procedure, so they haven't perfected it. It's a slow and agonising death I hear, but most that opt for it are so desperate to rid themselves from their half-life, they don't contemplate that, until they are barely more than a walking skeleton, their brain so rotted they have lost any shred of sentience," I continued, letting the full horror sink in.

Grace stared at me, mucus like tears falling from her one eye as realisation dawned on her.

"Please..." she begged.

I walked right up to her and stroked her head, feeling her bony skin through the thin flesh on her scalp, all resistance in her was gone, as she understood what was happening.

"But don't worry Grace, unlike most of your undead patrons I am not heartless, I wouldn't want to watch you suffer a long painful death," I said, hushing her.

I reached for a piece of the glass in the sink and quickly slashed her throat. She gurgled as it severed her already rotted vocal chords. As she slumped backwards into a cubicle, I followed arm raised, glass shard in hand. I raised the glass and stabbed her repeatedly, her chest, her face, anywhere I could. She fell to the floor, and I kept stabbing until my arm ached.

When I stopped she was no longer making any sound. The dead blood was doing its job, her body was decaying before my eyes, it was like watching a corpse rot in fast forward, the traces of demon blood unable to heal her and sustain her body any longer. I grabbed the Morshard back and put it back on.

I looked away from the putrid corpse and down at myself, I was covered in the thick ghoul blood, I couldn't go back out looking like this, if it was human blood it would be fine but ghouls blood would certainly raise questions. Also, I still had the issue of the glamour spell wearing off. My human eyes and flushed cheeks were not changing back so my fears that this was more than a temporary glitch were true. Both these issues were important but first I had to hide Graces body, I propped her up on the toilet bowl and closed the cubicle door firmly behind me. I went back to the sink and started washing myself up as best as I could, as I did, two girls stumbled in giggling. One of them headed straight for the cubicle where Graces was.

"That one's not working," I said, quickly stepping in front of it.

"Oh, okay thanks" she replied, before stumbling into the cubicle next door instead. With that, I quickly left. Grace would be discovered soon but I had managed to leave the scene and hopefully bought some time before anything could be connected to me.

When I returned to the bar I spotted Ted, he was having an argument with one of the vampire bouncers.

"How was I supposed to know she already had a vamp, girl was putting her neck all up in my face! It was a simple mistake, he's the one who got all Blade on me!" Ted argued, waving his arms about.

I grabbed his arm and lead him away. "We're leaving now anyway," I smiled apologetically at the bouncer who looked like he was about to teach Ted some manners.

I led us around the opposite side of the club to where Kristian and the others were sitting, hoping to avoid their gaze. As we made it to the main door, Joe noticed and called out.

"Leaving so soon?" he asked.

I replied without turning around. "It's not really my scene." As I strode off, I faintly heard Joe laugh and say. "You sound just like Dezzy."

I carried on walking, pulling a confused Ted along with me until we were on an empty street far from the sounds of Plasma.

"What's going on Scar? Why did we have to leave I could have handled that dude," he said unconvincingly.

"I need a favour and it's going to sound odd," I said calmly.

"What is it?" Ted asked curiously.

"I need you to turn me again, my vampirism is wearing off," I said, hoping Ted would just go with it. Unfortunately, he wasn't as stupid as he looked.

"That's impossible," he laughed.

"No, it's something that can happen," I insisted. "Think of it as an undead defect like ghoulism," I said nodding. He peered at me, his pale eyes widening in shock.

"Oh wow! Your eyes! And your cheeks! You're right, you're turning back!" Ted exclaimed.

"Exactly, so if you wouldn't mind I would like you to turn me again," I said, trying to move things along.

"You want me to sire you?" he said slowly as it finally dawned on him.

"Yes," I said abruptly, starting to lose my patience.

"And that will get rid of this defect?" he asked doubtfully.

"Yes," I repeated getting even more impatient.

"I dunno...sounds complicated, maybe you should go visit one of those ghoul clinics?"

"There's no need Ted, when you can do it for me now. If I wait it might be irreversible," I pleaded.

He contemplated this.

"Is that so bad? You could be my blood doll," he looked at me hungrily.

"Do you really think my brothers would approve of that?" I said threateningly.

His face dropped. "Oh yeah, erm okay, just give me a second." I tilted my neck towards him and he stared at it nervously, licking his lips as he grabbed me awkwardly. I waited bracing myself for the pain but nothing happened.

"Hurry up!" I urged.

"Okay okay, I just need a minute," Ted responded.

"What are you talking about?" I said frustrated.

"It's my first time," he said, slightly embarrassed. I sighed. Out of all the vampires, I had to choose one that was a virgin.

"Just bite me, then feed me your blood, it can't be that hard." I tried to reassure him.

"I'm worried I'll kill you by mistake," Ted said, slowly scratching his head.

"Then try not to," I said through gritted teeth.

"I.....I'm sorry, I can't do this," said Ted, before rubbing his hand over his face.

"What do you mean you can't? You're a vampire, it should come naturally to you!" I yelled at him, all patience lost.

"I know..but I don't perform well under pressure," he said shifting on the spot.

"What kind of vampire are you?!" I said in disgust.

"Look, there's a lot of high expectations to meet, they make it look easy in the films but it's a lot harder than it looks, I've never even had my own blood doll," Ted replied defensively.

"Look, just stick them in me and let your instincts take over. I'm sure you'll do fine," I said, nodding for reassurance.

"Okay, I'll give it a go," Ted stammered.

I closed my eyes and waited, I felt his cold lips touch my neck, then the sharpness of his fangs as he clumsily bit into my flesh, the penetration was messy and painful. He was nervous at first barely drinking from me, but then the demon in him awoke and he began taking deeper gulps, he was loud, slurping and growling, his hands were rough, grabbing me awkwardly making me twist my neck painfully, as he tried to get a better hold. The whole experience was unpleasant and it was taking far too long. I started to feel a little light headed, I no longer had the strength to stand and I felt myself go limp in his arms.

He carried on drinking regardless, I felt drowsy but I forced myself to keep a clear head.

"Give me your blood now," I urged, but he ignored me.

"Ted, it's time," I insisted.

But he continued to drink from me, it was like he couldn't hear me at all. I tried to push him off but he was too strong and I felt too weak and dizzy from blood loss. I felt a wave of panic hit as I realised what was happening. He wasn't going to turn me, he was going to kill me.

"Ted please!" I pulled his hair, scratched at his face but he just continued to drain my blood.

"Scar!" I heard a raspy voice cry out, before everything went black.

Chapter 19

~Jessica Sunday~
Day Seven as a Vampire

I awoke and immediately cried out in pain as I turned my neck, in a flash things were coming back to me, Grace, Ted, and finally the raspy voice before I passed out. And as everything focused into view, I saw familiar things, Herb was sitting there next to me, his murky green eyes filled with worry, the fireplace and sofas. I was back at Scarlet's house and was laid out on one of chaise longues, which meant I had to be in the sitting room. As my vision completely cleared, I turned to Herb, who was still waiting for me to say something. I pushed down the repulsion and irritation I felt for this weird, decaying freak and the freakish brotherly love he felt for me, or Scarlet should I say.

As I lay there and fully recalled the previous night's events, I was more worried than ever. I was running out of time and options, Ted had been a long shot that had almost killed me and Grace's earlier meltdown hadn't helped. I was still angry; if Ted had just grown a proper pair of fangs my plan would be complete. Instead I was stuck here in pain, still human, being babysat by a teenage zombie. I found the strength and sat up, clutching a hand to my neck. To my surprise, I could feel a wad of bandage, courtesy of Herb I assumed.

"I also gave you a small amount of Kristian's blood before you passed out, it's healed the worst of it," he rasped.

I glared at him, knowing I would have to give him some form of an explanation, which in itself infuriated me. It was the final day of the swap, things had not gone according to plan and to top things off, I had been caught by Scarlet's pubescent stunted freak. But I had to say something, I had to know what Herb had in store, surely he had to know I was not his mistress?

"Thanks...for saving me," I managed. "That Ted has some serious issues, he can't get a human to feed on so he tries to feed on me, can you believe it? I'm almost prone to agree with Kristian, fledglings nowadays are so confused they think they can turn on their own," I blagged.

I had heard Kristian rave on about fledglings enough times to make it realistic, but Herb was frowning or at least it looked like it. It was a lot harder to fathom the expressions of ghouls due to their decomposition.

"Ted said you asked him to turn you, he was really upset. He said he just got carried away as your blood is human. But you don't look human to me Scar, what's going on?" Herb pleaded.

"That's absurd, why would I ask him to turn me?" I said, feigning indignation.

"I'll tell you. Because you *are* human, because you're not Scarlet but merely look like her, you are an imposter."

A shock of fear ran up my spine.

The voice that suddenly spoke up, shattering my illusion, was not Herb's. It was Kristian's, I had not spotted him in the darkness of the room. He was sitting in the corner watching me as Herb did, I was in trouble now and panic was quickly filling me, as I desperately thought of something to say. I had always been so good at thinking up things on the spot but now my flawed human brain failed me. All I could do was sit there in silent fear, the charade was over in the most dangerous of ways. Kristian spoke again.

"Where is the real Scarlet? Where is my sister?" He asked dangerously.

"I am her," I said unconvincingly.

He suddenly stood up and walked towards to me, his pale eyes roving over my face.

"Hmm, why don't I believe you? Oh I know, perhaps it's because I never recall my sister having blue eyes or flushed cheeks, or red blood instead of black." He waved a wad of tissue at me, covered in dark red blood.

"If you kill me you'll never get her back!" the words came out in a panic, desperate and pleading, I hated myself for it, but my instinct to survive was stronger than any pride I might carry.

Kristian merely laughed.

"Are you trying to threaten a vampire you silly girl? I don't have to kill you to get information, I can drain you to the brink of death then bring you back again, over and over until I get bored of you or until you tell me what I want, whichever comes first," he grinned wickedly, light glinting off his fangs.

"Please! I'll tell you! Just don't hurt me, she asked for this, really she did." My voice trembled as I spoke, weak, I hated it.

I told them both everything. About Scarlet's proposal, how she had turned up on my doorstep and how, after I had agreed, she had cast a spell on both of us using blood magic, both of them remained silent while they listened, seemingly unswayed.

When I finished my story, Kristian smiled. "My little sister is quite the rebel after all, I must be rubbing off on her."

Herb however, scratched his chin nervously causing a chunk of green flesh to come loose. "But Scar will be in so much trouble, she has broken so many laws, they'll take her in for human intent."

"Who else knows about this? Did you know she was planning this, Herb?" Kristian said, frowning. Herb shook his head.

"No. I knew she wanted to be like them, that's why she would spend so much time above ground...that's why she started.." he trailed off fearfully.

"Started what? What was Scar doing?" Kristian pried. But when Herb failed to answer, Kristian rounded on him.

"Look! I can't help her if I don't know what she's been up to."

"She was hunting, she was feeding off the humans so she could feel what they feel, using flickers," Herb blurted out.

Kristian swore. "For how long?" he asked, raising his voice.

"Maybe months, she was doing it even before I found out," he said honestly.

Kristian took out a blood vap and popped it in his mouth, inhaling deeply and slowly breathing out the red plume of smoke as he took the information in.

"I thought that she was going to stop though, after what happened last time," said Herb huskily.

Kristian looked at him questioningly and Herb bit his lip causing brown blood to appear before continuing.

"The boy that died. The one that's been on the news, Scar fed on him that night," Herb said ashamed.

"She's the one that killed him! All this time Dante has been taking the blame for it, and it was Scar...I can't believe this!" Kristian was rarely ever shocked, but this news was too much even for a vampire as nonchalant as him.

"She didn't mean to kill him!" said Herb defensively.

"When she left him, he was alive, still breathing. She even called an ambulance for him before she left...she always made sure they were alive. She never wanted to kill them...just have a chance at being one of them." Herb stammered, coming to the defence of his mistress.

"She was stupid. And so were you! You should have told us as soon as it happened," Kristian chided.

Herb nodded sourly. "I never knew she would resort to this though...it's powerful blood magic's that she's used, she can't have done this alone."

Kristian's face was grim as he replied. "She's had help from a witch, that's the only way she could have conducted a spell so powerful as this. Herb, use all your ghoul contacts, someone must have seen Scar visiting the Witches Quarter over the last few months. When you discover who our helpful witch is, bring her here. I want to have a little chat with her."

Herb nodded, determination in his ruddy eyes. He turned and lopped off on his errands, moving surprisingly fast despite his deformities. Kristian turned to me again, as if suddenly remembering I was there.

"How long until this spell wears off?" he asked.

"Today. I mean today is the last day, but as you can see it's already starting wearing off," I said nervously.

"That means Scar could also be in danger. If she is among humans, when she suddenly turns back to her vampire self, who knows how they will react," Kristian considered, then eyed me curiously.

"Still can't believe you've been here nearly a week and we never knew, that must be some powerful mojo," he said, a hint of wonder in his voice.

I didn't say anything, he had figured out half the spell, but still hadn't considered the magic from the Morshard. The Glamour spell may have faded, but the protection spell might still work as far as I knew. Regardless, that was all I had left now...I was relying on it. Kristian continued talking down to me.

"So was it worth it? Do you, like all the others that come down here, want to be one of us? Were you hoping Scar would turn you?" Kristian had a sneer on his face as he spoke.

I shrugged.

"I had no expectations other than a new experience," I said calmly. To my surprise, he laughed at my response.

"You are a smart one," he said edging nearer. "What makes you think I won't just kill you? You're not registered, no one knows you are here except Scar and I," Kristian said menacingly, but I was not phased. I looked up and met his gaze.

"Because I have watched you for the last week and I know that you are many things. But a murderer is not one of them," I said coldly.

He merely smiled.

"Oh really?" he said. "If I'm to be honest, I'm fascinated with what you and my sister have done. It was risky, you would have to be half crazy or stupid to agree to such an endeavour. So tell me, which are you?" He said smiling.

"Your sister threatened me, I didn't feel I had a choice," I answered flatly.

"Is that a fact? Strange, you don't seem to scare easy," Kristian said observantly.

Before he could continue talking me to death, his demeanour switched. He stood straighter and cocked his head as if he had heard something. He suddenly looked up before dissipating.

"Cecile?!" I heard him yelling from upstairs.

With effort, I pulled myself off the chaise longue and stumbled towards the doorway. I climbed the stairs, wobbly at first, but gaining strength with each step. As I reached the landing and got to the doorway of Kristian's bedroom, I saw him. He was at the bed, shaking Cecile who lay there limp, her eyes rolled to the back of her head. A thick trail of blood and foam dribbled from her nostrils down to her chin.

"Come on, Cecile.." Kristian said. He shook her again, but she continued to flop backwards and forwards in his arms, like a dead fish. He gazed at her for a moment in shock before speaking.

"I heard it, I heard her heart stop beating.." Kristian said quietly. "We bought her back with us early as she said she felt unwell, I just thought she was blood drunk..." He touched a finger to the blood dribbling down her chin and sniffed it.

"Her blood is tainted. Someone has spiked her!" Kristian said loudly. As I stood there in the doorway, he turned and looked at me, realisation dawning on his face. He looked again at Cecile's dead body then to me, as he did I allowed myself to smile.

"You! But why? WHY?! What would be the point in killing a blood doll, my blood doll?!" He shouted at me. Still smiling, I started to back out of his room.

"I don't know what you're talking about," I said coyly.

Kristian put his hand gently on Cecile's forehead, before slowly rising up. He turned and paced towards me ominously. For the first time since I had arrived, I could see a flicker of emotion, it was hate. It was subtle but I knew the look all too well to dismiss it. The first time I had seen it, had been on my mother's face. She had tried to hide it then as well, but it had been too late. I had already known how she really felt.

Kristian moved closer and closer towards me, his mouth pulled back over his teeth, his face a mixture of anger and sorrow, he was going to kill me, perhaps he would take me in his arms and drain the blood from my veins. But before he got within arm's reach, he stopped. His normally perfect face was twisted with pain. Black blood began to run from his nose and his steps became wobbly. A look of fear and confusion crossed his face before he fell to the floor, like his legs had been swept from under him. He began convulsing, his back arched so violently, I thought he would snap in two. I watched curiously as he writhed in pain, his pale eyes were wide open, glaring at me as I stepped forward and stood over him. His face started turning a sickly grey as he lay paralysed. Standing over him, I reached into my bra and pulled out the syringe along with one of the vials from Mistress Varias. I shook the tiny vial in front of him, making sure he could see it.

"Witches Salt," I said with a smile.

The Witches Salt was poisoning him, Varias had told me, that a little would be enough to weaken a vampire, but I had added a bit more just in case, that explained why Cecile had died I thought to myself. Witches Salt was completely harmless to ordinary humans, but those who had vampire blood in them, like a blood doll, was another matter. Oh well, trial and error. As I continued to watch Kristian writhing in agony, I recalled Varias's magical explanation, but looking at it first hand, it seemed like a lethal chemical reaction. It had been easy to spike Cecile, a small amount of Witches Salt discreetly tipped into one of her drinks at Plasma while she took selfies of her and Mary.

Kristian tried to reach out towards me, his face concentrating as he held his hand out. I let out a short laugh, what was this fool trying to do? He couldn't even get up, let alone lunge at me! I suddenly felt pressure build up around my throat, there was a sharp pain and it was getting hard to breathe, he was trying to use his magic to choke me. I kicked him hard, I thought I heard something break, but I didn't care, it had the desired effect, the pressure around my neck ceased. As he continued to lie there in agony I scanned his face one final time. It seemed blood drinker or not, the look of fear was always the same.

Chapter 20

~Scarlet Sunday~
Day Seven as a Human

"Not seeing your friends today?" asked Mrs Young. I was curled up on the sofa, with Princess on my lap. I was watching a mindless cartoon, which so far had proven ridiculous, what possible life lesson could one get from a talking sponge? Yet I had been unable to stop myself from watching it all morning, it was a welcome distraction from the night before.

"You still look very pale," she observed. "Watching this rubbish isn't going to do you any good either, why don't you join your father and Leyna in the garden? I could bring you out an Ice Tea," she said with a smile on her face.

"I feel fine," I said, narrowly dodging her hand as she tried to feel my forehead. She dropped her hands and instead placed them on her hips.

"Well, in that case you can help me around the house instead of nursing your hangover on the sofa all day," I groaned and actually managed to sound like the real Jessica.

"I need you to sort out the drawers in the office, they are filled with old photos, Christmas cards and who knows what else. But it's all such a mess, I need you to organise them into albums and throw out any of the really old cards," she instructed.

"Can't you do it?" I asked, at the risk of coming across a selfish brat, the last thing I wanted to do right now was sort through photos of Jessica.

"No, because if I go through them I won't throw anything out, I will always think of a reason to keep something. I need your teenage ruthlessness to sort through the clutter. Anyway, you're the one who has been nagging me to let you have the room for a gym, the least you can do is help clear it out," she said matter of factly.

This is how I ended up sitting on the carpet floor in Mrs Young's office, sifting through piles of old birthday cards, school photos and old diaries. I flicked through one and saw it belonged to Mrs Young. I was about to cast it aside when something in the first excerpt caught my attention, so I read on.

3rd July 2008

I started this diary on the recommendation of Doctor Thompson, she feels writing down my feelings will help. I don't quite know where to start; this all seems like a nightmare. I just wish I could wake from it, I feel like I have failed as a mother somehow. My husband John is so easy going and thinks we have the perfect five year old child, but he doesn't know all the things I know, he doesn't know the other Jessica. At first I tried talking to him and suggesting we take her to a psychiatrist, I told him about the violent outbursts when she doesn't get her way, how she smashed my mother's wedding gift, a Wedgewood bone china tea set. His response was that she's at a difficult age and will grow out of it; he never cared for that tea set anyway. I sometimes feel scared when I am alone with her, I know it's an awful thing to say about your own child but sometimes she gets this look in her eye like she hates me.

I flipped over to the next page but there was nothing written until a couple of weeks later.

17th July 2008
Today the third babysitter handed in her notice after advising that Jessica had threatened to kill her with a pair of scissors after she refused to let her stay up and watch TV. When I confronted Jess she said she had been joking. Nevertheless I have decided to keep any sharp objects.

The next few pages were blank, the entries were sporadic as if she was only writing when she was particularly distressed. Again I flipped through until I found the next entry.

8th August 2008
Jessica has been much better lately, the new babysitter says she is a joy to be around and there have been no violent tantrums or any sign of erratic behaviour. My only concern is that she seems to have developed an unnatural obsession with death; she keeps asking questions about it. At first I thought it was natural to be curious, her grandfather had passed away recently. But then a week later our cat Smokey died and we buried her in the garden, the next day I found Jessica had dug her up and cut her open as if performing an autopsy. She said she just wanted to know what happened after you died, but I cannot get the image of her cutting up poor Smokey, out of my head, what normal child does something like that, especially to a pet? Other days she is sweet and endearing, dancing around the living room and laughing, it is like I have two children in her.

I stared at the neatly written words as a sudden realisation dawned on me, Jessica was two people, the human I had seen when I first visited her house, friendly and relaxed even when faced with a vampire in her house, and then the other one, a darker person that held morbid interests. Then it became clear, why else would a normal happy human girl want to change places so readily with a dead girl, that only lives by drinking the blood of the living. This was the part of Jessica that I had learnt about last night, the part that likes inflicting torture, the part that deliberately goes out with her friends looking for people to viciously attack and then film it. I turned to the next entry, unable to stop, now that I had started reading.

23rd August 2016
I haven't written for a few years, things seemed to be going so well. Jessica is now thirteen and we have another daughter who is three - Leyna. She is very similar to Jess to look at, but quieter than her sister was at that age, she almost never cries and doesn't like to be left alone. She dotes on Jess, following her everywhere even places she cannot get to which, I hope, is the reason for what happened today. We had to take Leyna to the hospital for a broken arm. She had been playing with Jessica in the back garden. Jessica said that Leyna tried to follow her and climb the big elm tree, but had fallen. I want to believe her, she seemed genuinely upset, she couldn't stop crying while we waited for Leyna to be x-rayed, and kept asking if she was going to be okay. Yet still, a small voice inside of me keeps asking the same question, is this Jessica's doing? I vowed I would move on and not keep blaming her. John thinks I am being unfair to not give her the benefit of the doubt but every time Leyna has a fall, cuts a knee, burns herself; I always wonder, was it really an accident?

The question mark glared out at me from the page. If Mrs Young's intuition had been correct, what kind of a person had Jessica grown up to be? How far was she willing to go to harm something or someone? I thought of Leyna and how she mostly avoided me, how she had frozen when I had hugged her and fled as soon as she had the chance and then I thought of the scar that ran across her stomach and Mrs Young's reaction when I asked about it. I heard Mrs Young approaching, so I shut the diary and shoved it back in the drawer.
"How're you getting on?" she asked.
"Fine, just reminiscing," I said.
She knelt over me and kissed the top of my head.
"You shouldn't be at your age, you've still got your whole life ahead of you," she said with a smile as she looked down at the scattered photos, bending down to pick one up of Jessica hugging a small white dog.

"I remember this! Your 12th birthday, you were so happy when you opened the box up and Daisy jumped out, I remember how much you cried when she ran away only a year later," she said distantly.

I looked at the picture, how could the Jessica I see here, the smiling pretty child, holding her puppy lovingly, become this other Jessica that I was starting to learn about.

"You've gotten through a lot, haven't you? It looks much better already" said Mrs Young, looking round the room.

"Can you do me one last favour? There's another box in the shed filled with yours and Leyna's baby pictures. Your father moved them there to keep them safe when the house was being re-decorated last year and I completely forgot about them," she said apologetically.

"Sure," I replied.

"The shed's a bit of a mess and needs sorting out and the roof has been leaking as well. I keep telling your father to fix it, I am worried the pictures will get damp and ruined," she said distractedly.

"I'll bring them in, don't worry," I said reassuringly.

"That's my girl," she said and gave me another kiss. "I'll make us something special for lunch, how about pancakes?" I tried not to grimace.

"Sounds great!" I replied as she walked out of the room.

I was greeted by an unpleasant musty smell when I entered the shed. Mrs Young wasn't kidding when she said this place needed a sorting out. I brushed and shook my hair as a giant cobweb tried to paste itself there.

I stared at the stacks of boxes that filled the shed, most were filled with old kitchenware and garden tools. In the last one, however, I found what she had been referring to, it was mostly old school books and another four photo albums. I was just about to lift the box and carry it out when I spotted a smaller box hidden at the back, completely covered in dust, it was taped shut. I might as well check this one I thought as I ran my sharp nail along the thick tape. I had thought the unsavoury smell had been due to the damp and dirt that seemed to fill the shed but as the cardboard flaps opened I was hit by the real source. It was something I had become accustomed to during my century and a bit as a vampire, it was the smell of death. I looked inside the box knowing that if I had been human I would have retched, it was filled with bones, animal bones. Some still had matted fur stuck to them and as I dug through them, I found a little pink collar with a gold medallion hanging from it. I turned it in my hands, the name *'Daisy'* was engraved upon its surface.

I closed the flaps and stood back, still staring at the box. I pictured Princess snuggling on my lap earlier, her large brown eyes gazing up at me with trust as I stroked her. I thought about Jessica killing previous pets just like her and stuffing their bodies in a cardboard box, keeping it near the house so she could what? Come in from time to time and relive it?

I grabbed the box of photos and walked back up to the house, I had to get back home, my true home. All this time I had been worried about Jessica getting harmed but now I was worried about the harm she could do to others. It seemed absurd, she was a human surrounded by vampires after all. These were supernatural beings, capable of killing at a word, not tiny puppies, she would be a fool to try anything, but learning what I did about Jessica, I wasn't entirely convinced. After everything I had just discovered, I had come to the conclusion, that Jessica was not sane and capable of anything.

I told Mrs Young, that I had decided to go out and see Hannah in the end. I hugged her goodbye, it was a disguise, I was really apologising. Saying sorry for having taken her daughter away for a week and sorry, that I would have to deliver her daughter back to her. I found Mr Young and Leyna in the garden soaking up the morning sun as they pieced a jigsaw together on the garden table. I hugged them both, feeling Leyna flinch as I did so, and now knowing why. I knew I should of gone straight home, but I had one more thing left to do before I returned. I closed my eyes and materialised, feeling myself fading was terrifying but I focused on my destination with determination and when I opened my eyes, I was standing next to Ben's hospital bed.

"What the?!" I spun round and saw Sam standing behind me with a cup of coffee halfway to his lips.

"How did you get in here?" he turned round at the door behind him then back to me.

"I don't have time to explain, but I can help Ben," I said.

"Jess, what are talking about?" he frowned, confused.

"I'm not Jess, you know I'm something different, you saw that the other night. But I promise I am not here to hurt you and I will be gone from your life soon, but before I go I can help your brother." I told him,

"I don't know what I saw the other night," he said shaking his head.

"Yes you do," I grabbed his hand and put it against my chest.

"Do you feel a heartbeat?" I asked softly.

He stared at his hand against my silent chest, he moved it to the left slightly, a baffled look on his face.

"You won't find it," I said.

"It hasn't beaten for over one hundred years. My true name is Scarlet and I'm a vampire, a Nosferatu, a creature of the night, Lestat, Edward Cullen... you get the gist?" I said, trying to get a response.

"What? That's ridiculous!" but I could see he was having doubts.

"I borrowed Jessica's body and she borrowed mine, she'll be back tonight," I promised.

"That's not possible, you can't just borrow a body?" said Sam, disbelief running through him.

"You don't have to believe me. But let me do one thing for you, let me help your brother." I stepped closer to the bed.

"Wait, what are you going to do to him?" he said, grabbing my arm to restrain me.

"Trust me. Let me do this for him...for you." I said.

He stared at me for a moment, his eyes searching mine, then he pressed his lips together in resolution and dropped his hold on me.

I bit into my wrist, just as I had with Penny, and held it over Ben's mouth. Droplets of blood fell between his half-parted lips. I held it over them until I was sure enough had been given. Then I turned to Sam.

"It will take a few hours but he will wake, I can't promise if he will be the same as he was before but it's the best I can do."

Before he could say a word, I started fading before him and just before I was gone he lunged forward and I faintly felt his lips touch mine, but when I opened my eyes I was alone again.

I had been very foolish, I had now revealed myself to two humans. But I would deal with those repercussions later, now I was far too busy thinking about how I was going to deal with Jessica. I made for the nearest Underdark entrance point, filled with determination, thoughts raced through my head. I had been so blinded by my own agenda that I had failed to see the truth behind Jessica, only someone who knew darkness already would be so comfortable in its presence. I had only seen what I had wanted to see. From an outsider's point of view Jessica was everything I wanted to be, who I should have been. But she was wearing a mask as much as I was; the laughing, happy girl was nothing like the girl I had come to learn about. The only thing that seemed to make Jessica happy was hurting people. She had started off doing it in secret, killing her pets and pretending that they had run away. Jessica was an attention seeker though, causing pain from behind closed doors was not enough, she wanted to gloat. This explained the bolder acts of violence as she matured, the reckless abuse on her sister and the random attacks on strangers which she filmed and posted on-line.

Her crimes screamed out for recognition, her need to hurt people was stronger than the fear of being caught, or was she just arrogant in believing that she would get away with it?

As I entered through the city gate, I was surrounded by the familiar scene of the Underdark and yet found it looked different. It had the same buildings and streets, the same undead inhabitants but it was as if I was seeing it through new eyes. I had left here a week ago, an institutionalised vampire, desperate to get out and live in the human world. Now, after all I had seen, it felt a relief to be back, as if the real evil lurked outside, and now that I was back underground surrounded by my fellow demons, I was somehow safer. Something was amiss though, as I walked through the city, signs of disturbance greeted me, worsening the further I walked on.

Smashed shops, fighting on the streets between Wardens and vampires were scattered throughout. What had happened here?

When I got home I was relieved to see the Vampire Quarter had escaped damage from whatever had caused the wreckage in the other Quarters. But as I entered the house I knew something was very wrong, I could smell the vampire blood straight away.

I found him upstairs with one of his blood dolls, I sensed he was the only one here, but even with that small blessing, I could not get over the sight of him lying there. I bent over his body taking in his still form, his skin had taken on a leaden grey hue was but still flawless, even in death. A faint hint of a smirk lingered on his lips. The fact that his head had been completely severed from his body was the only thing stopping me thinking he was about to sit up and give that low throaty laugh of his. Then it hit me, an unfamiliar tightness in my throat, a pain in my chest no… in my heart, my heart that I had thought to be as dead as the corpse in front of me. Before I could digest any more of what was going on, I heard a strange choking sound, I looked around until I realised the noise...was me. My body started to shake violently, as pure, unfiltered emotion took over me, far more potent than any flicker, far more real, far more painful. It was the worst kind of pain I had ever experienced, it was a breathless, soundless scream, deep within that robbed me of all sense. I felt wetness on my cheek and for a moment thought I must be bleeding somehow, but as I brushed my hand across it and stared in shock, I saw that it was not blood, but glistening tears that covered it.

"Awww how sweet, you've learned how to cry," came the mocking voice of Jessica from behind me.

I spun around and launched myself at her with a roar, pinning her against the wall, my hand gripping her throat. My grief turning into rage, the unfamiliar emotions pumping through me like a drug. It filled me with an urge to destroy and rid myself of the cause of all this, this human girl who, by all reason should be the innocent one in all this. It had been me, I was the one to corrupt her, to intimidate her to take my place in a world without light, to inflict upon her the emptiness of my existence, I was meant to be the monster in this tale. But I had not fathomed that this human might already live in the darkness, her mind might already be corrupted, this human might be more monstrous than myself.

The monster laughed as I held her, it was unnatural, not human not vampire but something else entirely, something that possessed a soul yet when I looked into its eyes could see and feel a coldness beyond the grave, beyond sanity. Then I felt pain, not the emotional pain but the sharp pain that reminded me I was still part of this world, I looked down and saw a syringe sticking out of my chest.

"Witches Salt!" said Jessica triumphantly, as I staggered back, pain shooting through my entire body like I was being burnt alive. I fell to the floor and began convulsing as it took full effect. Jessica stood over me, her head tilted to the side as she watched curiously.

"Such a simple thing, yet very effective, I can see why the distribution of it is banned among your kind," she continued gloating as I writhed in pain.

"You must have thought, I was so silly when I turned up with those table salt sachets, but one can learn a lot when determined enough, even in such a short space of time. You just have to ask the right questions. Your witch friend was very helpful in that respect, not just in providing me with the materials but also teaching me about vampires. See it's the demon you get your strength from, quite obvious really, that any humanity in you only serves to make you weaker." She bent down and wiped her finger across my cheek holding it up to show me a fresh tear that had run down it.

"Varias told me that some vampires could cry, that they were able to tap into parts of their former humanity. But she also told me why so many vampires never sought to do so. It isn't just the emotional floodgates that would ensue but...and this I found very interesting...it weakens a vampire - physically I mean. It makes your almost impenetrable bodies far more vulnerable to pain."

She walked over to Kristian's body, gave it a kick and retrieved the sword she had hidden under his body, then walking back over to me she held it above her head, blade pointing straight at my chest. I saw it rushing towards me as if in slow motion, the tip of the blade glinting in the candlelight. As the Witches Salt burned its way through my veins, I lay there frozen, a petrified corpse, as the sword came plunging down. The tip broke into my flesh and buried itself into my chest. I cried in pain, sounding more human than the human girl who, laughing as she did so, pushed the blade deeper, before giving it a savage twist. I couldn't cry this time, only gurgle as black blood came up from my throat, I coughed trying to expel it but my useless lungs failed me and I choked as my instinctive gagging reflex kicked in. I didn't need oxygen, I was under no threat of choking to death but it was not pleasant. The wound in my chest was of more concern though, but luckily for me, it had not pierced the heart, either Jessica was a bad aim or she was toying with me.

"I can only imagine how much pain you are in now, for someone who has lived a century without feeling anything this must be very traumatic. It must be very confusing for you, these new emotions you have suddenly opened yourself up to. But still, you did say you wanted to experience what it was like being a human right? And to think you have me to thank for it all," she said contemptuously.

She twisted the blade again, before pulling it out and raising it above her head.

"Where next? The leg? I hear being stabbed in the knee cap is quite painful," she contemplated.

With a huge effort I raised my hand and attempted to tap into my demon side by forcing her back with my will, but nothing happened. I tried again, a small shudder vibrated through the air around me, it wouldn't have been strong enough to lift a leaf off the ground. I stared at her, open mouthed and confused, she smirked and fingered the red stone hanging from her neck. I hissed angrily, of course, she was wearing the amulet, protecting her against the abilities of a vampire, rendering me powerless by my own doing. After all I was the one that gave her the damn thing.

"What a thoughtful gift this was, Scarlet," she said, before driving the sword into my knee cap. My enhanced hearing picked up every sound, the flesh slicing, the cartilage rupturing, the bone cracking. A cacophony of pain lead by my own cries of anguish.

"You sound pathetic!" said Jessica with disgust.

"You should be above pain. But no, you are so obsessed with trying to be human that you invite it," she spat.

She pulled the blade out with a sickening squelch, then held it to my throat.

"You're a lot more fun to play with than your brother was, he barely made a sound as I drove this into every part of his body," she said.

"Why? Why Kristian? Why not just me?" I asked as I pictured him being stoic to the last. He was a better vampire than me in all aspects.

"Blame your poor blood magic for that, if your spell had been better, the glamour would have lasted the full time it was meant to. And I would not have been discovered," she said angrily.

So, Kristian had found out Jessica wasn't me. He must have confronted her, causing her to switch into psychotic mode. He was dead because of me, I deserved to die, I had never been happy with my condition, but he had always embraced it, my own selfish desires had led to this. I stared at the blade accepting my fate as it came down once more racing towards my throat. I felt pain as the tip of the sword pierced my throat, but was then surprised when she removed the blade, I was still alive?! I turned my head sideways and retched. As I coughed up more of my own blood, I dared to lift my head and search for Jessica. She was still standing there, sword in hand.

She dropped the blade and knelt down beside me.

"I also learnt that a vampire's need for human blood increases when they are weak," she eyed my wounds critically.

"That's a lot of blood you're losing. The Witches Salt is stripping away your healing powers that would normally get you through such injuries."

She was right of course, my body was weakening. I was still alive but I wouldn't be able to move any time soon, the Witches Salt would eventually wear off but I would need a lot of blood before then. Father and Desmodeus would be busy with the riots, I had no idea where Dante, Herb or Mildred were, perhaps she had killed them as well, it was too much to even consider.

As if sensing my thoughts Jessica smirked.

"Your family won't be back any time soon to save you. The riots are only just starting. That servant of yours is out there looking for you, not a good time for a ghoul to be walking the streets of the Underdark, the FF will attack him on sight. Mildred is out there too, I made sure to send her on an errand, knowing full well, that she would be caught in it. Your brother Dante and the blood dolls with him will be trapped inside Plasma. If they leave, they will also be attacked, the FF are not overly fond of blood dolls from what I hear."

Her face loomed over me, it was a strange sight, she still partially looked like me. The long blonde hair framing her face was still mine, but her flushed cheeks and blue eyes were her own. Her features were beginning to change back also, the shape of her mouth and nose. She reached for the sword again, and I braced myself, but this time she sliced it across her arm, the flesh opening easily. Dark red blood began to seep out, the scent of it immediately causing my body to react. My fangs, which had returned, flared in preparation. She moved her arm towards me and I tried turning my head away with difficulty.

"Come now, Scarlet, don't be coy. I know how thirsty you must be," she cooed.

She grabbed my chin with her other hand, holding me in place and held the bleeding arm above my mouth. A few droplets fell onto my lips, I forced myself to keep them closed but the vampire in me started to take over, my jaws opened and in a half frenzy latched onto Jessica's bleeding arm. The blood rushed into my mouth and with it, her flickers. Shadowy figures formed into people, familiar people, her parents just as I knew them, her sister Leyna. I could feel it, the deep resentment she held for her little sister. Images of what I had read in the diary, Leyna crying in pain as Jessica took every opportunity to hurt her, it was senseless abuse. Jessica's joyous memories mixed with my feelings of disgust as I experienced the full, unedited version of her life.

The boys who she had cheated on Sam with, just because she could, the people she had bullied, like Penny and other faces I didn't know. Then one face I knew almost as well as my own, for it had haunted me the last week, the boy from Insomnia. Jessica stumbling into the alley and finding him where I had left him, looking around to see if anyone was there, then to my horror she covered his mouth and nose with her hands suffocating him, he struggled weakly still half conscious from the loss of blood and intake of alcohol. I pulled away and opened my eyes, focusing on Jessica sitting over me.

"You killed him!" I accused her.

"All this time I thought it was me but it was you, you came back and finished him off! Why? What reason did you have to take his life like that?" I yelled.

Jessica frowned contemplating this.

"Because I could, it was so easy that I was disappointed afterwards, I thought killing someone would be harder but then you had done most of the work for me. Still, I had expected him to hang on longer...to at least try and fight back," she said in disgust.

"This is what you hid from me when I first drank from you, it wasn't the salt sachets, you were hiding. It was the terrible things you had done." I said frantically.

The reality of it was astounding; all this time I had thought I was the evil one, I was the demon, the creature of nightmares but I had been misconceived, I'd been harbouring the real monster and I'd let her into my home.

"At first I thought he had been stabbed, there was always something going on at Insomnia, only the week before a boy had been bottled," Jessica mused.

"But then, when I saw it on the news here, I couldn't believe I had caused all this trouble, not only had I shaken the human world but also the undead world and that is quite an impact to have," she said arrogantly.

She stopped musing and looked down at her arm. "You haven't finished? You need to take more than that in order to turn me."

"What? I'm not turning you!" But even as the words left my mouth my mind disagreed.

"Oh you will, that Witches Salt not only weakens you but it gives me utter control over you, how else do you think witches control demons? Every command they give is obeyed because the demon is constantly being fed this, the blood they drink is laced with it. It's harder with vampires due to the human in them. This will wear off soon so you better hurry up," she said, thrusting her arm into my face again.

I felt the urge to do as she said but then another urge stronger than that stopped me, I turned my head and looked at Kristian's corpse again even in death, he gave me strength. I would not immortalise his murderer.

"Turn me. NOW!" she yelled, losing patience. I remained motionless, stubbornly staring at the bleeding arm in front of me.

"Do it!" she screeched shrilly.

"Why don't you do as I say?! The witch said it would work." She grabbed my face trying to prise my mouth open but failed. She looked around and grabbed the sword, holding it across my throat.

"If you don't turn me I will slice your head off just like I did with your brother," she threatened.

I felt the anger rise in me unbidden and as it did, I managed to start regaining control over my body once more. I moved my hand and grabbed the sword from her grasp. She flinched and jumped up, backing away from me as I slowly rose from the ground. I would not be able to use my blood magic on her, she was still wearing the amulet, but I could use my strength. Weakened as I was I would still be stronger than a human.

"You shouldn't be able to move!" she screeched.

As I pushed myself to my feet, I held the sword out and walked towards her. She backed against the wall as I pressed the blade against her throat, ready to do to her what she had done to my brother. But I couldn't do it, after all these years believing I was a killer. I knew how precious life was.

Jessica saw me hesitate, she kneed me in the stomach before pushing me away and running out the room. Even as I stood there hunched over, I knew I could have stopped her, despite the injuries and weakness, but then what would I do? I knew I couldn't kill her no matter how much I wanted to. I could hand her over to the Wardens, but then what I had done would come out and I would be charged with human intent. I sunk to the ground not knowing who or what I was anymore. As I sat there, the remainder of the glamour finally faded and I was once again Scarlet Lucard, the vampire. But I felt different, like a switch had been turned on inside me. I slumped to the floor and edged nearer to Kristian, grabbing his limp hand.

"I'm sorry," I whispered to him. "I had so much to tell you, I finally experienced life, I wanted to share it with you."

I sat there holding his hand. I don't know how long passed, time seemed irrelevant. Eventually I heard the front door open, someone else was here.

***

"Incompetence, that's what it is!" Dante stated in annoyance.

"To have kept us locked in there is simply ridiculous. What were the Wardens doing? That's what I would like to know! Surely it can't take that long to take down a gang of miscreants," he complained.

As he led the way into the house, Michael and Kristian's blood doll; Mary, followed in his wake.

"I'm just glad they did, I've never been so scared in all my life" said Mary dramatically.

"I bet Kristian's annoyed he missed it, he would have loved to see all those fledglings being dragged off to the Tower. I don't know why he left so early, he told me he was just going to drop Cecile back," said Mary sullenly.

Dante smirked to himself, he knew what his brother was like and how he enjoyed playing the emotions of the blood dolls like a harpsichord. With that thought in mind, Dante considered retiring to his room to do just that, Michael would be the perfect captive audience for a late night sonata. As he started making his way up the staircase, he suddenly felt that things were very wrong.

"Wait!" Dante said sharply. His sudden change of demeanour cut through the blood doll's conversation like a knife.

"Something's not right, something is not right at all!" An uncharacteristic grimace cracked along his normally marblesque features. Blood, It was blood he could smell but not just any blood, but the blood of one of his own.

"Michael! Stay here with Mary and, if possible, arm yourself." He knew that despite that, the humans would not have stood a chance, if the danger was as he perceived.

Starting with the lower floor, he abruptly opened and closed each room, surveying each of them in mere seconds.

Chapter 21

~Herb~
~Ghoul On the Run~

I knew something was wrong as soon as I turned down Victorian Street into the Trade Quarter. The FF were smashing the shop windows, other vampires, encouraged by the FF, were already looting and dragging merchandise out of the shops. One vampire, who was rolling a barrel of blood out of Norm's, spotted me.

"Got another one here skulking in the shadows!" he yelled out. I tried to turn and run but he pounced, knocking me to the ground.

"It's a Unclean!" he yelled to the others.

"Your kind are a plague and were never meant to be vampires. You need to be cleansed from our city," he pulled out a long dagger from the inside of his jacket.

I held my arms over my head and closed my eyes tight, waiting for the pain but nothing happened. When I opened them the vampire had dropped his arm with the dagger and was staring behind him, I followed his gaze and froze in terror. I should have felt relief at the arrival of the Wardens but it was hard to feel anything but fear when they were nearby, their pale faces gaunt and starved looking, their eyes slitted and black as the night itself. Vampires that embraced their true nature, physical manifestations of what lies inside us, darkness incarnate. They seemed to come from shadow appearing behind their victims, malformed jaws opening to reveal rows of needle like fangs that shred through vampire flesh like it was human, claws that burst through chests and out the other side, all the time they were silent, no snarls or hisses escaped their mouths, just the cries of their prey as they delivered death. The remaining looting vampires tried to flee but were quickly hunted down, horrifying screams revealing their fate.

I took the opportunity to scramble to my feet, pulled my hood up over my head and hurried down a side street heading to the Witches Quarter. As I looked round, I noticed it had been left mostly untouched. Maybe the FF feared them. Surveying the empty streets, there was no one around to ask, the rioting vampires and Wardens had scared everyone off. Even the shops had closed up. One store called 'Toil and Trouble', looked to have cleared out for good. I peered through the window into the dark and empty shop. It wasn't that unusual, many of the witches that came here would pack up and leave after a few months. Either fed up with the underlying hostility or simply wanting to return to their previous lives above ground, witches were still part of the living world after all. But something about this particular shop seemed familiar. Then I remembered, it was owned by a teacher at the Ghoul School. A 'Mistress Varias', Scar had mentioned how good her classes on Blood Magic had been. Now it looked like this Varias had done a runner, far too much of a coincidence for my liking.

On the way back I avoided the Trade Quarter and slipped into the ghoul tunnels under the city. These had been built when undead relations had been at their most fragile, even the Tribune didn't know about all of the tunnels. I was making my way down one below Tudor's row when I heard hushed voices. I froze and squinted in the dark, it was a couple of ghouls. I made my way towards them and saw it was Norm and Mildred, they were standing over the prone figure of a young ghoul, he was bleeding heavily. Mildred pulled me into a bony hug as soon as she saw me.

"Oh Herb, you're all right! I was worried you would be caught in this, never in all my years as a ghoul have I seen it this bad. They set fire to the Ghoul School again, this time there were students still inside, vampire students. They said those willing to study with ghouls should burn with them," she sobbed.

"What happened to him?" I asked, kneeling down next to the young ghoul.

"They broke in the Blooderie and began looting," said Norm. "I let them, hoping they would leave but then they started on the blood dolls I stock," he gave a husky choke and covered his face with his hands. "They killed them all! Then they went for Oscar, four of them dragged him out into the streets, they were beating him for a long time, I tried to stop them but they turned on me." I noticed he was oozing brown blood from several wounds. "Then Mildred was brought out, she had been ordering a case of free range blood for Master Dante. I've never seen the likes of it before, they were calling us filth and a burden on the rest of the undead."

"I don't know what would have happened if Ted hadn't shown up," said Mildred shakily. "He managed to fight them off of us, we took Oscar and ran for the tunnels. I do hope he's okay, he saved us all."

Oscar gave a small cough and spat out brown blood, Mildred bent down wiping his chin with her shawl.

"We have to stay in here until it blows over but I'm worried about this little one, he needs blood to heal properly," Mildred said quietly.

"I'll get it," I said without thinking.

"Herb, it's too dangerous! What are you doing out tonight anyway? I thought you were at home."

"I'll explain later, it's a long story, just stay here until I'm back, I'll stick to the shadows, most of them will be distracted by the Wardens anyway," I said sounding more confident than I felt.

I followed the tunnel until I found the exit I was looking for, climbing out, I saw with satisfaction I was inside 'Plasma'. It looked empty, I hoped the others had made it safely home. I was searching the bar when I heard a low moaning, I scanned the room but found no sign of anyone, then I heard it again, it sounded as if it was coming from the ladies toilets. I carefully opened the door and peeped inside, dragging itself across the tiled floor was a female ghoul or at least I guessed she was female, but she was so decomposed it was hard to tell, only a few pieces of flesh lingered on her skeleton. I carefully lifted her up into my arms and carried her out with me, grabbing a few bottles of blood and shoving them in my pockets on the way. I returned to the tunnels and made my way back to Mildred and Norm. Luckily, Oscar was now fully conscious and able to sit up, so I gave him a bottle of blood to drink. Mildred and Norm stared in horror as I placed the female ghoul gently on the ground.

"What did they do to her?" asked Mildred in shock.

"Not sure, but this is beyond our healing skills, she needs to see one of the flesh crafters," I replied.

We sat there in the dark resting, wondering how long this madness would last and when we could go back home. Or if we even had a home to go back to. Most of all, I wondered if Scar was back and if she was safe. I truly hoped she was.

Chapter 22

~Scarlet~
~Discovered~

Dante burst into the room and took one look at Kristian on the floor, his pale eyes moved to me widening as he took in my wounds.

"What on earth happened?! Did those bastards come in and do this?!" There was a fierceness to his voice.

I shook my head, not knowing how to begin explaining what had happened. He looked across at Cecile's dead body on the bed.

"Who...did this?" he whispered, unable to tear his gaze away from our dead brother. Mary ran into the room and screamed as she saw Kristian and then Cecile. She fell upon his body crying and wailing, the sight of it too much for her bear. I rose slowly and staggered out of the room, Dante kept staring at me, waiting for some form of explanation. When he didn't get one, he followed me out the door, occasionally looking back at the scene in confusion. When we were in the hallway I finally tried to form words.

"It was all my fault," I said, feeling the waves of sadness rising up again. Just then the sounds of Desmodeus and father entering the house sounded from downstairs. Dante hurried to meet them and lead them to the study. I waited in the hall by myself, unable to face them. When they exited they didn't say anything. Dante saw to my wounds, while Desmodeus brought me a glass of blood. I was taken to the parlour room and seated. The three of them sat patiently waiting for me to finish my blood and begin talking. The sound of Mary's crying was the only noise in the quiet house, it echoed like a banshee.

I finally found the strength and courage to speak. I started at the beginning, how I had met Mistress Varias from Ghoul School and had confided in her, my desires to be like the humans. That my desires had become an obsession as I started to hunt above ground, how I had thought I had killed that boy and instead of coming clean I continued on my selfish mission. I informed them, of how I picked a human and with Varias's help performed a glamour spell so I could get my wish, I could live as a human for a week. I told them that Jessica had seemed normal at first but how in the last couple of days I had started to become suspicious. I told them how I had come back earlier than arranged but had been too late, it seemed that Varias had not just been inclined to help me, but also Jessica, giving her Witches Salt to use against me, but for what purpose I still did not understand. After my tale, they sat there still in silence. It was Desmodeus who spoke first.

"I cannot believe you could be so irresponsible, inviting an unregistered human to our home, pretending to be you while you swan off above ground, to do what? Go to a school prom?"

I didn't argue back, he was right of course, it seemed so foolish now. I had risked so much for my own shallow needs.

"But the worse part is that you did this with the help of a witch? Have you not learnt anything from our histories? Treaty or no treaty, did you ever think to question why this Mistress Varias would help you? Everyone has an agenda, especially witches. They seek to rule us and you played right into her hands, and now Kristian lies dead because of it," Desmodeus continued coldly, sounding all the more like a true member of the Tribune.

"That's enough!" We all looked up in shock at father, his pale eyes were tired looking as he addressed us.

"Scarlet is not wholly to blame, she is young and has always been more drawn to the human within her than the rest of us. I knew this would make her more vulnerable to above ground influences, but hoped she would grow out of it. To be turned so young and never remember another life except for the one forced upon her, there was always the possibility that she would try and seek a human life," he said solemnly.

I was caught completely off guard, and I could tell from the faces of Dante and Desmodeus, that they were too. I couldn't believe how understanding he was being, he had just lost a son because of me yet he still defended me, he truly was a great man.

"And what about Dante? He had to endure days of questioning and accusations from the Tribune because they thought he had killed that boy, who turns out was the victim of Scarlet's night out," said Desmodeus.

"Scarlet did not kill the human boy Desmodeus," corrected father.

"She may as well have, she left him bleeding and vulnerable and then never even tried to tell us."

"We are all bound to make mistakes eventually brother, especially in our long lives. Our sister did not intend for this to happen. She left the boy alive, I was arrested because I had a track record for my own mistakes not for Scarlet's," said Dante.

Suddenly Herb burst in with Mildred; both looked bad even by ghoul standards. Herb was missing an arm and Mildred was nursing a deep wound on her head. Herb stared at me for a moment as if uncertain then he broke into a smile.

"Scar! You're back, it's really you!" He shuffled over to me and shocked me by giving me an awkward one armed hug.

I gave a weak smile back despite myself, he proceeded to bow before each of the household in respect, before frowning in confusion.

"Where's Kristian? He asked me to go find the witch, I went and looked, but she's gone. her shop is empty. I would have gotten back sooner to tell him, but I got caught up in the riots and.." he trailed off as he saw our grim faces. Father informed both of what had happened but I had to leave the room, I could not bear to hear it again.

I went upstairs and paced the hallway slowly to Kristian's room, the door was now closed. I opened it to see Mary was still there. She looked at me with a tear stained face.

"I'm sorry," was all I could muster before turning and closing the door. I went to my room and lay on the bed and for the second time that day, in over one hundred years I cried.

Chapter 23

~Jessica~
~Girl On the Run~

When I got to the Gate, there was already a queue, it seemed, that in light of the riots, security at the gates had been stepped up to accommodate fleeing ghouls and clamp down any potential vampire trouble makers. I tapped my foot and looked around trying to appear calm as I scanned the streets for any signs of Scarlet or her family. Riot or not, they would be back at the house by now and if not, it was only a matter of time. Scarlet would no doubt confess, feeling guilty over Kristian's death. It was her own fault, if she had prepared me better I could have been turned without resorting to such measures. I pictured her weeping pathetically, she would have a lot to explain. Hopefully, that would give me enough of a head start to get out of this city. But what would they do once she had told them everything? I knew the answer already, I would be hunted down by the Tribune. Desmodeus would probably make it his personal objective to see me brought back and tried. I pictured the gold faced judge looming over me; how did they punish humans? Their rule against killing humans, would surely not apply for a human that killed one of their own. The queue seemed to have stopped moving, what was taking so long? I peered over the line of undead and saw a ghoul being padded down and on the counter, lying open and being searched was a large suitcase. It was packed with blood bags but the security officer was ignoring these and instead inspecting a grey scaly looking sausage that was hidden at the bottom of the case.

"Er - Archie, come and look at this," he called to his colleague. "Looks like Demon meat to me."

Archie ambled over and sniffed it, before nodding in confirmation.

"That's Strigoi Salami all right," Archie confirmed. He turned to the ghoul commuter with a stern look on his face.

"You know the rules when clearing the Gate, no demon meats allowed through. Who knows what effect this could have if one of the humans ate it. Didn't you hear about the outbreak of Horn and Tail disease back in 1881?" Archie said authoritatively. They confiscated the offending sausage and moved the ghoul along.

Moments later, I had reached the front of the queue, the security officer looked me over with apprehension, he scanned my arm and stared at the screen before him. He squinted for a moment, before turning his head and calling over his colleague. He whispered something into his ear, before both turned and looked straight at me. My heart was pounding in my chest, it was good I still had the necklace on, even if I no longer looked like Scarlet anymore, the necklace at least still stopped me sounding and smelling like a human. The security officer motioned for me to come behind the desk as his colleague continued checking the other undead through.

"If you could come with me, please," he said, before leading me to a small cubicle behind the desk. Once inside he closed the door and faced me.

"I knew there was something different about you as soon as I saw you, but when I scanned your implant it confirmed it. But you look nothing like your picture," he said squinting again.

I looked around the room for a weapon of some sort, I could hit him and make a run for it. I thought about the risks, there were many more undead officials patrolling to when I first arrived and the gates had been reinforced with more security and additional check in procedures.

"Was it Flesh Fusions?" he asked.

"What?" I asked in confusion.

"Your skin, it looks so alive. I heard they can do that with corpse care treatments. I'm sorry but it just looks so natural and I'm thinking of getting something like that as a gift for the wife, she woke up in a better state than me but she has always hated her grey skin tone," he explained.

"Oh yes...right. Yes, that's right. Corpse care treatment from Flesh Fusions, this is the rose rub, but they have a nice peach pinch also," I lied smoothly.

"Interesting, they do the eyes also?" he asked thoughtfully.

"Er..yes. Brilliant blue is the shade," I said impatiently.

"Fascinating, well thanks for the info, you've convinced me, I'll book her in for a session there, I might even treat myself to some eyebrows" he replied, pointing to his browless forehead. "Think it might make me look more intimidating, security should be able to muster a good frown every now and then."

"No problem, glad to be of help," I said, given him a hurried smile and turning to leave.

"Hold on a bloomin' minute!" he shouted and I froze.

"They did your teeth an' all?!" he said dumbfounded.

"Yes, filed them down, it's a temporary effect but worth it," I said calmly.

"Amazing what they can do these days eh?" he said, shaking his head in wonder.

I nodded and made to walk away, this time he didn't stop me. I left the cubicle quickly and passed through the gate. Once I was on the other side I picked up the pace, the ghoul at the Exit station desk giving me a questioning look as I dashed past.

When I was above ground I ran and didn't stop until I was three streets away from the portal. With the adrenaline fading, I started to feel tired, so I slowed my pace to a brisk walk, before turning down a side alley. I couldn't risk going home, Scarlet knew where I lived and that would be the first place she would come. I would have to lie low for a bit, I could stay at Hannah's I supposed, but how for long? Suddenly my foot caught something and I was tumbling through the air, the ground coming up to meet me hard. I lay there for a moment dazed then put my hand out to push myself up, it came into contact with something sticky. I immediately pulled it back and looked to see what it was. Blood, fresh blood. I scrambled backwards, before my back hit something solid. I turned slowly, before seeing it was not something, but someone. I was face to face with the lifeless eyes of a human girl. Her brown hair had been brushed back exposing the neck, which had two puncture wounds. I pushed myself to my feet and made to run, still looking back at the girl's body, before hitting something for the second time. It was cold and hard, and it knocked me straight back down, I looked up fearfully and gasped. A woman stood over me, she was beautiful yet terrifying, her pale eyes fixed on me with a deadly smile. Her mouth widened to reveal sharp fangs, which were red with blood. Her hair was shaven and she wore an old-fashioned black dress with a white pinafore, also saturated in blood.

"I was wrong," she said, her voice was soft and almost childlike. "I've been searching for so long…" she pointed to the dead girl on the ground. "I thought that she was the one but she wasn't."

I tried to back away but she was fast, and was upon me in one move. I cried out in shock and my whole body started shaking as I broke into ragged sobs. She pressed a white finger to my lips, it felt like an icicle against them.

"Shush, my dearest. I will make it all better," she said, then frowned.

"I know you… I tried to make you better before. I will do it properly this time."

As she leant slowly into me, she opened her mouth, fully exposing her fangs. I opened my own mouth to scream but was silenced as she covered my mouth with one hand. I let out a small pitiful whimper, as her fangs pierced through my flesh. I could feel my blood being siphoned out of me, like before, only not like before. I was not in control, I was food this time. I am dead I thought to myself, before the darkness took over.

Chapter 24

~Scarlet~
~The Makings of a Monster~

    The next few weeks passed by in a blur. I went through the motions, accepting the hostility from those who still blamed me. Dante, father and Herb cast no judgment on me, which in a way, made it worse. I felt like I was being let off far too easy. Desmodeus on the other hand could barely look at me and I could understand why. He had spent his entire undeath dedicating himself to making sure the laws of our kind were obeyed and yet he had been unable to stop his own sister from violating those laws he held so precious. If news of what transpired got out, it would make him lose face as an authority figure and hinder any further elevation within the Tribune. Keeping it covered up however, was difficult, it would be hypercritical. Desmodeus was clearly torn by his loyalty to his beliefs and his loyalty to his family. Mildred, being a ghoul, never dared say a word about any of it, but I could see her disappointing gaze shift my way when she thought I wasn't looking, and truth be told, it bothered me more than I cared to admit. The worse of it though had been at Kristian's funeral, I had been wrong in thinking that vampires would have few to mourn their passing. It seemed as if half the Underdark turned up to say a final farewell to Kristian. I really had underestimated how many friends he a had, most of which he had made since staying underground. Dante had read some diabolical poetry that I felt Kristian would have appreciated, even if just to laugh at, while father performed his own ritual of knighting Kristian in death. I had felt even more of an imposter at this funeral than at Jessica's grandmothers, but I got through it.

    Kristian's surviving blood doll Mary had been dismissed to continue with her own life, but father had let her attend Kristian's funeral, she wore a black lace dress with a veil and wept continuously. Whether it was because she missed Kristian or because she thought her chance of being sired had gone, I was unsure. But who was I to judge? My time as a human had not given me much more insight, in fact I was more disconnected than ever. I kept thinking about Jessica, why she had done the things she had done and despite going over it again and again, I could never come up with anything. Her parents had seemed like nice people, her sister had shown me no cause to deserve the treatment she had received, and Sam...well Sam had been the one I thought about the most. The time spent with him, as short as it was, had been the best time in my long drawn out life, on those few occasions I had felt normal.

As my thoughts flitted between the people I had met during the life swap, Jessica was always the one I found myself wondering about the most. Had she returned home as if nothing had happened and gone back to her normal life? Was she still hurting people? I felt responsible, I had discovered a monster and released it back into the world. Desmodeus and father were both keeping a watch on her house, I had given them all the details of Jessica and they wanted to make sure there would be no further repercussions. But there was no sign of her; then it was on the human news that a young girl named Jessica Young had gone missing, she had left the house on Sunday and never returned. No one had seen her and no body had been found. It was a mystery. She must have left the Underdark, Desmodeus had searched the entire city and no sign had been discovered of a human fitting her description. But still, I had an uneasy feeling, that she was somehow still among us. As I walked through the Underdark, more than once I would see a blood doll with a passing resemblance to Jessica, only to look again and realise it was not her. She haunts me, along with her memories. I wanted to live as her and now, in a way, I always will. I shared her experiences and regardless of what may have happened between us, whatever becomes of her now, I know I am responsible.

At the end of it all, we had one final surprise in the form of the reading of Kristian's Will, which father had appointed Mikey to deal with. The entire household had been gathered into the parlour room to be present for the reading. A vampires will is created through a series of flickers and extracted on time of death, these legally binded memories can be hard to decipher and are often scrutinised for weeks prior by flicker experts which is most likely why we were only hearing about this now. Mikey who I had not met during Dante's trial introduced himself to me and also offered his services for pursuing a case of identity theft, the fact that I had been the instigator and that Jessica was missing seemed irrelevant to him.

"Your brother kept his affairs in good order, contrary to his carefree demeanour. He invested in a number of sensible businesses and property, ones that have prospered over the decades," Mikey informed us.

"Kristian had businesses?" Dante exclaimed.

"Indeed he did," said Mikey. "A Tattoo parlour in the Witches quarter and a Blood Den just off the Vampire Quarter as well as a vacant property in the Ghoul quarter that was being rented by a ghoul named Willy until his arrest."

"Kristian owned 'Willy's Waterhole?'" Dante turned to Desmodeus. "Did you know about this?"

Desmodeus shrugged. "I discovered it when I had to investigate Willy, but he had no knowledge that the ghoul was stocking dead blood, he never even bothered to do checks on any of the businesses so long as they were still bringing Drakmir in."

Mikey straightened his tie and cleared his throat before proceeding.

"To my eldest brother. Firstly, I give you my thanks, we may not always have agreed on things but I know you always have our families interest in mind and so I bequeath you my total savings to invest how you deem necessary. I have faith you will use it well."

Desmodeus bowed his head in respect.

"My Blood Den 'Dolls House' I leave to my brood brother Dante," continued Mikey. "So that he may turn it into his own pompous blood bar, as I know he always wished to have his own."

Dante sniffed before uttering. "He was always very thoughtful, I will truly miss our verbal sparring."

"My Tattoo studio 'Dead Canvas' I leave to my dear sister Scarlet and hope that she realises we all undergo changes, some are our choice some are not, but it's really how we let those changes define us that matters."

I thought back to him standing in 'Dead Canvas' lecturing me on the positives of undead living, never once had I considered he owned the place.

"Lastly," continued Mikey.

"It was your brother's wish that his only sired undead, a ghoul by the name of Herb be set free of his servitude and inherit the Waterhole, which includes the flat above it. He has also left a substantial sum to help start up a new business in its place."

All but father and Desmodeus gasped before turning to stare at Herb, who was looking at me in confusion. How was it possible that Herb had been sired by Kristian? Father had always stated that he'd been responsible for siring him. This raised a lot of questions, is this why Kristian had always been so hard on Herb? Had it been some form of coping mechanism? It can't have been easy having to look at Herb, a walking corpse and know you were responsible for that.

And so it was, that House Lucard lost two members of its household that day, the reading of Kristian's final will and testament, being the last of him in the house, even if only in flicker form. And also the loss of Herb, my ever loyal servant now free. However, it was not to stay that way for very long...

With Herb now a free ghoul, the household was in need of a replacement. So it was, that father took in Grace to act as Mildred's assistant, who thanks to Herb's quick action and the skilled flesh crafters at Flesh Fusion had survived her severe injuries. And while I believe Mildred could have managed without the extra help, father was adamant to keep Grace on as a second. Perhaps Grace's encounter with Jessica, meant she had a link to us, like it or not, or perhaps it was part of father's and Desmodeus' attempt to keep all knowledge of what had transpired within House Lucard. The fact that Mildred and Grace never seemed to get any work done, due to their incessant bickering wasn't considered a factor. Mildred liked things done in a certain way, Herb had at least come from the same era and had always gone along with this, but Grace was altogether different, and being a twentieth-century ghoul, could not fathom why Mildred insisted on sticking to her old, outdated methods. I had never seen Mildred so angry as she was when Grace brought home a steam cleaner. The two bickered incessantly over it, but to Grace's amusement Mildred had slowly come round and now would rarely be seen without it.

Grace wasn't the only new house guest, Ted was now renting a room with us as his old accommodation; which had been in the ghoul quarter due to their lower rental rates; had been burned down during the FF riots and father, again showing his softer side offered him lodgings in gratitude for helping the Wardens that night. Father had also sought to show me one more kindness. During his watch over Jessica's house he had seen a boy leave a letter on the doorstep, it had not been addressed to Jessica but to me, father had managed to keep it hidden from Desmodeus, who had already destroyed Jessica's phone, wanting to get rid of every piece of evidence. I remember feeling upset when Desmodeus did this, as it had been my only reminder left of Sam. I had deleted all the other photos of Jessica, but I had left the one with Sam in it and now I didn't even have that. So the letter was was a great gift indeed:

Scarlet,

I didn't know how else to get in contact with you, but I wanted to say thank you...that is, if this is all true, which is something I'm still struggling with. What I can't deny is the fact, that after you vanished before my eyes (another concept I struggle with) my brother, defying all the doctor's predictions, woke up, just as you said he would. He's back with us, words cannot describe how great that is, but I had to try. I also need some assurance I'm not going insane, I keep thinking about the other night on your doorstep (or Jessica's doorstep) when I saw you change, I should be terrified, but to tell the truth I'm not. I want to see you again, the real you.

Here are some photos from the play, I thought you might want them.

I hope this letter reaches you, if so please contact me, if even just to explain things, with Jessica missing I have a lot of unanswered questions, I think I deserve that. Is Jessica still with you?

Sam

The letter contained photographs taken from the play, the girl in the photograph was not the Jessica glamour, it was me. Pale and blonde, my lips stretched into a smile that for once didn't look unnatural or carnivorous. I read the letter a dozen times since receiving it and tacked the photographs up on the wall, much to Desmodeus's disapproval. He didn't know where I had gotten them from, but father had forbidden him from taking them from me. Four photographs were not much to show for being around over an century, but all the same I could not help smiling as I stared at them, pleased that now I had some proof of an existence. There was a gentle knock on the door and Dante poked his head round.

"Okay to come in?" he asked.

I nodded.

"Why are you using the door when you normally just materialise?"

He smiled.

"I thought it was about time I respected your privacy." Vlad was perched on his shoulder, his wing bandaged but on the mend.

"I'm sorry about Vlad," I said. I had seen what Jessica had done to him in her flickers, it was yet another thing resting on my conscience.

Dante waved a hand dismissively.

"What's done is done, Scar. You didn't know she was going to hurt Vlad or any of us for that matter, she was a human and we are known to underestimate them. We forget we were once like them and that they are capable of more than just being food," Dante said prophetically. He then scanned my face.

"For awhile your eyes were still a shade of blue, but you look yourself again, I hope you realise that isn't such a bad thing," he said softly.

I nodded in agreement and meant it. It felt good to be back in my own skin, which had reverted to its alabaster tone.

I no longer despised how I looked nor felt like I was a monster. I had seen the eyes of true evil and they were not those of my own. My inner conflict had subsided, I now knew humans could be outcasts too and that it was not what you were, that dictated your character, but your actions.

There was another knock on the door and Herb came in. Despite receiving his freedom and moving into his own accommodation, he would frequently visit. Although, it still took me a moment to adjust to his new appearance whenever I saw him. Mikey had advised him that if he was going to start his own business he would need to look the part, especially if he wanted to attract different types of clientele; such as humans and not just your average undead. So using some of the funds Kristian had left him, he booked a consultation with Flesh Fusions. Herb's face, despite being an unclean ghoul and suffering a severe form of decomposition, had always shown subtle traces of the boy he was before, but nothing would have prepared me for his full reconstruction. He looked like a normal boy you would see walking above ground, his skin was smooth and rot free, his eyes were a dark brown instead of murky yellow and his hair was no longer a few thin strands, but now covered his head in sprouts of short blonde curls, he looked like a cherub, even his cheeks were round and rosy and full of life. Dante shook his head in disbelief.

"It really is fabulous what they can do now with corpse cosmetics," he said.

Herb nodded in agreement.

"I've felt faceless for so long, it's hard to believe I'm me again," he wiped his eyes as they welled up. Herb had been even more emotional since the operation, it was as if the magical flesh had not only made him look more like a human, but act more like one as well. That illusion was swiftly shattered as he lifted up his hand and stuffed a shrivelled intestine into his mouth, tearing a chunk out of it. At that point, I knew Herb was still Herb. He handed me the glass of blood he was holding.

"Grace asked if I could bring this up for you as her favourite TV show is on."

It was plain blood, no added human condiments. Since the events of my return, I had not gone out and hunted above ground. I did as my family did and drank from the blood packs, I no longer needed that forced connection with humans. I had found something else to keep me connected, I had the letter from Sam. Dante eyed the blood thoughtfully.

"That reminds me I have a date with Michael."

"A date? You're finally admitting he's your boyfriend?" I asked, amused.

Dante rolled his eyes.

"I prefer not to use such base terminology to define what Michael and I share. His blood does wonders for my vampire well-being and that is all I shall say on the matter for now," and with a smile on his face, he began to fade into mist before my eyes. I sighed some things stayed the same. Like Dante had, Herb scanned my own face with his new eyes.

"Your skin has grown back now," he said.

I raised my hand to my cheek and felt the smooth skin. To help reduce the cost of Herb's surgery I had donated my own flesh, it had been unpleasant having the ghouls at Flesh Fusion hack away the foundation that gave me my human identity, along with seeing the parts beneath exposed as I carried on walking, talking and feeding. But thankfully vampires heal fast and it had been worth it; it felt good to give something back, instead of taking it for a change. I took a sip of blood as Herb updated me up on his affairs, Willy had left the Waterhole in a bit of a state so there had been some repairs needing doing, but now Herb was refurbishing it and relishing having ownership and free reign to decorate it how he wished. The shop itself was still a work in progress as Herb was indecisive of what business to venture in, not keen on running a Blood Den or Blood bar left him limited choices. I could relate to that, having not had much involvement in 'Dead Canvas' aside from signing the new lease. Dante was the only one who had dived straight in, immediately closing the 'Dolls House' down and erecting a stylish Blooderie in its place, which he aptly named 'Vanity Vein'. Since the Blooderie had been destroyed in the second bout of FF riots and Blue Bloods still refused Dante entry after his public trial; despite being cleared of all charges; he needed a new place to hold his 'Tastings'. He even went so far as to hire Norm, as his head Blood maker and showed out of character consideration to the previous blood dolls, by keeping them on as Burlesque dancers. Refurbishments were still under way but Dante was planning a big event for his first opening night scheduled in the next few weeks. I downed the glass of blood and stood up.

"Don't worry, I know I still can't come with you," Herb said, stepping aside.

"No, you can't come to the human clubs tonight, Herb," I said, confirming his previous statement. He bowed his head and made to walk out of my room dejected. I called out before he could take another step.

"You can, however, come to Plasma with me," I said.
His eyes widened.

" You're going to Plasma? I thought you hated the undead clubs," he said in surprise.

"I did, but I feel ready to give it a go," I said with genuine enthusiasm.
Herb smiled.

"What made you change your mind?" he asked.

"Someone once told me that it was fruitless to find the meaning of life in death, however, I've come to realise that even in death you only live once," I said with a distant smile. A tear formed in Herb's eye, he walked over to me, before placing his hand on my shoulder.

"I think Kristian would be happy you proved him wrong Scar," Herb said with a smile. I put my arm around him in a friendly embrace and we walked out the door.

I pictured the non-existent manuscript of my life and for the first time ever, I could see the beginnings of a story forming. A few precious sentences on a forgotten page. It was uncertain whether it would ever become more than that, but it was a start.

~*Epilogue*~

Mistress Varias surveyed the faces of the other witches in the circle, they had all shared the same vision, it was just as she had foreseen. Some had doubted her when she had insisted they help the vampire girl, but they had been proven wrong. She was the one gifted with the truest sight and she had seen what would follow.

She reached down and stroked Gron, who was purring in his kitten form. It had angered her, that the brother Dante had escaped the execution block and cleared his name and that Scarlet had avoided death at Jessica's hands, but she supposed, that getting rid of one of the Lucard's brood would have to suffice or now.

It was no matter anyway. They would all be suffering soon enough.

Printed in Great Britain
by Amazon